Honour Thy Father

Elizabeth
MURPHY

Honour Thy Father

CANELO

First published in the United Kingdom in 1996 by Headline Book Publishing

This edition published in the United Kingdom in 2019 by

Canelo Digital Publishing Limited
57 Shepherds Lane
Beaconsfield, Bucks HP9 2DU
United Kingdom

A CIP catalogue record for this book is available from the British Library.

Print ISBN 978 1 78863 531 8
Ebook ISBN 978 1 78863 477 9

Look for more great books at www.canelo.co

Printed and bound in Great Britain by Clays Ltd, Elcograf S.p.A.

In loving memory of Ted.

Chapter One

Anne Redmond glanced out of the wide window at the small white clouds in the blue sky and the sunlight falling on a cherry tree covered in blossom at the end of the long garden.

'This is how the first of May *should* be,' she said, smiling at her husband and three children gathered round the breakfast table in the window alcove. 'I hope you all remembered to say "White Rabbits".'

'*I* didn't. That's kids' stuff, Mum,' her ten-year-old son Gerry protested.

His father laughed. 'That's right, son. You're growing up now. Far more important to remember that May the first is Labour Day,' he said approvingly. 'I'll take you to see the parade later. We always get a good turnout in Liverpool and it should be even better this year with the general election coming up later this month.'

'I said "White Rabbits", Mummy, and I told Julie to say it,' Laura said loudly. Although only six and a half years old she was a stubborn, independent child and she looked defiantly at her father and elder brother.

Her mother only smiled and said easily, 'Then you and Julie should have good luck anyway, love.'

In 1955 the wartime food shortages were only a memory. The older children had eaten cornflakes followed by boiled eggs and there was a rack of toast and a dish of marmalade on the table. Anne was sitting beside her youngest daughter trying to coax her to eat but the tiny, fragile child turned away from all she offered and would eat only a small piece of toast.

With a sigh Anne lifted her down from her chair. 'If you're all finished you can go and play in the garden but hold Julie's hand, Laura, and don't let her sit on the wet grass. And don't you attempt to climb the cherry tree, Gerry, or you'll damage the blossom.' No use telling her happy-go-lucky son to look after Julie, she thought ruefully. Her words would go in one ear and out of the other although he loved his little sister, but Laura was more reliable.

John went upstairs and Anne began to carry the breakfast dishes into the scullery. At first the children just ran about the garden but then they gathered beneath the cherry tree trying to catch the petals which floated down from it like snow. Leaves like tiny fans were opening on the sycamore tree which grew beside it.

'I wouldn't spoil the blossom if I climbed the cherry tree,' Gerry said. 'I'd be careful.'

'Mummy said you would and she loves the blossom,' Laura said quickly. 'Leave it alone.'

'I'll climb the sycamore then. I'll climb right to the top,' Gerry boasted.

'Don't you dare, Gerry. It's too big,' Laura exclaimed.

'Don't, Gewwy,' Julie echoed, but he went to the tree.

He was a big, strong boy, tall for his age with a fresh complexion, blue eyes and fair curly hair. Laura had blue eyes and curly hair too but her hair was dark and her character completely different from Gerry's. He was placid and easygoing, usually content to be ruled by his strong-willed sister, but today he was determined to climb a tree.

He scrambled on to the wall behind the tree without difficulty and launched himself at one of the branches. From there he climbed higher up the tree. 'It's the gear up here,' he shouted. 'I can see nearly to the Pier Head.' He climbed even higher, then with the girls watching fearfully he began to crawl along a branch.

The next moment there was a loud crack, then boy and branch fell together, Gerry bouncing off the lower branches and coming to rest on the grass, flat on his back with his left arm bent awkwardly beneath him.

The screams of the younger children brought their mother racing to them, closely followed by their father.

'Don't move him. Have some sense,' John shouted as Anne fell on her knees beside Gerry and attempted to take him in her arms. John pushed her aside and she turned to comfort the sobbing girls, lifting Julie in her arms and drawing Laura close to her.

John hung over Gerry, frantically smoothing back his curls and shouting at Anne, 'Why weren't you watching them? He could have been killed.'

Laura's terror swiftly turned to anger and she flung her arms protectively round her mother's waist. 'It wasn't Mummy's fault,' she yelled at her father. 'She told him not to.' She glared at him so ferociously that he seemed taken aback but before he could speak Gerry opened his eyes.

'Oh, thank God,' Anne exclaimed.

John said gently, 'You'll be all right, son. We'll get the doctor and he'll give you something to take the pain away. Be a brave lad.'

Laura sighed with relief but she still scowled at her father and when he said, 'Ring the doctor, Anne. Tell him it's urgent', she kept her arm round her mother's waist as they went back to the house.

Within minutes, it seemed, the doctor arrived, closely followed by Anne's brother Joe and his wife Sarah who was also John's sister, and their two children David and Rosaleen.

When the ambulance arrived, Anne and John went with Gerry, leaving the other children with Joe and Sarah. Aunt Sarah took Julie on her knee. 'She's had a fright, poor little mite,' she said, cuddling the child, and Joe drew Laura to him.

'You've had a shock too, pet,' he said. 'But Gerry'll be all right. He's broken his arm and bumped his head but he'll be as right as rain soon.'

'Daddy shouted at Mummy,' Laura said resentfully, 'but it wasn't Mummy's fault. She *told* Gerry not to climb the tree.'

Anne was Joe's beloved youngest sister and for a moment he looked grim, then he said gently, 'Some people get excited when something happens and say things they don't mean, then they're sorry afterwards. Don't worry about it, love. Your mummy understands your daddy.' But Laura was not convinced.

Her cousin David had sat down in the corner and opened a book but Rosaleen, who was only six months younger than Laura, flung her arm round Laura's neck. 'Should we play "three coppa's out"?' she suggested and the two little girls went into the garden to play.

As they went, Laura heard her Aunt Sarah exclaim, 'I could murder our John. As if Anne wasn't upset enough without him shouting at her. Even the child noticed it.'

Laura followed Rosaleen down the garden and heard no more but indoors Joe said soothingly, 'Oh well, you know John, Sar. He speaks first and thinks afterwards but Anne understands him. Like Grandma says, actions speak louder than words and he's a good husband otherwise.'

'I'm not saying he's a bad husband,' Sarah said, 'but he's thoughtless and Anne's too soft with him.'

Joe laughed. 'Whose side are you on?' he teased her. 'I thought as his sister you'd be taking John's part.'

'Anne was my friend before she was John's wife,' Sarah retorted, 'and I feel responsible because they met through me. Our John should remember, too, that it's only eighteen months since your dad died so suddenly. He should be extra considerate with Anne.'

'Yes, that hit Anne even harder than the rest of us,' Joe said with a sigh. 'She was so close to him. His baby.'

'The trouble is Anne always puts the best side out,' said Sarah. 'She always seems so happy and light-hearted but *I* know how much she grieves for your dad and so should John.'

'I'm sure he does,' Joe said. 'It was just a moment of panic, especially as it was Gerry and he spoke without thinking.'

Julie had fallen asleep on her aunt's knee and Sarah gently laid her on the sofa where she continued to sleep. Laura and Rosaleen were still playing ball in the garden. They were close friends although very different in appearance and temperament and were classmates at the parish school. Rosaleen, reckless and extrovert, was a beauty with curling auburn hair and brilliant blue eyes. In contrast, sturdy, dark-haired Laura seemed withdrawn but her quietness could never be mistaken for shyness. Her features and expression, the tilt of her head, even the way she stood already showed her stubborn and uncompromising character.

4

Now they played together happily until they heard Laura's parents arriving home and rushed into the living room to meet them. Laura went immediately to stand protectively beside her mother but her parents seemed to be on good terms.

'Gerry'll be fine,' Anne said. 'He's had his arm set and they're just keeping him overnight to rest.'

'And to check him out in case he's concussed,' John said, but Anne gave him a warning look and nodded at the children and he added hastily, 'He was very plucky. The doctors were impressed with him, weren't they, Anne?'

'Yes, we were proud of him,' Anne agreed with a smile. Julie had woken and Anne took her in her arms. 'Has she been all right?' she asked Sarah anxiously.

'Yes, she fell asleep on my knee but she was getting a bit hot so I put her down on the sofa,' Sarah said. She patted Julie's cheek. 'You had a nice sleep, didn't you, pet?' Julie smiled shyly and nodded.

Rosaleen began to pull at Laura's arm. 'Come on, let's finish the game,' she said but Laura clung stubbornly to her mother.

Anne smiled at her. 'Yes, go and finish your game, love.' They went out and Sarah urged Anne to sit down and rest while she made her a cup of tea.

The two young mothers had become friends when they worked together as young girls, soon after leaving school, and the bond between them was strengthened when each married the other's brother. Now Sarah was solicitous with Anne, bringing her a steaming cup of tea and telling her not to worry about Gerry.

'Children are very resilient,' she said. 'Gerry will soon bounce back.'

'I'm sure he will,' Anne agreed. 'Nothing bothers Gerry for long.' Julie rested her head on her mother's shoulder and sucked her thumb. Anne smiled fondly at her. 'I wish she was more like that,' she said.

'She'll soon grow stronger,' Sarah comforted her. 'Don't forget she had a bad start being premature, but she'll soon catch up, you'll see.'

Anne looked at the child. 'She grows more like my mum every day, doesn't she?'

'Well, you're like your mum with that same Spanish look so I suppose Julie takes after both of you really,' Sarah pointed out.

'Yes, but I mean she's like Mum was in character too,' Anne said. 'Very quiet and gentle.' She smiled. 'Very different to Laura. She's as stubborn as a mule and she speaks her mind, young as she is. You should have heard her yelling at John this morning. Gerry's different again. Sails through life. Doesn't care if it snows.'

'Strange, isn't it?' said Sarah. 'No matter how many there are in a family, they're all different. Look at your family. Seven of you and all different in character although some of you look alike.'

'And the same with your family,' said Anne. 'All different.'

'Me and our John are as different as chalk and cheese,' Sarah agreed. 'Even to look at and Mick's different again, more like Gerry.'

'I hope Gerry's as successful as Mick,' Anne laughed. 'He must be nearly a millionaire by now.'

Sarah looked thoughtful. 'Our Kate, Anne. Do you think Rosaleen might be taking after her?'

'Not a chance,' Anne said. 'Rosa's full of life and high spirits but she's nothing like Kate. She was a little faggot even as a child, wasn't she?'

'Yes, and she was sly. Rosaleen's not sly, just the opposite,' Sarah said.

'I think Rosaleen's more like your Aunt Mary,' said Anne. 'Beautiful like her and the same colouring and look how *she* settled down with Sam. Any news from America?'

'Not from Kate,' Sarah said grimly. 'She never writes but Aunt Mary said in her last letter that Kate's third marriage is on the rocks now. I wish she hadn't told us. It only upsets Mum and Dad and Grandma and they can't do anything about it.'

'Yes, it would be better if she said nothing, especially as Kate never writes,' Anne said. 'Leave them in blissful ignorance.'

Sarah glanced at her. Anne's pale, clear skin looked even paler and there were dark shadows beneath her brown eyes. 'I'm a fool,' Sarah exclaimed remorsefully. 'I tell you to rest then I talk your leg off. I'll take Laura and Julie back with us, Anne, while you have a lie down.' Julie seemed sleepy again and Anne's arm tightened round her. 'I'll keep Julie with me, thanks all the same, Sar,' she said. 'I want to be sure she has no ill effects from the shock.'

'We'll take Laura with us anyway,' Sarah said. 'It was a shock for her, too, poor child, and she can get over it playing with Rosa.'

'Oh, Laura's pretty tough,' Anne said lightly. 'She'll soon shake it off.'

Sarah said no more but when she and Joe left for home with the children she held Laura's hand as they walked the short distance. When they arrived she gave Laura a large dish of ice cream with cream soda mineral poured over it. 'I know that's your favourite, love,' she said. 'And it'll help you to get over the shock of Gerry falling out of the tree.'

She made smaller dishes for David and Rosaleen and Joe joked, 'They're getting that, Laura, because they'd suffer from shock too if they didn't get any.' All the children laughed and Laura thought how nice her aunt and uncle were. I wish Uncle Joe was *my* dad, she thought, then felt uneasy. Too young to recognise her feeling as disloyalty she only felt that she loved her own dad *really*.

Gerry soon returned home with his left arm in plaster and in a sling and enjoyed all the attention this brought him. As it was his left arm and he would soon be taking the eleven-plus examination he was allowed to return to school where his easygoing personality had made him popular, so he enjoyed even more attention.

He was less pleased to be barred from the school football team and from other team games, but he still enjoyed wild games of cricket or rounders in the playground, using the bat one-handed. After school he often managed to slip out to play in the small park nearby, wild games of Relieve O or Kick the Can which meant that he often returned home with dirty and torn clothes, but John was proud of his son's recklessness. 'He's a real boy,' he announced fondly to the family.

Julie caught a cold which developed into bronchitis and Laura often woke to hear her mother moving about as she cared for the sick child. She heard her Aunt Sarah remonstrating with her mother one day. 'You shouldn't try to do it all yourself, Anne,' she said. 'You should waken John to take a turn.'

'He'd do it willingly,' her mother said, 'but I don't call him because he works such long hours and I'd be awake anyway if Julie was bad.'

'I'd look after Julie,' Laura said eagerly but her mother seemed annoyed. 'Little pitchers,' she said to Sarah then told Laura brusquely to go out to play.

Sarah worked part-time in a sweet shop but she was able to collect Laura and take her to school with Rosaleen so that Anne could stay with Julie. Sarah also brought Laura home. One day after school they arrived to find John and Sarah's grandmother, Sally Ward, with Anne.

'Is Julie worse?' Sarah asked in alarm.

Grandma said firmly, 'No, but John called in to tell us about Julie so I thought I'd come to let Anne get a night's sleep. Nothing more tiring than disturbed nights with a sick child.'

Sally Ward was a spare, upright old lady with white hair drawn back in a bun. Her late husband Lawrie Ward had fought all his life for better conditions for the poor of Liverpool and Sally had nursed the sick among them and comforted the bereaved. Her house had been destroyed by a bomb during the war and she now lived happily with her daughter Cathy and her husband Greg, who were John and Sarah's parents.

Anne smiled at her gratefully. 'Grandma says she'll sit up with Julie tonight and she's brought a lovely meat pie and some cakes from your mum, Sar.'

'She knew you wouldn't have time for cooking, girl,' Sally said.

'I'm very lucky. Sarah's done so much to help me and Laura's helped too, haven't you, love?'

'That's a good girl,' Sally said approvingly. 'There's no better blessing than a good daughter, like your Nana is to me.'

'What about me, Grandma?' Rosa said pertly. 'Am I a good daughter?'

'I think we'll have to wait and see about you,' Grandma said but Rosa was unabashed. She linked her arm through Laura's and they ran into the garden laughing.

Laura was often puzzled about her relations at this time, confused by the fact that her parents were doubly related to her aunt and uncle.

'Is Grandma your grandma too?' she asked Rosaleen.

'Yes, because my mum is your dad's sister and Nana and Grandma are their mother and grandmother. Your mum and my dad are brother and sister too but their mum and dad are in heaven.'

'You're very clever to know all that, Rosa,' Laura said, gazing admiringly at her cousin.

'My dad told me all about it,' Rosaleen said. 'He said it was as if me and our David married you and Gerry.' The two little girls rolled about on the grass, giggling at the idea, but later Laura thought wistfully that Uncle Joe was very different to her father. Uncle Joe was always ready to answer any question, even if he was busy with schoolwork to mark, but her father always seemed to be rushing about, getting ready to go out or talking to people on the telephone. He brushed questions aside, saying impatiently, 'Ask me later' or 'I'll tell you when I've got more time', but that time never came.

When John came home he was pleased to find Grandma sitting beside the sick child and he bent over Julie, anxiously smoothing back her hair from her forehead. 'What do you think, Gran?' he asked. 'She doesn't seem so hot, does she?'

'No, and Anne says she's not coughing as much,' Sally said. 'I think she's over the worst but I'll still stay the night. She needs watching and Anne must get some rest.'

John looked relieved and went to help Gerry with his homework before they sat down to eat. When the meal was over John began to fidget about the room. 'There's an important meeting tonight about the protest against the atom bomb,' he said finally. 'As long as you're here with Anne and the kids, Grandma, I may as well go.'

The old lady just looked at him over her glasses but Anne said quickly, 'Yes, go, John. They'll be making plans for the demonstration. We'll be all right here.'

He smiled at her gratefully and within minutes he was away. Laura scowled at his retreating back. He was going to go anyway, she thought, but he's afraid of Grandma. Mummy lets him do what he likes.

Julie was awake and Grandma sat with her while Laura helped her mother to wash and dry the dishes. 'Will Julie get better now Grandma's here?' she asked.

9

'I hope so,' Anne said with a sigh. 'Grandma's very clever. She helped a lot of sick people to get better in the days when they couldn't afford to call a doctor but you mustn't worry about Julie, love.'

'I worry about you, Mummy,' Laura said, putting her arms round her mother's waist, but Anne laughed cheerfully.

'No need to worry about me either, love. I'm as right as rain and anyway you're too young to be worrying about anything.' She gave Laura a quick hug and went out of the scullery.

Laura was carefully hanging up the tea towel when Grandma came in to wash her hands at the sink. 'Have you been helping your mam?' she asked. 'That's a good girl.'

Laura beamed at the approval in the old lady's voice and took her hand as they went into the back parlour where Julie's bed was drawn close to the fire. She had fallen asleep again and Grandma said comfortably, 'Never mind. Sleep heals. You can talk to her when she wakes up.'

They stood looking at the sleeping child. The high temperature had flushed her cheeks and made her lips unnaturally red and her dark hair clung in damp curls round her face. Her eyelashes lay like dark fans on her cheeks and Laura said wistfully, 'Julie's very pretty, isn't she, Grandma?'

'Aye, she's the model of your mummy's mother, Lord rest her,' Sally said. 'She has her quiet ways too.'

'Were you pretty, Grandma?' Laura asked innocently, looking up at the old lady. Her skin reminded Laura of the tissue paper in which her mother wrapped her treasures but her blue eyes were still bright although surrounded by wrinkles.

'I never thought so,' Sally Ward said with a smile, 'but Lawrie, your great-grandad – he said I was. I remember one time in a tearoom at Eastham, when we went for a day out. I was that nervous because it wasn't like it is now with Jack as good as his master. Those days you had to know your place and keep to it but that never bothered Lawrie. He took me to this tearoom and they were all so posh I felt real nervous and out of place but Lawrie said, "You're the prettiest girl in the room and I'm as proud as Punch." After that I felt as good as any of them.'

'I was named after him, wasn't I?' Laura said proudly. 'What was he like, Grandma?'

'Oh, he was a lovely lad. He had black curly hair and brown eyes and he was as happy as the day is long. But he had a feeling heart too and he grieved about the poor people round us, especially the children.' She was silent for a moment, absently stroking Laura's hand with her own, dry and brown-spotted with age, then she smiled.

'He could never keep a penny in his pocket. Many and many a time he walked home from the other end of the city after a hard day's work because he'd given away his fare and clothes! No matter how often I made him scarves or mittens or turned a coat from the market for him, he'd come home without them. "There was this poor little child, Sal," he'd say or "There was this poor starving feller in rags" and the pence'd be out of his pocket and the clothes off his back on to theirs.'

'He must have been very kind.' Laura hesitated then said doubtfully, 'Uncle Joe said Daddy was like him.'

'*Never,*' Sally Ward exclaimed. 'Lawrie never said a hurtful word in his life. It's into his head and out of his mouth with John without stopping to think.' She seemed suddenly to notice Laura's startled face and recollect where she was and she said more quietly, 'I see what your Uncle Joe means though. Your daddy tries to carry on what Lawrie tried all his life to do, to make life better for ordinary people just as Lawrie wanted him to do. I suppose all this union work and protesting about the bomb and that is what's needed now.'

'Daddy's always out doing that.'

'Aye, your daddy's a good man, child, but he hasn't been blessed with Lawrie's nature. Our old neighbour Mrs Malloy used to say that God broke the mould after he'd made Lawrie and she spoke true.' She fell silent, smiling reminiscently, and Laura sat quietly beside her, thinking of all that her great-grandmother had said, particularly her exclamation about her father.

Julie stirred and woke; Sally raised the child's head and gave her a drink from a feeding cup. 'You've had a nice sleep, love,' she said. 'Here's Laura come to keep you company.' Julie smiled at her sister and Laura began to tell her about a ladybird that she had seen in the garden.

Presently Sally went out and later Anne came to sit with Julie and sent Laura to bed. The talk beside Julie's bed was the start of a new closeness between Laura and her great-grandmother. The old lady loved to talk about the family and Laura heard a great deal about Sally's father, Matthew Palin, and more about Lawrie Ward.

Laura never tired of listening to these tales even when they were repeated and she was amazed that such an old lady could remember things so clearly. She said this to her great-grandmother but Sally only smiled and told her that these events were more real to her than what had happened last week.

There was another reason why Sally talked so often to Laura. Her sharp eyes missed little of what happened in the various families and she saw that Laura felt that she was less important to her parents than her brother and sister. John made no secret of his love and pride in his son and Julie's delicate health meant that Anne lavished attention on her. Sally could see that Laura felt left out. Anne and John were unaware of this so she tried to redress the balance.

She could also see that easygoing Gerry and sweet-natured Julie would have an easy path through life but Laura's temperament would make life hard for her. In the course of her long life Sally had known other people like Laura. Unable to compromise or to take the easy way, honest to a fault, they spoke the truth as they saw it and their bluntness often cost them friends although their honesty was rarely appreciated. Circumstances and childhood influences might soften such natures but the personality that they were born with could never really change.

Sally could see that this had been the case with John. Surrounded by adoring parents and grandparents as a baby, his nature had seemed sunny while he was given his own way in everything but as he grew this changed. His true temperament showed itself in clashes with his father and with employers and in his determination to do what he believed in, no matter what the consequences for himself and others.

Although Sally loved her grandson she knew his character well and she recognised those traits in Laura even now. She could see trouble ahead between the headstrong child and her father and she used these talks to build a special relationship with Laura. Anything she could do, she reasoned, no matter how little, to make Laura feel loved and wanted might give the child confidence to face the trials her nature would inevitably bring.

Chapter Two

In April 1955 Winston Churchill had resigned as Prime Minister and was succeeded by Anthony Eden, causing a general election to be called in May.

John was a dedicated member of the Labour Party and, in addition to his union work and protest meetings about the atomic bomb, he was fully involved with the election campaign. He undertook to address meetings and deliver leaflets on behalf of the Labour candidate which meant that he was out every night, usually until quite late.

Laura was pleased because her father's absence meant that she had her mother to herself more often but the rest of the family felt that too much responsibility was left with Anne.

Anne's eldest brother Tony Fitzgerald lived nearby with his wife Helen and two daughters and he complained bitterly to his brother Joe. 'I think Anne's getting a raw deal,' he said. 'John's never in and she's got all the worry about Julie and this business of Gerry's arm. She's left on her own to get on with it while John's out saving the world. It's just not good enough.'

'I agree,' Joe said, 'but Anne won't hear a word about it. Sarah tried to talk to her about it but Anne just said that she agreed with what John was doing and she wished she could do more in that line herself.'

'She's very loyal,' said Tony. 'I feel like tackling John myself. Telling him he's not being fair to Anne.'

'Wouldn't do any good,' said Joe. 'Sarah had a go at him too. Being his sister she could say more than we could and she really laid into him but she got nowhere. He's always so sure he's right.'

Although the adults were careful not to mention their disapproval before the children Laura gradually became aware of it. Abnormally sensitive where her mother was concerned, she was quick to notice a raised eyebrow or a meaningful glance when Anne's worries or John's activities were mentioned.

One day she overheard a snatch of conversation between her Aunt Sarah and Tony's wife Helen. They had spoken about Julie's health and Sarah said angrily, 'It's all such a worry for Anne and our John is never here with her. Always out campaigning for this, that and the other. Charity begins at home, I say.'

'But he's not out enjoying himself, Sarah,' Helen protested in her quiet voice. 'He truly believes in what he's doing and so does Anne, doesn't she?'

'Yes, but it's still wrong that she should be bearing the worry on her own,' Sarah said stubbornly.

They moved away without noticing Laura but she brooded on their words and redoubled her efforts to help her mother. Often she refused to play with Rosaleen so that she could stay with her mother until one day Anne said in exasperation, 'Oh Laura, for heaven's sake go and play. Don't be for ever under my feet.' Seeing Laura's stricken face she hugged her impulsively. 'I'm sorry, love,' she said. 'I shouldn't have snapped at you when you're trying to help.' She took a favourite chocolate biscuit from a tin and gave it to Laura but the child was not consoled and went away to cry in private.

Later, in bed, Laura decided that she would forgive her mother. It was her father's fault really because he was always out and her mother's lonely worries made her snap at her children, she told herself.

Unknown to the rest of the family, John had already been taken to task by his grandmother, Sally Ward. He had been addressing a meeting near to his parents' home and had called in to see them. He found that they were out but Grandma Ward, who lived with them, was at home.

'They've gone to the pictures,' she explained. 'I'd already seen the film so I didn't go. I'm glad you've called in, lad. I wanted a word with you.'

'That sounds serious, Gran,' John said, smiling. 'What have I done?'

'It's more what you haven't done,' Sally said. 'Anne's got too much on her plate with all the worry of a sick child and back and forth to the hospital with Gerry. She could do with you at home but you're never there, are you? It's too much worry for her on her own.'

'But I do worry about them too, Gran,' John protested. 'It's just that everything's happening at once. The general election and they've just announced plans to build *twelve* atomic power stations in the next ten years and Britain is going ahead with the hydrogen bomb. We've *got* to protest right now, Gran, and try to stop it. Anne feels the same way as I do about it.'

'But first things first, lad. You've got to think of your family,' Sally said.

'But I am thinking of them, Gran,' said John. 'What sort of a world will they grow up in if we don't fight these things? It'd be worse than anything Hitler could have done to us.'

'But things are getting better for ordinary people, John. No one's starving and you never see a barefoot child. Your grandad would be made up, I wish he'd lived to see it.'

'Yes, and we could lose it all just as quickly,' John said grimly. 'Go back to the way it was before the war. Men standing at the dock gates from four in the morning trying to get taken on or running like lunatics from one gate to another for half a day's work. I remember an old docker saying to me, "It's a terrible thing, lad, to hear your kids crying with hunger and not be able to do nothing for them. It takes away your manhood." Now I've got kids myself I understand how he felt. I swear I'm not going to let those days come back, Gran.'

'But they won't, lad, surely to God. People wouldn't let it happen.'

'They would, Gran. Already fellows are saying they don't need the union. They're too thick to see that it's only the union that keeps them from sliding back. It's still them and us. You know what they say. "The price of freedom is eternal vigilance." And it's even more important to fight the nuclear threat. To ban the bomb.'

'Yes, but don't neglect your family to do it, John,' Sally said.

'I don't neglect them,' John cried angrily. 'All that I'm doing is for them. To make a safer world for them and a better world for them to grow up in. And I work hard and provide a good home and all they need in food and clothes. You can't say I neglect them, Gran.'

A lock of dark hair had fallen over his thin, flushed face and he shook it back impatiently but Sally only said calmly, 'Sit down, sit down, lad.' When he sat down beside her she said gently, 'I don't want to fall out with you, lad. I know you mean well but I worry about Anne. You know I love the bones of that girl.'

'I know, Gran. But she's not on her own. Our Sarah and Helen are always at our house and you and Mum help her too. And you know what the Fitzgeralds are like. They wouldn't let the wind blow on Anne. Joe and Tony are there for anything she needs doing.'

'But they've got their own families to look after,' Sally pointed out. 'Your children are your responsibility, John, and you know Anne's still grieving for her dad.'

John took her hand. 'Honestly, Gran, you don't need to worry,' he said. 'If Anne was really on her own I'd stay in but I know she's not. And she agrees with me about these things. She wants me to go to meetings and on marches and deputations. If it wasn't for the kids she'd come with me. I'm always there at night with her anyway and we talk about these things and the worries about the children.'

Sally smiled ruefully. 'Well, I've always said no one should interfere between husband and wife and here I am breaking my own rule. It's true, John, nobody knows what goes on in a marriage but the people themselves. I should have kept my mouth shut. No offence meant, lad.'

'None taken, Gran. I know you only spoke out of concern for Anne and for my own good. Our Sarah tried to put her oar in but I soon told her where she got off. It's different with you.'

'But Sarah only spoke because she's fond of Anne, John. Your wife's a very loveable girl, you know.' She smiled and John grinned back at her.

'That's something we *can* agree on,' he said. 'Should I put the kettle on?'

'Good God, yes, and I'll get you something to eat, lad. Your stomach must think your throat's cut.'

Sally bustled about preparing supper and as soon as it was eaten John left. 'If Anne wants to know where I've been I'll say you kept me,' he said with a grin and she pushed him out of the door.

Later John told Anne about his conversation with his grandmother. 'Do you mind me being out so much, love?' he asked.

'Not a bit,' Anne assured him, then she looked sideways at him and a dimple appeared in her cheek as she laughed. 'Would it make any difference if I did?' she asked.

John looked up startled, and she flicked her fingers across his head. 'Idiot,' she said. 'Of course I don't mind. I only wish I could be out with you.'

'Only a week now until the election and things should be easier then. We'll be able to get out to the pictures or something.'

Anne nodded. 'Yes. The weather should be better soon and Julie won't be taking cold so easily. I wouldn't have wanted to leave her during the bad weather while her chest was so bad but once she gets over this spell we'll be able to go out.'

Sally gave no details of her talk with John but through Sarah she let it be known that there was no need to worry about Anne because she approved of John's activities and was quite happy. The family had great faith in Grandma's judgement and was quite satisfied.

'I think we've been fussing for nothing,' Sarah told Joe. 'Grandma says everything's all right and Rosaleen was talking the other day about Anne singing about the house.'

'She always did,' Joe said with a smile. 'Yet she would never sing at parties.'

Anne was blissfully unaware that her family had been critical of John and believed that Grandma's concern was due to her great age.

Julie's health improved as the weather grew warmer and at last she began to put on weight to everyone's delight. Gerry's arm healed well and soon the traumatic day in May seemed to be forgotten by everyone except Laura. Even for Laura the memory was buried by other events, two birthday parties to which she was invited and a happy weekend spent with her grandparents and her great-grandmother.

On 26 May the general election took place and, in spite of the efforts of John and other Labour supporters, the Conservative Party was returned with a majority of fifty-nine seats. John was less disappointed than the family expected because he was so caught up in the protests against the nuclear programme.

He had evidently heeded the words of his grandmother and once a week he and Anne went to the cinema or the theatre. Babysitters were always available to them and often Joe, who was a teacher, brought marking and did it while babysitting.

John and Anne took the children on an outing to New Brighton on a Sunday in early June. They all enjoyed it although Julie seemed nervous of the crowds as they boarded the ferryboat so the next Sunday they took a picnic to Sefton Park.

John took Gerry in a rowing boat on the lake while Anne and the little girls fed the ducks, then lay on the grassy bank in the sunshine. Later they went to the Palm House and the children were fascinated by the bananas and other tropical plants growing there.

'This is like the jungle, isn't it?' Gerry said. 'Some lad in our class said his dad fought the Japs in the jungle.'

'Don't say "some lad",' Anne corrected him automatically but she shivered in spite of the humid heat. 'This makes me think of that poor man Michael,' she said to John in a low voice. 'The son of Grandma's friend Peggy. Y'know, the one who's in the mental hospital. He never got over being a prisoner of war with the Japanese.'

John squeezed her hand. 'I know, love, but at least he's all right physically now. His mind might heal too.' He called Gerry and they left the Palm House but Gerry stopped before a statue of Linnaeus which stood outside it.

'Someday I'm going to be famous like him,' he boasted, 'and I'll have *my* statue in the park.'

'That's right,' John encouraged him. 'You can do anything you really want to do. Just work hard at school and you'll go far. You've got a good brain, son.'

Anne looked exasperated. 'He'll have a big head too if you don't stop praising him,' she exclaimed.

John was unrepentant. 'Nothing wrong with ambition. We should encourage it,' he said.

A protest march was organised when Britain and the United States agreed to cooperate on developing atomic energy and Anne wanted to join John on the march. John suggested taking Gerry with them but he was overruled and Gerry stayed with Sarah and Joe.

Laura hoped that her mother might suggest taking her instead but it was arranged that she and Julie should stay with their grandparents and great-grandmother. Laura was happy to spend more time with Sally and both girls enjoyed being petted and indulged by their grandparents, Cathy and Greg Redmond.

Greg Redmond was a quiet, gentle man, like John in appearance but very different in character and the children loved him. After lunch they all went into the garden, Laura weeding with her grandfather, while her grandmother helped Julie with a magic painting book.

'Look, Lawwa,' Julie called excitedly when colours appeared as she painted the page with water. 'It's magic.'

Laura was about to tell her that it was not magic and explain what happened but Greg touched her then put his finger to his lips and gave a conspiratorial wink. Laura smiled at him and only said, 'Yes, it must be.' She looked again at her grandfather and giggled then carried on helping with the weeding, feeling close to him and grown-up because of their shared secret.

In September the class to which Laura and Rosaleen belonged was moved up to the Junior Girls School. There was some reshuffling of pupils and Laura found herself sharing a desk with a girl who was unknown to her.

Eileen Unsworth was an adored only child and although school uniform was compulsory her doting mother had dressed her hair to make her stand out from the rest. Two large white bows adorned the top of the girl's head and two even larger were on the ends of her plaits.

Eileen sat preening herself beside Laura for a while then, unable to bear her indifference, she whispered, 'Do you think I'm pretty?' Laura examined her then said bluntly, 'No, you're not.'

Eileen burst into loud sobs and the teacher hurried over to them. 'What is it, dear? Is it a pain?' she asked Eileen.

The girl pointed at Laura. 'It's her, miss. She said I'm not pretty,' she sobbed.

'That was unkind, Laura,' the teacher said, then told Eileen to stop making so much noise. 'The rest of you get on with your work,' she told the class. 'You must tell Eileen you're sorry, Laura,' she went on.

Laura scowled. 'But she's not pretty,' she protested. 'She asked me and I told her she wasn't.'

'Er, beauty is in the eye of the beholder,' the teacher said reprovingly. 'It was unkind to say such a thing.'

'But it was the *truth,*' Laura insisted. Fortunately the bell rang for playtime. The teacher sent Eileen out with the rest of the class but kept Laura with her.

'You must try to be a little more tactful, dear,' she said, and when Laura gazed at her blankly she explained, 'Just say yes to a question like that. That's what you are expected to say.'

'But it's not true. She's not pretty.'

'You didn't think so but other people might not agree with you,' the teacher said. 'Eileen's mother, for example.'

'But it was me she asked,' Laura said stubbornly.

Suddenly the teacher lost patience. 'Think of how the other person feels before you speak in future, Laura,' she said crisply. 'Otherwise you're going to be very unpopular.'

She departed to the staff room and Laura joined Rosaleen in the playground, still scowling, but Rosaleen only laughed about the incident. 'Fancy asking you of all people,' she giggled. 'She must be daft. Come on, it's your turn in the rope.'

Laura joined in the game and the incident was not mentioned again but after playtime Laura found that she had a different deskmate. Eileen had been moved to the other side of the room and Laura thought darkly that Mary Morgan, her new deskmate, had better not ask her any soppy questions. If she did she would get a truthful answer no matter what Miss Turner said.

Fortunately it seemed unlikely that Mary would ever ask Laura's opinion on anything. She was a dreamy girl who paid little attention to anybody around her, living in a world of her own.

The twenty-first of October was the second anniversary of the death of Patrick Fitzgerald, the father of Tony, Joe and Anne and of their two sisters and two brothers who had left Liverpool. It was also the anniversary of the death of their mother who had died ten years before her husband. Tony, Joe and Anne and their families attended seven a.m. Mass and afterwards, unwilling to part, went back to Anne's house for breakfast. Those old enough to receive Holy Communion had fasted from midnight so they did full justice to the meal prepared by Anne, Sarah and Helen.

As Anne went through from the kitchen where the children were eating to the dining room the post arrived and she carried the letters through to the dining room.

'A bumper post today,' she said, looking at the postmarks. 'Two from Canada, one from Runcorn, one from Ireland. Nothing from Maureen.'

'It might come later,' said Joe. 'Although it must be very difficult to get letters off at all from where she is now and practically impossible to time them for a special day.'

'I know, Joe. I wasn't moaning. I just hope she got my letter today.'

'Did you write to her? So did we,' said Sarah.

'And so did we,' Tony chimed in. 'Let's hope she gets all the letters from home today. She deserves to.'

'She does indeed,' the others agreed.

Maureen, their unmarried eldest sister, had cared for their father until his sudden death when she closed the house and went to work for Sue Ryder with displaced persons, particularly the orphaned and abandoned children in devastated Europe.

'I'm amazed that the others have timed their letters so well,' Sarah said. 'Sit down, Anne, and enjoy them. Helen and I can see to everything.'

Anne opened the letter from Ireland first. Her other sister Eileen was living in Wicklow with her second husband Martin O'Hanlon and the letter was warm and loving, recalling happy times with Pat Fitzgerald when all his children were young.

Eileen had gone through a bad time when her RAF husband Whitey was killed within a month of their marriage and the family were delighted that she was now happily married to Martin, a kind and gentle man who was a bookbinder in Dublin.

One of the letters from Canada was from their bachelor brother Terry and the other from another brother Stephen and his wife Margaret. Stephen had emigrated to Toronto to join Terry. Both letters recalled the gentle giant Pat Fitzgerald who had been a loving

22

father to all of them and their dear mother who still lived in all their hearts.

Anne wept as she read them and then passed them on as there were messages in them for Tony and Joe but she laughed aloud when she read the letter from Runcorn. It was from her cousin Theresa with a note enclosed from her widowed Aunt Carrie who now lived with her daughter Theresa and her husband Jim, and their six boisterous children, in Runcorn New Town.

'Theresa's a case,' Anne exclaimed. 'She never changes, does she?'

'Remember her and Eileen when they were young?' Tony said. 'The things they used to get up to.'

'And the fellows they went out with,' Helen laughed. 'They left broken hearts all over Liverpool but they didn't give a toss.'

Everyone was laughing and Anne said impulsively, 'Wouldn't Mum and Dad be pleased to see us all here having a laugh together?'

'I was just thinking that,' said Tony. 'Mum and Dad would be pleased to see us all still so close even though some have had to move away. With the letters, I mean,' and everyone agreed.

A few days later a brief but loving letter came from Maureen and Anne was delighted to learn that her letter had been included in a batch delivered to the camp a few days before the anniversary. 'I wanted to keep it until the twenty-first,' Maureen wrote, 'but I couldn't resist opening it. It gave me strength for that day.'

She spoke about the sufferings of the displaced persons among whom she worked and Anne determined to redouble her efforts to raise money for the cause, if only in thanksgiving for her good fortune in having been born in a loving family in Liverpool.

She felt that she had much to be thankful for. Gerry's arm had healed perfectly and Julie seemed to grow stronger every day. She was eating more and had been free of colds for several months. Their savings were growing and John talked of buying a family car, although Anne was quite happy with their outings by train or bus or ferryboat. Laura was doing well at school and she was perfectly healthy and happy, thought Anne, blissfully unaware of the problems which Sally Ward could see so clearly.

Anne's peace of mind was soon shattered, however. Laura, who had always had a good appetite, suddenly decided to be faddy about her food. It started one Sunday dinner time when Laura refused to eat cabbage.

'But you've always liked cabbage. Eat it up, love. It's good for you,' Anne pleaded.

'Eat it,' John said impatiently. 'I'm not having good food wasted. Plenty of children would be glad of it.'

'They can have it,' Laura declared. 'I don't want it.'

John slapped her arm. 'Don't be so hard-faced. Eat it up, every bit of it.'

'You always liked cabbage before. This is just the same,' Anne said.

'I don't like it now,' Laura said, her lip out-thrust mutinously.

'*Eat it!*' John suddenly roared and banged on the table. Julie broke into loud frightened sobs but Laura only clamped her lips firmly together and glared down at her plate.

'Look what you've done now. You've upset your little sister,' John shouted as Anne tried to comfort the child.

Laura shot a look of contempt at her father then stared back at her plate. *He* upset Julie, she thought, and he's trying to blame me.

Anne had managed to calm Julie by taking her on her knee and now she said pleadingly to Laura, 'Eat it, love. Just for me. You don't want to upset Julie, do you?'

'*I* didn't upset her,' Laura muttered.

She would have eaten the cabbage to please her mother if her father had not ordered, 'Give it to her every meal until she's eaten it, Anne. She gets nothing else until it's eaten. When I think of the starving children in the world.'

He doesn't care about starving children, Laura thought angrily, clasping her hands beneath the table. He just wants to make me do what *he* wants and I'm not doing it.

Laura sat with her head bent, making no effort to eat and Anne said helplessly, 'The rhubarb tart will be ruined, John.'

'Serve it then, love,' John said. 'Laura can have hers when she's eaten her cabbage.'

Anne put Julie on her chair again and brought the rhubarb tart and a jug of custard to the table. Julie refused the pudding and Anne felt unable to eat any while Laura sat glowering at her cabbage so only John took his portion and began to eat.

Anne knew that he might as well have been eating sawdust but she was at a loss to know how to resolve the situation between her husband and daughter, both equally stubborn.

Gerry, who might have caused a diversion, was out training and his meal was being kept hot for him so it was a relief to everyone when the door banged and his loud cheerful voice was heard.

'How did you go on, son?' John asked eagerly when Gerry had plumped down beside Laura.

'Great,' Gerry said as his mother placed his meal before him. 'I was the fastest even on the sand.' He began to eat, then glanced at Laura's plate from which she had eaten everything but the cabbage. 'Gosh, don't you want your cabbage?' he asked and when she shook her head he snatched up her plate and emptied her cabbage on to his own plate. 'I'll have it,' he said boisterously. 'I'm starving. Doesn't half make you hungry, running.'

It all happened so quickly that for a moment everyone at the table was stunned and the silence seemed to strike Gerry. 'What's up?' he asked cheerfully.

A smile twitched the corners of Anne's mouth as she said, 'Nothing, son. Nothing at all.' She collected Laura's plate and put a portion of pie and custard before her. 'Would you like some more, John?' she asked.

'No thanks. I'll make a pot of tea,' he said, disappearing into the scullery and Laura ate her pudding with even more enjoyment because she felt that her father had been outwitted.

Later, when Laura had gone to Sunday school with Rosaleen, John grumbled to Anne, 'She thinks she got the better of me over the cabbage, y'know. She's a stubborn little faggot.'

'Yes. I wonder who she inherited it from,' Anne teased him. 'Thank God for Gerry's appetite.'

'Yes, he solved it that time,' John said, still angry. 'But I'm not having it, Anne. Refusing good food for a whim.'

'All children go through these phases,' Anne said but she tried to avoid another confrontation between Laura and her father.

John was often late home and Anne tried to have the children's meal over before he arrived but it was not always possible and Anne grew to dread Sunday dinner when all the family ate together. Cabbage disappeared from the menu but that incident had been only the opening round in the battle between Laura and her father.

In vain Anne tried to persuade John to ignore Laura's fads and to coax Laura to eat the food she was given. The vegetables that replaced the cabbage were refused by the stubborn little girl and at every meal there was a scene between Laura and John. Nobody, least of all Laura, realised that it was an unconscious effort by her to gain the attention that was lavished on Julie when she was unable to eat.

Anne was in despair and felt that the only person she could confide in was Sally Ward, partly because she was discreet but also because she loved and understood both John and Laura.

'I don't know what to do,' she told Sally. 'I try to serve meals at different times but sometimes we have to eat together and there's a row every time. I've tried giving her different veg and I only give her tiny portions but she won't even eat that and now she's started refusing meat.'

'All meat?' asked Sally.

'So far only lamb. She says she doesn't like the veins in it. John says she must be given nothing else until she eats it but I can't let her go hungry. I know how stubborn she is.'

'So you give her other food?' Sally said.

'Only jam butties or a sandwich. I feel awful about going behind John's back but I can't let her starve. I can't eat myself while this is going on but of course that doesn't worry John,' Anne said resentfully.

To her surprise Sally agreed with John. 'If it was just one thing that she really baulked at it'd be wrong to force her to eat it but it sounds as though you do your best to humour her and she finds something else to be faddy about,' the old lady declared.

'Yes, I'm at my wits' end,' Anne said. 'Gerry solved it the first time and saved face for both of them but now neither of them will give in and they're both so stubborn.'

'Good God, girl, you're talking about a child of nine and her father,' Sally exclaimed. 'Don't put them both on the same level. John's entitled to respect from his children.'

'I can see both sides,' Anne confessed. 'I thought you might advise me, Grandma.'

'Tell John you'll handle it,' Sally told her, 'and deal with Laura's fads yourself. Tell her you know that it's not that she *can't* eat but that she won't and you're not having it.'

'But what if she won't eat even then?' Anne said doubtfully.

'Tell her she'll get nothing else and keep to it. Hunger's a good sauce, girl, and she won't starve. She's had too many years of good feeding behind her. It's not the food. Laura's determined to defy her father and he's determined not to let her and he's right. You'll be making a rod for your own backs if you let her get the upper hand of you now, girl, and it'd be bad for the child herself.'

Anne sighed. 'I think you're right, Grandma, and I'll try it. The hardest part will be convincing John.'

'Tell him the cook's going on strike if he doesn't agree and he'll soon toe the line,' said Sally and they laughed together.

Anne put the plan into operation immediately and hardened her heart when Laura looked at her reproachfully or she heard her sobbing in bed. Sally took the opportunity to talk to Laura on her next visit.

'Your mum said you've started turning your nose up at good food,' she began and when Laura nodded Sally said sternly, 'That's something I can't abide to see. If you'd seen what I'd seen you'd never refuse food. Children dying long before they were your age because they never had enough to eat.'

'That was a long time ago,' Laura muttered.

'Not all that long, miss,' Sally said sharply. 'There was a time when your Nana was a little girl when it took me all my time to find enough to feed her and her sister and we were well off compared to some. Plenty of children lived and died without ever knowing a full belly.'

'Perhaps they just didn't like the food,' Laura said. She had never seen her grandma so angry.

'Don't talk like a fool,' she snapped. 'It'd do you good to go short. I'm talking about hungry barefoot children that would eat mouldy bread if they could get it, crying with hunger pains and their mams crying with hunger themselves and having to listen to their children suffering and nothing to give them. Think of your house with no food in the cupboard, nothing at all and no way of getting it and no fire or warm clothes either. You don't know you're born.'

Laura sat with her head bent and Sally said more gently, 'I can't expect you to realise I suppose. You've never known anything but plenty but my Lawrie worked all his life to do away with that sort of poverty. It broke his heart to see those children but I suppose it's soon forgotten.'

She looked sad and Laura said impulsively, 'I just didn't know, Grandma. I *will* eat all my dinners, honest.'

'That's a good girl. Your mam works hard cooking nice meals for you, love, and your dad works hard to get the money to buy the food,' Sally said. 'I know you don't want to upset your mam.'

Laura seemed subdued when she returned home but she ate all her meal. Anne had a quiet word with John so nothing was said and peace reigned.

Chapter Three

The food war was soon forgotten in excitement when Rosaleen and David came to stay for a week. Sarah and Joe had gone to Dublin to visit Anne and Joe's sister Eileen and her husband Martin O'Hanlon. After eight childless years Eileen had given birth to identical twin boys in Dublin's Mater Hospital and Sarah and Joe had gone to help when she returned home.

'I'd love to go to Eileen,' Anne said wistfully, 'but I daren't leave Julie.'

'Eileen understands that,' Sarah assured her. 'You're helping by taking our kids for a week.'

'I'm glad to have them and Laura's made up,' Anne said. The week passed too quickly for Laura. Rosa had dancing lessons twice a week and on those evenings Laura visited Sally. There were no main roads between the two houses so she was able to go alone. Sally had suffered with arthritis for many years in her arms and shoulders but now her legs were affected so walking was difficult and she welcomed Laura warmly.

Laura enjoyed her visits to her great-grandmother and Anne encouraged them. She felt that the wise old lady knew how to guide her difficult child and when Laura asked about the relationship between the people in Grandma's family stories she advised her to ask her father. 'He could tell you better than me,' she said. 'It's *his* family,' and rejoiced when she saw John drawing up a family tree for Laura.

On a day that was a school holiday Laura went after lunch and found her grandmother alone. 'It's Grandma's day for the pictures,' Cathy explained. 'You can help me to get a nice tea ready for her and Mrs Burns when they come back.'

For many years Sally and her old friend and former neighbour Peggy Burns had visited the cinema on one afternoon a week and a cafe either before or after the performance. Now that they were both in their eighties they found the journey and the cafe visit too much but fortunately Greg, who was managing director of his firm, could arrange his work so that he was free to drive his mother-in-law and her friend to the cinema. Later he collected them and brought them back for a meal prepared by his wife.

Laura liked Mrs Burns. She was as small and fat as Sally was tall and spare and she often joked that they were like Laurel and Hardy.

'Although I'm the daft one,' Mrs Burns told Laura. Peggy Burns and Sally had lived next door to each other for many years until their houses had been destroyed by the same bomb during the war, fortunately while they were taking shelter elsewhere.

Sally had moved in with Cathy and Greg and Peggy had gone to live with her granddaughter Meg and her husband. Meg was a very pretty but slightly retarded girl, brought up by Peggy after her parents' death, and it was a great relief to Peggy when Willie Smith wanted to marry Meg and look after her. They had all lived amicably together until Peggy took a house to provide a home for her son Michael when he returned from a Japanese prisoner-of-war camp. Unfortunately his experiences at the hands of the Japanese had left him broken in mind and body. Although he recovered physically, his mental state was so bad that eventually he had been admitted to a psychiatric hospital. He had been unhappy there and Greg had managed to get him transferred to the psychiatric wing of a smaller hospital.

Laura enjoyed helping her grandmother to make sandwiches of home-cooked ham and tinned salmon, and to lay the table with these and small dishes of pickled onions and beetroot, small home-made meat pies and various tarts and cakes, and also a glass bowl of tinned fruit and one of trifle. 'Mrs Burns likes her food,' Cathy explained as Laura surveyed the table.

'She must do,' said Laura.

All was ready when Greg ushered in the two old ladies.

'Oo, we've got company today,' Peggy exclaimed when she saw Laura. 'Have you been helping your nana, love?'

Laura nodded and Cathy fussed about her mother and her friend, settling them at the table.

'Was it a good film?' Laura asked.

'Yes,' Peggy answered, 'but I always enjoy the Palladium no matter what's on, don't you, Sal? It's more homely than the town pictures and they've got Cinemarascope and terrier sonic sound just as good as the Futurist or any of them.'

Laura glanced at the adults but no one appeared to notice Peggy's mispronunciation or attempted to correct her as Laura felt her father would have done. Peggy went on happily, 'Rosaleen's not with you then today, love? She's your best mate, isn't she?'

'Yes, my very best friend,' Laura said. 'She's gone to an extra dancing class.'

'I thought that was what she did,' Peggy said. 'I seen her one day in Breckfield Road with a parcel like shoes under her arm. I thought that was where she was off.'

Greg winked at Laura. 'Mrs Burns would have been a great detective if only she'd been a man,' he said solemnly.

Peggy laughed loudly. 'Go on with you,' she said, giving Greg a playful push. 'I keep my eyes and ears open, that's all.' They were all laughing and Laura felt warm and comfortable. I wish our house was like this, she thought, then corrected herself. It *is* like this until Dad comes in.

Greg went out to the hall to telephone his office and Peggy proceeded to tell many tales about the background to scandals and events in the city and anecdotes about her neighbours.

'Eh, you're as good as a music hall turn, Peg,' Sally said, wiping tears of laughter from her eyes.

Peggy, suddenly serious, said with a sigh, 'We might as well laugh while we can. None of us knows what's in front of us. Poor Nellie Ashcroft got took to the Kirkdale Homes last week.'

'What were those girls thinking of?' Sally exclaimed. 'Surely one of them could have looked after her. She was a good mother to them.'

'None of them ever give tuppence for her,' Peggy said. 'She was always just a handrag to them and to him and all. Never treated her proper. Only the size of sixpenn'orth of copper, he was, and thought he was the whole cheese.'

'I remember Mr Ashcroft when he was the air raid warden,' Cathy said. 'Strutting round like a little bantam cock. He thought he was running the war.'

'Aye, well, he was lucky. He dropped dead at work,' Peggy said. 'None of them girls have visited poor Nellie Ashcroft, Sal.'

'Greg would take you and Peggy to see her if you want to go, Mum,' Cathy said.

Later Cathy often regretted her impulsive suggestion but at the time the two old ladies welcomed the idea and Greg readily agreed to take them whenever they wished.

'Let me know when you want to go,' he said. 'I'm just going in to work to sign some letters but I'll be back to take you home, Mrs Burns.'

'Eh, he's a proper gentleman, isn't he?' Peggy said when he left. 'The way he always calls me Mrs Burns. And a good man too, and all done quiet like. No banging a drum or waving a banner like your John but he does more good in his own quiet way. He puts me in mind of Lawrie.'

'Lawrie could bang a drum if he thought it was needed,' Sally said. 'And our John is trying to carry on where Lawrie left off.'

'But Lawrie was never a big-head like John,' Peggy declared and Sally tutted and nodded at Laura.

'Oo, I forgot – he's your dad,' Peggy exclaimed. 'Don't take no notice to me, girl. I never open me mouth without putting me foot in it. Me and your dad are old sparring partners, that's all.'

Laura left as soon as the meal was finished and as she ran home she hugged the thought to her that Mrs Burns considered her father a big-head. Later when she was helping her mother to fold clothes she talked about Mrs Burns.

'She's funny, isn't she, Mum? The things she says.'

Her mother laughed. 'Yes, she's a real character. She's had a hard life but she's always kept cheerful. She and Grandma have been friends for years although they're so different.'

'She said that her and Daddy are old sparring partners,' Laura said, darting a quick glance at her mother before turning back to the clothes. 'What did she mean?'

'They disagreed about the atom bomb,' Anne informed her. 'Daddy didn't think it was right to use it and neither do I but Mrs Burns's son was badly treated by the Japanese and she agreed with using it.'

Laura opened her mouth to ask further questions but her mother said quickly, 'That's enough now, Laura. I've told you all that because you have a bad habit of nagging until you find out all you want to know. It's not nice in a little girl so I don't want to hear any more.'

Laura stood looking down and scowling with her lower lip thrust out and Anne laughed. 'I wish you could see yourself. You must have better things to think about than old arguments. Rosaleen wants to show you her new dance.'

Laura said no more but she heard her Aunt Sarah discussing the visit to the Kirkdale Homes and determined to be at the house in Wastdale Road when her great-grandmother and Mrs Burns returned. She hoped that Mrs Burns would say more about her father.

She again helped her grandmother to prepare a meal but when the two old ladies returned they both looked white and upset and neither spoke until Cathy and Greg had settled them in chairs and brought cups of tea to them.

'Thanks, girl,' Peggy said in a subdued voice. 'Thank God for a cup of tea. That's proper shook us up, hasn't it, Sal?'

Sally nodded and Cathy said gently, 'Was Mrs Ashcroft bad then?'

'Bad enough,' said Peggy. 'But it was them others. A great big ward full of old women and nearly all of them outa their minds. Oh, God, girl, it'd break your heart. Proper knocked the stuffing outa me and your mam, seeing and hearing that.'

'Senile dementia they call it,' Sally said. 'Crying and screaming and shouting for their mams. And the worst of it, poor Nellie Ashcroft and a few others in their right minds having to lay and listen to that night and day.' Her hand shook as she lifted the teacup and Cathy sat on a stool beside her.

'Try not to think of it, Mam,' she said gently. 'Was Mrs Ashcroft pleased to see you?'

'She broke her heart crying when she first seen us,' Peggy said, 'but then she ate some of your cake, Cathy, and enjoyed it. The nurse took the rest to mind for her because she said the other old women would pinch it off her.'

'The nurses do their best,' Sally said. 'Good job someone'll do the work but it's hopeless. It's something comes on in old age. I kept thinking that them women might have been the same as us a few years ago.'

'By God, I'd go outa me mind if I thought I'd go like that,' Peggy exclaimed and everyone was too upset to notice anything odd about her remark.

Cathy said swiftly, 'Well, at least neither of you would go in the Homes. Your Chrissie wouldn't let you go, Peggy, and neither would any of the others. Even now Chrissie wants you to live with her, doesn't she?'

'Yes, but I want to have a home for Michael if he comes out of hospital. Chrissie says he'll be welcome there and I know he will but he might be better on his own with me,' said Peggy. 'We're lucky, Sal. We've both got good children.'

She was quiet and subdued for a while but before long she became more cheerful and laughed and joked as usual, but everyone noticed a change in Peggy from the day of the visit to the Kirkdale Homes. It was not repeated but Cathy went alone to visit Mrs Ashcroft and reported that she was sinking fast. She died less than three weeks after the visit by Sally and Peggy.

The time for Gerry's 11-plus examination was drawing near and John became increasingly worried about his prospects, but Gerry was unperturbed. He did the homework he was given as rapidly as possible then escaped to play with his friends.

'It might be all the better that he's not worried about it,' Anne consoled John and she was proved right. Gerry remained unconcerned about the examination and in due course he was selected for a place at St Edward's College.

He went off happily and confidently on the first day of term, wearing the school uniform of purple blazer and cap and grey short trousers. His only complaint was that the college played rugby football, not soccer.

Julie started school and, now much stronger, easily survived all the usual childhood infections but she was still very shy and nervous with strangers. Anne worried about her and urged Laura and Rosaleen to watch over her at playtime, as their playground adjoined the Infants' playground, but her concern was unnecessary. Julie was still very small for her age but her gentle manner and sweet smile made even her small classmates feel protective towards her and she made many friends.

Laura had been once to the dancing class with Rosaleen but it was not a success. She lacked Rosaleen's natural grace and coordination and grew more awkward when the teacher criticised her. 'Now, Laura, no scowls here,' the teacher trilled as Laura stood with her lower lip out-thrust. 'Only pretty pretty smiles allowed in our happy little group.'

Laura looked at her with disgust and refused to go to the class again. 'She's too soppy,' she told Rosaleen, 'and she makes me feel as though my feet and hands are twice their size.'

In vain Rosaleen urged her to try again. 'It'll just come to you,' she said but Laura's mind was made up.

She went even more frequently to see Grandma, encouraged by Cathy, although Anne and John worried that the visits were becoming too frequent. 'Don't let Laura be a nuisance to Grandma,' John said when Cathy came alone to visit them. 'She gets very tired now, doesn't she?'

'She gets a bit low in spirit because of the way Peggy is,' Cathy said, 'but she enjoys Laura's company. She talks about the days of her own childhood and ours and Laura's always interested even though she's heard the tales before. They're on the same wavelength and it does Grandma a world of good.'

'Is Peggy no better then?' Anne asked. 'What exactly is wrong?'

'Nothing you can put your finger on,' Cathy said. 'She just seems to have lost heart. Ever since she went to the Kirkdale Homes it seems to have preyed on her mind – the way those women were. I wish to God I'd never suggested them going.'

'You did it for the best,' Anne consoled her. 'And if they hadn't gone she could be worrying because they didn't go to see their friend.'

'Maybe, but it all seems to have started then,' said Cathy. She sighed and picked up her handbag. 'I'd better go. I don't like to leave Grandma on her own for long. Let Laura come and cheer her up whenever she wants to.'

Later she spoke to her mother about Peggy. 'She's gone so quiet,' Cathy said. 'I was just saying to Anne I'm sorry I ever suggested going to the Homes.'

'You did it out of a kind heart, girl,' Sally said. 'And at least we let poor Nellie Ashcroft see that everyone hadn't forgot her.'

'But Peggy hasn't been the same since,' Cathy said.

'No, she hasn't,' Sally agreed. 'It upset me to see them women but it seemed to cut Peggy to the heart. Anyhow, Greg says he'll take her and the two daughters to see Michael on Sunday so that might cheer her up.'

Greg took Peggy and her daughters to see Michael Burns as planned and after dropping the daughters at their homes he brought Peggy to his own house for tea.

Sally and Cathy welcomed her affectionately. 'How was Michael?' Cathy asked as she poured tea.

Peggy sighed. 'He looks well but he never knew it was us till I said we was his mam and his sisters, then he put his arms round us and kissed us. He looks happy though, doesn't he, Greg?'

'Yes, he does,' said Greg. 'You see, Peggy, he's blocked off the past and the future in his mind but he's quite happy living in the present, the doctor said. He enjoys his food and sitting in that lovely garden and he's made friends there.'

'I seen you talking to the doctor, Greg,' Peggy said. 'I don't like to ask to see the doctor and they never tell me nothing anyhow. What else did he say?'

Greg sat down by Peggy and said earnestly, 'He said that Michael is improving but it's a long process. At first he forgot his friends if they went away to the toilet even but that doesn't happen now and that's encouraging. He's fine while he's awake. It's when he sleeps that those nightmares start but there's always someone on hand to calm him and the treatment is helping him.'

Peggy had sat with her head bent as he talked but now she looked up into his face. 'An' he thinks it'll take a long time? Will they keep him there, Greg?'

'Yes, until he's completely cured,' Greg said quietly. 'It might take years but you could see he was quite happy and the staff are fond of him.'

'I'm glad, lad,' Peggy said simply. 'I've been worried about having a home for him to come to but if he's cured he can go to one of the girls – or the lads.'

'Yes. If you want to plan to live with your daughter there's no need to worry about Michael,' Greg said.

Peggy said no more and a little later Greg took her home. After they had gone Sally sat looking into the fire until Cathy said gently, 'Another cup of tea, Mum?'

Sally looked up and smiled at her daughter. 'No thanks, love. I'm just thinking. Peggy's not planning on going to Chrissie's. I think she's clearing the decks, as your dad would say.'

Cathy made no patronising protest. 'I thought that, Mum,' she said. 'She knows Meg's safe with Willie Smith and now she doesn't have to worry about Michael.'

Sally nodded. 'And at least Peggy's got a family that think the world of her. Not like poor Nellie Ashcroft. I keep thinking of her and them girls, Cath. Well, they're born but they're not buried, as Mrs Mal used to say. Maybe their own children will treat them the same way.'

'Maybe,' Cathy agreed. 'Should we take a run down to our John's or our Sarah's after and see the children?'

Sally laughed. 'Yes, I'd like that but poor Greg, he'll be sorry he ever bought that car.'

'No, Greg'll enjoy seeing the children too,' Cathy said stoutly.

Cathy telephoned Anne and it was arranged that they would go to Anne's house and Sarah and Joe would be there with their children too. 'So that I can put Julie to bed if she gets tired,' Anne said.

The visit was a success and Sally seemed greatly cheered by being with the children. David went immediately to his grandfather and told him about the book he was reading and experiments his class had made but the girls gathered round Sally and Cathy.

'Do your new dance for Grandma and Nana, Rosa,' Anne suggested and Rosaleen performed a graceful dance.

'Very nice,' Cathy exclaimed as they applauded. 'A pity you didn't like the dancing, Laura.'

'I thought it was daft,' Laura said bluntly, 'especially when Miss Honey was saying "Think of leetle leeeves fluttering down, now we are all leetle leetle leeeves fluttering" and she did this.' Laura waggled her arms and jumped about but Rosaleen fluttered gracefully beside her with outspread arms and dainty steps.

All the adults laughed and Gerry, who had just come in called, 'Rosa *looks* like a leaf fluttering, Laura, but you look like a conker falling on someone's head.'

'Aye, well, Rosa's good at the dancing and Laura's good at knitting,' Sally said swiftly. She turned to Anne. 'I can't get over how quick she picked it up, even cable stitch, and lovely and neat too.'

Laura smiled with delight and Cathy hugged her. 'You must have inherited the knack from Grandma, love,' she said. 'Remember the beautiful knitting you did for us, Mum?'

'Yes, but I was never the same after I broke my arm,' Sally said. 'The rheumatics got into it and I could never do the fine sewing or the complicated knitting after that, although thank goodness I could still do the everyday sort of work.'

'Tell the girls how your arm was broken, Mum,' Cathy said.

Sally demurred. 'No, they want to be out playing, not listening to those old tales.' But Laura and Rosaleen clamoured for the story.

'It was a long time ago,' Sally said. 'The First World War. Just before your dad was born, Laura. Luckily I'd already made his shawl.'

'And you wore that shawl to be christened, Laura, and so did Gerry and Julie,' said Anne.

'So did I and so did David and Rosaleen,' Sarah added, smiling, 'and now it's been put away for the next generation.'

'Go on about your arm, Grandma,' Laura urged.

'People were very stupid,' Sally said. 'A ship called the *Lusitania* was sunk by the Germans and a mob of people went round wrecking the shops of anyone they thought was German. Poor Mr Solomon who had a sort of pawnbroker's shop by us was a Polish Jew but they wrecked his shop too. I went to tell him they were coming and they set about me as well.'

The children's eyes were wide with horror. 'Did they get put in gaol?' Rosa asked.

'I wish I'd been there, Grandma,' Gerry said fiercely. 'I wouldn't have let them hurt you. Did they kill Mr Solomon?'

'No, but they stole all his stuff,' Sally told them. 'And he was a real good old man too.'

Laura stroked Sally's arm. 'Did it hurt a lot when your arm was broken, Grandma?'

'Well, it did hurt, love, but it was more the inconvenience of it as it was my right arm. Still, it did me a good turn because your nana was married and in her own house then but she came home to help me because I couldn't cut bread or peel potatoes or anything. Your grandad was in the army so she moved in to live with us and that's how your dad came to be born in our house.'

'But what about those wicked people? *Did* the police lock them up?' asked Gerry.

'No, they all scarpered when the police came near. I think they were ashamed of themselves.'

'All this going on and we were stuck away in heaven,' Rosaleen said with an aggrieved air.

The adults laughed but Gerry said scornfully, 'You get dafter every day, Rosa.'

'It'll be a long time before she's as daft as you,' Laura retorted quickly.

'Now, now, only pretty pretty smiles here please,' Anne said in parody of the dancing teacher and made them all laugh.

Sally was cheered by the visit but only days later Peggy caught a cold which swiftly became pneumonia and within two weeks she was dead.

'She didn't make no fight of it,' her daughter Chrissie sobbed to Sally and Sally comforted her.

'It's the way she wanted to go, girl,' she told her gently. 'We saw them women in the Kirkdale Homes with their minds gone astray with old age and your mam dreaded an end like that.'

'I know,' Chrissie said. 'She never seemed the same after that day and she worried about going like them.'

'And now she's gone peaceful with her mind easy about Meg and Michael,' said Sally. 'Don't wish her back, girl.'

Chrissie dried her eyes. 'She had a hard life, me mam, but she really enjoyed herself these last few years. She thought the world of you and your family, Mrs Ward, and youse were all good to her. Them trips to the pictures and coming back for her tea and then before that the way Mary in America paid for youse to go to the cafe after the pictures. Me mam'd never had such a good time.'

'I was glad of her company,' Sally said. 'We went through a lot together, me and Peggy, and we never had a cross word from the day she moved in next door to me all them years ago.'

She wept a little and Chrissie said, 'We're all thankful for what you done for her and to Mr Redmond an' all. Taking us to see our Michael and getting him into that good place.'

'He'll still take you to see him any time you want to go, Chrissie,' Sally said. 'I think he told Robbie that at the funeral.'

'Yes, he did,' said Chrissie. Suddenly she bent and kissed Sally. 'Look after yourself. Good people are scarce. You and Mr Ward – all you done for people...' She could say no more but fled sobbing, leaving Sally upset yet comforted.

Chapter Four

Laura was surprised that her great-grandmother showed so little distress at Mrs Burns's death but Anne explained that old people learned to accept death. 'Grandma knows that Mrs Burns enjoyed her life. She had a loving family and a peaceful end and she was ready to go. That's what everyone wants for people they love,' she said.

Anne was trying to prepare Laura to face loss herself but Laura took a different meaning from her words. Her mother was old, Laura thought, not as old as Grandma but *old*, well over thirty, yet she didn't accept death.

Often Laura saw signs that her mother had been weeping and Anne would explain that the smell of St Bruno tobacco or an old song had reminded her of her dead father. But perhaps that was just an excuse, thought Laura. Perhaps it was really her father who made her mother weep. But Laura was less ready now to blame her father for everything. Since he had drawn up the family tree for her he had become more interested in her and shown his approval of the time she spent with Grandma. Laura had responded by being more obedient and less ready to argue. Anne was happy about the new harmony in the family and, always an optimist, decided that Laura's awkwardness had been just a passing phase.

Laura still tried to dominate Gerry at times but since starting at the college he had become more independent and refused to allow Laura to rule him as she had once done.

He spent less time at home now as he was involved in so much at the college: athletics and cricket in the summer and cross-country running in the winter. So much homework was given by each master that most of his time at home was spent on it and there was little opportunity for the talks with him that John had always enjoyed. As a result he spent more time with his daughters but the fragile peace between himself and Laura was soon broken on a night when John was late home from work.

Laura had woken with earache and Anne brought her downstairs, partly to avoid disturbing Julie and partly because she felt that Laura needed company. She settled the child in a chair by the fire, giving her an aspirin and a filled hot water bottle wrapped in a towel to hold close to her ear.

John was still not home. He was the personnel officer at a large factory and had spent a frustrating day trying to reconcile management and employees to avert a threatened strike, with little success. It was late when he left work, still raging at what he considered their stupidity. He went straight to a committee meeting where he was immediately involved in a row with a councillor so he arrived home in a foul temper. He began to pour out his troubles to Anne but she said calmly, 'Tell me about it later. Eat your dinner now.'

'I don't want it,' John said but Anne protested.

'You must eat, John. You'll feel better.'

'*I don't want it!*' John shouted. 'Can't you understand English?'

'Don't yell at Mummy,' Laura shouted from the depths of the armchair. John looked round in amazement, seeing her for the first time.

'Don't speak to me like that,' he snarled. 'And don't look at me like that either.'

'Leave her alone,' Anne said. 'She's got earache.'

'Then why isn't she in bed?' said John.

'I thought she needed company but *now* she'll be better in bed. Come on, love,' Anne said, picking up the hot water bottle and taking Laura's hand. As they left the room Laura looked back triumphantly at her father, unseen by Anne.

Upstairs Anne tucked Laura into bed, arranging the hot water bottle near her ear. 'Go to sleep now, love,' she said quietly. 'The pain will soon go with the aspirin and the heat. Goodnight.' She kissed Laura and went out, closing the door behind her.

The look from Laura as she went out had left John clenching his teeth and trembling with fury. 'I'm not having it,' he burst out as soon as Anne appeared. 'Speaking to me and looking at me like that. Would you have been allowed to speak to your father like that at her age?'

'My father never spoke to my mother like you spoke to me,' Anne said, sitting down and picking up her knitting.

For a moment John looked startled then he said plaintively, 'After the bloody day I've had, tearing myself apart for those boneheads at work, then I was late leaving so I went straight to the committee meeting and Philips was only waiting for me to come to start a row about procedure. I thought I'd get some sympathy at home but I wish I'd gone to the pub instead.'

'So do I,' said Anne. 'You could have had another row there and worked off your bad temper before you got here.'

John stopped pacing about and looked at her. 'I suppose I shouldn't bring my troubles home with me,' he muttered.

'Of course you should,' Anne said. 'And you know I always listen but you should control your temper, especially in front of the children.'

'I didn't see her there,' John said. 'But the way she looked at me as she went out, with her nose in the air and sort of disdainful. We'll have to do something about her impudence. You're far too soft with the kids, Anne.'

'It's a habit I've got into I suppose,' Anne said dryly. 'I've been too soft with you for years but you've never objected to that.'

'Too soft with me?' John echoed. 'But I've never given you any reason to complain, have I?'

Anne sat with the knitting resting in her lap looking at him quizzically and John crouched down beside her.

'I'm sorry I spoke like that tonight,' he said, putting his arms round her. 'But it's unusual for me to be bad-tempered with *you,* isn't it, love? It was just that I was at the end of my tether. That performance from Laura was just too much altogether.'

His rudeness to her came before he saw Laura but Anne only said, 'She's too much like you. That's the trouble.'

'Like me?' John exclaimed, astounded. 'She's less like me than any of them, except for her hair.'

Anne only shrugged and smiled then asked if he wanted his dinner.

'In a minute. I'll get it out of the oven. Listen, Anne, I do *try* to watch my temper, you know,' John said humbly and Anne put her arms round his neck and kissed him.

'I know. And you *are* better. A few years ago you wouldn't have discussed things.' She laughed. 'You'd have said your piece then you'd have been out of the door before I could speak. Going walkabout, as your Mick called it.'

John smiled but Anne could see that an unwary word could soon inflame his temper again and she said briskly, 'Sit at the table,' and standing up she took his dinner from the Aga and lifted off the plate covering it.

She went into the scullery and John could hear her whistling an Irish jig. 'You sound like your Eileen,' he called and she reappeared smiling.

'God, yes, she could whistle,' she said. 'I remember her whistling to a blackbird once and the bird whistled back. They kept it up for ages.'

Upstairs Laura lay tense trying to hear what was happening downstairs, but even when she slipped out of bed and opened the bedroom door the solid old house made it difficult to hear more than a distant murmur. Once she thought she heard her mother laugh but decided she must be mistaken. What if it was a cry for help?

After a while she crept along the landing then down a few stairs until she could peep through the banisters. The living-room door was slightly open and she saw her father light two cigarettes and hand one to her mother, who was smiling up at him as he bent over her.

As Laura watched in amazement she heard her father say casually, 'Dad's thinking of getting a television set. Now Grandma can't get out much he thinks it'll be a fresh interest for her.'

'It's a good idea,' Anne said. She laughed. 'Gerry'll never get any homework done. He'll be round there by the minute.'

John turned as though to walk into the hall and Laura ran lightly back up the stairs and jumped into bed. Grown-ups, she thought in disgust. You never knew where you were with them. She thought her mother would have told her father off and yet they seemed like good friends. No wonder Rosa said they were all mad. Anne would have been amused to know that Laura decided that her mother was far too soft with her father.

In previous years the families had gone to the grandparents' house for Christmas dinner but in 1957 Sarah decided that it was too much for her mother and invited Cathy and Greg and Sally to her house. They were joined by Anne and John and their children and Helen and Tony and their two daughters.

Sarah and Joe lived in a big old house with large rooms and they were able to seat sixteen round her large dining table fully extended. It was a happy occasion and everyone made an extra fuss of Sally who was becoming more frail although as bright and cheerful as ever.

Cathy and Greg were happy because they had received a Christmas card and a short letter from their daughter Kate in America, who was now Mrs Capaldi.

'We don't know whether he's in the Mafia or a successful ice-cream merchant,' Greg joked, 'but apparently he's a millionaire.'

Kate had met and married her first husband, the American Gene Romero, when he was stationed at Burtonwood during the war. She had returned to America with him but the marriage had not lasted. Now John said grimly, 'Let's hope he'll be firmer with her than Gene was. He was too soft with her altogether.' He suddenly caught Anne's glance and they both smiled.

Cathy said with a sigh, 'Yes indeed. I hope poor Gene meets someone who can make him happy. He deserves it. We wrote to him and his parents and had lovely cards and letters from them.'

They had just finished the meal when the telephone rang and Joe came for Sally. 'It's Mick ringing from York,' he explained. 'He wants to speak to you first, Grandma.'

Sally was still nervous of the telephone but soon they heard her laughing and exclaiming, 'Mick, you're a case. You never alter, lad.' She talked for a few more minutes then called Cathy and Greg to the telephone and came back to the family smiling.

'Eh, that lad. He never changes. Just as mad as ever. He must be a millionaire by now but there's not a ha'porth of difference in him.'

'Why should there be?' John demanded. 'Money's not that important.'

'Only when you've got none,' Sally said dryly and John was silenced. When Cathy and Greg came back Sarah and John went to speak to their brother and Cathy announced that Mick and his wife Gerda would come home for New Year.

'That's something to look forward to,' Anne said, 'Always plenty of laughs when Mick's around,' and everyone agreed.

Another family party was held at the grandparents' house at New Year when Mick and Gerda arrived. Helen and Tony and the girls were invited because Tony was Anne and Joe's brother so his family was always treated as part of the Redmond family too.

Before the party Laura visited Grandma and was shown old photographs of Mick and Gerda. She knew that they were wealthy but not why. Now Sally explained that the slim, elegant Gerda was a qualified accountant and that Mick, laughing and looking devil-may-care in RAF uniform, had opened a plastics factory after the war and made his fortune.

'He had Cathy's heart broke when he was little,' Sally said. 'The mischief he got up to. You never knew what he'd do next but there was no harm in him. The house went quiet when he went.'

At the party Laura thought that Grandma was right. There seemed to be continuous laughter wherever Mick was and Anne in particular seemed completely relaxed. She always seemed happy but Laura, sensitive to her mother's every mood, could see that she was always nervous in family gatherings in case John said something controversial.

Now John seemed as charmed by Mick as the rest of the family. When Mick asked if he would be going to London for the inauguration of the CND movement, John said eagerly, 'Yes of course. It's what I've been saying since Hiroshima, that nuclear weapons should be banned and I'm made up that other people think so too.'

'So that's the secret of your unpopularity, John. You're always ahead of everyone else,' Mick joked.

Anne looked anxious but John only laughed. 'Perhaps it is,' he said.

He was sitting near his grandmother and she said firmly, 'Your grandad used to say he marched to a different drum because he was often out of step with other people but they came round to thinking the same as him in the long run. When he wanted pensions for widows and sick pay when men were off work they thought he was mad but it all came in the end. Maybe John marches to a different drum too.'

Mick thumped John's back. 'He always did but keep it up, John. The world needs people like you to balance all the fools like me.' The next moment he was telling a joke that had everyone laughing but Laura looked at her father with new respect.

Shortly before midnight Greg went out as he had done for many years carrying coal and salt, then as midnight struck he returned. The door was opened to him by Cathy and he kissed her and said, 'A happy New Year, love. God bless all here,' before going to kiss Sally.

All the children had been allowed to stay up to see in 1958 and everyone spilled out into the road to join neighbours in listening to the hooting of the ships on the river and the sound of church bells, while wishing each other a happy New Year amid much hilarity.

Sally went out too but only for a moment then she returned to her chair by the fire, accompanied by Cathy and Laura. 'Go back to the family, Cath,' she urged her daughter. 'Laura will stay with me, won't you, love?' Laura nodded, feeling proud and important as she sat holding her great-grandmother's hand.

The table had been laid with traditional New Year fare: spare ribs and sandwiches of home-cooked ham and bunloaf and mince pies. Drinks were in the kitchen and the family soon surged back to toast the New Year and to eat the food.

'Gosh, I'm starving,' Mick exclaimed.

Gerda said reprovingly, 'But Mick, it's such a short time since you ate a large meal.'

'He's got hollow legs, girl,' Sally said. 'We always said so, didn't we, Cath?'

Cathy nodded and smiled.

Helen sat down beside her. 'This bunloaf is delicious, Mrs Redmond,' she said. 'I know you gave me the recipe but mine never turns out like this.'

'It's just luck sometimes,' Cathy said. 'I was baking all the time when they were all at home and it wasn't only Mick who had hollow

47

legs. John was as bad, and so were Sarah and Kate for that matter, and they'd have eaten anything. If friends were coming to tea I baked the same sandwich cakes that had turned out perfect for the family and they turned out as flat as flukes.'

Helen laughed. 'That must have been annoying.'

'It certainly was, especially when I made them again for the family and they turned out well. I must have tried too hard for visitors.'

'Perhaps I'm trying too hard,' Helen said. She looked over to where Mick crouched down surrounded by all the children. 'Just look at the children's faces,' she exclaimed. 'Whatever is Mick doing?'

'Conjuring tricks, I think,' Cathy said as Mick pretended to take a small flag from Julie's sleeve. 'Hasn't Julie improved this past year?'

'Yes. She looks really healthy now,' Helen agreed. 'I'm so pleased for Anne's sake – and John's,' she added hastily, realising that she was speaking to John's mother.

'Yes, it was a worry for them. Thank God Gerry and Laura are healthy too so they've got nothing to worry about.'

They were still watching the children and the next moment Mick stood up. 'Well, kids, I'm going to get a drink now and we'll have another game later.' The children dispersed and Moira came to her mother with her arm round her sister.

'Laura always spoils everything,' she said angrily. 'Uncle Mick was taking a ball from Dilly's pocket and the kids all thought it was magic but Laura said she saw it up his sleeves.'

Helen and Cathy glanced at each other and Helen put her arm round Dilly who looked tearful. Moira, who was now a tall girl of fifteen, went on, 'She's always the same. When we all went to see *Peter Pan*, and Peter and Wendy were flying to Never-Never Land, all the little kids thought it was magic but Laura had to say that she saw one of the actors fastening wires to Peter and Wendy's backs so they could fly. She spoiled it all.'

Cathy sighed. 'I'm afraid Laura's eyes are as sharp as her tongue.'

'She's just too honest,' Helen said soothingly. 'She doesn't mean to upset anyone.' She kissed Dilly and said to Moira, 'Why don't you organise a game of I Spy, love?'

'I wish Laura wasn't so outspoken,' Cathy said when the children had gone. 'She can't seem to help herself but she's such a good child really. She's so patient and loving with Grandma and she's really helped her to get over losing Peggy.'

'I know. She never means to hurt,' agreed Helen. 'She just speaks the truth as she sees it. She'll probably grow more tactful as she grows older.'

'Let's hope so,' said Cathy. 'Moira's lovely with Dilly, isn't she? A real big sister.'

Helen smiled. 'Yes, she is. Of course Dilly's very sensitive, you know. By the time she came to us when she was four she'd lost her mother and been in the orphanage for a year so it's no wonder she's easily upset.'

'I'm sure she'll soon outgrow that,' Cathy said. 'She's settled down so well with you, no one would ever know she wasn't born to you and Tony. You've done a good job with your girls, Helen.'

Sarah and Joe came to talk to them and soon all the parents began to collect their children to go home.

'I think it'll be eleven o'clock Mass tomorrow,' Joe said. 'We'll all need a lie-in.'

Nothing had been said about Laura's comments concerning Mick's conjuring tricks so Anne walked home feeling happy that the family gathering had gone well.

In February John travelled to London for the inaugural meeting of the Campaign for Nuclear Disarmament and returned home very excited. 'It was great, Anne,' he declared jubilantly. 'Do you know how many were there? Five thousand. They'd booked Central Hall for the meeting but they needed four other halls for the overflow meetings.'

'Where did they all come from?' asked Anne.

'All over the country. The speakers were Bertrand Russell, Canon Collins, A. J. P. Taylor, J. B. Priestley, Sir Stephen King Hall, all brilliant, well-known men.'

'I've just been reading a book by J. B. Priestley,' Anne exclaimed. 'I didn't know he was opposed to the bomb.'

'Everyone is, Anne, who thinks for himself,' said John, 'but these are all men who are at the top of their professions. The government and in fact the world will have to listen now and get rid of this evil. There's going to be a march to Aldermaston in Berkshire to the Atomic Weapons Research Establishment to protest.'

His eyes were shining and Anne kissed him impulsively. 'I'm made up, love. At last we'll feel as if we're getting somewhere. All those important men must give some weight to the protest, mustn't they?'

'It's the numbers, Anne. That's what's important. Like Grandad used to say, little drops of water when they come together can make a mighty river to sweep all before it.'

John's euphoria made for a very happy atmosphere in the house. Anne recalled a remark made by the prime minister Harold Macmillan the previous year. 'Most of our people have never had it so good,' he had declared. At the time John had disagreed, saying that there were still people in the country who were badly housed and poverty-stricken in spite of the welfare state. 'And the nuclear threat still hangs over everyone,' he said. 'We could all be wiped out just by someone touching a button, so everyone's afraid.'

Anne had not argued with John at the time although she felt that most people simply refused to think about the atomic bomb. Now she felt that the prime minister was right especially where her own family was concerned. The three children were healthy and happy, John was earning good money, they had a house where they were happy and were part of a close and loving family. God has been very good to us, she thought, and touched wood then laughed, thinking that she was covering all the options.

Now even John had to agree that life was better for ordinary people. In his earlier Christmas broadcast the Pope had urged the suspension of nuclear tests and now with the establishment of CND John felt that world opinion was at last recognising the dangers that had worried him so much.

Money was more plentiful because jobs were available for everyone, and the spectre of destitution because of old age or illness which had haunted people had been lifted by the provisions of the welfare state.

In Liverpool there seemed to be an air of change and excitement. Groups of adolescents, now known as teenagers, gathered at milk bars and cinemas with money in their pockets from better wages and more free time. Many older people disapproved of these young people but John was pleased to see them, even the 'teddy boys' wearing what Peggy Burns had said were known as brothel-creeper shoes, 'duck's arse' hairstyles and Edwardian-style suits. John contrasted them with the groups of ragged young men of pre-war days without jobs or hope and rejoiced to see these signs of a better life.

With the provision of school milk and school meals, even the poorest children seemed better fed and most were comparatively better dressed. John watched boys in the parks playing with a real football instead of a pig's bladder or rolled up newspapers, many of them wearing football boots and he recalled the children of the 1930s in broken boots or torn pumps and ragged clothes. He felt that much of what his grandfather had worked and hoped for had come at last.

Chapter Five

Sally's visits to the cinema ceased when Peggy died and as her arthritis became more severe she was soon virtually housebound, unable even to use the large wooden knitting needles on which she knitted blanket squares for the Sue Ryder Appeal.

She had many visitors, with Laura the most frequent and welcome, and Cathy was the loving and attentive daughter that she had always been, but there were times when Sally was necessarily alone. The television set that Greg had bought her helped pass the time and soon he and Cathy enjoyed watching it too. So did Sally's visitors and before long Tony had bought a set but John and Joe decided that it was not the right time for them to buy one.

David had now joined Gerry at St Edward's College and their fathers thought that television would distract them from their homework. Rosaleen and Laura would soon be taking the 11-plus examination so they also had homework to do. Sarah and Anne had agreed with their husbands until they realised that the boys were slipping away each night on various pretexts to watch television at other houses.

'A lot of people seem to have sets now,' Anne told John. 'I think Gerry might as well watch at home as tell yarns to get out to other houses and anyway I don't like him bothering other people.'

'But you shouldn't allow him to go, Anne,' John said. 'He can't be doing his homework properly.'

Anne was tempted to retort that John should stay at home in the evenings to watch Gerry but for the sake of peace she only said mildly, 'Perhaps you should have a talk to Gerry about it.'

John agreed and knowing Gerry's ability to cajole his father Anne was not surprised at the outcome.

'I think we should buy a set, Anne,' John said. 'We can afford it and Gerry tells me that there are some very good programmes on wildlife and things like that. The other kids talk about them because they are a help with their schoolwork and boys who haven't seen the programmes are at a disadvantage. What do you think?'

Anne smiled and agreed to the purchase reflecting that Gerry knew exactly how to manipulate his father. If only Laura would do the same, she thought ruefully, instead of charging into battle, but Laura would probably despise such tricks and think they were dishonest.

The television set was an immediate success and Anne was amused to see that John was as enthusiastic about it as he had been doubtful before. A short time later Sarah and Joe, too, bought a set. It needed careful budgeting as Joe's salary as a teacher was small but the little Sarah earned by working part-time in a sweet shop helped. Joe was still doubtful about the benefits, however. He said some of the boys he taught watched too much television and often fell asleep in school so he and Sarah limited the time that their children watched. 'It can't be good for their eyes anyway,' Sarah said.

After school one day Laura went back to Rosaleen's house and they settled down to watch television. Some time later Joe came in and watched with them but when the programme finished he switched off the set. 'I think that's enough for tonight,' he said. 'I hope you are both working hard at school. It's not long to the eleven-plus so this time is important, you know, girls.'

Laura was fond of her uncle and she smiled at him but as soon as he left the room Rosaleen burst out, 'Preaching, preaching, that's all we ever get in this house. *You* don't have this all the time, do you?'

'What about *my* dad?' Laura demanded. 'Always going on about *something*. Uncle Tony said he's trying to save the world single-handed. I know he was only joking but it's true.'

'Well, at least you don't have family prayers every night like we have,' said Rosaleen.

'Only because my dad would never be home for them. He's always at some meeting or other,' said Laura. 'Not that *I* mind,' she added with a toss of her head.

Rosaleen giggled. 'They'll get a shock when they see our reports,' she said. 'Sister Mary Angela is always telling me off and old Mixers has had it in for you since the first day in her class.'

'I know. If I was a genius she'd still give me bad marks but I don't care. She should have been glad I told her,' said Laura.

'She wasn't though,' laughed Rosa. 'Small hope for us for the eleven-plus.'

On the first day of the new school year the new class mistress for Laura and Rosaleen had been Miss Mixley, a teacher who was nearing retirement and was noted as a strict disciplinarian. She had written a passage on the blackboard and told the girls to write it into their English exercise books.

Laura had raised her hand. 'There isn't an "a" in independent, Miss Mixley,' she said.

To her surprise, the teacher glared at her, her neck and face suffused with red. 'What's your name, girl?' she rapped.

'Laura Redmond, miss,' Laura answered, smiling nervously.

'Well, *Laura Redmond*, you can take that satisfied smirk off your face. I made that mistake deliberately to test the class and I'm sure the other girls noticed it. Isn't that so, girls?'

'Yes, Miss Mixley,' they chorused cravenly, except for Rosaleen.

'*I* didn't notice it,' she said loyally. 'I'd have copied it in my book as you told us to, miss.'

'So we have one girl who is stupid and one who thinks she is smarter than everyone else because she was the first to shout out. I notice that you were both ignorant enough to address me as "miss" while the classmates whom you despise had the courtesy to address me correctly as Miss Mixley. Remember, pride goes before a fall.'

She rubbed out the letter 'a' and substituted an 'e' and from that day onwards she never missed an opportunity to find fault with Laura and Rosaleen.

Laura was truly amazed by the teacher's reaction. 'I thought she'd just made a mistake and she'd be glad to know before we all copied it in our books,' she said but Rosa was more cynical.

'She made a mistake all right but it wasn't deliberate,' she said. 'She just didn't want to admit it.'

Before long Rosaleen was also in trouble. The girls were allowed to bring games or favourite books to school on Friday afternoons and Rosa brought her current craze which was a hula hoop. At playtime she was demonstrating her skill with it, having tucked her dress into her knickers for her more elaborate contortions, when she was suddenly pounced on by Miss Mixley.

'Disgraceful,' she panted. 'Adjust your clothes at once and come with me to Sister Mary Angela.'

The headmistress had been watching from a window and was waiting for them with a grim expression and her hands tucked into the sleeves of her habit.

'How dare you?' she began. 'I will not have such vulgar and unladylike behaviour in my school. You are a bold, immodest girl.' Rosa stood with her mouth open in amazement as the tirade went on, with Miss Mixley supplying a Greek chorus in the background.

The nun concluded by saying, 'I know you have good Catholic parents who will be as shocked as I am at such behaviour. I can only think you must have been mixing with bad companions.'

'She's very thick with that impudent girl, Laura Redmond, Sister,' Miss Mixley said ingratiatingly.

'Indeed. Then they must be separated,' the headmistress ordered.

'But she's my cousin,' Rosa said indignantly.

The nun ignored her and Miss Mixley said meekly, 'I've done what I can, Sister. I don't allow them to sit together.'

'I will speak to the class later,' Sister Mary Angela said and the teacher hustled Rosa back to the classroom.

There was no opportunity for Rosa to speak to Laura but shortly before the class was dismissed the headmistress swept into the classroom and called Rosa to her.

'Rosaleen Fitzgerald today disgraced her class and her school by immodest behaviour in the playground. I know you were all scandalised, girls, and worse than that she has shown a bad example to the younger girls.'

She paused impressively and Laura was about to start forward and shout her indignation but her deskmate gripped her arm and hissed,

'*Don't.*' She bent her head and scarcely moving her lips she said, 'Don't play into the old cow's hands. You'd only make it worse for Rosa.'

Amazement kept Laura silent and rooted to the spot. In the eighteen months that she had shared a desk with Mary Morgan the girl had hardly spoken and had seemed to live in a world of her own. Now she gave Laura a quick wink and before Laura had recovered it was all over and Rosa was saying 'Sorry' airily and returning to her desk.

'Do you mean Miss Mixley – the old cow?' Laura whispered under cover of the headmistress's stately departure.

'No, the nun. Do you think I'll be struck down?' Mary asked with a smile.

'No, but she should be,' Laura said indignantly. 'She must be bad-minded to tell Rosa off just for showing her knickers.'

Neither Laura nor Rosa told their parents about their troubles at school, and Rosa was unconcerned about the reprimand from the headmistress but Laura was still indignant on her behalf. One day when she was sitting with her great-grandmother she confided in her about it. 'I think it was terrible, a nun making a show of Rosa like that,' she said.

'My father was never one for organised religion and neither was Lawrie, so I feel the same,' said Sally. 'I don't know much about nuns but they're spinsters the same as that teacher so they're bound to be narrow-minded. Don't you worry about Rosa, child. It would be like water off a duck's back to her.'

Laura was wide-eyed. 'But aren't you a Catholic, Grandma?'

'No, love. It was Greg your grandad who turned Catholic after the Great War on account of a Catholic man he admired named John Savage. Your nana went with him and it's been a comfort to both of them but I was happy the way I was. Of course your mam's family have always been strong Catholics.'

'I never knew,' said Laura. 'I knew you didn't go to Mass but I thought that was because you were old.' She smiled at Sally, thinking that there was no end to the surprises she could tell about the family.

Laura had not intended to tell anyone about the way Miss Mixley treated her but suddenly she found herself telling Sally about the incident with the blackboard. 'Honestly I wasn't trying to be clever like she made out, Grandma,' she said. 'I just thought it was a mistake and she'd be glad I told her.'

Laura's eyes were full of tears and Sally said gently, 'Don't take it to heart, girl. She was just trying to cover her own mistake by turning on you.'

'That's what Rosa said,' Laura murmured. 'But the other girls—'

'Don't bother about the other girls,' interrupted Sally. 'If they've got a brain in their head they'll see through her the same as Rosa. Try to be more like Rosa, love. Let it all run off you like she does.'

'I wish I could, Grandma, but I can't stop thinking about things like that. Anyway, Miss Mixley is always picking on me so I can't forget it.'

'Aye, people go on about respect for teachers but I say people have got to earn respect,' said Sally. 'If she starts again, love, don't answer back but just think to yourself she's a narrow-minded woman who doesn't know any better.'

Laura impulsively kissed her and Sally held her close. 'Eh, I enjoy talking to you, love,' she said. 'I don't know what I'd do without you.' Laura was warmed and comforted by these words and often thought of them when she was troubled.

Laura had gone home when Cathy returned and Sally told her daughter of Laura's troubles, knowing that Cathy was always discreet.

'It's strange,' mused Cathy. 'Most people would think that Rosa was the most sensitive of that pair because Laura's so outspoken. Yet she feels things far more than Rosa does.'

'She does,' agreed Sally. 'It's just that she comes right out with things. It's not that she doesn't care about other people's feelings but she doesn't stop to think. Like our John.'

'I know, Mam. And she worries if she *has* offended someone,' said Cathy.

'She's got a lot of feeling, Cath. Look at the way she comes to see me to keep me company. I'm sure she gives up many a jaunt because she thinks time might lie heavy for me now. And God knows I love the bones of that child, Cathy.'

'Yes, she's got a loving heart, especially for you, Mam. It's just that she's too honest for her own good.' She sighed. 'And Rosa's too pretty for hers. Our Sarah worries about her. With Rosa's looks and her character she can see trouble ahead.'

'No use crossing your bridges before you come to them, girl,' Sally said. 'Plenty of time yet before Sarah needs to start worrying and the girl's been well-reared.' She slipped suddenly into the easy sleep of old age and Cathy gently tucked a rug round her before going quietly away.

It was obvious to everyone that Sally was daily becoming more frail but only Cathy and Greg knew how much pain she endured because of the arthritis. She said nothing of this to the family who all visited her frequently even Mick and Gerda, travelling from York to see her. They heard nothing from Kate in America but Sally had always liked her least of Cathy's four children and was only distressed because Cathy and Greg were upset about it.

Sarah called every day and John was a frequent visitor. Although Laura was her favourite, Sally enjoyed the visits of all her great-grandchildren. She had never been a reader and now her hands were too twisted to support a book but she enjoyed the stories that David read aloud to her and Gerry could always make her laugh. When he formed a skiffle group he brought them along one night to play for her and Sally laughed until she cried.

'Whatever next?' she gasped. 'A tea chest, a brush handle and a rubbing board. Eh, it's a long time since I laughed like this, lad.'

Gerry was not offended. 'My dad got me the tea chest and the brush pole, Grandma,' he said. 'And he took me to this old lady's house to get the washboard. You should have seen the stuff in the cellar. Dolly tubs and dolly pegs, Dad said they were, and every size of washboard hanging up even a tiny little one she said was for collars. She used to have a washerwoman.'

Sally's eyes met Cathy's but they said nothing until the group had gone, then Sally said, 'You could have knocked me down with a feather when the lad said that about our John. I thought he'd be keeping Gerry's nose to the grindstone with schoolwork.'

Cathy agreed but when they spoke about it on John's next visit he said, 'He might as well enjoy himself. All the kids are crazy about skiffle now. I think I was too serious when I was his age.'

'That won't ever be Gerry's trouble – being too serious,' Sally smiled. 'Eh, we *did* laugh, didn't we, Cath? But the lads didn't seem to mind.'

'Do you know where they practise? In the Fitzgeralds' old house in Magdalen Street. That tall, dark lad, Peter Taylor – his family live there now. You know how Anne's dad did the cellars up for an air-raid shelter? That's where they practise,' said John.

'Anne'll be pleased to know that,' said Sally. She sighed. 'They had happy days, the houseful of them there, and now they're all scattered and their father and mother dead.'

'Yes, but they all keep in touch and they've got happy memories anyway,' Cathy said. 'And we're lucky. John's got a good wife and our Sarah a good husband from that family and we think the world of Anne and Joe.'

Just before Christmas the news came that Sally's other daughter Mary had died suddenly in America where she had lived for many years. Sally received the news calmly. 'Better this way,' she said. 'Sam's a good husband, none better, and he's waited on her hand and foot. She'd have been lost if he'd gone first.'

Cathy nodded. 'He says that in his letter. Says he's glad he was spared to look after Mary to the end and that she went without pain or a long illness.'

'Aye, he's a good lad. It was a lucky day for our Mary when she met him again on that ship.'

'Poor Sam,' Cathy wept. 'I remember the way she treated him when they were young but he always loved her. What will he do? And no children to comfort him either.'

'He has his work,' Greg soothed her. 'That will be his lifeline and knowing that Mary is safe. She won't be the one left alone.'

Sally looked at Greg cradling Cathy tenderly in his arms. Did Sam ever know? she wondered. Did Greg realise? No, she thought. It was only me and Mary knew her secret. That she had hungered for Greg all her life and would have stolen him from her sister if she could. She's taken her secret to the grave and no one will ever hear it from me. Sally closed her eyes and drifted off to sleep.

She was now almost completely bedridden. Daily she seemed to become smaller and her limbs more twisted but she clung tenaciously to life. She had a loving and gentle nurse in Cathy, helped by Greg and the rest of the family and Laura spent even more time with her.

One day when Laura arrived Sally was propped up in bed with a number of faded photographs spread about the quilt.

'I've just been looking out a photo of our Mary,' Sally said. 'I lost most of my photographs when my house was bombed but luckily I had a few in my handbag.' She handed a photograph to Laura of Mary wearing a cloche hat and a coat with a huge fur collar, standing beside a large limousine.

'Was she very rich, Grandma?' Laura asked.

'Aye. Sam always made sure she had everything she wanted. Even after the crash in twenty-nine he started up again and she had all she wanted, houses and servants and big cars. She always had big ideas even as a child and I worried about her but she got what she wanted and a good man as well. She was always lucky.'

She picked up another photograph. 'I'd have been broken-hearted to lose this,' she said. It was of her wedding day and showed her standing beside the seated figure of Lawrie with her hand resting on his shoulder. Both of them stared unsmilingly at the camera.

'Why didn't you smile, Grandma?' Laura exclaimed. 'Although he looks as though he's going to smile.'

'You weren't supposed to smile in those days,' said Sally. 'Although, mind you, Lawrie could never keep his face straight for long.' She gazed fondly at the photograph. 'Eh, he was a merry-hearted lad.'

Laura picked up a snapshot of Cathy and Greg standing beside their bicycles. Cathy was laughing with her head thrown back and her hands on the handlebars and Greg stood close to her, his right hand on his own bicycle and his left hand covering Cathy's. He was smiling down at her and Laura said with surprise, 'Nana and Grandad haven't really changed, have they? They still smile the same way.'

Sally agreed, thinking that it was Greg's smile that had caused the damage with Mary. As Peggy Burns once said, it would turn your blood to water but luckily he never realised the effect it had.

She picked out a faded sepia snapshot. 'That was in my handbag,' she said. 'It's the only one I've got of my father.'

Laura studied the photograph carefully. It was of a group of men in working clothes wearing flat-buttoned caps, except for the foreman who wore a bowler hat. The group of men looked awkward and self-conscious but even in the faded photograph Matthew Palin stood out. He was standing a little apart with arms folded and head flung back, staring challengingly at the camera.

Cathy had come to look at the snapshot and she laughed. 'The other men look nervous,' she said, 'but he looks as though he didn't give a damn.'

'Aye, that's how he was as a young man,' Sally said. 'He had his own ideas about what was right or wrong and he wasn't afraid to speak out, no matter who he offended. That was taken when he worked at Cammell Laird's.'

'I remember him chiefly when he was a sick old man in the parlour,' Cathy said.

Sally sighed. 'He was a fine big man before he had that stroke. He worked at the shipyard right up to then, but he had to trim his sails a bit as he got older, let things pass sometimes that he thought were wrong, for the sake of his family, in case he lost his job. He was always a good father to us, but a strict one, mind you.'

'You've had your share of men speaking out and getting into trouble for it, Mam,' Cathy said. 'Dad told me once that your father was in trouble with his boss on one occasion at least and I know you had a hard time when Dad lost his job for trying to form a union.'

'And I grumbled about it,' Sally said. 'I was always sorry afterwards that I did, because I realised it was the only way men could get any justice by standing together. I thought Lawrie should put us first, but as he said, it was better him taking the risk. He only had two children and I could do a bit of sewing. Most of the other fellows had big families in them days. Still, it's all water under the bridge now and I did back Lawrie up in the end.'

She looked up at Cathy with a twinkle in her eye. 'What do you mean anyway – the men in the family? What about you and your suffragists?' Cathy laughed and Sally said to Laura, 'Your nana was a real firebrand when she was young. Going to meetings and giving out leaflets about votes for women.'

'Did you go to gaol, Nan?' asked Laura.

'No, love, it was the suffragettes who did that,' said Cathy. 'We campaigned by peaceful means but we made a lot of fuss and I think we did as much to get the vote as the suffragettes.'

'And now here's your son marching and carrying on,' said Sally. 'And I think our John's the worst of the lot.'

Laura was amazed. 'I didn't know we had such an interesting family,' she said, and the two older women laughed.

'Aye, not much chance of a quiet life in this family,' said Sally.

Chapter Six

In March 1960 Sally was eighty-seven years old, still clinging to life, and still able to greet her visitors with a smile and an inquiry about their family or themselves. Bodily she grew ever more frail but her mind was as sharp as ever and often her dry wit flashed out.

It was a beautiful spring day when Greg summoned all the family to Sally's bedside. 'It's her heart,' he explained. 'The doctor says the strain of the arthritis pain is too much for it and it can't carry on.'

Sally was lying propped up in the bed on pillows arranged to give her least pain but she did not seem to be suffering now. Her eyes were closed at first then she opened them and looked at the family gathered round her bed.

'Eh, I'm a lucky woman,' she said. 'I had a good father and the best of husbands.' She smiled round at them. 'And a lovely family. God has been good to me.' Her glance rested on Laura at the foot of the bed and she tried to lift her hand. Cathy drew Laura to sit beside Sally and touch her hand and she stayed there when the other children were sent from the room.

The room was quiet except for the shallow breathing of the dying woman and the soft fall of ash from the fire. Sally seemed to have drifted away again but her hands moved restlessly over the quilt. She had slipped down in the bed and Cathy gently lifted her against the piled pillows.

Sally seemed to rouse again briefly and in a thread of a voice she said again, 'Yes, a good life.' She looked up into Cathy's face. 'But I'm glad to go, girl. He's waited a long time, my poor lad.' She drifted off again, restlessly plucking at the quilt and murmuring, 'Lawrie lad. Oh, Lol.'

Finally her hands were still and her quiet breathing ceased. Cathy bent and kissed her then drew Laura forward.

'Say goodbye to Grandma, love,' she said gently. Bemused, unable to realise what had happened, Laura kissed Sally's soft lips then Cathy drew her away and held her in her arms as the rest of the family said goodbye to the indomitable old lady who had meant so much to them.

For Laura the following days passed in a blur. Afterwards she could remember little of them, not even the funeral except the smallness of the coffin and the crowds of people who attended it. A brief notice had been placed in the *Liverpool Echo* and the family were amazed at the response.

'I knew Mam helped people,' Cathy said, 'but I never knew there were so many and that they would still remember and be grateful. The number of people who've been here to tell me how kind she was to them and the ways she helped them. I can't get over it.'

Greg put his arms round her. 'That's the best kind of monument,' he said. 'To be remembered like that. Mam didn't live her life in vain.'

Cathy wept. 'It reminds me of the crowds who came to my dad's funeral. A lot of them were councillors and people like that who he'd pestered to get help for people but there were hundreds of poor folk as well. Do you remember, Greg?'

'Yes, and it was such a bitter day and your mam was worried about them,' said Greg.

'She thought Dad would have been upset because they didn't have warm clothes or good food inside them for such a freezing day to stand about in the cemetery,' Cathy sobbed.

'Never mind, love. There was no one as badly off as that for Mam's funeral and that was partly because of all the good she and your dad did throughout their lives,' said Greg. 'Don't cry, Cath. Think of the pain Mam was in, and it would have got worse.'

'I know,' Cathy said, drying her eyes. 'I'm just selfish. Crying for myself, I suppose. Greg, I don't know what I'll do without her and poor little Laura'll miss her more than anyone.'

'I tell you what we'll do. We'll have a little holiday and take Laura with us. The school can't object now the eleven-plus is over and it'll cheer her up.'

'We'd better take Rosa as well,' Cathy said practically. 'We can't make any distinction between the girls and she'll be company for Laura. Where should we go?'

'I thought perhaps Gloucester. It's lovely at this time of the year with all the blossom out or Devon or Cornwall.'

'I think the seaside would be best for the girls,' Cathy said, her thoughts successfully diverted from her loss. Anne and John and Sarah and Joe were enthusiastic about the plan and Torquay was decided on.

Laura was less enthusiastic. I don't want to go away to forget Grandma, she thought rebelliously. I want to stay here and think about her but Greg asked her to help him in his garden and took the opportunity to talk to her.

'We won't forget Grandma when we go away, love,' he said quietly. 'She'll still be with us. She'll always be with us because of the happy memories we have of her.'

'But why are we going away now to enjoy ourselves?' asked Laura. 'As if – as if we were celebrating.' She found it hard to explain what she meant but her grandfather seemed to understand.

'For Nana's sake really, pet. You know she's lived with Grandma or very near her all her life so she'll miss her very much – even more because she's had to do so much for Grandma lately. She'll be lonely and she won't know what to do with the empty hours. If we have a break she can start afresh when we come back.'

'And she can do different things. Come and see Mum and Auntie Sarah or work in the hospital again,' Laura said eagerly.

'That's right, and I hope you'll still come and see us,' said Greg. 'I know it won't be as often as you came to see Grandma but Nana needs you too, you know.'

'Oh, I will,' Laura promised and Greg began to talk about Torquay and nearby Brixham.

The holiday was a success and soon after they returned the results of the eleven-plus examination were announced. Laura and Rosa were informed that they would be going to the senior school, now known as a secondary modern school.

Their parents were disappointed but Anne said to Sarah, 'I'm glad that if they had to fail the exam, they both failed. At least they'll still be together.'

'Joe doesn't like it called pass or fail,' Sarah said. 'He's always said it was selection but most people still see it as pass or fail. He thinks the eleven-plus should have been delayed until the secondary modern schools had the same facilities as the grammar schools but I think they're catching up now.'

'I'm not worried really. St Joseph's is a good school and Mr Harris is an excellent headmaster.'

'The Doyles' eldest girl over the road is head girl there this year and she's a credit to the school,' Sarah said. 'A really nice, polite girl and so good with the younger children. If Rosa turns out like that I'll be happy.'

'Let's hope they both do. I know the discipline is good and the kids are happy there.'

'That Rafferty woman came in the shop yesterday. You know her daughter's going to Everton Valley. You should have heard her sympathising with me. I said St Joseph's was a good school and she said all smarmy, "Yes, but I know Colette will be in good hands with the nuns and the girls get an extra polish from a convent grammar school."'

'What did you say?' exclaimed Anne. 'I'd have felt like planting her.'

'I said, "My children don't need to go outside their own home to be polished, thank God. There are no rough diamonds among the children in *our* family."'

Anne laughed heartily. 'Sarah, I didn't know you had it in you. What did she say?'

'Nothing. She just went as red as a beetroot and flounced out.'

'Good for you, anyway,' said Anne. 'I can't stand that woman and it's only the uniform she wants to swank about. The education means nothing.'

Laura and Rosa were unconcerned. 'I knew we wouldn't pass,' Rosa said. 'And the parents don't seem to mind.'

'I'll bet Sister Mary Angela tipped them off,' Laura laughed. 'The nuns, I mean.'

Rosa drew herself up and placed her hands in imaginary sleeves. 'Oh, Sisters,' she said, in the nun's tones, 'you won't want those bold girls Laura Redmond and Rosaleen Fitzgerald disrupting your school. Let them go elsewhere and we'll pray they'll improve with the help of God.'

Laura was helpless with laughter. 'Oh Rosa, you sound just like her. I'm glad we're not going to the grammar. I remember Aunt Helen being worried when Moira first went there because of all the loads of homework every night and all the dos and don'ts.'

'I think I'm allergic to nuns,' Rosa announced. 'I'm glad we're going to St Joe's.'

The holiday in Torquay had been such a success that at a family gathering it was decided to arrange a family holiday for when the schools closed. Joe would be free and John and Tony arranged their holidays for the same fortnight. They were able to book adjacent caravans in North Wales and Cathy and Greg promised to spend weekends with them.

Tony and Helen's eldest daughter Moira, now a tall eighteen-year-old, had left her convent grammar school after taking A levels and was hoping to go on to university. Her adopted sister Dilly had been at the same school for a year and Moira came on holiday with the family so that she could spend more time with Dilly to whom she was devoted.

Gerry, now fifteen years old, was reluctant to join them and sulked for the first few days. The skiffle group had been disbanded and he had formed another group with Peter Taylor and two others. Gerry was the drummer and his drum kit was kept in the cellar of the Taylors' house in Magdalen Street but he practised on every available surface with cutlery, knitting needles, anything he could lay his hands on.

He announced that Rory Storm and the Hurricanes with Ringo Starr as drummer were playing at Butlin's Holiday Camp at Pwllheli in North Wales. 'Why can't I go there with my mates?' he complained.

'Because you're only fifteen and you're coming with us,' Anne said. 'And don't think you can get round your father either. You're not going off on your own with that crazy gang so just forget it.'

Gerry sulked for a couple of days, then in spite of himself he began to enjoy the holiday. A van delivered fresh milk and freshly baked, hot crusty bread every morning and everything else could be bought from the camp shop.

Sarah was unable to bathe because of an early bout of rheumatic fever and it was too cold for Julie but everyone else rushed to bathe every morning before breakfast.

They came back ravenously hungry to piled plates of buttered crusty bread and masses of egg and bacon and sausage cooked by Sarah and whoever had volunteered to stay with her. There was tea brewed in an enormous teapot and home-made marmalade and jam.

In later years those meals were often recalled with nostalgia. 'Nothing has ever tasted as good as that food,' someone would say. 'Nectar and ambrosia. That was a great holiday.'

Only Laura had reservations about the holiday and that was because of two incidents with her father. In June there had been a disastrous fire in Henderson's, an exclusive department store in Church Street, Liverpool's main shopping area. Eleven people lost their lives and the tragedy was still fresh in everyone's mind. The family talked about it as they sat on the sands after a picnic lunch.

'I often think about those poor people going out that morning to work or to shop, never dreaming that it would be their last day,' said Sarah. 'You'd wonder how such a thing could happen.'

'And in such a lovely shop,' remarked Helen.

'It wasn't a shop I ever used,' Anne declared. 'I went there once years ago when the children were small for a maternity bra and the assistant was horrible with me.'

'They could be very snooty,' agreed Helen. 'Not all of them but some of them thought they were superior just because the customers were wealthy.'

'She treated me like dirt,' said Anne. 'Nowadays, of course, I'd soon sort her out but then I was vulnerable. She made me feel poor and shabby and really inferior.'

'Don't talk rubbish, Anne,' John said angrily. His face was red and congested.

'I know what you mean, Anne,' Helen interjected quickly. 'We were easily intimidated when we were young. Makes me almost glad to be middle-aged.'

68

Anne disregarded John's angry words. 'I think the truth was I interrupted her talking to some sort of floor walker, a man in black coat and striped trousers and she was mad.'

'She probably fancied him and you nipped a little affair in the bud,' laughed Sarah.

'The joke was that she swanned off somewhere leaving me waiting and a girl and her mother came in to return a bra. The girl was quite nervous, whispering to her mother that she didn't think they'd change it. The assistant came back and just said rudely to me, "No we haven't one", then went gliding up to them with a smarmy smile on her face.'

'They must have thought it was their lucky day,' Sarah giggled.

'Yes, and she had her eye wiped because she thought she'd make a sale,' Anne said. 'I never went back there though.'

John was still scowling and Tony looked annoyed. Laura sat near the group with Julie and Dilly and she glared at her father. I wish Auntie Helen hadn't rushed in, she thought. I'm sure Uncle Tony was mad and he was going to say something about him talking to Mum in that bullying way.

Later when they were in their own caravan, the argument was resumed.

'What were you playing at?' John demanded. 'Saying you felt poor and shabby and inadequate.'

'But I did,' protested Anne. 'I can understand why people let themselves be pushed around. You lose confidence when you're at home all the time with just young children.'

'Nonsense,' John exclaimed. 'You're talking rubbish, Anne.'

'No, I'm not. You just don't understand. If you come up against people in authority, especially if they are bullies, you can't stand up to them. They treat you as though you're inferior and you feel that you are. I'm not talking about myself now but I've seen it with other people.'

'You were talking about yourself today,' John said violently. 'Making a fool of yourself and making little of me.'

'Making little—? What are you talking about?' Anne gasped.

'Making out you were poor and shabby as though I couldn't provide for my family,' John said. 'Letting your brothers see how badly their precious sister was treated.'

'It wasn't anything to do with providing. They all knew what I meant. About when I was ill after Julie was born.'

'No need to rake that up and remind people,' said John, changing ground. 'I know your family blamed me for that.'

'Now *you're* talking nonsense,' Anne began, but then she paused. 'Oh, John, don't let's quarrel and spoil everyone's holiday.'

'Then be more careful about what you say,' John retorted.

Laura could hear the quarrel clearly through the thin walls of the caravan and she longed for her mother to make a cutting reply but she only heard her father say in a different tone, 'Would you like a cup of tea, love?'

Probably the raised voices had been heard in the caravans on either side but no one mentioned them.

Another day Gerry and David went missing and provoked more discord between Anne and John. The two boys were not as close friends as their sisters were but as the only boys in the holiday party they were thrown together and became closer.

On this day they had strolled along the beach turning up stones to examine small crabs and collecting curiously shaped stones and shells. They wandered further than they intended and as nobody had seen them go the adults became worried when the tide began to come in strongly.

'It's not like David,' Moira said. 'He's always so careful not to worry his mother.'

'It's probably Gerry's idea,' Anne said.

'Yes, Gerry's a natural leader,' John put in quickly, 'and David's a follower but Gerry'll look after him.'

Laura saw an expressive glance between Tony and Joe but Joe only said quietly to Sarah, 'They've probably gone to the camp shop for sweets or ice cream. They had money in their pockets.'

'I hope so. Could they be trapped by the tide, Joe?'

'Not on this beach,' Joe reassured her.

Fortunately it was not long before they saw the boys approaching them from the bridge over the railway line which lay between the camp and the sea. David said immediately, 'Sorry, Mum. We walked further than we realised and when the tide came in we thought it would be quicker to get a bus back from the road.'

'David was panicking in case you were worrying but I knew you'd know we were all right,' Gerry said cheerfully.

'We *did* worry,' Anne rebuked him. 'Be more careful in future.'

But John said impatiently, 'I told you there was no need to fuss. I know my son. He can look after himself and anyone else who tags along.'

Again Laura saw glances exchanged between the adults although nothing more was said, and Anne saw them too. Later in the caravan when John began to scoff at the panic about the boys she said quietly, 'It was David who showed sense although he's two years younger than Gerry. He was the one who suggested the bus back.'

'Nonsense, they could have walked back in no time – or Gerry could without David holding him back.'

'With the tide in? It would have taken them twice as long,' Anne said. 'I wish you wouldn't boast so much about Gerry, John. People will think we're daft.'

'What do you mean?' John demanded.

'Saying he's a natural leader and all that. We shouldn't brag about our own.'

'Don't talk daft. I wasn't bragging. Just stating a fact,' John snapped. Anne said no more but Laura lay in bed fuming. Just you wait, she thought. Another few years and I can get a job. I'll take her and Julie away and you'll never be able to talk like that to her again.

All the family were fond of John although they were sometimes irritated by his remarks but they said nothing, partly for Anne's sake and partly to preserve harmony in the family. John was quite unaware of giving offence.

When Cathy and Greg came for the weekend he behaved like the loving son he was and exerted himself to make his mother's visit as enjoyable as possible. Later, when Julie suddenly developed a high temperature, he was loving and supportive with Anne, so that her brothers saw the better side of his nature.

'He's just obsessed with Gerry,' Joe said tolerantly. 'No half measures in anything with John but there's no harm in him.'

'He runs off at the mouth a bit but it doesn't seem to bother our Anne, that's the main thing,' said Tony. 'She seems happy enough.'

They were all sorry when the holiday ended and decided that they must do the same again another year. Julie had recovered quickly and everyone agreed that they felt in better health because of the sunny days by the seaside. It had also provided a break between the time of deep grief for Sally and a return to normal life, although she would never be forgotten.

In September Laura and Rosa settled happily into their new school. Freed from Miss Mixley's sniping, Laura made good progress and her new teacher Miss Watts found her bright and responsive. She gave Laura the praise and encouragement that she needed at that time.

Rosaleen was equally happy. She developed a passion for the male teacher who took them for art and worked hard to please him. He carefully gave her no encouragement but her hard work and talent merited praise which he was too just to withhold. Rosa treasured his words and wrote them in her diary to be read and reread and repeated to Laura who said nothing to spoil her dreams.

Both joined a youth club and spent happy hours there, playing table tennis, dancing to records or just talking with others in the bar where they could buy soft drinks and tea.

Laura was still uninterested in boys but Rosa revelled in the admiring glances of the young boys and in being in great demand for the dances. She was an excellent dancer in addition to being outstandingly pretty and boys stationed themselves strategically near the girls for when the youth leader announced the next dance.

Laura was still unable to dance well but sometimes one of the losers in the race for Rosa would ask her to dance. 'I should be called Laura the next best thing,' she announced without rancour to Rosa. 'They're willing to have their feet trampled on just to ask me about you.'

The only drawback to the youth club, the two girls decided, was that their fathers insisted on meeting them, taking it in turns to escort them home. When Laura grumbled, Anne told her that she should be glad that her father cared enough to cut short a meeting to walk her home but Laura only scowled.

'Other people don't have their fathers meeting them,' she muttered. 'It's not far to walk home.'

'Far enough at ten o'clock at night at your age,' her mother said firmly. 'If you don't like it you can stop going to the club until you're older.'

Rosa was equally resentful on the nights when they were met by her father. She frequently complained to the group of boys who surrounded her and wanted to walk her home and she also complained of having to join in family prayers when she returned home. Yet when one of the boys said, 'Here's Holy Joe come to meet you,' she was furious and refused to speak to the boy again.

Laura had been chosen for the school netball team and for the Handicraft Group who made items for the Christmas fair and the garden fete. They also knitted and sewed baby clothes which were distributed to various charities. All these interests helped Laura to bear the loss of her beloved Grandma, although sometimes she would be overwhelmed by longing for her. When something happened which Sally would have enjoyed hearing about, or when she had a problem and needed Sally's advice, the realisation that she had gone would sweep over Laura, leaving her devastated.

She went frequently now to see Nana, finding it easier after the first few visits when she was unable to bear to look at Grandma's chair. Gradually she realised that Cathy, always so quiet and unobtrusive, had many of Sally's qualities.

John had called to see his mother on the way home from work one evening and later over the meal at home he said casually, 'Mum's still missing Grandma badly but you know I think she might blossom out a bit now. Grandma was such a strong-minded woman that I think Mum was a bit overshadowed. She might come out of her shell a bit more now.'

To Laura this seemed like a criticism of Grandma and she scowled at her father but before she could speak her mother answered him. To Laura's dismay she seemed to agree with him.

'I know what you mean, John,' she said. 'Grandma was always the centre of that house and Nana was content to have it that way but now she'll be the centre. It's wonderful that there was never a cross word between them in all those years.'

'My dad said that the other day,' said John. 'He said that even in Norris Street, their first house, Mum spent most of the time at her mother's. Then when they got the house opposite Grandma's in Egremont Street they were made up and spent even more time together. When Grandma was bombed out and came to them, she just fitted in naturally.'

'Could have been tricky though. Two women in one kitchen,' said Anne.

John laughed. 'I know, but they were both always so anxious to stand back for each other that it *had* to work. Must make it even harder now for Mum, though.'

Laura watched and listened, glad that she had not rushed in to argue with her father before she heard the rest of the conversation. But it was a funny thing to say about Grandma, she thought, that she was a strong-minded woman. She was just Grandma and there would never be anyone like her again. Her eyes filled with tears but she blinked them away.

Chapter Seven

The boys in the youth club were all caught up in the craze for pop music and some of them, like many other boys in Liverpool, went to Hessy's music shop to buy a guitar. The fatherly salesman there was an accomplished guitar player and he taught the rudiments of playing to the boys, most of whom had no idea how to play.

Constant practice followed and although few could read music they became reasonably accomplished guitar players. When a group from the club was booked to appear at a local church hall Laura and Rosa and most of the other girls went along to support them.

The two cousins were afraid that their fathers would insist on meeting them and pleaded to be allowed to come home with the crowd.

'It makes us look daft, as though we are little kids or as though you don't trust us,' Laura grumbled to her father. Rosa was complaining at home too and Joe decided to speak to the youth leader.

'I'll be there to see that they behave themselves,' the young man told him. 'They'll all come home together so they'll be quite safe.' The parents were reassured and Laura and Rosa were delighted.

'Free at last,' Rosa said dramatically and Laura was pleased because she felt that her father had been outwitted.

Gerry suffered none of these restrictions and seemed to Laura to be able to do whatever he pleased. Although a natural athlete, he managed to be sufficiently inept at trials for the college rugby and cross-country events to avoid being chosen for the main teams. His chief sporting interest was soccer and he was determined that he would be free on Saturday afternoons to play with a local team. This widened his circle of friends to include many who were involved in the music scene in Liverpool.

The groups broke up and re-formed, with guitarists and drummers moving from group to group, but Gerry was still with his original group who practised enthusiastically in the cellar of Peter Taylor's parents' house in Magdalen Street.

Gerry did the minimum of homework and made little effort with his schoolwork. The Christian brothers who taught him told his parents bluntly that they were disappointed in him. Nobody was surprised when he managed only two low-grade O levels but Gerry, still smiling, was unperturbed.

He left school at sixteen years old and easily found a job in the office of a fruit importer in the city centre.

'I thought you'd have been looking for a job in Hessy's or Rushworth's,' said Laura but Gerry shrugged.

'No, I'd have to work Saturdays,' he said. 'With this job I can play footy on Saturday afternoons and we're hoping to get bookings for the group Saturday nights.'

'You're not as soft as you look,' Laura told him, impressed.

Gerry's group now called themselves the Merrymen and began to get bookings at church halls and small clubs on Saturday nights and Gerry was becoming known as a good drummer. The pay for these gigs was only between two and four pounds but it paid for the petrol for the van to transport their equipment and for large platefuls of curry and chips at an all-night cafe after the performance.

In contrast to Gerry, David was an immediate success at the college. He found the work easy and enjoyed it and every Speech Day he was one of those who mounted the stairs to the platform of the Philharmonic Hall to receive a prize. Laura wondered that her father could accept this situation so easily, but she decided that he had realised that Gerry would never shine academically, so he had encouraged him in his musical ambitions. There was always the chance that Gerry would make the big time and meanwhile it would be seen as his choice rather than academic failure.

She said something of this to Rosa but she disagreed. 'I think your dad's just soft about Gerry and lets him do whatever he wants,' she said. 'Anything to make him happy. But you can't see any good in your dad, can you?' She laughed but Laura had an uncomfortable feeling that Rosa believed what she said.

David had played the violin and the flute from an early age and at the college he began to learn to play the cello. He was asked to join a string quartet and John mocked him to Anne. 'A string quartet and a debating society,' he said. 'What sort of interests are those for a youngster? I'm glad my son's a real lad with normal interests.'

'Philistine, you mean,' Laura retorted. She was helping her mother to clear the table.

Anne said quickly, 'Everyone's different, John. David's been studying music since he was eight and our Joe probably influenced him. He always liked light classical music.'

'Seems a namby-pamby sort of life for a lad,' John said but Anne changed the subject by talking about a forthcoming visit by Mick and Gerda. They had driven up from York frequently during the last months of Sally's life, staying at the Adelphi Hotel and spending every day from breakfast onwards with Cathy, Greg and Sally. Now Mick was concerned about his mother who had grown thin and pale since her mother's death, although she always appeared cheerful in company. He and Gerda had travelled up to urge Cathy to spend a holiday with them in York. She thanked them but refused. Even a few days of Mick's cheerful company, however, did much to raise her spirits.

'Mick was always a rip and he hasn't changed,' Cathy said laughingly to Anne at a family gathering on the Sunday night. 'The risks he took with that first little plastics factory he opened after the war! Good job his dad and I didn't know at the time. We'd have been worried to death.'

'It paid off though, didn't it? He's so successful now, but I think he'd have been successful whatever he did. He's so clever.'

'And he's lucky. He always was. The antics he got up to but he always got away with them and then they told us at the college that he had a photographic memory. He only had to look at a page of print to remember it, so that was a big advantage.'

'Pity none of the younger ones have inherited that gift, although David's very clever,' Anne said. 'Sarah says Gerry is like Mick but I think that's because he doesn't care if it snows. He hasn't got Mick's brains.'

'Grandma always said that Mick could charm the birds off the tree.' Cathy looked over to where Mick sat. Laura and Rosaleen and Dilly, with Gerry and David, surrounded him and they were all laughing and looking admiringly at him. Slim, elegant Gerda sat at a little distance with Moira and seemed to be talking about cosmetics as they examined the contents of a small make-up bag from Gerda's handbag.

'That's another way he's lucky,' Cathy said. 'Gerda's a lovely girl and a good wife. It's a pity they haven't any children. They're so good with young people.'

'Perhaps it's their choice,' Anne said. 'They travel a lot, don't they?'

'Yes, they do,' Cathy agreed. 'I don't like to say anything to them so I don't know why they're childless but I still think it's a pity.'

'Never mind, there's still time.'

Cathy smiled at Anne and pressed her hand. 'Mick's not the only lucky son I've got. Our John's been well blessed with a wife like you, Anne. He's a more complicated character than Mick, love, but you've made him very happy.'

Anne smiled and blushed. Then, as Sarah came into the room with Julie, Cathy said, 'And Sarah's got a good husband, too. I think the world of Joe. Greg and I are lucky to see three of our children well settled. The less I say about our Kate the better. I don't know where we went wrong with her, Anne.'

'You can't blame yourself,' Anne said.

Sarah came to them with Julie and Anne held out her arms to the child. Although nearly eleven years old, Julie was still small and thin with a timid air. 'Did you have a good sleep on Nana's bed, love?' Anne asked and Julie nodded. 'She hardly slept at all last night,' Anne told Cathy. 'The wheezing was keeping us all awake. You feel as though you want to breathe for her.'

Cathy kissed the little girl. 'Never mind, pet. Asthma is something people grow out of.'

Julie looked longingly at the group round Mick and Sarah said immediately, 'Come and see Uncle Mick.' Julie clung to her hand as they approached Mick and held her head down but Sarah raised her eyebrows at Mick and nodded down at the child.

Mick understood and made no effusive greeting, only took Julie on to his knee and said cheerfully, 'We're just talking about a bad boy who climbed on to a roof to catch a pigeon.'

'It was *you*,' the others chorused but Julie hid her face against Mick's chest.

'All right, it was me,' he agreed amiably. 'That's how I know so much about it. Anyway, this pigeon had a broken wing and I wanted to put a splint on it. I tried to catch it and it fluttered up on to a wall. I climbed after it but it fluttered away again and again until I was on this big high roof with some glass missing. I reached out again and it fluttered off but I'd reached too far and I fell through the roof and finished up in hospital.'

'What happened to the pigeon?' David asked.

'I think it was codding me,' Mick said. 'It probably wasn't injured at all but it had young near where I was so it decoyed me away. Birds do that, you know. Anyway, I wasn't worrying about the pigeon when I found myself in hospital.'

'Were you there long?' Laura asked.

'A day would've been too long,' Mick said. 'It wasn't like Alder Hey. I couldn't believe it when I went to see you there, Julie. Nice nurses and toys and pretty pictures on the wall. My hospital was like a barracks and the nurses were like soldiers. And the sister – wow!'

'Wasn't she nice?' asked Rosa.

'Nice! She was like a dragon and everyone was terrified of her. When she came in the doorway I wouldn't have been surprised to see horns on her head and flames shooting from her mouth.'

'Was she a dragon or the devil?' David said, laughing.

'A bit of both,' Mick said solemnly. 'The worst features of both. She wouldn't have been allowed in Alder Hey, I can tell you.'

They were all laughing, even Julie, and later Anne said gratefully, 'Thanks, Mick. Julie didn't need to go in hospital this time but it's bound to come. You'll have made her feel better about it.'

'Don't worry so much about her, Anne,' Mick said gently. 'She must be pretty tough to have got through what she has and I'm sure she'll grow out of the asthma too.'

'I hope so. And I hope she grows out of her shyness. That's something that's never bothered the other two and they're both so healthy as well.'

'She will,' Mick said confidently. 'Julie had a bad start, didn't she, but she'll catch up. I know when she was born Mum and Dad didn't think she'd live but here she is.'

'I know. She was so tiny and premature.' Anne smiled. 'You're right Mick. I should be counting my blessings.'

'That's more like it,' Mick exclaimed. 'You don't look like yourself when you're not smiling, Anne. What was it your Uncle Fred used to call you? Happy Annie.'

'Oh, Uncle Fred,' Anne said laughing. 'What a character. He never opened his mouth without putting his foot in it but he was smashing. We all missed him when he died.'

Laura looked at her uncle admiringly. Mick's clear skin was tanned from foreign holidays and his teeth were very white and even. His fair hair was still thick and curly and he was well tailored with gleaming shoes but it was none of these things that made him so attractive, Laura decided. It was his air of vitality and cheerfulness that drew everyone to him and made them feel better after contact with him.

She looked over to where her father and Sarah were standing together talking. How could brothers and sisters be so different? she wondered. Aunt Sarah with her sweet smile and quiet manner was different to Mick but just as nice and her father was different to both of them. Even now he seemed to be laying down the law, Laura thought, ticking off points on his finger as he talked to Sarah. She nodded and smiled but John's body was tense and he frowned in concentration as he earnestly made his point.

Why does he make such a big thing of everything? Laura thought scornfully. He never talks to people, just lectures them. Everybody else is enjoying themselves.

'Take that look off your face, Laura Redmond,' said a voice in her ear and she turned, startled to find Rosa beside her. 'Why were you looking daggers at your dad?' Rosa asked. 'What's he done now?'

'Nothing. I didn't think I was. I was only wondering why he makes such a big deal of everything. He's so different to your mum and Mick although they're brothers and sister.'

'Well, you're different to Julie and Gerry,' Rosa pointed out. 'And I'm certainly different to David, the pride and joy, but so what? Come on. Nana wants us to help.'

Everyone was sorry when Mick and Gerda returned to York but they promised to come again soon and to telephone frequently. Sarah had told Gerda that Rosaleen and Laura were experimenting with make-up. 'It's no use forbidding it,' she said. 'They only do it after they leave the house. Rosa forgot to wipe hers off one night and she came home looking like a clown.'

Gerda showed the girls how to make up their faces skilfully and gave them some of her own cosmetics but though the girls admired Gerda they thought their own efforts made them look more striking. They were grateful for the gifts of scent from Gerda and even more for the money slipped to them by Mick 'to buy yourself a frock' but the cosmetics were relegated to the back of a drawer.

Their Friday and Saturday night visits to various clubs and concerts were now accepted by both sets of parents, although they were told that they must be home by eleven o'clock. 'What can we do?' Sarah said. 'All the other kids of their age go to them and I suppose they're safe enough in a crowd.'

'But they're getting later all the time coming home,' Anne said. 'It's a good thing John had gone to bed when Laura came in last Saturday.'

'I know. Joe read the riot act to Rosa but she's got an answer to everything.'

It was fortunate that they were unaware that although Laura still walked home with the group Rosa was rarely with them. There was great competition between the boys to walk home with her and she usually said lengthy goodnights to her latest choice. Laura was often in trouble for being late because she loyally waited for a signal from

Rosa before returning home to keep up the fiction that they had been together.

With the money from their uncle they bought dresses in the same style but a different colour, Rosa a green one and Laura a blue. They were straight shifts, sleeveless and ending just above the knee. The dresses had a drawstring just below the bust, tactfully undrawn at home but in the cloakrooms of various halls drawn tight to emphasise their developing busts. With a liberal application of mascara and pale lipstick and hair piled high in a beehive they felt that they were the acme of style and sophistication.

Most of the girls wore similar dresses or short tight skirts and tight sweaters and had beehive hairdos but as the weather grew colder most of them put on the navy duffel coats that they wore for school. These were discarded in the cloakrooms and make-up applied with a heavy hand and the girls emerged, telling each other that they looked fab.

Gerry's band, the Merrymen, had become more professional now. Gerry was on drums, Peter Taylor was the lead singer and also played guitar, and they had two more guitar players, Michael and Martin Hogan, who were twin brothers. Peter was a tall, dark and handsome boy and his appearance on stage always brought screams from the girls in the audience. Gerry was an object of devotion to many of the girls and the twins had their followers but Peter was the main attraction.

He was a frequent visitor to Gerry's house and Anne always talked to him about her old home and the happy years she and her family had spent in Magdalen Street. Sometimes Gerry was out when Peter called and Anne was puzzled until Gerry laughed and told her that Peter was probably hoping to see Rosaleen.

'But she's only a *child*,' Anne exclaimed. 'Your Aunt Sarah wouldn't like a boy hanging round after her.'

Gerry laughed even more heartily. 'You must be kidding, Mum. Peter's not the only one. Anyway, she should be flattered.'

'You'd better warn him off, Gerry, I mean it,' Anne said. 'Tell him her parents won't like it. She's far too young to be thinking of courting.'

'Mum, you slay me,' Gerry laughed but fortunately at that moment the telephone rang and he left the house.

Anne wondered whether she should warn Sarah but decided in her usual fashion that 'least said, soonest mended'. Gerry could be mistaken or it could be a passing fancy on Peter's part so there was no point in worrying Sarah and Joe. The kids are enjoying life so much, she thought, I don't want to throw a spanner in the works. Gerry would never forgive me if I said something and the group broke up.

Although Gerry was friendly with the twins Michael and Martin, Peter was his closest friend. Gerry spent a lot of time at Peter's house while his elder brother Jim was home from sea.

Jim had fought in Korea during his National Service and had become eager to see more of the world so he became a seaman. He always brought the latest records home from New York or Hamburg and the boys played them over and over again, although Jim's taste was for jazz.

'That's what I call music,' he said to them. 'I used to go to the Cavern in Mathew Street when the Merseysippi Jazz Band played there. God, it was great! We were packed like sardines and the water was running down the walls but the jazz! It just lifted you out of your skin.'

'You should come to the Cavern with us when we've got a free night,' Peter said. 'Some great groups on, Faron and the Flamingoes, the Beatles, the Fourmost,' but Jim refused.

'No, I looked in one lunchtime,' he said. 'The music's all right if you like R and B and rock but the place was full of young kids. For the jazz we went in our lunch hours from the shipping office and got a pass out for the pub during the evening sessions. Different scene altogether.'

Gerry and Peter were fascinated by Jim's tales about the clubs in Hamburg. The Beatles and other local groups had played the Hamburg clubs and they thought that it was the place for the Merrymen to find fame. They made a record at Percy Phillip's recording studio in Kensington and they begged Jim to take it to Hamburg on his next visit and try to interest a club owner.

'I'm not exactly on good terms with them,' Jim said laughing. 'Especially if Mick Mulligan's one of the crew. He could start a fight in an empty house and we usually finish up getting thrown out. The last time it took five fellers to get him out and he was still shouting, "I've been thrown out of better places than this, y'know". Anyway most of them are dead rough.'

'We wouldn't care as long as we got a start there,' Gerry said eagerly. 'We've played at some pretty rough places here anyhow, haven't we, Peter?'

'Yes, scruffy maybe,' Jim said. 'But I'm talking about *rough*. Where it's not soft drinks but mind-benders. LSD and that sort of stuff and a knife pulled at the drop of a hat.'

'We wouldn't play *that* badly,' Gerry laughed, but Jim refused to take the record. He promised to ask around but that was all. Nevertheless, Peter and Gerry talked constantly of the prospects in Hamburg. Michael and Martin were less enthusiastic.

'It'd mean leaving home and giving up our jobs,' they said doubtfully.

'We'd have to leave home if we had to do National Service like our Jim,' Peter said. 'And we wouldn't need jobs if we were famous.'

The twins were unconvinced. They were completely different in appearance, Michael quiet and dark and Martin red-haired and extrovert, but they were united in their resistance to the idea of playing in Hamburg.

'There are more chances here in Liverpool,' Michael argued. 'We all know groups no better than us that have been taken on by managers. We just need a bit of luck.'

'And a bit of patience,' his brother told Gerry. 'You always want everything yesterday.'

Gerry was annoyed but the following evening he heard something which made him think that Michael might be right; it was from an unlikely source – his Uncle Joe. Sarah had left some heavy shopping at Anne's house and Gerry carried it home for her. Joe was searching in a vase on the mantelpiece for a flint for his lighter and he asked casually, 'How's the band going, Gerry?'

'All right, thanks,' Gerry said.

Joe, still searching, asked, 'Have you heard of Brian Epstein from Nems in Whitechapel?'

'Yes, he's a manager – managing groups I mean,' Gerry said eagerly. 'Haven't you heard about him? He manages the Beatles.'

'I thought I'd heard the name,' said Joe. 'I believe he's signed Fred Marsden's lads. You remember that do we went to in the Dingle, Sar? Fred played the ukalele – or was it a banjo? And later the young lad played the electric guitar and sang.'

'Fred and Mary. Yes, I remember,' Sarah said. 'She was a nice woman, Mary, and that kid was good.'

'Remember when he was jumping about singing and he pulled the plug of his guitar out of the socket? But he kept right on singing and strumming while Fred put the plug back in the socket. We were pulling Fred's leg about the way he stood back with his arms folded beaming – y'know, "That's ma boy."' Joe laughed heartily.

Before he could say any more, Gerry broke in, 'Are you sure? They've definitely been signed by Brian Epstein?'

'Yes, Fred's older boy plays the piano, I think, and there are two other boys in the group, Nick Phillips said. Do you know them?'

'Yes. Gerry and the Pacemakers. We've done gigs at places they've been but they're way ahead of us. They do places like Litherland Town Hall now.'

'Your turn next, Gerry,' said Sarah. 'Perhaps you'd better call yourselves Gerry and the Merrymen.'

'It'd have to be Peter and the Merrymen,' Gerry grinned. 'We practise in his cellar and use his dad's van. His dad used to drive us about until Peter got his driving licence.'

'That cellar,' Sarah sighed. 'Your mum's family used it as an air-raid shelter during the war, Gerry. Your Grandad Fitzgerald made a smashing job of it.'

'Yes, he did,' Gerry agreed and turned towards the door. 'I'll have to go now. The lads are waiting for me,' and he sped away.

He was anxious to tell the news about Gerry Marsden to Peter and even before the twins arrived they had decided to postpone their dreams of Hamburg for a while.

'It's only a few years since they were a skiffle group glad to get a booking,' Peter said. 'It just shows you what can happen.'

Michael and Martin agreed with him when they arrived and Martin said, 'All you need is a bit of luck.'

'*And* talent,' Peter said. 'We'll all have to work harder at the rehearsals so we'll be ready for our bit of luck when it comes.'

It was fortunate that Anne had known nothing about the Hamburg scheme as she had enough to worry about with Julie's health at this time. The winter of 1962 started early and Julie contracted a chest infection which quickly became a severe bout of bronchitis. She recovered before Christmas but seemed even thinner and had no energy.

Snow fell on 28 December and the cold increased. Tony and Helen gave a New Year's Eve party but Anne stayed at home with Julie and Laura went with Rosa and her family. Gerry was with the Merrymen who had a booking in Bootle.

Just before twelve o'clock John went out carrying coal and salt and returned to let in the New Year as church bells rang and hooters sounded from the ships on the River Mersey.

Anne had built up the fire and laid out spare ribs and bunloaf and she and John sat either side of the fire with Julie swathed in blankets in the armchair between them.

'This is nice, isn't it, pet? Our own little party,' Anne said and Julie smiled happily. She held a glassful of hot blackcurrant drink, John had whisky and Anne Babycham and they solemnly clinked glasses.

'Here's to nineteen sixty-three,' John said. 'I think it's going to be a very exciting year.'

He was obviously thinking of Gerry but Anne said quietly, 'I'll be glad when January and February are over.'

'The weather might improve. And at least we've got a good stock of coal now.'

'When haven't we?' Anne laughed. She always said that coal was an obsession with John. His mother and even more his grandmother had known what it was to be short of coal and both had always ensured that their coalholes were always full.

John smiled but said, 'Seriously, though, Anne, coal could be short if this weather lasts. The railways and the roads could be blocked.'

'Wouldn't be only coal in that case,' Anne said. 'But we'll cross that bridge when we come to it. This is supposed to be a party. Turn up the telly, John.'

Scottish dancers appeared on the screen and the sound of bagpipes filled the room. 'Isn't it wonderful,' Anne said. 'When you think that all that is happening in Scotland and yet it's here in this room.'

'A girl in our class has a kilt like that,' Julie said. 'With a big pin in it. Can I have one, Mum?'

'Yes, they look nice and warm. I'll get you one, love, but it'll have to be a lot warmer than this before you go back to school.'

It had been arranged that Laura would stay with Rosa, and Gerry at Peter's house, so Anne and John and Julie went to bed.

Laura had been enjoying the party until a woman with greying fair hair spoke to her. 'You must be Anne's daughter,' she said. 'I'm Mrs Wilson, a friend of your Auntie Maureen. Have you heard from her lately?'

'Yes, Mum had a letter last week,' Laura told her. 'We sent her a parcel of clothes with a Mickey Mouse shirt in it and she said a little boy fancied it so much she let him keep it although it came down to his feet.'

'She's still abroad with Sue Ryder then?' said Mrs Wilson. 'And still happy. She said she was when she wrote to me but that was a while ago.'

'She must be. If she wasn't she could come home. She's not a nun or anything.'

'I suppose you're right,' the woman agreed, looking amused. 'Your mother's not here tonight?'

'No, my sister's been sick so Mum stayed at home with her,' explained Laura.

'I'm sorry she's not here. I was looking forward to seeing her again. I always said Anne lighted up a room when she came in. She was always so happy and full of life. Who did you come with, love?'

'My cousin Rosa and my Auntie Sarah and Uncle Joe,' said Laura. They looked over to where Sarah and Joe stood talking to another couple. Joe had slipped his arm round Sarah's waist and they were looking at each other, laughing at something.

'Eh, they're a happy couple,' said Mrs Wilson. 'I always liked Joe and he's turned out a real good husband. I always say to my girls look for a man that'll *cherish* you, that's what's most important. Never mind what he earns or anything else. If he'll *cherish* you, you'll be happy.'

Someone came to speak to Mrs Wilson and she moved away but Laura stood thinking of what she had said. It was true that Uncle Joe cherished his wife. Quietly and unobtrusively he was always on hand, to take heavy dishes from her or to find her a seat near the fire or just to be there if by any chance she stood alone.

That's the difference to my mum and dad, Laura thought angrily. If they were here, Dad would be in a corner arguing with someone, taking no notice of Mum and not bothering whether she needed him or not.

'Here you are,' Rosa suddenly exclaimed. 'I've been looking for you. Come and see the dresses Moira's made. They're fab.'

Laura promptly forgot her gloomy thoughts and spent a happy time in Moira's bedroom, admiring her clothes. Moira gave each of them a skirt and sweater she had outgrown and a can of hair laquer. 'They'll be out of fashion by the time Dilly's old enough,' she said.

The celebrations at twelve o'clock soon followed and at the end of the party Laura and Rosa admitted that they had thoroughly enjoyed themselves. 'I'm not going to tell my dad that though,' said Laura.

They had wanted to go to hear their favourite group and on to a teenage party, and Laura felt that they could have persuaded her mother and Rosa's parents, but her father had been adamant that they were too young and must go to the family party.

'He's probably forgotten all about the argument by now,' Rosa said carelessly, 'and you're bound to let it out that it was a fab party.'

It was only as they prepared to go home that Laura remembered Mrs Wilson's words. Joe wrapped his big woollen scarf round Sarah's neck and over her head and she protested, 'Joe, I've got a scarf under my coat. You need this.'

'No I don't,' he said and tucked her hand firmly under his arm. 'Rosa, take your mum's other arm and you hang on to me, Laura.' Giggling and laughing, occasionally breaking into song, they picked their way, slipping and sliding on the frozen snow but supported by Joe, and exchanging greetings with other groups of people.

When they reached home they all had a hot drink and Laura and Rosa went up to share Rosa's bed. Rosa was soon asleep but Laura lay awake thinking over the evening and Mrs Wilson and the word cherish. She thought of the woman's words about her mother and how true they were. She *did* light up a room but she was certainly not cherished and she should be.

Why did she marry him? Laura wondered. There must have been lots of men who wanted to marry Mum so why did she pick him? And why did *he* marry? He doesn't love her and cherish her, he only cares about himself.

Her old dream of providing a home for her mother and Julie revived and seemed much closer. Only a few more years and I'll be working and able to take them away, she thought. He can *pay* someone to skivvy for him and he won't even notice we've gone, especially if Gerry is still at home, and *I'll* cherish her.

Making happy plans for the future, Laura fell asleep.

Chapter Eight

The bitter weather continued and grew even worse. There were further falls of snow which quickly froze, farms were cut off, trains derailed and road travel became almost impossible. Shortages of food and fuel followed, sporting fixtures were abandoned and even the River Mersey froze.

Illness was widespread and in spite of Anne's care Julie became ill again. The sound of her wheezing breath filled the house and in early January she was admitted to Alder Hey Children's Hospital.

At the same time, Sarah developed bronchitis, complicated by a heart condition caused by an earlier bout of rheumatic fever, and she was also admitted to hospital.

It was a nightmare time for both families as worry over the invalids and daily hospital visits were added to the misery of the conditions and shortages and the difficulty of keeping pipes unfrozen and clothes dried.

Julie recovered quickly and within weeks she was discharged to be nursed at home but Sarah's illness was more serious. At first she was in a bed near the door where she could be seen from the sister's office but when she was out of danger she was moved further up the ward.

Joe had to attend a parents' meeting one night and Rosa had a cold so Laura and John went to visit Sarah while Anne stayed with Julie.

The ward was frantically busy and Sarah wept as she told them of the old people brought in from unheated rooms only to die within days or even hours.

'Is nobody doing anything about it?' John demanded.

'I don't know, John. There are so many old people living alone not able to cope and everything is stretched with this awful weather,' said

Sarah with a sigh. She looked at Laura's shocked face and said more cheerfully, 'It's not all doom and gloom though. The woman in the next bed and that big fat woman opposite are a real pair of comedians. They have us in fits sometimes, even the nurses.'

They talked about Anne and Julie for a few moments but John was obviously uneasy and before long he strolled up the ward and spoke to several of the patients who had no visitors.

'I suppose you and Rosa can't get out with this weather,' Sarah said to Laura but she shook her head.

'It's not the weather. We didn't want to go out while you and Julie were very sick but everything's still going on. Gerry's got bookings every night, all over the place.'

'I know you've been a good help to your mum and Rosa's helped Uncle Joe but you'll have to get out and enjoy yourselves as soon as the weather's better.'

'We went out at the weekend,' Laura assured her, feeling that she was receiving praise under false pretences.

John had now gone to see the doctor and sister in the sister's office and Laura watched him, fuming. What's he doing now? she thought. He's supposed to be visiting Auntie Sarah.

John returned just before the end of visiting. 'Sorry, sis,' he said to Sarah. 'They say it's nobody's fault with these old people but I'm sure *something* can be done to help them.'

The next time they visited Sarah she greeted John with a smile. 'So you got something done to help old people on their own, John?'

'I only talked to some of the men at the factory,' he said. 'We raised some funds and got a rota going to visit them. I had to tread on a few toes to get the names and addresses but I'm not worried about that.'

'Joe said a lot of people are sympathetic but you get things done and very efficiently too,' said Sarah.

John shrugged. 'It was the others really.'

Rosa was loud in praise of John and Laura said grudgingly, 'I suppose he's got good points but I still think charity begins at home. He doesn't look after Mum properly.'

'But your mum's able to look after herself,' Rosa protested.

91

'But he doesn't *cherish* her,' said Laura stubbornly. 'Like that woman at your party said. Like your dad with your mum.'

'Oh, *them*,' Rosa exclaimed. 'You wouldn't want them as soppy as that. I suppose they'll be even worse now. No fools like old fools.' They giggled together.

With both invalids out of danger and improving fast, Laura and Rosa felt free to go out again and enjoy themselves, encouraged by Anne and Joe. 'We've missed a *whole* month,' Rosa mourned, and they decided to play truant on 4 February to go to what they later found was the Beatles' last lunchtime session at the Cavern.

A bitter wind whistled down the narrow canyon of Mathew Street and the girls huddled together for warmth as they queued but felt that it was well worth it when they were finally admitted.

They could scarcely speak when it was over. They tottered out, their throats sore from screaming, exhausted by emotion and excitement but huge-eyed with bliss.

'If I died now I'd die happy,' Rosa croaked and Laura nodded in agreement. They stumbled towards the bus stop, still carrying their coats and oblivious of the cold.

Suddenly their arms were gripped. Laura's father was staring at them in horror and anger. 'What the hell?' he began. Laura tried to pull her arm away but she was gripped too hard.

John signalled to a passing cab and pushed both girls into it, then followed, giving his own address. 'You're coming to our house to clean yourself up before your father sees you,' he told Rosa grimly. 'He's got enough to worry about without this.' He glared at Laura. 'And you! What the hell are you doing parading through town got up like a clown or a streetwalker? Why aren't you at school? And those dresses! Are you mad?'

Both girls were too stunned by the suddenness of the confrontation to speak and John's eyes raked them. 'That muck on your faces,' he said angrily. 'Do you realise what you look like? A pair of tarts and dirty scruffy ones at that. Just asking for trouble. By God, there are going to be some changes made, I can tell you.'

Laura found her voice. 'We only went to the Cavern,' she said sullenly. 'Everyone goes. There's no need for such a fuss.'

'Isn't there?' John shouted. The taxi driver looked round and he said more quietly, 'You're just children and you've got yourselves up like this.' He shook his head. 'Sagging school too. I tell you, things are going to change. You've had too much of your own way.'

Rosa smiled at him and said coaxingly, 'We only went because we thought we mightn't have another chance, Uncle John,' but he refused to be mollified.

'I'm surprised at *you*, Rosa. You know how ill your mum's been and how worried your dad's been about her. I thought you had more feeling for them.'

The taxi stopped and John thrust the fare and a tip at the driver and marched the two girls into his house. There was no one in the kitchen and he went into the hall and listened then came back to the girls who were standing together, looking mutinous.

'Go upstairs quietly,' he hissed, 'and get that muck off your faces before anyone sees you. You look *grotesque*.'

The girls slipped quietly upstairs. They heard Anne's voice from Julie's bedroom. They looked at each other for the first time and Rosa began to giggle.

'Gosh,' Laura exclaimed, looking in the bathroom mirror, 'I didn't realise our mascara had run like that.'

'No wonder he said we looked like clowns,' Rosa said as they surveyed their streaked faces. 'We'll never hear the end of this.'

'*I* won't, anyway,' Laura said grimly. 'But I don't care. We got there anyway. He can't take that away from us.'

'No,' Rosa sighed sentimentally. 'I'll remember it all my life.'

They kept their voices low as they smeared cream on their faces then wiped it off and washed thoroughly. Then Rosa whispered, 'I'll have to go and change before my dad gets in. Are you ready? I'm not going downstairs by myself.' Laura slipped into her bedroom and changed rapidly then they crept downstairs.

John was sitting by the kitchen table and Rosa said meekly, 'I'll have to go home now, Uncle John.'

'Aye, you'd better,' he said grimly. 'But don't make any plans to go out with Laura because she won't be going out.'

'Are you going to tell Dad?' Rosa asked.

'Yes, but I won't worry him more than I have to. Something's got to be done about you two though.'

Laura went to the door with Rosa to say goodbye. 'I hate him,' she whispered. 'But don't worry. Your dad will be all right.'

Rosa grimaced. 'He'll pray all over me,' she whispered back. 'I don't know which is worse.'

'*Laura,*' John called and Laura shut the door as Rosa sped away.

Anne came downstairs. 'I didn't realise you were home,' she said to John. 'And Laura!' She glanced at the clock.

'She should be still in school,' John said grimly. 'I met her and Rosa in town, sagging school, so I brought them home.'

'Oh, Laura,' Anne said reproachfully. 'I thought you had more sense.'

'We went to the lunchtime session at the Cavern. It was the Beatles. Everyone else goes,' Laura said sulkily.

'Where's Rosa?' asked Anne.

'I sent her home with a flea in her ear,' John said. 'I've told them, Anne. They'll be better apart. They've had too much freedom and they've taken advantage while we've been worried about Julie and Sarah.'

'No, we haven't,' Laura flashed. 'We didn't go out while they were very ill.'

John glared at her. 'Don't use that tone to me, madam. I'd expect you to show some shame after what I saw today but you're too impudent for that.'

'Why? What did you see?' Anne asked in alarm.

John said dismissively, 'Oh, muck caked on their faces like a pair of clowns or streetwalkers. They were a disgrace but don't fuss about it.'

Anne was indignant. 'It sounds as though there's something to fuss *about*. I'm surprised at you, Laura, and Rosa, too.'

'I told Rosa she should have had more thought for her father,' John said. 'Joe's got enough on his plate but I think this one's the ringleader. She leads Rosa astray.'

'It's probably six of one and half a dozen of the other,' Anne said. 'Perhaps they're a bad influence on each other.'

Laura gazed at her mother, feeling betrayed. I'm sure Mum doesn't really think that, she thought, so why is she siding with him?

'I've told Rosa not to make any plans to go out with her and I mean it,' John stated. 'In future I'm going to keep a closer watch on her. She'll stay in where I can see what she's up to.'

'That's if you're ever in yourself,' Laura retorted. The words seemed to pop out of her mouth, surprising her as much as her parents, but her father reacted with a stinging slap across her face.

'Go up to your room and stay there, you impudent faggot,' he roared.

Laura turned and fled.

'Oh John,' Anne said reproachfully and started after Laura but there was a frightened wail from Julie and she turned instead into her bedroom to reassure her.

Laura rushed into her room and slammed the door behind her then flung herself on her bed and gave way to a torrent of tears. I hate him, I hate him, I hate him, she told herself, burying her face in the pillow to muffle her sobs. After a while she lifted her head and heard her mother talking to Julie.

Again Laura was overwhelmed with tears. I can't bear it, she thought. I don't care about him but now Mum has turned against me. She thought of her mother looking reproachfully at her then siding with her father even when he struck her. She had been too shocked and upset to realise that Anne had been following her and thought she had simply come up to Julie. She wept afresh as she compared the way her mother had spoken to her and the gentle tones she used to Julie and felt herself unloved and unwanted.

When she could cry no more she went into the bathroom and sluiced her face with cold water then combed her hair. *He's* not going to see me looking upset, she thought defiantly. She examined her face in the mirror and was disappointed to see no trace of John's slap on her cheek.

The house was silent and it seemed a long time before Laura heard voices and the clatter of dishes from the kitchen. A little later there was a knock on her bedroom door and her mother came in carrying a tray with a plateful of beef casserole and a glass of milk.

Laura longed to apologise to her but could only say perversely, 'I thought it would be bread and water.'

Anne shook her head. 'Laura, love, why are you like this?'

Laura could only scowl and mutter, 'Is Julie all right?'

'Yes. I was going to go to the hospital with your dad tonight to see Auntie Sarah and leave you to mind Julie but Dad won't hear of it now.'

'Does he think I'll corrupt her or something?' Laura said angrily.

'He doesn't think you are responsible enough,' her mother answered calmly. 'And can you blame him, Laura? He says you must stay in your room and he'll look after Julie. I'll go to the hospital with Uncle Joe.'

'There's no need for that. You know there isn't, Mum. It's just spite,' said Laura and Anne looked vexed.

'Don't speak like that about your father,' she said. 'Eat your meal before it gets cold,' and went out of the room without a backward glance.

Again tears poured down Laura's face. Why do I say things like that? she thought. I can't help it. They just pop out. Why can't I be like Rosa and let it all run off me like water off a duck's back? She never bothers about answering, just says 'Sorree' then floats off and forgets all about it. Suddenly she thought of her and Rosa's faces streaked with mascara running over their made-up cheeks and with a sudden swing of mood she began to laugh, then ate her meal with enjoyment.

Joe and Sarah took Rosa's escapade more calmly than John. Joe taught fifteen-year-olds and knew about the hysteria of the girls who followed the groups and of the new mood of freedom sweeping through that generation. The sweet shop Sarah worked in was patronised by girls from a nearby school and she knew many of them. On morning duty she saw them with faces free of make-up and with neat hair on the way to school, and when she did an occasional evening duty she saw the same girls heavily made up with hair lacquered in huge beehive hairstyles, but they were the same happy, likeable girls.

John was annoyed that Sarah and Joe seemed so unconcerned. He had not intended to go into detail about the appearance of the two girls but he was unable to resist telling of the grotesque picture they had made.

'They looked like streetwalkers,' he said. 'I got the shock of my life. They put themselves in danger, going round like that.'

Joe laughed. 'They all get themselves up like that,' he said. 'You're taking it too seriously, John. They're just young and daft. They all scream when they go to watch these groups, not just on television, y'know.'

'It's unhealthy,' John said with distaste.

'You don't say that when the girls scream at Gerry's group,' Sarah retorted.

'But they don't—'

'Of course they do,' Sarah interrupted him. 'Gerry and Peter were laughing about it when they were here the other day.'

John was silenced for a moment. He was proud of Gerry's many bookings but he saw little of his son. Gerry was often out when he came home from work and even when Gerry had a rare free evening he himself was usually out at one of his meetings.

He was shaken by jealousy at the thought that Sarah seemed to know more about Gerry than he did. He tried to conceal it but Anne glanced at his face and said soothingly, 'It's only a phase anyway. Look at the way Moira's settled down at university and she was crazy about Bill Haley and people like that when she was younger.'

'But she didn't get up to any of these antics,' John said, recovering.

'Of course she did. She was at the Odeon when he appeared there and the police were called.' Sarah laughed. 'They thought it was a riot because so many seats were wrecked but it was only the kids going mad, screaming and carrying on, dancing in the aisles in their bare feet.' She laughed again. 'Ours haven't done anything like that yet.'

Joe, Anne and Sarah were laughing but John was still annoyed and determined not to let the matter drop. 'What about the truancy?' he demanded. 'I thought as a teacher you'd be concerned about that at least.'

Joe shrugged. 'It's not a regular thing,' he said.

'How do we know? I just happened to catch them this time.'

'Rosa told me. They missed a lot of Beatles concerts in January while we were all so worried and they took the chance of going to the lunchtime session at the Cavern. You know what they're like about that group.'

'I thought it was the Swinging Blue Jeans they were mad about,' said Anne. 'Or that lad from Bootle. Billy J. Kramer. They're the photos Laura has up in her room.'

'I think it's a fresh craze every week,' said Sarah, 'but the Beatles are the main ones. The lad on the drums, Ringo Starr, is Gerry's idol too, isn't he?'

John was even more annoyed by Sarah's apparent knowledge of Gerry and he said angrily, 'You didn't see the girls or you'd be more worried. They were just asking for trouble. I tell you, I'll be watching Laura like a hawk from now on and I'd advise you to do the same with Rosa.'

Suddenly Joe and Sarah both became angry, Joe because Sarah was not yet fully recovered and he knew that she already worried secretly about Rosa's combination of beauty and recklessness, and Sarah by John's criticism of Rosa and what she saw as interference in her family affairs.

'You'll have to alter your own lifestyle then, won't you?' Joe snapped. 'Maybe even spend some time at home,' he added sarcastically.

Before John could speak Sarah said angrily, 'Thanks, John, we don't want any advice from *you* about our children. Rosa's been well brought up and she knows how to behave. You look after your kids and leave us to look after ours.'

'I think we're all taking it too seriously,' Anne said hastily. 'After all, we all did daft things when we were young and look at us now.'

Sarah realised that Anne was trying to keep the peace so she laughed and agreed. 'Yes, we're all model citizens now, aren't we? Mind you, it's a different world for kids these days. Plenty of money in their pockets and jobs and no threat of call-up.'

'That's true,' said Joe. 'Well-paid jobs and plenty of them too so if they don't like the job they're in they can just leave and get another.'

'When you think what we had to put up with from Miss Meers at the cake shop,' Anne said laughing. 'These kids don't know they're born.' The conversation turned to other topics for a short time, then Anne and John left.

Joe went to the door with them but when he came back to Sarah he shook his head. 'God, I was never so near thumping John as today. Damned stupid fuss about nothing but he goes on and *on*. So damned intense about everything.'

'I know and he annoyed me trying to tell us how to bring up our kids,' said Sarah. 'The cheek of him.'

'Yes, that really got under my skin,' Joe agreed.

'I felt tempted to tell him where he was going wrong with his own. I can understand that Anne has to give most of her attention to Julie but it's wrong that John dotes on Gerry so much. He's always picking on Laura.'

'I don't think he picks on her so much as ignores her. But I tell you what, Sar, he doesn't seem to know much about what Gerry's doing these days, does he?'

'Because he's never in,' Sarah said. 'Always out saving the world. That's why he doesn't know what's happening around him with the kids. I don't know how Anne puts up with it. I'd kill him.'

'But he's a good fellow really,' Joe said, belatedly remembering that John was Sarah's brother. 'He means well but he's just tactless. He takes things too much to heart.'

'I don't suppose he'll change now,' Sarah sighed. 'He's been like that as long as I can remember but I'm glad we didn't properly fall out today.'

'So am I.' Joe hugged her. 'What we must do now is concentrate on getting you really well again.'

'A bit of better weather and I'll be fine,' Sarah said. 'We all will.'

Anne and John walked home in silence. Anne felt that they had come very close to a complete rift with Sarah and Joe and was determined to warn John to be more discreet but he seemed unusually subdued. She wondered whether some of the home truths he had heard had hit their mark and he was regretting taking the girls' escapade so seriously, or whether he felt that Gerry had drifted away

99

from him. When he suddenly announced that he intended to withdraw from a visit to a factory social club she felt sure that it was to see more of Gerry but she said nothing.

'I'll ask Bill Brewer to give the talk instead of me,' he said. 'Time I delegated more anyway.'

'Yes, and Bill's very keen, isn't he?' Anne agreed peaceably, reserving judgement on John's good intentions until she saw how long they lasted.

Laura believed that her father was spending more time at home to watch her but it was the revelation that Sarah knew more about Gerry's affairs than he did that had decided John to cut down on his evening meetings. For a while he checked Laura's homework and questioned her about her activities but his vigilance soon relaxed and he said no more about parting her from Rosa. Anne had told him that he might offend Sarah and Joe and that anyway the girls usually went about in a group.

John was still often detained at the factory on union matters but on the night of the CND talk by Bill Brewer he made a determined effort to be at home in time to sit down with the family for the evening meal.

'Where are you off tonight then, Dad?' Gerry said, eating his meal rapidly.

'I'm not out. I've asked another fellow to give the talk tonight.'

'Good. Time you slowed down a bit,' Gerry said cheerfully.

Anne shook her head at him. 'You're the one who needs to slow down. Out till all hours then getting up for work the next day.'

'Never mind, Mum. Wait until we hit the big time then I'll give up my job and stay in bed all day.'

Julie giggled and Gerry began to tease her about her homework. In spite of her long absences from school, Julie had passed the eleven-plus and had been selected for a place in the same convent grammar school as Dilly, Tony and Helen's daughter, and seemed happy there.

'About time for a haircut, isn't it, son?' John said, looking at Gerry's mop of fair curls.

Gerry laughed. 'No. There's no short back and sides now, Dad. Everyone's grown their hair.'

John seemed about to protest but instead he asked where the Merrymen were playing.

'At a club called the Cherry Tree,' Gerry told him. 'It's a bit minty but it's a booking.'

'I might come and see you,' said John and Gerry looked alarmed.

'Not there, Dad. It's a dive.' He looked at John's dark suit. 'You'll have to get some gear if you want to start clubbing it,' he laughed.

Laura had not spoken at all but now she said suddenly, 'The oldest swinger in town.'

John glared at her.

'You could come some night next week,' Gerry suggested. 'We've got a few good ones then. The Grafton and the Orrell Park. You could pretend to be an agent. Wave a cheque book.' He laughed and John smiled uncertainly.

What's happening here? he thought. A little while ago *I* was the one who made the decisions. He'd have asked me if he could grow his hair and stay out so late but suddenly *I'm* being told what to do. He felt uneasy and disorientated. He looked down the table to Anne, who smiled and said cheerfully, 'I wonder how Bill will go on. I hope he doesn't get stage fright.'

'A lot of fellows are into CND, you know, Dad,' Gerry told him. 'And David says a lot of them at the college are too.'

'It's daubed all over the entrance to the Cavern,' Laura said. 'Y'know, CND and the symbol.'

'I'm glad to hear it. Everybody'll be affected if they go ahead with these bomb tests.'

Later John said to Anne that he seemed to have alarmed Gerry by suggesting going to listen to the Merrymen.

'It's just that you'd probably stick out like a sore thumb from what I've heard of these clubs,' Anne said. 'They're all so young and you wouldn't be able to hear properly with the noise and the screaming girls. Not a bit like the caelidhes we used to go to,' she laughed.

John smiled then said ruefully, 'Come to think of it, I wouldn't have wanted my dad there either.'

'I tell you what though, John, these kids have got it made. They seem to think the world's their oyster and it is. Like Joe says, they've got plenty of money and good jobs and they do what they like and get away with it.'

'I know. I was thinking that tonight and I don't know how the hell it happened.'

'It's because they're all the same. They've all got money in their pockets and it's given them the confidence to demand their own way and get it. They just sort of take it for granted and that's made them all independent.'

'Like Gerry with his long hair,' said John. 'He didn't ask me, just told me.'

'Well, he is eighteen, John.'

'Yes, but we didn't make our own decisions at that age. We were still treated as children.'

Anne looked at him quizzically. 'How old were you when you went to Spain to fight?'

'Yes, but I had to do it on the quiet. Pretend I was going to Paris for the weekend or my dad would have stopped me.' He thought for a moment. 'Mind you, he told me the night before I left he knew what I was up to but he said as long as Mum wasn't upset I should do what I believed in.'

'I always admired your dad,' Anne said softly.

'Yes, I have to admit he was good about that. Not many fathers at that time would have taken that line.' He lit two cigarettes and handed one to Anne. 'Now that I'm at this stage myself I think I understand him better or at least I have more sympathy for him. Mind you, it's harder now. We're living in a different world.'

'I'm made up for the kids,' Anne said staunchly. 'This is the time to enjoy life while they're young. I hope the good times last for ever. We were kept down too much.'

'As long as things don't go too far the other way,' John said. 'Some of these television programmes seem to be making out that anything goes. It's fuddy-duddy to have any morals.'

'I didn't like that programme, *That Was The Week That Was,* mocking religion. But those sort of people always had way-out ideas. Strange lives, and they've got the chance now to air their ideas, but ordinary people see them for what they are.'

'Our generation do, Anne, but kids are easily influenced. They'll think it's clever and fashionable and try to copy them.'

'No, they've got more sense.'

'Don't be too sure. Businessmen don't spend money advertising soap powder and stuff like that on TV unless they know they can influence people. It's the thin edge of the wedge.'

'It won't last,' Anne said cheerfully. 'They'll just go too far and get knocked back. Why, I nearly wrote in about that programme, I was so shocked, and lots of people must have felt the same. Some with more influence than me and others who *did* write in. They can't afford to stir up a hornet's nest like that and get away with it.'

'I'll tell you two who need watching,' John said. 'Our Laura and Rosaleen. Joe and Sarah seem to wear blinkers.'

'You're wrong, John,' Anne said positively. 'Rosa's too pretty for her own good but they're both good girls. They won't come to any harm.' John shrugged, unconvinced, but Anne had lost interest in the argument. At this time her thoughts were often with her beloved sister, Maureen, whose health was failing. She was to return shortly from the refugee camp to a hospital in England.

Chapter Nine

The snow at last began to melt on 16 March and soon the hard winter was succeeded by a lovely summer. Laura and Rosa had both obtained Saturday jobs to supplement their pocket money, but while Laura stayed in the same job in an estate agent's office, Rosa flitted from one job to another, rarely staying more than three weeks anywhere.

Gradually the girls were drifting apart although they remained good friends. They were nearing the end of their schooldays. Rosa showed a flair for art and design and hoped to go on to the College of Art and she was still interested in dancing and also had vague plans for an acting career. She had twice appeared in pantomime with others from her dancing school at Liverpool Empire.

Laura shared none of these interests and was uncertain about a career. After a visit to Julie in hospital she thought briefly that she might become a nurse but she was dissuaded by a nurse friend of Moira's.

'You'd never stand it,' the nurse told her frankly. 'The discipline and being told off for something you hadn't done. You'd be crowning Sister with a bedpan.'

Laura had to agree but could think of nothing else. She was not ambitious and thought she would be happy enough in any type of office work.

As the two girls grew older, the difference in their temperaments showed more clearly and made them less close. Laura's feelings were deep and complex. She loved Julie and worried about her, yet she had to struggle not to resent the amount of love and attention given her sister by their mother. She was proud of Gerry but she felt it unfair that he had so much freedom and she had so little.

Her anxious protective love for her mother was deep and never wavered and she longed to shield her from any unhappiness. Her feeling for her father swung between love and hate, or what she told herself was hate, only to feel ashamed that she had used the word about her own father. Often her confusion was compounded by an act of kindness and compassion by her father or evidence of his care for his own mother.

Everything was black or white to Laura at this stage and she spoke as she thought, often with devastating effect, but although she regretted giving offence she was unable to compromise.

Rosa was completely different. Light-minded and light-hearted, she did whatever she wanted to do without thought of the consequences and was untroubled by the effect on other people. She lacked the imagination to put herself in another's position and understand their feelings and she never felt deeply enough to care.

Everyone was charmed by Rosa, even the girls in their group who lost boyfriends to her, because it was obvious that Rosa did nothing to draw them away. Her beauty and charisma did that.

The group of friends who had stayed together since their youth-club days were gradually breaking up. Rosa had been the first to go out alone with a boy but soon others within the group began to pair off.

Laura stayed within the group and still regarded the boys only as friends. She was impatient with the constant giggling discussion about the boys among the other girls.

'I think they're daft,' she told Rosa. 'We have far more fun in a crowd.'

'You know what you are?' Rosa laughed. 'You're a late developer.'

'It's more that you're an early developer,' Laura retorted. 'And you've given the others ideas.' But she still loyally covered for Rosa when she was out late on a date.

As time passed, Laura found that she had more in common with her cousin David than with Rosa. They shared a love of books and David had a dry wit which Laura appreciated. He played cello in the college orchestra and was studying hard, hoping to be accepted for Oxford or Cambridge. He had no time for visiting clubs but he collected records of the Beatles and Roy Orbison and had lately become interested in soul music.

'A bit of everything,' the girls teased him. 'How can you enjoy the stuff you play on the cello and like all those records as well?'

'Easily,' David retorted. 'One doesn't shut the other out and I mostly buy ballad-type music anyway.'

'It's no use playing records in your room,' Rosa said. 'You've got to *hear* them to really appreciate them. Come to the Cavern.'

David responded to the challenge and had the foresight to buy tickets for the Cavern for 3 August when the Beatles and another of his favourite groups, the Escorts, appeared there.

The warm city streets were thronged with young people as David and the girls walked along North John Street. Crowds filled Mathew Street as they turned off for the Cavern but only ticket-holders were admitted. The Beatles had become even more popular since appearing on television's *625 Show* and on numerous radio programmes.

'Good job you got the tickets, David,' Laura said as they pushed through the crowd. 'We'd never have thought of it.'

'Whew, it's hot, isn't it?' David said. 'Might have been better to go to the Grafton last night to hear them.'

'No, the Cavern's better,' Rosa said but when the performance was over David again regretted not going to the Grafton Rooms instead.

'I agree the music sounds great and it's a fabulous atmosphere but it *stinks*,' he complained.

'No it doesn't,' Rosa said indignantly. 'You've got no soul. That smell's fab. So exciting. You just *know* you're going to have a fantastic time as soon as you smell it.'

'What? BO and mustiness, that's all I could smell,' David said. 'And the heat and the water running down the walls. No thanks. I'll stick to records.'

'There's a heat wave on, you goon,' Laura said but David only laughed.

Although it was midnight, the streets were still full of young people strolling around in the warm, scented air, wearing every style of fashion – young men with long hair in gaudily patterned shirts and winkle-picker shoes or clog-style sandals in bright colours and girls in bright shift dresses and elaborate hairstyles.

They met many people they knew and exchanged greetings or stopped for a few minutes to talk. Everyone seemed happy and suddenly Rosa threw back her head and raised her arms. 'Isn't this great?' she cried. 'Oh, I'm so glad we live now.'

'"Bliss was it in that dawn to be alive,"' David began and Laura finished the quotation. '"But to be young was very heaven."'

They all laughed then linked arms and ran through the side streets from sheer joy in living. Older people talked of a new Elizabethan Age after the Queen's coronation in 1953 but to the young people now it seemed that the Golden Age had arrived. Everything was changing and youth was coming into its own.

A friend of Moira's was a typist in a cotton brokers' office in the Cotton Exchange where all the clerks wore dark suits and bowler hats. The office boy had been reprimanded for wearing a leather jacket and string tie for work and had left, only to become the hugely successful Rory Storm of Rory Storm and the Hurricanes. He later went back to visit the office wearing designer clothes and driving a white Rolls-Royce and was surrounded by the dazzled office girls. Incredulous and dismayed, the sober-suited male clerks watched with envy.

Everyone dreamed of following his example and boys and girls were determined not to be pushed around. Bewildered supervisors and senior staff now looked in vain for the deference they felt was due to them.

Laura and Rosa felt cheated that they had missed most of the years of the Beatles in Liverpool although they followed their triumphant progress elsewhere with pride and there were many other Liverpool groups for their adulation.

Their tastes were now different and by the time Rosa moved on to the College of Art, she followed the more raunchy music of the Rolling Stones and the Kinks. Laura still preferred the local groups, the Escorts, the Searchers and Billy J. Kramer and the Dakotas.

Laura had seen little of her silent deskmate, Mary Morgan, in recent years but on her first day at a business college in Rodney Street they met again. Relief at seeing a familiar face made them greet each other eagerly and soon they became close friends, although Laura's loyalty to her cousin Rosa never wavered.

The country was rocked by the Profumo scandal at this time and Mary said she was sick of hearing about it. 'Who cares what those sort of people get up to?' she said. 'They just haven't got enough to do. My father keeps on about the devil finding work for idle hands and Sodom and Gomorrah but he can't get enough of the details.'

'My dad's on about the political angle all the time,' said Laura. 'And my Uncle Joe, y'know, Rosa's father, he's back and forth like a yo-yo switching news broadcasts off. Rosa says the newspapers are like lace curtains because he cuts out any articles that give too many details. Trying to protect her innocence.'

'He's a bit late for that, isn't he?' Mary said but at a warning glance from Laura she said no more.

Mary was fascinated by the easy hospitality of Laura's family. The first time she went home with her she was warmly welcomed by Anne and introduced to one of her numerous relatives who had called with her two daughters and they all sat round the kitchen table drinking tea and eating fruit cake and small buns. Before long they were joined by Julie with two friends from the netball team and later by Gerry and Peter Taylor. Julie had outgrown her childhood weakness and was now strong and healthy although still very shy but she talked to Mary.

Mary was sorry when Laura took her off to her bedroom to listen to records, especially as Gerry and Peter had been talking about the Iron Door Club where they met up with other pop groups after their gigs.

'I thought you wanted to hear my Beatles records,' Laura said. 'You can hear those two any time. They're always gassing.'

'*I* can't,' Mary said, but she said nothing about wanting to stay in the warm and friendly atmosphere of the kitchen.

Mary had never mentioned her own family but the following day she began to talk about her home.

'It's very different to yours,' she told Laura. 'Very formal and we hardly ever have visitors. I don't think my father has any friends.'

'Are you an only child?' Laura asked.

'Good heavens, no. I'm the one he's ashamed of though, because I failed the eleven-plus. My eldest brother James is at Sidney Sussex, Cambridge, and my sister Angela is reading maths at Oxford. It was bad enough when Luke only got Lancaster University but when I went to St Joe's he just wanted to draw a veil over me.'

'My Uncle Joe says it isn't pass or fail, it's just selection and the secondary moderns should have the same standards as the grammar schools, the same facilities,' Laura said.

Mary looked sceptical. 'Try telling that to people like my father.'

'My brother was at St Edward's College but he left after O levels. Julie's at Notre Dame although she missed a lot of school because of illness,' said Laura, 'I'm the odd one out but that's nothing new.'

'That makes two of us,' said Mary. Now that she had spoken about her family she often talked about them to Laura who was surprised to find that there was great hostility between Mary and her father. I thought I was the only one who didn't get on with her father, she thought, but Mary's dad sounds much worse than mine.

She quickly realised that although their feelings about their fathers made a bond between them their attitude to their respective mothers was very different. In contrast to Laura's own deep love for her mother, Mary seemed to feel only contempt for hers.

'She's just a doormat – a handrag,' she declared. 'He treats her like a servant and she accepts it. No spirit at all.'

'Was she always like that?' Laura asked curiously.

'I don't know. She was by the time I was old enough to realise what was going on but maybe she wasn't always. Our James had a row with my father last year and afterwards when my mother was crying he said she should stand up to him. He said, "People take you at your own valuation. If you behave like a doormat he'll treat you like one."'

'I think that's true,' said Laura. 'What did your mum say?'

'Just cried,' Mary said contemptuously. 'And then she said he shouldn't argue with my father because it only made him worse. James said being allowed to get away with it made him worse, but my mother started crying again. Said you can't argue with a steamroller and James would go back to Cambridge and she'd have to bear the brunt of the row. Does your Gerry argue with your dad?'

'*Gerry*?' Laura said. 'My dad wouldn't argue with *Gerry*. Everything he does is perfect in my dad's eyes. Mind you,' she added honestly, 'it's very hard to argue with Gerry. He's so easygoing.'

'I thought all your family were easy to get on with – those I met,' Mary said. 'Everyone seemed happy.'

'That's because my dad was out. And my mum's a very happy person, everyone says so. Not because of him though but because that's her nature.'

'But she stands up to him?'

'Not exactly,' Laura said. 'She just gives in to keep the peace, I think. She's far too soft with him and she puts up with his bad temper and his selfishness but not because she's afraid.' She paused, finding it hard to explain her parents' relationship and instead she asked about Mary's family. 'I know James stands up to your father but what about Angela when she's home from Oxford and your Luke?'

'Angela hardly opens her mouth when she's home,' Mary said. 'And our Luke might as well be in Lancaster all year. He always gets holiday jobs that keep him away from home.'

'So your mum misses out on her children as well as having to put up with your dad,' Laura said bluntly.

They were sitting in a small park eating their lunchtime sandwiches and Mary stood up and brushed crumbs from her skirt. 'Don't be trying to make me feel sorry for her, Laura Redmond. I reckon he couldn't have been like this when she married him. She let him become a domineering bully and we've all had to suffer for it. Don't worry. I don't let it get me down. I keep out of his way as much as possible and as soon as I can support myself I'll be off. Get my own place.'

'That's my plan too,' Laura said eagerly. 'As soon as I can I'll get a place where I can take Mum – and Julie if she wants to come. Where she'll never have to put up with his bullying again.'

Mary looked at her in surprise and seemed about to speak but then as she took in Laura's shining eyes and happy smile she shrugged and stayed silent.

They set off for the college, passing a record shop which was belting out the Beatles record 'She loves you, yeah, yeah, yeah'. Four girls walking along together were singing in unison with it and Mary suddenly exclaimed, 'What are we doing worrying about those things on a day like this? The sun's shining, everyone's happy. Come on, race you up the hill.'

They raced up, giggling and pushing each other, and arrived for their classes breathless but cheerful again. Laura was happy at the college and worked hard, determined to qualify for a well-paid position which would bring her dream of independence nearer.

Mary went to Laura's house several times but said she felt embarrassed because she was unable to ask Laura to visit her home. Laura brushed this aside.

'Don't be daft,' she said. 'Our place is just handier for playing records, that's all.'

Mary's father was uninterested in music so they had never owned a gramophone but in Laura's home there was a radiogram in the sitting room and also a record player in her bedroom, a Christmas present from her Uncle Mick.

Laura's Aunt Maureen had worked abroad since soon after the end of the war, first in the chaos of Europe then in the Middle East, but her health had failed and she had returned to England. She was now staying with her sister Anne to be nursed back to health before she decided on her future. A situation like this brought out the best in John's character and, watching him with Maureen, Mary wondered why Laura was so hostile to her father.

She said so when they had retired to Laura's bedroom but Laura said indignantly, 'Oh yes, he can be very nice with other people. It's the way he treats my mother that I object to. And the way he treats me.'

Mary looked round the bedroom. Although small it was freshly decorated with wallpaper that matched the pretty curtains and the bedspread on the divan bed. There was a small wardrobe and dressing table and David, who liked working with wood, had built a long desk under the window to hold a typewriter and the record player.

'I don't think you've got much to complain about,' she said. 'All this and you can do what you like. Bring anyone home.'

'You're forgetting the fly in the ointment,' Laura said. 'My father. He might seem all right fussing over Aunt Maureen but you haven't heard him laying down the law to Mum and me and snarling at us when something doesn't suit him. Everything else is more important than Mum. He doesn't care about her at all. Street angel, home devil, he is, like my grandma used to say.'

'Didn't she have any time for him either?' asked Mary.

'She thought the sun shone out of him,' Laura said. 'Oh, I see what you mean. That was just a phrase she used, not about him but about other people. He was her grandson, you see.'

'I wouldn't mind changing places with you,' Mary said. 'Your dad bought that typewriter for you, didn't he?'

'Only so I could increase my typing speeds,' Laura said quickly but Mary shrugged and said she would wait a long time before her own father ever did anything like that.

Although Laura had refused to accept Mary's opinion, in spite of herself doubts began to creep in, especially after she was present during a conversation between her mother and her aunt.

'I'm so glad to see you settled so happily, love,' Maureen said. 'John's a good man and your children are a credit to you both. John hasn't changed – as enthusiastic as ever.'

'Still tilting at windmills, Mick says,' Anne laughed. 'He's very much involved with CND and organising demonstrations.'

'And he's right. I'm surprised to see how little people in this country care about the bomb, Anne. I met a woman who did relief work in Hiroshima after the atom bomb was dropped there and you wouldn't believe the horrors she'd seen. We were all experienced workers, we thought we'd seen everything, but what she described! And even then she said there were worse things she couldn't bring herself to talk about.'

'I know,' Anne said. 'John's got copies of pictures from there. Man's inhumanity to man!'

Maureen's pale cheeks were flushed and she said with unusual vehemence, 'I admire John for the work he's doing for CND, Anne, and I don't think his brother should skit at him. Saying he tilts at windmills. It's a good thing there are people like John in the world.'

'It was only a joke. Mick's very fond of John and he respects what he does. We all do. I help as much as possible with the paperwork and I go with him to demonstrations when I can.'

'I'm glad, pet,' Maureen said, smiling at her. 'I remember just after the war when John spoke out against using the atom bomb, when we all accepted what we were told. That it was necessary to finish the war with Japan.'

'Yes, and Peggy Burns fell out with him because their Michael was in a Jap prison camp. He fell out with a few people after that because he was so against the bomb but he was made up when CND started with famous people like Bertrand Russell and J. B. Priestley supporting it. And the crowds that turned up! It gave him hope.'

'What does CND stand for?' Laura asked.

It was Maureen who answered. 'The Campaign for Nuclear Disarmament, love. I hope you take an interest in it too.'

'I think my father does enough for all this family,' Laura said sharply, thinking of the time that he spent at CND demonstrations and meetings which she felt should be spent with her mother. She realised that her mother and aunt were looking at her in surprise and added hastily, 'I think Mum makes the sacrifices, being on her own while Dad's at Aldermaston and all over the place.'

'He doesn't go to enjoy himself,' Anne said. 'And when am I ever on my own anyway?'

Maureen said nothing but looked thoughtfully at Laura, making her feel uncomfortable.

'Auntie Maureen's very serious, isn't she?' she said to her mother when they were alone. 'Do you think she disapproves of us because we enjoy ourselves?'

'Of course not,' Anne said. 'Maureen was always quiet and devout but she was never a killjoy. It's just that she's seen such awful misery in her work with Sue Ryder. We must seem frivolous to her, the men so excited about winning the Cup and us only thinking of things for our houses and clothes.'

'So she *does* disapprove?' Laura said.

'No, love. She just says she feels bewildered. Values are so different.'

As the days passed, Laura felt that her mother was probably right, and that her aunt only rejoiced to see them happy. She was not so sure that her aunt approved of her personally. John was more forbearing than usual while Maureen was present and without realising it Laura took advantage of the situation to answer back to him. 'You just don't understand,' she said impatiently when John complained that she had been late home the previous night. 'We're not living in the Middle Ages now.'

John kept his temper. 'Good thing for you we're not,' he said, 'or I'd have locked you up long ago.'

Maureen said nothing but she looked reproachfully at Laura who felt her face grow red.

'I'll be glad when she's better,' she told Mary. 'She just looks at me but she makes me feel a heel.'

Laura was puzzled that Maureen seemed so much older than her mother. Her hair was grey and her face lined and one day when she was helping Maureen to wind wool she tried to ask her tactfully about it.

'You're not a bit like Mum, are you?' she said. 'Even though you're sisters.'

'We were very alike when we were young,' Maureen said. 'Like our mother. Like Julie and David are now. They both resemble my mother, almost like Spaniards, but that's because my mother came from the west of Ireland. It's a legacy from the sailors of the Spanish Armada who were washed up on that coast and married Irish girls.'

'But you're not alike now,' Laura persisted. 'Are you much older than Mum?'

Maureen smiled. 'Yes. Eleven years. I'm fifty-five.'

'Is that all?' Laura exclaimed, then bent her head over the ball of wool. I've put my foot in it again, she groaned inwardly, just when I was trying to be tactful, but Maureen seemed to notice nothing.

'Yes, your mum still looks very young,' she said. 'She's had her worries and troubles but she's always had your dad beside her looking after her. "Honour Thy Father" our Lord says and you should have no difficulty in honouring yours, Laura. He's a good man, one of the best.'

Laura kept her head bent and said nothing and Maureen changed the subject by showing her the pattern she was about to make.

After that, Laura avoided being alone with her aunt and this was made easier because as she grew stronger Maureen spent more and more time either at church or at the Cenacle Convent in Wavertree.

'If I can't work for those poor people, I can pray for them,' she said to Anne with a smile.

A few weeks later Maureen waited until she was alone with Anne and John to tell them that she had been told that she was in the first stage of a disease which would eventually cripple her. She had decided to enter a convent which was a few miles away in open country as a guest.

'They take a few ladies, some elderly, some in my situation and some who just want a quiet, peaceful life, where they can take part in the religious observance of the Order. They have an infirmary where they can nurse their guests when the time comes.'

Anne burst into tears and flung her arms round Maureen and John put his arms round both of them.

'Hush, love, hush,' Maureen said. 'It's nothing to cry about. I'll be very happy there. If I can't work in the field at least I'll know my prayers will be helping and I'll have no need to worry about the future.'

'But why can't you stay here?' Anne wept. 'I'd nurse you and you could still go to church or the Cenacle.'

Maureen hugged her. 'Your heart's good, love, and I know you mean it but believe me this is the best way. I prayed for guidance. And I'm not entering an enclosed Order,' she said, smiling and giving Anne a little shake. 'I'll be able to come and see the family whenever I want and you can come and see me. It'll work out well, you'll see.'

'But this illness, Mo? What is it?' Anne asked. 'Is there no cure?'

'Not yet, love. It's what they call a degenerative illness. It might be very gradual and I could live a normal life for a long time yet or it might progress very rapidly. No one knows and, honestly, I'm prepared. Whatever it is will be God's will and I hope I can accept it cheerfully. Now if you don't mind, love, I'll just go up to my room for a while.'

It was impossible for Anne to see this as Maureen did and she raged and cried while John tried to comfort her. 'Maureen has the right to make her own decision, love, and she's shown great courage, I think,' he said quietly. 'Try to accept it and don't make it harder for her.' And with a great effort Anne grew calm.

When Maureen came downstairs a little later she said immediately to John, 'I'm sorry, John. I've been very thoughtless. I was intent on my own affairs. I forgot that your mum and dad are celebrating their golden wedding next month. Can we keep this between us three until after that? There isn't a vacancy yet anyway because the nuns also take women for short periods for convalescence and they're booked up until after Christmas.'

'Thank God,' Anne said in such heartfelt tones that John and Maureen both smiled at her and Maureen kissed her.

'Perhaps I shouldn't have said anything at all yet but I thought I should tell you as soon as possible. Will it be hard to say nothing?'

'No, of course not, Mo,' John said. 'It'll give us time to get used to the idea before we involve the rest of the family. And don't forget, if it doesn't work out you can always come back here and know we'll be delighted to have you.'

'You're a good fellow, John,' Maureen said and Anne kissed him impulsively.

'I second that,' she said.

Chapter Ten

Mick and Gerda frequently travelled from York to spend a weekend with Cathy and Greg and Mick was full of plans for celebrating their golden wedding in October. He planned a large party in the Adelphi Hotel with as many of his parents' old friends present as he could trace, as well as all the family, but Cathy demurred.

'I wouldn't like a big fuss, Mick,' she said.

'But wouldn't you like to see all the friends of your youth, Mum? All the people you knew at the time of your marriage?'

Cathy looked at Greg and said sadly, 'We'd love to, Mick, but there's hardly anyone left now. So many were killed in the First World War – ours was a wartime wedding, remember – and others were scattered because of it. Norah in Morecambe is about the only one I've kept in touch with from those days.'

'Makes you realise,' Mick said. 'The Second World War was bad – a lot of my friends in the RAF bought it, but the fourteen–eighteen war wiped out a whole generation. You were lucky to survive, Dad.'

'I was and I was never even wounded,' Greg said. 'Yet so many were killed who were a loss to the world, never mind their families. People like Noel Chavasse, the Bishop of Liverpool's son. He was awarded the VC twice, the second one posthumously, but he would have been such a force for good in the world. A wonderful man.'

'And the poets like Wilfred Owen,' Mick said, but then he smiled and hugged his mother. 'We don't want to be talking about unhappy things. Are you sure you wouldn't like a big party, Mum? What about the friends you've made since then, and neighbours, people like that? I know there aren't many relations.'

'No, thanks all the same, son,' Cathy said.

'That's something I've often noticed, Mick,' Greg said thoughtfully. 'Families are either like the Fitzgeralds, a big family in themselves and with dozens of relations, aunts and uncles, cousins and second cousins, or like us. Neither your mum nor I have any relatives to speak of. There never seems to be a happy medium.'

'That's true,' Cathy said. 'My mother had a sister and two brothers, all dead, the boys when they were children, and my dad was an only child. I only had one sister, Mary, and as you know she's dead. There's only her husband Sam in America now.'

'And I was an only child,' Greg said quickly before America was mentioned again but all their thoughts had turned to Mick's sister Kate in America who seemed to have vanished; their letters had been returned for over a year.

'John and Sarah are lucky,' Mick said, 'marrying into the Fitzgerald family. Means they're both honorary members of that enormous tribe.'

'They're lucky in more ways than one,' Cathy said. 'I think the world of Anne and of Joe.'

'Yes, Joe and Sarah are perfect together,' Mick agreed. 'And Anne – she's just what John needs. She's the strong character there.'

Greg took his pipe from his mouth. 'I've often thought that. If John had married someone like himself it would have been a battleground and with anyone weak it would have been a disaster. Anne understands him. The way he goes at things, he's either up in the clouds or down in the depths and Anne can deal with him in both moods.'

'*You* never had any patience with him,' Cathy said angrily to Greg. 'You make him sound like a monster.'

'I know what Dad means, Mum,' Mick said quickly. 'Anne always seems easy and pleasant but she's very well-balanced. You know what John's like. She knows when to treat him gently and when to be firm with him. I think he'll meet his Waterloo with young Laura though,' he added laughing.

Cathy smiled, her momentary anger over. 'She hasn't got involved with any causes, anyway, thank goodness. Too busy enjoying herself.'

'And that's how it should be,' Mick said. 'But to get back to the party, Mum. You're sure you wouldn't like one in the Adelphi?'

'No thanks, son,' Cathy said again.

Mick consulted John and Sarah and it was decided that a family party should be held in Sarah's house.

'These big old rooms are perfect for parties,' she said. 'And Mum needn't be involved in any of the preparations. They can just come and enjoy themselves.'

They told Cathy of the plan and she agreed. 'I do want to celebrate it, love,' she said. 'I just didn't want a lot of fuss.'

Mick later spoke quietly to his father about inviting his Uncle Sam to the party. 'It's easier to get here from America now,' he said.

'But Sam is over eighty and more or less housebound these days,' Greg told him, 'although his mind is still clear, thank goodness. He never really got over Mary's death.'

'She was a doll, wasn't she?' Mick said. 'I remember her coming when I was a kid. I thought she was like a princess and Sam was a nice guy. Very generous.'

'Too good for her,' Greg said forcefully. 'She was selfish to the bone. I think Sam saw her faults but he loved her anyway. Fell in love with her when they were very young and he never got over it.'

'You make it sound like a disease,' Mick said, smiling at the thought of love in connection with these old people. 'You didn't like her?'

'I was charmed by her as everyone was,' Greg said stiffly. 'But she hurt her parents and your mother and I find that hard to forgive. They could often have come to visit because Sam worked like a dog to make money for all she wanted but it didn't suit *her* to come home. Sam was different. We're very fond of Sam.'

'But if he's housebound there's not much point in inviting him,' Mick said. 'I didn't want to mention America to Mum until I'd checked with you because of our Kate.'

'No way of getting in touch with her, I'm afraid,' Greg said with a sigh. 'Your mum wonders where we went wrong with her but Kate was just Kate. As selfish as Mary but without someone like Sam to keep her straight.'

'I was away in the RAF when she was growing up,' Mick said, 'but I don't know why Mum blames herself. If anyone spoiled her it was that old fellow who lodged with Grandma and paid for Kate's dancing lessons.'

'Old Josh,' Greg said. 'I don't know, Mick. I think character is inborn but sometimes circumstances make a difference. We all liked Gene Romero when she brought him home but marrying him and moving to America after the war was a mistake. She just went wild.'

'Plenty of girls married GIs and went to America and it worked out. Kate brought a lot of grief to the Romero family before she went off with that other fellow and they'd been very good to her.'

'Yes, I'm ashamed of that,' Greg said, 'but we could do nothing about it.'

The golden wedding was not mentioned in letters to Sam but he remembered. A few days before the date a parcel arrived from him containing Rolex gold watches for Greg and for Cathy but it was the letter that was enclosed which caused more excitement.

Sam wrote: 'As you know I lost touch with Kate some time ago, I think because I warned her against Capaldi and I was proved right. I feel I might have been the cause of her breaking with you but I have managed to trace her. She has divorced Capaldi and has remarried and I am assured that her husband is a man of good character. His name is Doolan and he is of Irish descent. I have been in touch with them and they have promised to visit with me in the near future as they live less than three hundred miles from me. Kate will be writing to you soon.'

'Thank God,' Cathy exclaimed, dropping the letter and flinging her arms round Greg. 'She's safe. I've imagined all sorts of things happening to her on her own there.'

'So have I,' admitted Greg. 'Isn't Sam a good fellow? We can stop worrying now, love, and really enjoy our celebration.'

All the family were relieved for the sake of Cathy and Greg but Sarah worried that their hopes might be raised only to be dashed again by Kate.

'I can't believe she's changed,' she said to John. 'She'll only write if it suits her.'

'Yes, but don't forget Uncle Sam seems to be calling the tune. I don't think he's as wealthy as he used to be but he's still a rich man and Kate will want to keep well in with him.'

'I'm surprised that she ever lost touch with him.'

'I think it was more that he cut her and that Capaldi character off. I'm sure Sam bailed her out several times after she left Gene Romero and he'd probably had enough.'

'Remember when Sam and Mary came here when we were young?' said Sarah. 'I thought he was smashing but I didn't like Mary.'

'I thought she was charming,' John said. 'So beautiful and elegant yet so friendly.'

'Yes, to you, because you're male. She even tried to get off with Dad.'

'Don't be daft. You're imagining things,' John said. 'A woman like that.'

'No, I'm not,' Sarah protested. 'I think Grandma knew and maybe Sam but Mum didn't and Mary didn't get any encouragement from Dad.'

'You dreamt that one,' John scoffed. 'An adolescent fancy.'

Sarah decided that it was wiser to say no more. John in a temper was quite capable of confronting her father with this, she thought.

John took the opportunity of the discussions about Kate to point the moral to Laura. 'Now you see why I'm strict with you, Laura,' he said. 'You see the grief my sister's caused Nana and Grandad and other people just because she was spoiled when she was young. I do it for your own good.'

'Didn't stop you spoiling Gerry, though, did it?' Laura muttered, flouncing out of the room.

'Gerry's not spoiled, is he?' John appealed to Anne and Maureen. 'Look how he took his disappointment like a man over that agent and the way he's settled down with this new group.'

Anne and Maureen agreed with him.

The Merrymen had been disbanded some months earlier. An agent had wanted to sign them to go on tour and Peter and Gerry were willing to give up their daytime jobs and sign up but the Hogan twins had refused. They were younger than Gerry and Peter and were still apprentice electricians and their father had insisted that they finish their training.

'Keep on with the music part-time,' he said, 'but finish your training and make sure you've got a trade to fall back on. This music business could end tomorrow.'

Peter and Gerry tried hard to persuade the twins to take a chance but they were obdurate. 'I agree with my dad,' Michael said. 'I think we'd be mad to give up now when we're so near the end of our time.'

Martin added, 'Dad's kept us while we've been on peanuts as apprentices so he has a right to have a say.'

By the time the argument was resolved the agent had lost interest but Peter and Gerry were now too unsettled to carry on as before.

'We'll never get a chance like that again,' Gerry told his family. 'We've had offers before but Peter's dad always told us not to sign until he'd seen the contract and with some of them we'd really have been ripped off, working like dogs and the agent taking the money, but this was genuine. He's one of the top agents and dead straight but he won't be messed about.'

Michael and Martin Hogan left the Merrymen, Peter had an offer as lead singer with a well-known group and Gerry was warmly welcomed as drummer with another group and immediately went on tour with them.

Wayne and the Wildmen were very different from the Merrymen and the bookings meant constant travel all over England and Scotland. The other members of the group seemed able to sleep in the back of the van carrying their equipment or in the sleazy digs provided for them but Gerry found it hard to adapt to their lifestyle.

'You've had it too soft,' the manager jeered when he complained.

Very little of the promised money materialised but they were told to be patient. Soon they would be in the really big money, living like millionaires. 'Look at the Beatles,' the manager told them. 'Money no object now but they had to do these sort of gigs first.'

Sometimes Gerry was so exhausted that he accepted a pill from one of the lads who took them freely. Just to get me through tonight, he told himself. I'm not going to make a habit of it.

After some argument, Gerry managed to get a night off for the golden wedding party, as the group were playing Birkenhead just across the Mersey from Liverpool, but the family were shocked at his appearance.

'Are you getting proper meals?' his mother asked anxiously. 'You look so thin.'

'Just as well,' Gerry said cheerfully. 'I take up less room in the van and it's a tight fit with my drums.' But he found it so hard to keep awake in the comfort of home that he took one of the 'uppers' he had been given by one of the group.

Everyone was in high spirits for the party. Early the previous day Cathy had opened her front door to find a strange couple on the step with their luggage. It took her a few minutes to recognise Kate in the small stout woman in a bright Crimplene trouser suit, with large spectacles and short hair.

'*Kate*!' she cried. 'Oh Kate, love,' flinging her arms round her and hugging her close, then drawing them into the hall.

Greg had been working in the back garden but had come into the kitchen for water and heard the commotion. He came through to the hall and welcomed Kate more coolly but realising that her husband was uncomfortable, he shook hands with him and smiled at him warmly. 'Jim Doolan,' the man said, as Kate made no attempt at introductions. 'I guess we shoulda phoned you up first.'

'Not at all,' Greg said, ushering them into the living room. 'Leave your luggage, I'll attend to it.' Cathy was offering tea or coffee and Greg said quietly, 'You stay and talk, Cath. I'll see to it when I've washed my hands. I've been gardening,' he explained to Jim.

'You should get together with my pop,' Jim said. 'He does it for a living.'

'Lucky man,' Greg said smiling.

Kate had been chattering nonstop about their journey but when they were settled with cups of coffee and there was a pause, Cathy asked if they knew about the party.

'Of course. That's why we're here,' Kate said.

'Sam staked us,' Jim said abruptly. 'I couldn't afford it and he said it was important so I accepted but I don't take handouts. That's why I didn't want Kate to contact Sam. I thought that was what she was after and I wasn't having it.'

'I'm glad you made an exception this time,' Greg said warmly, 'although I admire your principles. Sam knew how much we worried about Kate.'

'Yeah. Of course I didn't know about Kate's English family,' Jim said. 'Tighter 'n a clam when she wants to be, this little lady,' but he smiled fondly at Kate.

Jim was a stocky man not much taller than Kate, with what Greg thought of as an Irish face – ruddy complexion, blue eyes and dark hair growing in a widow's peak on his forehead. His chin was firm and the glance from his blue eyes very direct and Cathy and Greg liked him more and more.

'Mick wanted to have a big party in the Adelphi,' Cathy said. 'But we wouldn't have liked that. We're having a party at Sarah and Joe's instead. Those big old houses are great for parties.'

'They're still together then, Sarah and Joe?' Kate asked.

'Of course,' her parents said in unison.

'Sarah was engaged to Joe's brother during the war,' Kate told Jim, 'but she chucked him after the war and married his brother.'

'It wasn't like that, Kate,' Cathy said warmly. She turned to Jim. 'Sarah and Terry were only friends really. It was just a joke that he wanted her to be his girl but when he was taken prisoner at Dunkirk they were sort of paired off by everyone. Our Sarah and Joe were in love for years but they couldn't say anything until after the war.'

'They acted very honourably,' Greg said, 'but when Terry came home it was easily sorted out. He'd made a friend in the camp and they wanted to try their fortune in Canada so Sarah and Joe could marry at last.'

'They were lucky,' Jim said. 'A lot of girls married in wartime out of a sense of duty and then suffered for it.' He looked at Kate and Greg wondered what she had told Jim about Gene Romero.

All the family were amazed at the change in Kate's appearance but they soon decided that her character was unchanged. Everyone liked Jim Doolan and the general opinion was that he was the strong man that Kate needed. He charmed everyone at the party by singing in a true tenor voice old favourite Irish songs – 'She is Far From the Land' and 'The Snowy-breasted Pearl'.

'Mam's favourite,' Maureen and Anne wept, although they enjoyed the songs.

'Don't they bring it back, the parties at Uncle Fred's and our house,' Joe said. 'Ah, God be with the days of our youth.'

'Fancy you knowing those songs in America,' Rosa commented.

'You're of Irish descent, though, aren't you, Jim?' Joe asked.

'You can say that again,' Jim said laughing. 'It's a real thriving Irish community where we live. Third or fourth generation but they're more Irish than the Irish.'

'They're American as well,' Kate said sharply. 'That's more important.'

Laura took an instant dislike to her Aunt Kate and avoided her as much as possible. 'I can't stand posers,'she told David. 'And hasn't she got a good opinion of herself?'

Rosa was indignant that she had often been compared to Kate when she surveyed her aunt's dumpy figure and weather-beaten skin. 'I'm insulted,' she said to Laura, 'if people think I look like that.'

'She wasn't fat when she was young and her hair was red then like yours,' Laura told her curtly.

She had quarrelled with Rosa a few weeks previously and they had to make a show of friendship for the party but Laura found it hard to pretend. They had been able to conceal the quarrel from the family because Anne had been busy with Maureen and Sarah had tactfully reduced her visits while Anne was nursing her sister. Joe often called to see Maureen but Laura was confident that she and Rosa were not discussed.

The cause of the quarrel was Rosa's latest boyfriend whom she had met at a party given by a friend from the College of Art. Laura had been taking a short cut through a narrow alleyway in the medieval part of the city when she had come upon Rosa and the man standing together smoking.

'Oh, Laura,' Rosa said airily but she blushed and dropped the cigarette quickly, grinding it under her heel. 'This is Ricky Hewlett.' To the man she said briefly, 'My cousin.'

Laura was too surprised to speak but the man said, 'Hi' and blew a cloud of smoke in her face. His hair was long and greasy and he wore grubby jeans and a sweater, with a wispy beard and dirty bare feet in scuffed sandals.

Laura looked at him with disgust and he stared back at her offensively and put his arm round Rosa, pressing his hand on her breast.

'I'll see you,' Laura said abruptly to Rosa and walked away but before she reached the bus stop she heard hurrying footsteps and Rosa caught up with her.

'I was just coming anyway,' she said breathlessly. 'Those were herbal cigarettes we were smoking.'

Laura looked sceptical. 'I knew they weren't Park Drive,' she said. 'But *herbal*! Oh Rosa, what are you doing with a creep like that? Where did you pick him up? You can do better than that.' She wanted to point out to Rosa that she could have practically any man she fancied so why bother with Ricky. She was genuinely fond of her cousin and worried about her but Rosa was bitterly offended.

'He's a very interesting and talented man,' she said.

'And very dirty,' Laura retorted. 'And I suppose he supplies you with those disgusting cigarettes. *Herbal*. You must think I'm soft.'

'I knew you'd think that,' Rosa said. 'That's why I came after you in case you carried tales.'

'When have I ever carried tales?' Laura demanded. 'I've covered up for you but never again.'

They were now at the bus stop and the row continued until the bus arrived and went on in hissing undertones all the way home. As they stepped off the bus, Rosa said angrily, 'You know what's wrong with you, Laura Redmond? You're jealous.'

'Jealous! Of that specimen?' Laura exclaimed. 'You must be joking.' She turned and walked rapidly away and Rosa went home by another route. They had not spoken to each other since.

There was a core of truth in Rosa's last remark which Laura was unwilling to admit but it made her more angry with her cousin. Rosa had dated many of the boys in the loosely knit youth-club crowd to which Laura still belonged and many more would have liked to date her.

Laura had gone out in a foursome with Rosa and a friend of her current date on several occasions in those days, and had occasionally been to the cinema with a boy but she was friendly rather than romantic with them. She had never envied Rosa and though she often laughed at Rosa's transports over whatever boy had taken her fancy she was always willing to cover for her with her parents.

There was a girl in their group named Monica, a fat girl with heavy-lidded eyes and a sleepy voice. She had a reputation for being tactless but the others only laughed at her blunders. 'Monica's so dozy. She never realises when she's putting her foot in it,' they said, but other people, never Monica, suffered from her *faux pas*. After Rosa had moved out of their orbit to the College of Art, someone commented that she would be missed by the boys in their own group.

'Yes. Laura should get plenty of dates now,' Monica said sleepily. 'All the fellows will want to take her out to keep in touch with Rosa.'

'*Monica*,' someone said laughing. 'You're the limit.'

Laura laughed with the rest but it made her suspicious whenever she was asked for a date. Even the slightest reference to Rosa put her on the defensive and the evening usually ended with a row. 'You're as prickly as a bloody hedgehog,' one boy told her angrily and when Laura flashed back, 'I just don't like being used,' he was honestly amazed.

Secretly Laura wondered whether she would ever be wanted for herself and for the first time she envied Rosa as she flitted from one boyfriend to the other, often juggling two or three at once.

Mary was not very successful with boyfriends either. She could be as blunt as Laura on occasion and she watched every boy she went out with for any trait which reminded her of her father.

'Who needs them anyway?' she said to Laura. 'I'm not keen on the moonlight and roses stuff and I'm not anxious for marriage like a lot of girls. It's too much of a gamble.'

Laura knew that she could not agree with Mary but for once she held her tongue and simply nodded.

Kate and Jim stayed on for a few days after the golden wedding party, then went to Ireland to the birthplace of Jim's great-grandfather. They were all sorry to see Jim go but found it much easier to part with Kate. She had become aggressively American and constantly told them how backward and old-fashioned England seemed to her. She offered

Cathy recipes containing types of meat and flavourings unknown to her and talked of pumpkin pie and blueberry compote. 'You've never made them?' was her amazed cry until John showed his impatience.

'What are you so surprised about?' he said forthrightly. 'You lived here until you were nineteen. You know what sort of food we eat.'

She abandoned the recipes then and talked instead of her fully tiled kitchen and all her labour-saving devices and the much superior lifestyle she enjoyed in America.

'The sooner she goes back there the better,' Sarah said privately to her mother. 'She's become a real pain.'

Cathy agreed but said that she was pleased she had seen Kate again and now knew that she was safe with a good husband. She was also glad to know that Sam was comfortable and was being cared for by a married couple.

'Jim says they are more like friends than servants. We know they've been with Sam for years. The man was born in Athol Street off Scotland Road and the woman's from Sheil Road way, so Sam will be at home with them, and they'll be good people coming from Liverpool.'

'Don't let Kate hear you,' Sarah laughed. 'You know everything good must be American.'

'Good job she thinks so as it seems she'll spend her life there,' her mother said calmly. 'Mind you, Sar, I wouldn't like her kitchen. It sounds more like a hospital.' She looked round her own comfortable, shabby kitchen. 'This suits me much better.'

Sarah hugged her. 'And you've cooked some lovely meals here for all of us – and not a bit of ground hogmeat in any of them.' They laughed together and Kate sailed to Ireland blissfully unaware that they were not heartbroken to see her go.

Mick urged his parents to travel to America to see Sam and offered to pay their fares but they refused.

'We're too old now, Mick,' Cathy said. 'We've never travelled and I'd be very nervous. Anyway, I'd be worried to be so far away from Sarah.'

Sarah had become increasingly breathless and had been advised by her doctors to have an operation to open the mitral valve in her heart. Admission to hospital seemed imminent so Mick said no more.

'We're very fond of Sam,' Greg said. 'He's one of the best. We used to speak on the phone occasionally until the stroke affected his speech and letters aren't quite the same.' He sighed. 'I'd like to be able to tell him how much we appreciated his kindness. Tracing Kate and sending her home like that for the party.'

'Gerda and I might have a holiday in the States next year,' Mick said. 'I could fix it to see Sam and tell him. I'd have to make sure he didn't think we were after his money. Tell him how well we're doing.' He laughed heartily and Cathy and Greg smiled.

'It'd be the truth anyway, thank God,' Cathy said. 'And John and Sarah are comfortable too.' Her dimples showed as she laughed. 'We might have been born too early for aeroplanes but I know your generation think nothing of flying. It's a different world.'

'It's nice to come home to the old one though,' Mick said, hugging her.

Chapter Eleven

Gerry was twenty-one in January 1966 and his parents had planned a party for him but he was away on tour in Hamburg.

'I wish the Merrymen had stayed together,' Anne said. 'I worry about him with this crowd. He doesn't seem to be able to please himself at all and he doesn't look well, either.' She had been concerned about Gerry's loss of weight and the dark shadows under his eyes when he arrived for the golden wedding party but later in the evening she had been relieved to see that his spirits were as high as ever. She was unaware that they were the result of the pill he had taken.

She had been talking to Maureen but Laura joined in the discussion. 'I don't know why they're always on tour. Plenty of venues in Liverpool for them. The Litherland Town Hall, the Orrell, the Grafton, as well as the Cavern, and there are clubs opening all over the place. It's fab here now.'

Both women laughed and Maureen said, 'I think you're right, Laura. Joe was telling me the other day about the kids in his class. One of them said, "It's the gear in Liverpool, isn't it, sir? It's like being drunk all the time."'

Anne agreed that everything seemed to be going right for Liverpool. Local groups dominated the charts and success stories could be heard on every side. Young people were proud to see contemporaries they knew personally, although under different names – Billy J. Kramer, Cilla Black, Gerry Marsden and the Pacemakers – appearing on television and felt reflected glory from the success of the Beatles in America.

Older people were happy too. Everton Football Club were League Champions 1962–63 and Liverpool Football Club 1963–64 and Liverpool won the FA Cup in 1965. The Redmond and Fitzgerald families were all Everton supporters except John who predictably followed Liverpool, so everyone was happy.

Trade was booming and jobs plentiful and the dark days of hand-to-mouth casual labour seemed to have gone for ever.

'I wouldn't change places with Rockefeller,' an old ferryman told John as he boarded the ferry one day.

'Neither would I,' John replied without hesitation.

Early in the New Year Maureen told the rest of the family of her illness and her decision to live in the convent guest house. Anne was still opposed to the idea and her eldest brother Tony and his wife Helen agreed with her but Joe supported Maureen. They had always been close friends and he understood Maureen's need for independence and for the support of the religious community who shared her acceptance of the will of God.

'But why go to strangers when we're all here to look after you?' Tony argued.

'Maureen knows that,' Joe said firmly, 'but she must be free to do as she wants. If it doesn't work out she knows she will be more than welcome with any of us.'

'Thanks, Joe,' Maureen said. 'I'm grateful to all of you but Joe's right. This is the best way I can cope and anyway I'll be able to see you all very often.'

Soon after Maureen left, Sarah was admitted to hospital for the operation on her heart. She had found any exertion increasingly difficult, becoming very breathless and tiring easily, and she had been forced to give up the job in the sweet shop. Frequent bouts of bronchitis had decided her doctors that an operation could not be deferred any longer and she was admitted to have the mitral valve opened.

The operation was a complete success and she returned home six weeks later, declaring that she had been promised a new lease of life and that she intended to enjoy it to the full.

While all this was happening, there was constant contact between the relations, which meant that Rosa and Laura were thrown together, more especially as Gerry was away so often on tour and David was abroad for a year with the Peace Corps before going on to Cambridge.

Rosa seemed to have completely forgotten their quarrel but Laura found it more difficult. Ricky Hewlett was never mentioned but Laura suspected that Rosa was still seeing him. She worried about her cousin but Rosa talked freely about her other dates and Laura consoled herself that there was safety in numbers.

Laura and Mary had now completed their training and both had found well-paid jobs, Laura in a shipping office and Mary with a firm of importers in the same office block in the centre of Liverpool.

Out of her first month's salary Laura bought small treats for all the family. 'You haven't won the pools, love,' her mother protested. 'This is money you've worked hard for,' but Laura enjoyed giving.

Mary's father demanded a large share of her salary but she and Laura still had enough money now to buy the fashionable clothes that they craved and to finance their visits to clubs and discos.

Mary told Laura that she intended to save something every month to enable her to leave home as soon as possible, but Laura was less anxious to leave home now. While Maureen lived with them John had controlled his temper, although often provoked by Laura, and since Maureen had gone they had avoided confrontation. Both had been too busy, John with the general election when Labour had been elected and with Sarah's operation, and Laura because she was enjoying herself so much.

She was now nearly eighteen years old, tall and slim with long legs which showed to perfection in the mini skirts she wore. John had objected to the first one but Laura told him that it was comparatively long. 'Have you seen Rosa's?' she asked.

On his latest visit home Gerry had told her that she had improved. 'I could fancy you myself,' he told her, adding with brotherly candour, 'pity you always look as though you're ready for a fight.'

Later Laura carefully studied her face in the mirror. Her blue eyes were fringed with long dark lashes, her nose was straight and her skin and teeth were good but she was unable to see why Gerry thought she looked aggressive. She asked him before he left but he said he was only joking. 'No, tell me,' she insisted.

'It's just the way you hold your head, I think,' he said. 'The way you look at people. Don't worry about it. Nobody'll try anything on with you anyway.'

She studied his face then said impulsively, 'You've changed, Gerry. Why don't you come home? Don't go back to Hamburg,' but he only shrugged and turned away.

Anne was worried about Gerry too. 'He looks ill, John,' she said.

John agreed but he told her that Gerry said the manager had promised that he would get English bookings for them as soon as the present contract in Hamburg was finished. 'He didn't want to tell you because they've been let down before but I think it's better for you to know,' he said and Anne was glad there was some hope at least of her son coming back to England.

Laura and Mary saw little of the friends from their youth-club days now and when Laura was escorted home from a club and asked for a date she had the satisfaction of knowing that these young men had never met Rosa. They were usually brief affairs but Laura told Mary that this suited her. 'I wouldn't want to be serious with any of the fellows I've met so far although they're all right for the odd date.'

She often thought about Gerry's remark about 'trying it on' after a scuffle with one determined young man and fending off another who had attempted first to force his tongue into her mouth then down her ear and then pulled down her top and bra and put his mouth against her breast.

Laura gave him a blow across the head which rocked him back and told him furiously to clear off.

'You wanna move with the times, grandma,' he shouted as he stalked away.

And Laura shouted back, 'Not with a clot like you, I won't.'

She laughed about it in the office the next day but one of the girls said seriously, 'They expect it now though. Not just hugs and kisses any more. In fact, after a couple of dates most of them expect to go all the way.'

'So what? As long as you're careful,' another girl said. 'All those rules – nobody bothers now. People are more broad-minded. Look at the telly. Anything goes.'

133

'If they think I'm going all the way with them, they've got another think coming,' Laura said. 'It strikes me it's the fellows who are all for changing things.'

'I'm surprised any fellow had the nerve to try it on with you, Laura,' a girl named Tricia said. 'I thought you'd only have to give them one of your looks.'

'What do you mean, one of my looks?' Laura said, puzzled, and the other girls laughed.

'What my nan used to call a look as good as a summons,' Tricia said. 'And you don't know you're doing it half the time, do you?'

Before Laura could answer, another girl said to her, 'You're behind the times, you know, Laura. You'll never keep a bloke these days if you're too strait-laced. Nina's right. They expect girls to be broad-minded and nobody thinks anything of it now. Do they?' she appealed to the other girls.

'*I* do,' Laura said firmly. 'And if that's all a fellow wants he can sling his hook as far as I'm concerned.'

'Wait till you really fall for someone, then we'll see,' Tricia laughed, but their tea break was over and they returned to their desks.

Gerry came home briefly in early March and the family were horrified to see how ill he looked. He insisted that he was having a great time in Hamburg and the group were going down a bomb and had been asked to stay on for another tour.

He was still telling himself that he only took his 'Bennys' to keep him going through the long hours on stage so he brought few home with him and suffered accordingly. Anne and John were alarmed by his trembling hands and sudden sweats and asked him to visit the family doctor but he refused irritably.

'Even his character's changed,' Anne said fearfully. She was even more alarmed when Mike Millward, a guitarist with the popular local group, the Fourmost, died in March at the age of twenty-three. 'It *can* happen even at that age,' Anne said. 'He was a big, strong lad too, six foot four and full of life.'

'It was cancer with that poor lad, Anne,' John said. 'I think it's something different with Gerry but still serious. The way his hands tremble and his eyes look terrible. So bloodshot and the pupils are like pinpoints. He'll have to see a doctor.'

When Anne heard Gerry vomiting the next morning and saw how he trembled as he came from the bathroom she decided to ask the family doctor to visit whether Gerry liked it or not.

The doctor was an old friend and when Anne described Gerry's symptoms he told her he would go up and see Gerry alone. 'What are you taking?' he asked bluntly as soon as he had examined Gerry.

'Only the odd pill to get me through a performance,' Gerry said sullenly. 'I'm not *ill*.'

The doctor questioned him closely about the type and number of pills he took. Gerry knew only the slang names – blues, Dexys, purple hearts, Bennys – but as he talked to the doctor he realised for the first time the number and variety of drugs he had been taking.

'What about grass, reefers?' the doctor asked.

'Yes, but that's nothing, is it?' Gerry said defensively. 'Everybody smokes them.'

'What about the hard drugs? Cocaine?' the doctor said and heaved a sigh of relief when Gerry denied ever trying them. 'You're lucky then,' he said grimly. 'You can become an addict with one shot of cocaine and then you're in real trouble. Now you've got a chance to sort yourself out.'

He sat and talked seriously to Gerry for some time but when he went downstairs he said nothing to Anne about the drugs. 'Overwork and bad living conditions,' he said. 'He needs rest and a nourishing diet. I'll give you a prescription for some tablets but you must be in charge of them. Don't let him have more than the prescribed dose.'

'He couldn't take more. He's very sensible,' Anne said in surprise but the doctor insisted that she took charge of the tablets.

'It's easy to forget you've taken one,' he said, 'and take another. I'll call back this evening for another look at him.'

John was at home when the doctor returned. After seeing Gerry again he told Anne and John about the drug taking. 'I'm going to admit him to hospital,' he said, 'because he has some of the symptoms of TB but don't be alarmed. Even if it is TB, we have the drugs to treat it now.'

He gave Anne some instructions about sterilising dishes and when John accompanied him to the door the doctor said bluntly, 'Damn fools, these lads. Knocking themselves about, couple of hours' sleep in twenty-four, drugs to keep them going, jumping about on stage and snatching bits of food when they can. They don't value their health until they lose it.'

Gerry seemed resigned to entering hospital and surprisingly unconcerned about being away from the group. 'They'll have found another mug to take my place,' he told his father. 'We missed the boat, y'know, Dad. That first agent who wanted the Merrymen – that was a reputable outfit, good managers who looked after the lads and only took their fair cut. This lot are cowboys. Don't give a damn about us and all the money we make goes into their pockets, not ours.'

'Never mind, son, you live and learn,' John said. 'Put it down to experience and when you're well enough, find a better group.'

'I'm still under contract to them,' Gerry said but John told him not to worry.

'Just get fit again. I'll sort that out,' he said.

Laura and Julie came in to see Gerry but he told them not to kiss him. 'I'm getting a little bell,' he joked. 'Unclean, unclean.'

'You sound more like yourself already,' Laura said. 'And you don't even know yet whether it is TB. Are you worried about missing your bookings?'

'No. To tell you the truth I've been feeling so bad that I was just glad to come home and forget it,' said Gerry.

There was general relief in the family that Gerry had been admitted to hospital to receive expert care. Joe had suspected the drug taking since the golden wedding party and was surprised that John had been blind to it. 'He just couldn't believe it could happen to Gerry, I suppose,' said Sarah.

Gerry's youth and his previous good health meant that he recovered very quickly but his manager's attempt to hold him to his contract failed. John had many useful contacts from his work with trade unions and the CND and threats of investigation made the agent speedily release Gerry from his contract. He was known as a good drummer and soon joined another group which played mostly local gigs with an occasional tour.

Great changes were taking place in Liverpool with much demolition. 'This lot are doing more damage than what Hitler done,' an old woman grumbled but it was the demolition in the Everton area that worried Anne.

'I know Julie seems fine now but I'm sure all the dust can't be good for her,' she said to John and he agreed.

They discovered that Sarah and Joe had also thought of moving, because the neighbourhood seemed to be changing.

'Might be the time to go while we can still get a good price for the houses,' John said. Once the idea was mentioned, events moved very quickly.

They often spent days at the north end of the city at Crosby or Freshfield shore near the mouth of the Mersey. 'Should be a healthy place to live, all those sea breezes,' Joe said. 'And there are plenty of houses similar to these. Big, solid old houses and there's a good train and bus service.'

Both families owned their houses, thanks to Pat Fitzgerald, father of Anne and Joe, and within a short time they had found suitable property in Crosby in two adjoining roads.

Laura and Rosaleen both approved of the move when they found that there was easy access to city clubs and to Litherland Town Hall and Orrell Park Ballroom. Laura's office building was within a few minutes' walk of the train station and Rosa could easily reach the College of Art.

Julie had gained nine O levels and was staying on to do A levels. Joe, who taught at a city centre school, had offered to drive her in each day.

All seemed set fair and the sale of Sarah and Joe's house went through without a hitch, but just before the contracts were exchanged the buyer of Anne and John's house was forced to withdraw because of a break in the chain of house selling. Another buyer was quickly found but in that short time the house in Crosby had been sold. They found another house in the same road being sold by a widow but their surveyor found a small amount of dry rot in the window frames.

The vendor dropped her price and the dry rot was easily dealt with but the mortgage was refused until the work was complete. John's temper grew steadily shorter. 'We only need a small mortgage, for God's sake,' he raged. 'When you think what we've put down it's bloody ridiculous.'

Anne's nerves were stretched too and the difficulty with the mortgage seemed the last straw. She burst into tears. 'I'm sorry we ever started this,' she wept. 'I don't want to leave this house. Dad was so pleased to buy it for us and we've been happy here.'

'For God's sake, Anne, talk sense,' John exploded. 'You were the one who wanted to move, for Julie's sake. You caused all the upheaval for all the family, our Sarah as well, and now you want to change your mind. We're going and that's flat.'

Laura had rushed from the other room at the sound of his voice and she flung her arms protectively round her mother.

'Don't you talk to Mum like that,' she yelled. 'She can stay here if she wants to. I don't want to go anyway.'

'So that's it,' John shouted. 'I might have known. All that about your dad but it's to suit this one.'

Anne was looking at Laura in surprise. 'I thought you wanted to go, love,' she said and John's temper reached boiling point at being ignored. He grabbed Laura's arm and shook her.

'You can clear off. Do as you like,' he snarled, 'but we're going. I'm not being ruled by your moods.'

There was a rap on the kitchen door and a voice called, 'Anybody home?' The next moment Joe walked in and stopped amazed at the tableau before him, John panting with rage, his face red and congested, and Laura's arms protectively about her weeping mother.

Joe's smile vanished. 'What's going on?' he demanded, crouching down beside Anne.

She turned from Laura to press her face into his shoulder. 'Oh, Joe,' was all she said.

'I'll tell you what's going on,' John said loudly. He swallowed deeply. 'After all that's gone on, your sister has decided now that she doesn't want to move just because this madam doesn't want to go.'

Anne raised her head. 'No, John, no,' she protested.

Laura glared at her father. 'That's a lie,' she said fiercely. 'Mum doesn't want to go and you're trying to force her.'

John took a threatening step towards her as Anne again tried to speak but Joe said authoritatively, 'Calm down, calm down, everybody. There seems to be a misunderstanding here.'

Anne sat up straight and wiped her eyes. 'It's me, Joe,' she said. 'It just came over me – you know, Dad and all the happy memories. We left our troubles behind when we came here. I suddenly didn't want to leave.' Her tears flowed again.

'I know, love,' Joe said gently. 'We're sorry to leave our house too. The kids grew up there but it's time to move on. You know that, don't you, pet?'

Anne managed a watery smile. 'I know, Joe. It was just all the hassle and I started thinking. I'm just daft.'

John and Laura were still glaring at each other but Joe ignored the tension and said conversationally, 'I thought you were keen to go, Laura. Rosa is.'

Laura looked away from her father. 'I was,' she muttered. 'But if Mum doesn't…'

Anne hugged her and smiled at John. 'I'm sorry. It was just a brainstorm,' she said lightly. 'I'll make a cup of tea.'

Joe had brought some papers connected with the sale of the houses and the two men studied them but later Joe contrived to be alone with Laura. They walked round the garden in the gathering dusk.

'I was surprised to hear you speaking to your dad like that, Lol,' Joe said. 'You should show him more respect, you know.'

'You've got to earn respect,' Laura muttered. 'He's a bully.'

'No he's not and you know it. He's got a short temper but he's had a lot to try him lately,' said Joe. 'Anyway, it sounded as though you were doing some bullying yourself when I walked in.' He smiled and Laura's sullen look faded.

'I was just mad at the way he spoke to Mum,' she said.

'That's between your mum and dad. They understand each other. But you should respect your dad because he's your father and because he's a good father to you. Do you respect my judgement?'

'Of course, Uncle Joe,' Laura said, slipping her hand through his arm.

'Well, *I* respect your dad more than anyone I know. He's got courage and integrity and a compassionate heart. He's never been afraid to stand up for what he believes in even when it meant being on his own and he's been proved right like his grandfather often was. They were a bit ahead of their time, that's all,' said Joe.

'I know all that,' Laura said impatiently. 'It's the way he is at home. The way he treats Mum and us.'

They were standing by a tobacco plant which glimmered in the dusk, breathing in its perfume, and Joe said, 'Did you plant this?'

'Yes, all this border,' Laura said proudly. 'All the back garden, really, and Mum does the front one.'

'Your dad had a beautiful garden when they lived in Huyton when they were first married,' Joe told her. 'It was a council estate and nobody had much money but your dad started a gardening club so they could exchange plants and cuttings. It was generous of him to hand over to you when you showed an interest.'

Laura laughed and squeezed his arm. 'All right, Uncle Joe. I get the message.'

Joe smiled too. 'I thought you would. You're an intelligent girl but just on a short fuse like your dad.'

Laura was about to protest but thought better of it and they strolled back into the house.

'What on earth were you doing out there in the dark?' Anne asked. 'Just sniffing the tobacco plants and talking about gardening,' Joe said. 'Time I was off, Anne. Hope everything goes smoothly from now on, John.'

'I hope so. We've had our quota of setbacks,' Anne said cheerfully. 'Tell Sarah that Julie and I will be down early tomorrow.'

'I'll walk down with you,' Laura said suddenly. 'Is Rosa in?'

'You must be joking,' Joe said. 'But Aunt Sarah'd like to see you. We don't see much of you busy young ladies lately.'

They walked down companionably and Joe said suddenly, 'Don't worry so much about your mum, Lol. She's always been a happy person and she's still the same. I suppose we all spoiled her a bit because she was the baby but it did her no harm.'

'But she has too many worries,' Laura said. 'And what you said about Dad. All these causes. It means Mum's on her own while he goes on demonstrations and all that.'

'She doesn't usually let worries get her down. This business with the mortgage was just the last straw for both of them.'

'I know she doesn't often cry,' Laura admitted.

'When we were kids we had a toy, might even have been from when our mum was a child. Micky Dripping, we called it. It had a clown's face and a round body, must've had lead in the base or something because if it was knocked down it just came upright again. We used to call Anne Mick Dripping because she always bounced back.' He laughed heartily.

Sarah showed Laura large cardboard packing cases which had been filled and labelled dining room, kitchen, front bedroom, etc., in black felt-tip pen. 'We'll have unpacked these when you move so you can use them,' she said. 'Isn't Uncle Joe organised? Marking them all like that. Typical schoolteacher.'

It was a phrase that Rosa often used about her father though less fondly than Sarah, Laura thought, and as though reading her mind Sarah said with a sigh, 'I wish Rosa was still with your crowd, Laura. I don't like this College of Art crowd. They're too way-out.'

'They're just posers, most of them,' Laura said. 'No harm in them,' but she thought uneasily of Ricky and his 'herbal' cigarettes.

She had much to think about when she strolled home later. She loved and respected her uncle and although some of his views were unpalatable to her she was too honest not to admit that he was right.

When she reached home her mother was in the scullery and her father was sitting at the table in the kitchen studying papers. She went to stand beside him.

'I'm sorry I spoke like that, Dad,' she said gruffly.

John looked up in surprise and after a moment's hesitation he said, 'I'm sorry too. I didn't mean that about you going. We're all a bit fraught, I think, with this move.'

'Mum didn't say that because of me,' Laura murmured.

John nodded. 'I realise that.' He seemed about to say more but he restrained himself.

As Laura went to the scullery to her mother, she wondered whether her uncle had also talked to her father but knew that she would never find out if he had.

Julie was wildly excited about the move. Now that her O levels were over, she was free to help Sarah with the packing and the preparing of the new house. Sarah and Joe's house in Crosby was vacated two weeks before they were due to leave their present house so they could lay carpets, hang curtains and do some decorating before they moved in. Julie went every day with Sarah and enthused about the house to Laura. 'It's beautiful. Really bright and sunny. All big windows and bags of space. I love the little park and it's so near and so is the shore. I'm sure we'll be happy there, Lol.'

'Let's hope you're as enthusiastic about our house when we finally get in,' Laura said dryly.

'Of course I will be,' Julie said. 'It's almost exactly the same only I can go all over Auntie Sarah's house and see how good it is.'

Only weeks after Sarah and Joe moved, the Redmonds were able to follow them. The widow who was selling the house to them was going to share a flat with her sister and so was unable to take all her furniture. She offered curtains and carpets and the furniture to John for a sum which he felt was too small.

'That's not enough,' he told her. 'You're doing yourself. Talk to your brother about it.'

'I make my own decisions,' the tiny lady told him. 'I'll be quite satisfied with that price.'

John was uneasy. 'I feel I'd be taking advantage of her and she's a widow,' he told Joe.

'Offer to pay her removal costs then or offer a higher figure,' Joe suggested but the widow was adamant.

'I appreciate your concern but my sister agrees with me that I'm asking a fair price,' she said firmly and John had to content himself with sending a bouquet of flowers to greet her in her new home with her sister.

They were all happy in the house from the first day and they were still only a few minutes' walk away from Sarah and Joe who were equally happy. An impromptu party took place on the first Saturday night after they moved in when some of Laura's friends came to see the house and so did Julie's friends.

David was home and he came down with some of his and Gerry's friends although Gerry was in Newcastle. Anne supplied huge plates of sandwiches and the boys cider and wine. Laura's crowd had intended to go on to a local club but they were enjoying themselves so much that they stayed.

At twelve o'clock there was no sign of the party breaking up and David came to where Anne and John were sitting in a small morning room. 'Why don't you go to bed?' he suggested. 'I'll keep an eye on things.'

'But David, we can't do that,' Anne exclaimed. 'Julie should be in bed and what about her friends? Their parents will be worried to death.'

'It's all right. They've all rung home to ask if they can stay and their parents have agreed,' he said calmly.

Anne looked helplessly at John but he only said, 'Make sure they keep the music down then, David. We don't want to offend the neighbours so soon.'

'But how will they get home?' Anne asked.

David said easily, 'Don't worry about that, Auntie Anne,' and they found themselves being ushered upstairs.

Anne thought she would lie awake worrying but she and John were both asleep within minutes. The house was silent when they woke at eight o'clock but a peep into Laura's room revealed three girls asleep on the bed. There were others asleep in Julie and Gerry's rooms and downstairs boys lay on sofas and chairs or in sleeping bags on the floor.

'Where did all this bedding and the sleeping bags come from?' Anne whispered to John as they picked their way among the sleeping bodies.

'Probably from our Sarah's,' John whispered. 'Some of it's ours but David must have slipped home.' As though on cue, David came in the back door carrying two large loaves and a large parcel of bacon. 'Hi,' he said. 'I'll make you a cup of tea then cook this stuff.'

'We'll all have a cup of tea and then I'll cook it,' Anne said. 'They're all still asleep anyway.'

'They'll soon wake up when they smell the bacon,' David prophesied and he was right. John had taken out a huge teapot and marshalled rows of mugs and teacups and David made toast while Anne cooked bacon.

The girls drifted downstairs and joined the boys in drinking tea and eating the seemingly endless flow of bacon sandwiches and they were all still sitting about when Anne and John went off to ten o'clock Mass.

When they arrived home their guests had gone and the house was transformed. Dishes had been washed and put away, the cooker cleaned, the rooms vacuumed and tidied and cushions plumped up.

The only sign of the party was one broken glass neatly arranged on the draining board and a box of chocolates and a packet of small cigars on the coffee table.

Julie and Laura were waiting to make tea and toast for them and Anne looked at Julie's pink cheeks and starry eyes and joked, 'You can't have had much sleep but it doesn't seem to have done you any harm, Ju.'

'Oh, Mum, it was the best night I've ever had in my whole life,' Julie said ecstatically.

'That's because you tapped off,' Laura teased her.

Anne and John said in unison, 'Don't be silly.'

Julie made no protest.

Although it was hard for her parents to believe, that night Julie had met the man with whom she would spend the rest of her life. Peter Cunliffe was a friend of David's, six years older than Julie, but there had been an instant rapport between them.

For Anne and John the idea of their young daughter being considered old enough for courtship was only one of the bewildering events of that night.

'I just can't believe that we went meekly off to bed and left them partying all night,' Anne said to Sarah.

'I tell you what,' John added, 'your David's a case. The way he organised us! He should go far.'

'He should indeed,' said Joe. 'Do you know how he got the bread and bacon? Went on his motorbike to a cafe on the dock road and talked them into letting him buy bread and bacon from them. He might seem quiet but he's got the cheek of a robber's horse.'

Anne laughed. 'I think we've started something anyway. I think that's the first of many parties. I'll have to make sure I've always got plenty of bread and bacon in.'

Chapter Twelve

Rosa was annoyed that she had missed the party when Laura told her about it. 'An all-night do and I missed it,' she said. 'You might have told me about it, Laura.'

'It was just an impromptu thing,' Laura protested. 'I went down for you but you'd already gone out. The crowd and Julie's friends would have gone home early only your Dave and his crowd came and got things going. It really was fab though, Ros.'

'Don't rub it in,' Rosa said. 'But we could have one in our house, couldn't we? Mind you, I don't see Holy Joe going off to bed like your dad did.'

'I wish you wouldn't call Uncle Joe that. It's not true. I know he does a lot in the church, SVP and that, and he's devout like Aunt Maureen but he's not narrow-minded. I think he's smashing.'

Rosa shrugged indifferently. 'I suppose so,' she said but her attention had wandered. 'You know that very dark fellow, friend of David's? The one they call Mogsy? I've made a date with him for tomorrow night.'

'What about Neil?' Laura asked.

'What about him? He doesn't own me,' Rosa said.

'No, but he's lasted longer than the others. And Ricky. What about Ricky?'

'What about him?' Rosa said again, but her voice was cool.

Laura knew that Rosa was still seeing the abominable Ricky, as she and Mary called him, although he never called at Rosa's home to pick her up when they went out together or returned with her later, but she decided not to purse the subject. I'd probably get my head bitten off, she thought, and said only, 'How long is Mogsy staying at yours?'

'A few weeks,' Rosa said. 'He's fab. Those eyes and that dark-brown velvet voice. Really swoon making.'

Laura laughed. 'My God, Ros, you get worse. Where on earth did you learn that tripe? Dark-brown velvet voice,' she mimicked.

'You know what's wrong with you, Laura Redmond?' Rosa said. 'You haven't got an ounce of romance in you,' but she laughed.

They parted at the corner of the road and Laura walked home slowly. No romance, she thought ruefully. Little does she know. My trouble is that I've got plenty of romance but no technique and a big mouth. She thought of Sean, one of the boys at the party whom she had fancied and who seemed interested in her yet they had never managed to get together. When she had gone into the kitchen for glasses, he had followed her and looked appreciatively at her long legs as she reached up into a cupboard.

'Want any help?' he asked.

Laura, flustered at finding him so close, said only, 'Can you reach those glasses?'

'I'd rather watch you reaching for them,' he joked.

'I'll ask someone else then,' she snapped back.

There was an amazed silence and before she could say anything to retrieve the situation Monica appeared beside him. 'Laura's very independent, aren't you?' she said in her sleepy voice, taking Sean's arm and drawing him away.

Laura was still standing by the open cupboard when David dashed into the kitchen. 'You found some, Lol. Great.' He rapidly filled a tray then looked at her where she stood as though transfixed. 'You all right?' he asked and Laura nodded and managed to smile.

For the rest of the evening, whenever she saw Sean, Monica was close beside him and several times she saw Monica looking at her then talking to Sean. Probably dripping something in his ear about me being allergic to men or something, she thought bitterly, but it's my own fault. I had my chance and blew it.

'How did that Monica get in here?' she said angrily to Mary. 'I know I never asked her.'

'She's a pain, isn't she?' Mary said. 'She's got a talent for sliding into parties. Thick and Thin must have escaped tonight.'

'Thick and Thin' was the nickname by which two inseparable although unlikely friends were known. Bert was a podgy and unprepossessing youth with thick lips, snub nose and thin sandy hair already receding. Denis was small and thin with a reputation as a ladykiller. Monica had attached herself firmly to them and as the friends refused to be separated they were now a trio. A wit had suggested that they should now be known as Thin, Thick and Thicker.

Now Laura walked home thinking of events at the party and vowing that Monica would never gatecrash again but she was too honest with herself to believe that it was all Monica's fault. I'll just have to watch my tongue, she told herself.

When she reached home her father was crouched in front of the television set and he waved his hand impatiently when she tried to speak. 'I'm watching this,' he snapped but a few minutes later he exclaimed, 'My God just look at this.'

The screen was filled with running figures and bodies with blood streaming from head wounds were being pulled along the ground. 'I knew it, I knew it,' he said excitedly. 'They've been sitting on a powder keg for years just like South Africa.'

'Where is it?' asked Laura.

'*Where is it?* Northern Ireland, of course,' John shouted. 'Don't you take *any* notice of what's happening around you? It's been going on for a year, starting with a civil rights march – a *peaceful* civil rights march – and you haven't even noticed.'

'But they're all white,' Laura said.

'It's religious discrimination, not race,' John said. 'Catholics are second-class citizens. Boards outside shipyards and factories say "No Catholic need apply". No jobs, no vote, no fair share of housing.'

'Why do they put up with it then?' Laura said. 'That must be against the law.'

'Oh Laura,' John sighed. 'What do you think all this is about? Grow up, for God's sake. You can't be as thick as you sound.'

Laura bounced out of the room, slamming the door behind her, but the argument was resumed over the evening meal. 'I can't believe that you know nothing about what's happening in Northern Ireland, Laura,' her father said. 'The papers and the telly have been full of it for weeks.'

'If it was anything about pop stars she'd know all about it, wouldn't you, Laura?' Anne laughed. 'To each his own.' But this only enraged John more.

'What about you, Julie? Do you know about what's happening?'

'Only because we did it at school in current affairs,' Julie said truthfully. 'I haven't read about it or watched the news.'

'I despair of your generation,' John declared. 'What about the atom bomb? Do you know that China, *China*, has exploded an H bomb? That they did underground tests and last year they tested thermonuclear weapons? Do you take no interest in what's happening in the world?'

Julie's thoughts had evidently wandered away from the argument; she sat thinking of Peter Cunliffe and smiling dreamily to herself. Anne watched her indulgently but Laura said aggressively, 'I don't see what that's got to do with us.'

'*Don't* you?' said John. 'Don't you? I'll tell you what it's got to do with you, madam. Do you think I'm fighting to have it banned for my own sake? It's not my generation who are going to suffer.' He banged on the table. 'It's yours and your children's and your children's children. That's who I'm fighting for,' he said passionately.

Laura suddenly remembered a discussion with David and his friends and she said with a world-weary air, 'What's the use of worrying? If so many people have the bomb it only needs a finger on the button and we'll be blown away anyway. No future for us.'

Anne rapped the table. 'Look, can we stop this *now*. How can we digest our food with a discussion like this going on? I haven't cooked this good meal for it to be wasted.'

Even John had to grin and the conversation turned to pleasanter subjects but after the meal he said earnestly to Laura, 'There is hope for the future, you know, Laura. We can fight the people who are producing the bomb and those who are buying them. I'll give you something to read about the CND.'

Laura, who had only been quoting David and his friends and had never seriously thought about the atom bomb, except to be irritated by her father's CND activities, was taken aback. For once she managed to swallow a retort and only nodded.

A little later John came to her with a foolscap envelope full of papers and some pamphlets. 'Read these, Laura, and you'll see that something can be done if everyone pulls together.'

For a moment Laura felt ashamed that she was deceiving him but then she thought that it was his own fault for being so gullible. And he thinks *I'm* thick!

Laura put away the foolscap envelope and promptly forgot about it. Life was far too full and exciting for her to think of anything but dates, discos and parties. She approved the move to the new house even more when she found that many of the boys she had met could be seen at the train station every morning. Most of them worked in the business centre of Liverpool near to the River Mersey.

A few days after the party she was delighted to meet Sean on the platform and they sat together for the fifteen-minute train journey to Liverpool. They found that the shipping office where Sean worked was only a few minutes' walk from the office building where Laura worked, both near the station. They finished work at the same time so arranged to travel home together.

Sean asked if they could meet at lunchtime but Laura refused as she had arranged to meet Mary, but she was flattered by the request. She was almost too excited to work but she said nothing about Sean in the office. Her sharp tongue had made her a few enemies there who she knew would be only too pleased to scoff if her hopes failed to materialise.

She met Mary as arranged and as they walked down to the Pier Head to eat their lunchtime sandwiches Laura poured out every detail of the meeting with Sean and their conversation on the train. Her eyes were darting about, hoping to see Sean among the crowds from the various offices pouring down Water Street, but he was not to be seen.

Mary seemed unimpressed. 'Got a big opinion of himself though, hasn't he?' she said. 'Monica was buttering him up like mad at your party and he was lapping it up.'

Laura was instantly angry. 'How do you make that out?' she demanded. 'Just because he listened to Monica. Have you ever tried to get away from her?'

Mary was surprised by her vehemence but she shrugged and said diplomatically, 'I know she's a leech. Look at Thick and Thin. I'm sure they've tried to get away often enough.' She appreciated that Laura had kept her promise to meet her for lunch, although she was obviously smitten with Sean and must have been tempted to meet him.

A few weeks earlier they had found a small grassy slope between two riverfront warehouses and they sat there to eat their sandwiches and watch the shipping in the river, then lay back on the grass to sunbathe. It was very pleasant with the sun beating down and a warm breeze coming off the Mersey and they lay quietly, each dreaming her own dreams. All too soon it was time to return to the workaday world.

Laura began to tell Sean about it when they met at the station but he broke in to complain that he had been blamed for a mistake in a bill of lading which had been made by another clerk. 'It's always happening,' he said. 'The office manager's got it in for me.'

'Why?' asked Laura.

Sean seemed surprised by the question. 'Who knows?' he said. 'Might be a bit of jealousy because the boss talks to me about football sometimes.'

'It seems a bit petty to be jealous just because of that,' Laura exclaimed and Sean smiled self-consciously.

'Actually it was because I played for the office team and scored the two goals which meant we won the shield,' he said. 'The boss was made up.'

'I didn't know you had a football team,' Laura said, looking at him admiringly.

'We haven't really but someone donated the shield and all the offices got teams together to play for it. Grayson Rollo were favourites but we won it,' he said. He looked smug and Laura suddenly remembered Mary's words about his big opinion of himself. She firmly dismissed them. Mary knew nothing about him.

The train was crowded and they were both standing crushed close together. As the train swayed, Sean slipped his arm about her and smiled into her eyes. 'A good excuse,' he whispered as a middle-aged woman nearby strained to hear their conversation.

Their faces were close together and he put his mouth close to her ear. 'I love your colouring,' he whispered. 'Blue eyes and dark hair. Very fetching.'

Laura smiled at him. 'It's the same as your own,' she whispered and he grinned.

'Maybe that's why I like it,' he said.

Laura's spirits rose. If he can skit at himself he can't be big-headed, she thought.

They walked from the station hand in hand and stood at the corner of the road near Laura's house, talking for more than thirty minutes. 'I must go,' Laura said several times and they parted reluctantly, arranging to meet again later.

Laura walked home as though treading on air. She had meant to conceal her excitement from her parents but she was unable to resist telling them about meeting Sean at the station. Julie had received a letter from Peter Cunliffe and John looked from Laura's flushed cheeks and shining eyes to Julie's glowing face and joked, 'It must be the Crosby air, Anne.'

Anne smiled and agreed but both parents were secretly dismayed. They felt that Julie was too young to be receiving love letters and worried that Laura might be hurt.

'She's so all or nothing about everything,' Anne said to Sarah a few days later. 'She's been out with a few boys before but it never meant anything. This time she's really gone overboard. I just hope the lad feels the same or she'll be badly hurt.'

'Don't worry,' Sarah consoled her. 'Sean seems very keen and he's a nice lad. He wants to spend all his free time with her, doesn't he?'

Anne held her teacup in both hands, thoughtfully watching a bee exploring a nearby flower. 'You know what worries me, Sarah? At present Laura can't see a fault in him but when the first glow wears off she's likely to tell him a few home truths. You know what she's like – she can't help herself. It might break things up between them and she'll be broken-hearted.'

'Don't cross your bridges before you come to them, Anne,' Sarah said gently. 'It may never come to that but if it does Sean will know her well enough by then to know that she doesn't mean it.'

'I hope so,' Anne said with a sigh.

'Anyway, if she's so much in love she won't say anything to hurt him, will she?' Sarah argued.

Anne looked at her quizzically. 'It doesn't stop John. He still comes out with things he regrets later but maybe you don't think it applies with us.'

'Oh Anne, you know that's not true. There's never been anyone but you for our John and he's always been fathoms deep in love with you. You know that.'

Anne nodded. 'There was never anyone but John for me, and I knew it was the same for John, but we had a few rows in our younger days when he sounded off at me. Mind you, he was always sorry afterwards and I knew he didn't really mean it. I knew that what we had was rock solid and all that was just surface stuff that didn't matter. He's a bit better now, though not much, and I know he can't help his nature.'

Sarah looked solemn and Anne suddenly threw back her head and laughed aloud. 'Our kids wouldn't believe this,' she said. 'Two old matrons like us solemnly talking about love. They'd split their sides laughing.'

'I know,' Sarah agreed smiling. 'They think they've cornered the market as far as love is concerned. But don't you find it's worse worrying about them than when we were going through it ourselves?'

'Yes, and it seems to have come so suddenly. I'm not ready for it. I remember Bridgie Phelan saying, "Jasus, I'm a grandmother and I hadn't even got used to being a mother yet." Anyway, I'll take your advice, Sar, and stop crossing my bridges before I come to them.'

For the moment it seemed there was no need for Anne to worry. Julie watched anxiously for the twice-weekly letters from Cambridge and carried them away to her room but she always reappeared glowing with happiness, her eyes like stars. Her schoolwork was not affected and she was working hard for her A levels.

Laura's happiness was unbroken too. She still had lunch with Mary a couple of times a week and on the other days she met Sean and spent a blissful lunch hour with him. She was able to see him nearly every evening too as Mary had fortunately begun a relationship with a young man in the importer's office where they both worked.

Laura and Sean parted more readily now when they walked home from the station after work, knowing that they would meet again within a few hours. The constant sunny days gave way to beautiful, balmy evenings and often they walked down to the shore to sit on the sandhills which had been warmed by the sun, wrapped in each other's arms. They made a little nest for themselves, revelling in the seclusion and silence as they watched the changing colours of the sky as the sun slowly dipped below the horizon and colour drained from the river.

'I'd love to go to sea,' Sean said suddenly one evening as they watched a ship making her way majestically down the river to cross the bar. 'I wonder where she's bound for. It's the wide wide world out there.'

'Not now surely,' Laura said. 'I mean you don't want to go now, do you?'

For a moment Sean hesitated then he sighed and said, 'Oh well, it's just a dream, I suppose. I'll probably spend my life behind a desk but sometimes when I'm doing ship's documents I wonder about the places they're bound for.'

'You wouldn't see much of them if you went to sea,' Laura said, ever practical. 'A fellow in our office went to sea for years and he said they saw nothing but the ports. And not much of them because they were usually into the nearest bar.'

'Oh Laura, you're so down-to-earth,' Sean said half exasperated and half rueful and Laura suddenly raised her face and kissed him.

'I know,' she said gently. '"Tread softly for you tread on my dreams."'

He laughed quietly and hugged her. 'Laura, you can always surprise me,' he said.

Their courtship had now assumed a regular pattern, with meetings every night except Thursday when Sean went for football training. He came to the house every night to meet her but left her at the gate during the week. On Friday and Saturday nights they went to a disco or club, either locally or in Liverpool, and on those nights Sean came with her into the house. Anne prepared a tray of supper for them and they sat in a small room at the back of the house playing records.

At first Anne or John or both stayed up until Sean left at about two o'clock or later but as time went on they began to go off to bed and leave the young people still playing records.

John was more uneasy about this arrangement than Anne. 'I don't like it,' he grumbled. 'I think we're asking for trouble,' but Anne tried to reassure him.

'It's what they all do nowadays,' she said. 'At least we know Sean is a respectable boy and I'm sure Laura will be safe with him. Anyway, John, if they want to misbehave they can easily find places to do it. It's less likely under our roof.'

Laura also took Sean to meet her grandparents and he was warmly welcomed by Cathy who was delighted to see Laura looking so happy. Laura suspected that her grandfather had some reservations about Sean although he was always very polite.

She had been to Sean's home several times. His mother was a widow and he had three older sisters who plainly adored him. The home seemed to revolve round Sean and his wishes and Laura was shocked to find herself thinking, no wonder he's so big-headed, although she dismissed the thought immediately.

These unwelcome thoughts sometimes intruded when they were at clubs or discos. Sean seemed to know everyone and to be popular with both sexes. 'He's a cracking footballer,' Laura was often told by various young men and girls seemed to flock round him.

Several times on packed dance floors girls managed to insinuate themselves between her and Sean and he appeared to welcome them. I wish it was still fashionable to dance cheek to cheek like in the olden days, Laura thought, but the present style of detached dancing seemed to suit Sean.

Mary's earlier assessment of Sean that he had a big opinion of himself often returned to haunt Laura when she saw him preening himself in the attention he received but always she thrust the thought away. Nevertheless, she was much happier when she and Sean were alone together and most of the summer passed for her in a happy dream.

She saw little of Rosa. One evening shortly after she met Sean they were standing on the platform waiting for the train to Crosby when there was a sudden stir among the home-going crowds. Young men who had been slouching against the wall stood up and smoothed their hair and older men straightened their spines and their ties.

Rosa moved easily through the crowds wearing a tiny mini skirt in green leather and a skinny rib jumper with a green leather jacket slung round her shoulders. She carried an artist's folder and her head on her long slender neck moved from side to side as though she was searching for someone and was unaware of the admiring glances from everyone. Her shining red hair hung to her shoulders and she wore knee-length soft leather boots.

'My God, what a beautiful girl,' Laura heard a man nearby say and she was proud when Rosa saw her and came to her. 'Laura!' she exclaimed.

When Laura had introduced Sean, Rosa gave him her hand and a dazzling smile then said smoothly, 'Nice to meet you. I'm just looking for a friend,' and moved away with a pat on Laura's arm.

'Lovely, isn't she?' Laura said and Sean grinned.

'Yes, and tactful too,' he said, and Laura's fears subsided.

Although Laura saw little of Rosa now she began to hear disquieting tales about her wildness and the crowd she now mixed with. People were afraid to tell her about Rosa's wilder exploits, because she instantly sprang to her cousin's defence, but Mary said seriously one day, 'Your Rosa's riding for a fall, you know, Lol. There's nothing too mad for that crowd she hangs round with. They're into drugs and mixed up with the police and everything.'

Laura knew that Mary was not simply repeating gossip but was truly concerned and she asked if she had any details. 'I know she's still seeing that Ricky Hewlett,' she said, 'although she has lots of other dates.'

'He's the centre of it, I think,' said Mary. 'I can't understand Rosa. A lovely girl like her who could have anybody but he's a real Svengali. I'm sure he supplies her with drugs. Have you seen her lately – the way she dresses?'

'I've seen her at home a few times but she always seems to be in a dressing gown,' Laura said. 'I know my aunt's worried about her because she's as thin as a lath.'

'There's more to worry about than that,' Mary said grimly. 'She even looks wild. The rig-outs she wears!'

Laura felt ashamed that lost in her happy dreams she had failed to see what Mary saw so clearly about her cousin. 'I'll try and talk to her,' she promised. 'It's a wonder her mum and dad have missed seeing it, though.'

'She'll have been well tutored by the abominable Ricky on how to deceive them,' Mary said.

'Yes, and they're so full of this holiday they might not watch her as carefully,' Laura said.

Sarah and Joe were planning to spend two weeks in Ireland with Joe's sister Eileen during the school holidays but Rosa refused to go with them. 'I was bored stiff the last time we went,' she said. 'Nobody of my age but those twin boys who only talk to each other.'

Joe had suggested that Anne and John and their two daughters came with them but John was too tied up with his political activities and neither of the girls wanted to go. Laura was unwilling to leave Sean and Julie expected to see Peter Cunliffe during his vacation.

Finally it was decided that Anne would accompany Sarah and Joe and Rosa would stay with her uncle and aunt, Tony and Helen. Laura decided that if possible she would drop a hint to her uncle or aunt about Ricky Hewlett, blissfully unaware that her hints had all the finesse of sledgehammers.

John was inclined to be grumpy about Anne going on holiday without him, feeling that she should have waited for him to be free so that they could go away together, but he said nothing. He showed his displeasure by criticising the meals the girls prepared.

Julie was apologetic but Laura suggested that he should try his hand when he complained that the potatoes were too salty and the chops tough.

'I'm working,' he said, outraged.

'So am I,' Laura retorted, 'but I still try to help Julie when I come home. She's got enough on just running the house and doing the shopping when she's not used to it.'

'We need your mum here,' John grumbled.

'That's the trouble,' Laura said swiftly. 'We've been spoiled. Mum's always done too much for all of us.'

'That's true,' Julie agreed in her quiet voice. 'I've only realised it since she's been away.'

'So have I,' said Laura. 'We'll all appreciate her more when she comes home.' She looked at her father with a challenging air but he chose to ignore it.

Laura told Sean about her worries about Rosa and he suggested that she consulted her grandmother. 'She's Rosa's nana too, isn't she?' he said.

'Yes, but Rosa's staying with the Fitzgerald side of the family and Aunt Helen and Uncle Tony have two daughters themselves. Moira's engaged, getting married in the spring, and Dilly's two years older than me and Rosa. I think I'd better speak to them.'

She had an opportunity when her Aunt Helen called with a large homemade steak pie and two fruit pies. 'Just to help out with the rations,' she said with a smile.

'I don't know how you managed when there was rationing,' Julie exclaimed. 'I can't manage when I can buy what I like.'

'It's surprising what you can get used to,' Helen said comfortably. 'But you're doing very well, love.'

Helen, who was a keen gardener, went into the garden with Laura to look at her plants and when she said gently, 'You look tired, Laura. Are you worrying about something, love?' Laura blurted out her fears for Rosa. 'I haven't heard or seen anything of this Ricky,' Helen said thoughtfully, 'although she seems to have dates every night with a different young man.'

'Most of them are harmless,' Laura said. 'Even some of them from the college, although she seems to be mostly with a really wild crowd from there. I worry because she's so *gullible*, Aunt Helen. She believes everything they tell her.'

'Don't worry so much, love,' said Helen. 'Rosa's a bit like a chameleon, you know. She changes to merge with her background. She went off with that wild crowd one night and you never saw such a get-up. Even black lipstick and black eyeshadow but they were all the same. About seven of them crowded into one car but they didn't need to worry about crushing their clothes,' she laughed.

'They're just daft really,' Laura said, 'but if you get an evil fellow like Ricky he can manipulate them.'

'Rosa doesn't spend all her time with them. When Mogsy came up from Cambridge to see her at the weekend she looked completely different. Very smart and fashionable but *normal*. Mind you, Uncle Tony said he'd seen wider bandages than the mini skirt she was wearing, but she's such a lovely girl. She can get away with anything.'

'Perhaps I'm worrying about nothing,' Laura muttered but she was not convinced.

'I'm glad you *are* concerned about her,' Helen said. 'You're a good girl, Laura. Her mum wishes she was still with your crowd but she thinks this is just a phase with Rosa. She only has another year at the college and she might settle a bit more after that.'

Laura was not too pleased to be described as 'a good girl'. Makes me sound like a real pudden, she thought, but aloud she said, 'If Aunt Sarah's not worried, I suppose I shouldn't be. It's just a feeling I've got about that Ricky. They'll be home soon, won't they?'

'Yes. You'll be glad to see your mum,' Helen said.

'Dad will,' Laura laughed. 'He doesn't think much of our cooking.' Helen only smiled but after she had gone and Laura thought over their conversation, she remembered Helen's smile.

Suddenly, with the added perception she had gained through her feelings for Sean, she realised that her father's grumbles about the food were only a smokescreen. What he was really missing was the affection and daily companionship of his wife.

Chapter Thirteen

The holiday in Ireland was a big success and the travellers returned looking fit and well. Helen and Tony declared that Anne looked ten years younger.

Her eyes sparkled when she recounted details of the holiday and John slipped his arm round her. 'I'm glad you enjoyed it so much,' he said.

Anne kissed him. 'The only drawback was that you weren't with me. I wanted all the family there. They'd all have enjoyed it,' she said.

'What are the twins like now?' Julie asked.

'Paul and Pat? You should see them. The image of each other, very tall for their age and dark. They work in a pub at the weekend.'

'But they're only about fourteen, aren't they?' John exclaimed. 'They shouldn't be working – and in a pub of all places. I'm surprised at Martin.'

'But they love it,' Anne protested. 'There were about a dozen young lads in this big place on the outskirts of Dublin collecting empty glasses, darting around in long aprons and really enjoying themselves. I said they looked very young but Martin just laughed and said, "It puts a few ha'pence in their pockets and they love it." And they do, John.'

'It's still sweated labour,' John said but Anne laughed at him.

'You should see the tinkers. You'd be having a protest march,' she teased him. 'Martin and Joe and the lads went to see something on the Quays and Eileen and I waited for them by the Ha'penny Bridge one day.'

'Is it a real bridge?' asked Laura.

'Yes, over the River Liffey,' said Anne. 'I'd just taken a packet of cigarettes out and offered it to Eileen when two young tinker girls came up. "Would you ever have a few ha'pence, m'aham?" one of them whined, and I was just going to give her something but Eileen stopped me. "We've no change at all so be off with yez," she said in a thick brogue. You should have seen the change in the girls. One of them snatched two cigarettes out of the packet. "I'll have a cigarette so," she said and they ran off laughing and pushing each other.'

'Did they look poor?' John asked.

'Destitute,' said Anne. 'One minute you'd have been getting up a collection for them, John, and I'd have given to it, but the next! You could see they enjoyed every minute of their lives.'

'Sounds as though I'd be out of my depth.'

'No, you wouldn't. You'd love it, John. The talk. They're all so articulate and well informed, even the kids. They knew more about world affairs and English affairs than I did but you'd have been in your element. Eileen and Martin love living there. He's doing well with the bookbinding and she has a job in a bookshop in Dublin.'

'Sarah and Joe seem to have enjoyed it too,' John said.

'They can't wait to go back. Joe hired a car and we drove to some lovely places but the next time he says he'll go to County Mayo in the west where our mother was born.'

The euphoria of the holiday lasted for several weeks but soon various problems quenched it. Gerry was now travelling the country doing gigs in places from Torquay to Glasgow, but although he came as near Liverpool as Manchester, he never came home. His letters and phone calls became fewer and Anne and John were increasingly worried.

Sarah and Joe were worried too. Joe had been into town one day to the museum in William Brown Street to arrange about a school visit and decided to walk through St John's Gardens to take the train home. He rounded a large statue to see Rosa and Ricky sprawled on a seat behind the statue in attitudes of complete abandon. Rosa lay along the seat with Ricky sprawled across her, his mouth open and his wispy beard blowing in the wind.

Joe stood for a moment rooted with shock, then with a cry he rushed forward and hauled Ricky roughly away from Rosa, then shook her. She was obviously drunk or drugged. She opened bleary eyes but seemed unable to focus on him.

Ricky had toppled off the seat when Joe threw him aside but Joe ignored him and frantically tried to rouse Rosa. After a few moments he dashed out of the gardens and managed to stop a taxi. Looking at his distraught face, the driver offered to help with Rosa.

They almost carried her to the cab and Joe asked for Walton Hospital. 'There are nearer ones, you know, squire,' the man said but Joe shook his head. He had a faint memory of reading that Walton Hospital had a drugs unit and by now he was sure that Rosa was drugged.

This was confirmed when they reached the hospital. Joe asked the doctor if it could be the first time for Rosa and this was her reaction. The doctor shook his head. 'First time for the hard stuff possibly,' he said, 'but she's probably been experimenting. LSD, Benzedrine, that sort of thing. They all do, the young fools.'

'But what happens now?' asked Joe. 'Will she need a clinic, something like that?'

'No. We'll just admit her overnight and keep an eye on her,' the doctor said. 'It's not an overdose so she won't need the stomach pump.'

Rosa still looked ill and was very subdued when her parents collected her the following day from the hospital. She stubbornly refused to answer any questions about the drug she had taken or about Ricky, but Joe told her firmly that he would see that she broke completely with Ricky.

'What happened to him when you hauled me away?' she asked.

'I don't know and I don't care,' Joe said bluntly. 'I hope he was picked up by the police.'

Rosa said nothing but her mother suspected that her anxiety to return to the college was because she wanted to find out about him.

She shared her worries with Anne who was equally worried about Gerry. 'I'm sure he's back taking that stuff,' Anne said. 'He's changed so much, never coming home or writing or phoning. John's talking about finding out where they're playing and going to see him but I'm afraid he'll make a scene and fall out completely.'

'I feel the same with Joe,' Sarah sighed. 'He says he's only going to see that Ricky and warn him off but I'm afraid he'll lose his temper and batter him. I can't believe this is happening to us, Anne. I know pop stars and society people dabble in these drugs but I never thought our kids would be affected.'

'There's so much money in it for the creatures who bring the stuff into the country, that's the trouble,' said Anne. 'No one's safe from them.'

Sarah told Joe about the conversation that evening but he reassured her. He had a friend in the local police who was now a chief inspector and Joe had told him about Ricky. 'Don't worry, we'll feel his collar for him,' the policeman had promised. 'Let him know we've got our eye on him and that should scare him off.'

Although Sarah was reassured, Joe felt too angry and worried to leave the matter entirely to the police. John offered to come with him to see Ricky and to bring a man he knew through his trade union work.

Nelson was a local boxer, born in Liverpool of Jamaican parents. He was a huge black man and a successful boxer but outside the ring he was quiet and gentle. 'That creep won't know that though,' John told Joe. 'Nel will put the fear of God in him. He hates drugs and anyone who deals in them.'

Joe kept watch on Ricky and the three of them surrounded him one night in a quiet alleyway. 'You keep away from my daughter Rosa,' Joe said ferociously, 'or you'll be sorry, I'm telling you.'

Ricky cowered back against the wall. 'You touch me and I'll have you for assault,' he squeaked.

Nelson leaned forward and gripped the front of Ricky's dirty jersey. He lifted him up with his feet dangling and said quietly but venomously, 'And all the other daughters too, man, with your filthy drugs. I don't like drug dealers.' His face was on a level now with Ricky's, who stared back at him like a frightened rabbit.

Nelson lowered him to the ground and Ricky gasped, 'I don't. I only have a few little tablets.'

'It wasn't a little tablet made my Rosa so ill,' Joe roared, starting forward, and John restrained him with difficulty from punching the evil little man.

'Listen,' John said to Ricky. 'He wants to kill you. There's three of us here and a dozen more who'd like to take you apart, mate. The police know about you too but they wouldn't look too hard for you if you went missing.'

Joe broke away. 'I've got to have one swipe,' he cried, throwing a wild punch which lifted Ricky off his feet.

Nelson hauled him up again and held him at arm's length. 'What do you think, John?' he said while Ricky squealed in terror. John was still struggling with Joe and Nelson lowered Ricky again. '*Blow*,' he said contemptuously and Ricky scuttled away.

'Remember what we said,' John shouted after him and Ricky's speed increased.

'Thanks, lads,' Joe said, straightening his clothes. 'I should have seen him by myself though, given him a bloody good hiding. I'd have felt better.'

'I'll bet he's had plenty of those in his time,' John said. 'This will have frightened him more.'

Joe turned to Nelson and shook hands with him. 'Thanks, Nel,' he said. 'I think you had the most effect. He'll think twice before he risks crossing you again.'

'They turn my stomach,' Nelson said, 'fellers like that. I asked around about him and they say he starts kids on poppers then gets them on the hard stuff. He's on it himself. Did you see his arms?'

'I didn't notice,' said Joe. 'Thank God I walked through the gardens that day.'

'Aye, she had someone's good prayers that day,' Nelson said simply and sincerely. He put his hand on Joe's shoulder. 'You saved her, Joe, and she'll realise it in time.'

'Thanks,' was all Joe could say huskily, then he and John left Nelson and took the train home.

A few days later Joe's policeman friend phoned him to tell him that Ricky had left Liverpool. 'He knew we were on to him and he scarpered,' he said. 'But we've put the word round about him.'

Joe said nothing about his confrontation with Ricky and he was sure that Rosa had not heard about it. She continued to be subdued and miserable and refused to take phone calls from the faithful Neil or any other boyfriends. 'Tell him I'm out,' was her refrain when her mother called her to the phone.

Summer had given way to autumn with gales and heavy rain and Laura and Sean's trips to the shore were now only a memory. Instead they occasionally went to a club during the week and on other nights went to the swimming baths then sat in the small room at the back of Laura's house playing records.

'Do you think this fellow's a bit mean?' John asked one night when Anne returned to the kitchen after taking a supper tray to the 'lovebirds', as she and John called them.

'I think he's just anxious to keep fit,' Anne said.

'Not much fun for Laura, though, is it?' John grumbled but Anne only laughed.

'I think she's happy just to be with him,' she said lightly.

Sean's obsession with fitness was in preparation for the football season and Laura was dismayed to discover that he played for two teams, for his school's Old Boys team on Saturdays and for a League team on Sunday. For a while they continued to go to a nightclub on Friday nights, and on Saturday evenings they met up at a local pub, but Laura saw nothing of him during the day at the weekends.

They had occasionally made a foursome with Mary and her boyfriend, a droll character named Danny, which they had all enjoyed but now Laura was unable to make any plans with Mary as Sean's life seemed to be dominated by football.

The Friday nights at a club were dropped because he wanted an early night in preparation for Saturday's game and Saturday nights usually meant a meeting with his teammates and their wives and girlfriends, when the day's match was discussed and analysed *ad nauseum*. If they played away matches there was no meeting at all.

Laura was hurt that he seemed to find it so easy to forgo her company but she told herself that it was just the first enthusiasm at the start of the season and things would soon be back to normal. Sean suggested that she come to watch a home match but warned her to wrap up well because the ground was very exposed.

She borrowed a sheepskin coat from her cousin Dilly and wore boots and a scarf wound round her head. She was glad of its concealing folds when Sean attempted a shot at goal which went wide.

'Greedy bugger,' a man beside her growled. 'There were three men in a better position than him but he won't pass to anyone else.'

'No, he thinks he can do better from thirty yards than another feller from five,' another man agreed. 'Right bloody big-head he is.'

Laura's cheeks burned and she pulled the scarf forward to hide her face as the men continued to criticise Sean.

'Look at him, thinks there's a scout here from a bigger club,' one muttered as Sean tried another shot at goal.

'Pass to your mates, you greedy so and so,' the other men roared.

Laura dodged behind a bigger man in case Sean looked round but he ignored the shouts. The big man was shouting abuse indiscriminately but the first two men concentrated on Sean.

'Chicken!' one of them yelled. 'Look at him,' he added. 'The way he chickened out of that tackle. I wouldn't have him in the team.'

'Looks like a bit of a poof the way he's always poncing around,' the other man said.

I can tell you you're wrong about *that*, Laura thought grimly but she worked her way through the crowd away from the two men, unwilling to hear any more. She remembered comments when she and Sean were with his teammates about Sean hogging the ball. At the time she thought they were praising him for working hard but now she could see a different meaning. But it's not true, she thought loyally. Sean's not like that. He was just trying to do his best to score for the team and those two men were determined to pick on him.

The match finished with a 1–1 draw and as the players came off the field Sean came over to her. He was covered in mud but he smiled at her. 'Glad you came?' he asked. Without waiting for a reply, he said eagerly, 'What did you think of my game?'

'Very good,' she said. 'I was impressed.'

He smiled again and looked down at his muddy strip. 'I'm going for a shower and I'm promised a lift home. If you'd like to wait, I'll see if they can squeeze you in.'

Laura shook her head. 'No, I'll get off. See you later.' She kissed him and turned away to catch a bus home but her spirits had lifted. Now she knew why Sean was trying to score the goal himself. He was trying to show her what a good player he was. She wished she could see the men who thought he was trying to impress a football scout and put them right and she hummed to herself as she waited patiently in the bus queue.

Although Laura made excuses for Sean, her loyalty was tested to the limit during the following weeks. She saw less and less of him. They still travelled to work together, but he had joined a squash club and stayed in town two nights a week to play with friends from the office, so she travelled home alone.

He still played football on Saturdays and Sundays but Laura stopped going to watch him or meeting with his teammates and their wives and girlfriends. Sean had no doubt about his popularity but Laura was soon uneasily aware that many of the jokes about him were meant to wound. She was hurt by them but Sean seemed unaware, armoured in his own conceit.

As time passed their outings decreased until she was only seeing him on one or two evenings a week, and travelling to work, when they were often joined by friends so had no private conversation.

On Friday night they usually went to a cabaret club but on two occasions Sean fell asleep during the acts. Laura woke him roughly. 'I'm glad you find my company so exciting,' she snapped but Sean only laughed.

She was too proud to protest or ask to see him more often but she was bitterly conscious that she needed his company more than he needed hers. If he loved me, he'd want to be with me, she thought but she was confused because when he was with her he was so loving. He resented any attention paid to her by other young men too and made it clear that she was his girlfriend if anyone became too friendly with her. That must mean that he loves me, she told herself, but the honesty which was often her undoing suggested that it might mean only a dog-in-the-manger attitude.

Her temper grew ever shorter and the uneasy truce between herself and her father was soon broken. John was worried about Gerry and it needed very little to cause a quarrel between them.

The rest of the family tactfully ignored Laura's problems but John said one evening, 'Are you staying in *again,* Laura?'

Laura's temper flared immediately. 'Everyone's not like you,' she snapped. 'Got to be out every night.'

Battle was joined right away with Anne and Julie vainly trying to keep the peace. Finally John shouted, 'I'm sick of pussyfooting around, not mentioning the way that fellow's behaving. Get rid of him, Laura. He's no good to you.'

Laura rushed out of the room closely followed by her mother and when they reached Laura's room, Anne took her in her arms. Laura was crying bitterly and at first Anne only held her, murmuring, 'Oh love, love,' and rubbing her hand round and round on Laura's back, but when she was calmer they sat on the side of the bed.

'Your dad doesn't mean to hurt you, love,' Anne said gently. 'He's a bit tactless but it's only because he's worried about you. We all are.'

'There's no need,' said Laura, still weeping, but lifting her head proudly. 'I'm glad Sean is so fond of sport. It's not as if he's off after other girls.'

'No, I know that,' Anne agreed, 'but it makes for a dull life for you, love. Why don't you take up a sport or go out with your friends when Sean's not free?'

Laura drew away and looked down at her clasped hands. 'He doesn't like me going to clubs without him,' she muttered. 'And anyway, I never know which nights he's playing squash.'

Anne was furious but tried to control her anger. 'But he can't expect you to stay in waiting for him to decide to see you,' she said forcefully, then as she saw the expression on Laura's face she said hastily, 'I think Dad hoped you would take an interest in CND.'

'*I* would?' Laura gasped. 'Whatever made him think that?'

'You said you were worried about the bomb,' Anne said but Laura laughed scornfully.

'I've got more sense,' she said. 'What do they think they can do? If the top dogs decide they want the bomb they'll have it and they won't take any notice of people waving banners or lying in the road like at Aldermaston.'

'But it does have some effect,' Anne protested. 'You know Dad often quotes his grandfather's remark that little drops of water together make a mighty river. Politicians need our votes so they *will* listen if enough people protest. Don't forget, you have a vote now too.'

'But it's an obsession with him,' Laura said, forgetting the cause of the quarrel. 'You don't really think it's such a danger, do you?'

Anne was silent for a moment then she said quietly, 'Do you remember the man Dad worked with whose wife took thalidomide? Their baby was born without arms or legs and with a malformed liver. He died after two days but I'll never forget the day Dad rang me to tell me. The man had told him that Alder Hey Hospital had many babies without limbs.' Anne's eyes were full of tears as she looked at Laura. 'I remember I was ironing. We didn't know about thalidomide then and we thought it was caused by nuclear fallout. I just sat there stunned for a minute then I was so *angry*. I wanted to go to Parliament, scream at them to stop it, lie down in the road, march, do something, anything, to stop them testing the atom bomb.'

'But it wasn't nuclear fallout,' Laura said.

'Not that time but things like this happened in Hiroshima and Nagasaki after the atom bomb was dropped. I always felt Dad was right to oppose it but it never really came home to me until that day, Laura. It was like a pit opening under my feet.'

'I never really thought about it,' Laura said. 'I only said that about the bomb wiping us all out because David's friends said it.'

They had moved away from the subject of Sean but now Anne said gently, 'Speaking of them, don't you think we should have another party? Everyone seemed to enjoy the last one. Perhaps when David's home for Christmas. I'm sure Julie would be keen.'

'She certainly enjoyed the last one,' Laura said dryly. They stood up and Anne hugged her daughter again.

'Think about what I said, love. Get some other interests,' she urged but Laura only nodded.

After her mother had gone, she perched on the deep window seat and stared out at the garden, filled with shame as she thought of how her behaviour had appeared to other people. She thought of her mother's words, 'He can't expect you to stay in waiting for him to decide to see you.' Her mother would never say that to hurt her but only because she was stating a fact. I must seem like a right wimp, Laura thought, feeling more and more depressed and humiliated as she recalled comments made about her and Sean.

'Proper little sultan, isn't he?' one girl had laughed when Sean had turned to Laura on the train and informed her that he was not playing squash so they could go out that night. Other remarks returned to her, some merely flippant and some malicious, and gradually her depression was replaced by anger, as much with herself as with Sean.

What is wrong with me? she asked herself. Where is my pride, my self-respect? Me, Laura Redmond, letting myself be picked up and dropped like an old glove when it suits him. Deliberately she let herself think of all the traits in him that she had refused to acknowledge, his selfishness, his massive conceit, his thick skin which made him able to ignore remarks from people who detested him and his confidence that she would be waiting gratefully for his notice when he spared her an evening.

I don't even like him, she thought with a shock of surprise. I never really loved him, not the fellow he really is, only some romantic dream that I fitted round him.

She stayed staring unseeingly from the window for a long time, then as darkness fell she turned away, her mouth set in a determined line. From now on things would be different but she would not give him the satisfaction of a scene. She could imagine him thinking, perhaps even saying, that she wanted more than he was prepared to give. She would let the affair fade away.

With Laura, to think was to act. She deliberately took a later train the following morning and applied for another job in the same building that had been advertised. She was interviewed immediately and accepted and told that she could start as soon as she was free.

She handed in her notice when she went back to her office. The supervisor was so annoyed that she told Laura that she could leave at once.

Mary was amazed when Laura told her at lunchtime that she was starting at the new office the following day. 'I didn't know you were thinking of a change,' she said. 'Halkin and Breen are a good firm to work for though. They have flexitime, you know.' She glanced sideways at Laura. 'I suppose you won't want that though, will you? You'll want to be on the same train as Sean.'

'Not necessarily,' Laura said airily. 'To tell you the truth, I'm finding him a bit of a bore lately.'

'Thank God for that,' Mary exclaimed, too surprised to be tactful. 'I'm glad you can see it at last.'

'He's not *that* bad,' Laura said, affronted. 'He can be very nice but I'm a bit cheesed off with all the sport. It's not my scene.'

'Nor mine,' Mary agreed hastily. 'Listen, are you seeing him tonight? Danny's started evening classes. We could go out and celebrate the new job.'

'Good idea,' Laura said. 'I'd like that.'

Sean was not on the train but when she reached home her mother was pleased to hear about the change of job and even more about her date with Mary. She said nothing about Sean and neither did Laura.

She enjoyed the night out with Mary and realised how much she had missed the light-hearted banter of the crowd they met and the music.

Sean was waiting on the platform the following day and said immediately, 'Were you off work yesterday? You didn't get the train yesterday morning.'

'No, I went in later,' Laura said casually. 'I've changed my job. The same building but a better firm, Halkin and Breen. I start this morning.'

Sean was astounded. 'But you didn't tell me,' he complained. 'I didn't know you were even thinking of it.'

Laura shrugged. 'It was just on impulse,' she said. 'The job was advertised so I applied.' She laughed. 'I thought I'd have to work a month's notice but old Simmonds was so mad. She bounced in to Mr Clark, then said I could go immediately.'

Sean was evidently annoyed. 'You must have had *some* idea,' he grumbled. 'You never even said you were fed up at work.'

'I don't think we ever discussed *my* work,' Laura said. 'But I wasn't fed up. I just saw a better job going. It's more money and flexitime, luncheon vouchers and so on, so it's a good move for me.' She said nothing about wanting to get away from the girls who knew of her unsatisfactory affair with him.

She was supposed to work for a month before starting flexitime but on the first day a large order came in at twenty minutes to five and she willingly stayed with some of the other staff to complete the documentation for it.

'You've been a good help,' one of the men told her, yawning and stretching when they finished. 'The ship's sailing on Wednesday. Fancy coming for a drink with us at Riley's?'

Laura agreed and they all went along to a pub near the station for a drink. There were eight of them, men and girls, and they decided to go on to a singing pub where they would get something to eat but Laura said she would go home. 'Another time,' she said and they assured her that they often did this when they worked late for any reason.

Her mother was pleased to hear of the visit to Riley's and the invitation to go on to Flanagan's. 'You should have gone, love,' she said. 'Get out as much as you can.' Again she said nothing about Sean but Laura looked quizzically at her and they both laughed.

Laura had said nothing to Sean about her night out with Mary and she decided not to mention her visit to Riley's. She was uncertain whether she was yet ready to tell Sean how her feelings had changed towards him. Although during the day she was determined to finish with him, during the night she often lay awake, thinking of their early days together. I'm sure he loved me then and I loved him, she thought. Sometimes she wept at the thought of never seeing him again and wondered whether she was right to end their affair.

With daylight her mood always changed. She remembered his selfishness and his cavalier treatment of her and decided that enough was enough. She was as annoyed with herself as with Sean.

Why did I allow it to happen? she thought. I've been a fool but I'll put an end to it, yet with uncharacteristic lack of determination she postponed it from day to day.

Chapter Fourteen

Many of Laura's friends had paired off during her months with Sean and she had wondered whether she would lead a very lonely existence without him. It seemed like fate that suddenly she was invited out so often.

The other half of their semi-detached house was occupied by an elderly couple who were often visited by their numerous family. Laura had become friendly with the neighbours when she was gardening and especially friendly with their granddaughter Claire who was the same age as herself. Claire often stayed with them for the weekend.

Claire lived in Southport, a few miles further up the coast, and the weekend after Laura's first week in her new job, she suggested that they should go to one of the clubs there the following weekend.

'Toad Hall or the Sandgrounder,' she said. 'We'd have a good time in either of them. What about next Saturday?'

Laura agreed, feeling that events were sweeping her along quicker than she intended. She had already agreed to go out with friends from the office to celebrate a birthday, and with Mary on one of Danny's night-school nights, and Sean knew nothing of any of it.

She had avoided him by travelling on a different train in the morning and evening, feeling that she needed more time to think, but she was due to go for a meal with him on Sunday night. I'll have to say something to him, she decided, but when Sunday came there seemed to be no opportunity.

Laura's resolve to finish with him hardened as she listened to his non-stop conversation about his own affairs and she wondered how she could have blinded herself to his conceit earlier. She had only seen him once during the week and that had been for a session at the swimming baths when he had left her at the gate with a casual kiss.

He had played five-a-side one night as well as his two evenings of squash but he only said perfunctorily, 'Hope you weren't too fed up because I had so much on this week, Lol.'

'No, I had things to do myself,' she said but he seemed to take no warning from her tone.

'Good, good,' he said. 'The five-a-side was brilliant. I really enjoyed it. I was more fit than any of them and I'm sure our swimming helped.' He smiled at her but Laura turned her head away from him.

Am I supposed to be pleased that I've helped to make him more fit so that he can go out without me even oftener? she thought indignantly, but Sean seemed unaware of any atmosphere. He vigorously applauded the singer and laughed heartily at the comedian. He seemed so sure that he had not offended in any way that Laura wondered whether perhaps she was just being awkward and unreasonable, but as she thought of the lonely week she might have had, her resentment grew. No thanks to him I wasn't at home every night, she thought.

In the scramble for taxis after the show there was no opportunity for conversation and in the taxi Sean began immediately to talk about football. In the light of the street lamps as they passed, Laura could see his complacent smile as he bragged of his triumphs and she grew more and more angry.

When the taxi stopped at her gate, she said abruptly, 'Keep the taxi, Sean. I want an early start tomorrow. Goodnight.' With a peck on his cheek she jumped out of the taxi and slammed the door. She thought he might follow her but he was evidently anxious to save face with the taxi driver and they drove away as she entered her front door.

That's it, thought Laura. Finish. I'll tell him about my other plans but I won't quarrel with him. I won't give him the satisfaction of thinking I care enough to quarrel with him. I'll just let it fizzle out like I planned. Before she fell asleep she thought bitterly that Sean might not even notice her absence. She had seen so little of him lately.

It seemed as though she had only been asleep for a few minutes when she was awakened by a thunderous knocking on the front door. She switched on the light and fell out of bed and into her dressing gown, then looked at the clock. Six o'clock. On the landing she met her mother and Julie, her father was already running downstairs, tying his dressing-gown belt.

They leaned over the banisters as he opened the door and they saw two policemen on the step. 'Mr Redmond?' they heard and John nodded.

The policemen came into the hall and Anne ran downstairs closely followed by the two girls. 'Gerry?' she said breathlessly.

The elder of the two men said soothingly, 'Now don't get too upset. He's been in a bad accident but he'll be all right.'

They went into the dining room and the policeman asked more formally if Gerald John Redmond was their son. John seemed too stunned to speak and it was Anne who answered the questions, then began to press for details of the accident.

The policeman told them that the group had been driving back to their flat when their van had skidded off the road and into a tree. The driver had been killed outright and the front passenger had died on the way to hospital but Gerry and the two others in the back had been less severely injured. They could give no further details, only that the three young men were in hospital a few miles outside Birmingham.

The older man turned to Laura. 'Make your mum and dad a cup of tea, love,' he said. 'Put plenty of sugar in it.'

Laura and Julie went into the kitchen and John began to bombard the policemen with questions but they said they could tell him no more. They had been asked to inform the parents or next of kin but had been given no further details. Anne asked if they had any idea how serious Gerry's injuries were. The policemen were soothing but vague. The girls returned with the tea, with some for the policemen too, and John and Anne decided to set off for the hospital as soon as possible.

The policemen left and Anne and John were soon ready to set off. Laura looked at John's shaking hands and blurted out, 'Are you fit to drive? Should I ring Uncle Joe?'

'No, no, I'm all right,' John said impatiently.

'Let them know though,' Anne said, 'and ring Nana. We'll ring you as soon as we've seen him.'

As they left, the old lady from next door appeared with a thermos flask and a parcel of food. 'Try to eat, dear,' she said to Anne. 'Carbohydrate is good for shock. God go with you.'

'We should have thought of that,' Laura said.

'You had other things to think about, dear,' Mrs Barret said quietly.

'It's not seven o'clock yet,' Laura said. 'Did that hammering on our door disturb you? I don't know why they couldn't use the bell.' The first shock was wearing off and she wanted someone to be angry with to relieve her feeling.

'One of them was very young,' the old lady said calmly. 'It probably seemed more dramatic to him.'

Laura and Julie sat by the phone all morning willing it to ring but it was silent. 'I should have rung the office,' Laura said, 'but we'll have to keep the phone clear in case Mum's trying to get through. We can't ring the relations yet either.'

'It'll be better to wait until we know more anyway,' Julie said. 'Oh Laura, I'm terrified about what they'll find there. If two of them were killed, it must have been a bad crash.'

'But Gerry was in the back. That makes a difference,' Laura consoled her but her own imagination was suggesting terrible possibilities to her.

It was lunchtime before the call came from their mother. 'Gerry's all right,' she said immediately. 'His foot was trapped in the wreckage so he's been in the operating theatre but he's come round now and he's spoken to us.'

'Will he lose his foot?' Laura asked fearfully but Anne reassured her.

'No, but his left arm is broken and also some ribs. One of the other lads had head injuries. He may be transferred to Walton and if so they might take Gerry too but nothing's settled yet. Are you all right?'

'Yes, Mum. What about you and Dad?'

'All right but what a journey. We'll probably stay tonight. I've no more change now but I'll let you know—' She was cut off.

The girls hugged each other and cried with relief. 'I was afraid the policemen were just being kind. Letting us find out gradually,' Julie said.

'I'll tell you something,' Laura said gruffly, 'I'm not having any kids. All that hassle before with Gerry and the worry Rosa's caused. It's not worth it.'

Julie smiled through her tears. 'I'll bet you change your mind,' she said. 'I'd like six children.'

'Six!' Laura exclaimed. 'I'll bet *you* change your mind too.' They felt light-headed with relief that their worst fears were unfounded, so they were able to sound quite cheerful when they telephoned their grandmother and their aunts and gave them details.

Laura phoned the office and told the office manager what had happened and he urged her to take time off while she was needed at home. 'Just keep me informed,' he said. 'I hope all works out well.'

'Isn't he nice,' Julie said. 'You made a good move when you went there, Lol.'

'I did,' Laura agreed. They were sitting at the kitchen table drinking tea and she cupped her hands round the mug and looked pensively out at the rain-soaked garden. 'I only moved because of Sean, you know,' she said abruptly. Julie looked surprised but said nothing and Laura went on, 'I decided I was going to change my life, break with him, and I started by getting a new job away from that crowd in Bellamy's and their snide remarks about him. I did that right away but here I am still dithering about finishing with him.'

'It's a big decision,' Julie said gently.

'It shouldn't be. I usually know my own mind and it's not as if it's the love affair of the century or anything.' Julie was gazing at her sympathetically with her big brown eyes and suddenly all the details of the football matches, the squash and now the five-a-side poured from Laura.

'Even the swimming,' she said bitterly. 'That wasn't my idea. He just decided we'd go as part of his keep-fit programme and I went along with it meekly. We hardly ever go out but it – well, it doesn't bother him. He doesn't really care whether he sees me or not.'

'I'm sure he does,' Julie protested. 'He's just caught up with all this sport.'

'But that's what I mean. The sport is more important to him than I am. If he really cared about me he'd want to see me as often as he could, wouldn't he?'

'I'm sure he does love you, Lol,' Julie said earnestly. 'But he just hasn't got his priorities right. A lot of fellows go crazy about sport because they just haven't grown up properly but he does really love you, I'm sure.'

'I wish I was,' Laura said, trying to smile. 'I haven't told anyone else how I feel except Grandad. I didn't tell him really, I just hinted. I know Grandad was doubtful about Sean and I asked him why one day and he said that Sean reminded him of a joke he'd heard. Someone said about a married couple, "It should be a happy marriage, they're both in love with him." I got the message.'

'That doesn't sound like Grandad,' Julie exclaimed.

'I know, but I think his idea was that he was being cruel to be kind. I've got to admit it, Sean is a big-head. I can see all his faults during the day and I decide to finish with him but then during the night I lie awake thinking of the other side of him and I dither about and do nothing.'

'But do you have to finish with him?' Julie asked. 'Can't you go out with Mary and Claire on the nights when he's out and see each other when you can?'

Laura shook her head. 'It wouldn't work. I haven't told him about going out because I know it'll mean a row.'

'I don't see why,' said Julie. 'If he's doing his own thing, why shouldn't you do yours?'

'Because he's very jealous. Even in the baths he got a cob on because a fellow was fooling around, grabbing my legs, and he goes mad if I dance with anyone else or even talk to them at a club. I'd like to think it was love but I think it's just his vanity.'

'Oh Laura,' Julie said. She sat with her head bent, drawing a pattern in spilled tea on the table then she looked up. 'This lying awake at night changing your mind,' she said. 'Why don't you have hot milk and codeine tablets when you go to bed and you'll sleep through the night?'

Laura laughed aloud. 'Julie, you slay me. I thought you were so romantic and I was waiting for something sentimental then you tell me to take hot milk and codeine.'

Laura's laughter was slightly hysterical and Julie said practically, 'I think we need something to eat.'

A few minutes later there was a knock at the back door and Sarah appeared. 'I've brought fish and chips,' she said. 'I thought you might not think of eating.'

'You must be a mind reader,' Laura said. 'We were just saying we should eat.' As they bustled about laying the table and buttering bread, they told Sarah all that had happened since they were awakened by the knock on the door.

'What a shock for your poor mum and dad – for all of you,' Sarah said. 'Thank God the news is no worse.'

'It must have been a terrible crash,' said Julie. 'I keep thinking of those other poor families, of the boys who were killed, I mean. That might have been us if Gerry had been in the front.'

'Yes, but he wasn't,' Laura said. 'His injuries sound bad but not dangerous.'

'And he's young,' Sarah said. 'He'll soon heal. I hope he's transferred to Walton. When your mum rings again, Laura, get the phone number from her and ring her back. Then she won't have to worry about her change running out.'

Laura was pleased to have her aunt with them and to discuss practical details. She felt relieved to have spoken about Sean to Julie and yet she felt self-conscious with her sister and wondered why she had suddenly confided in her. Sean was not mentioned again.

Later, when Sarah had gone, Julie telephoned Peter and Laura went next door to see Mr and Mrs Barret. They were pleased to hear that Gerry was not in any danger and sad that the other young men had died. 'Such a waste,' Mr Barret said. 'Parents must be glad their sons haven't got to go to war any more but the roads are getting as bad as Flanders fields.'

'And so near Christmas,' Mrs Barret said. 'Why do so many tragedies happen at Christmastime?' She indicated a large casserole dish beside the oven. 'I've made a chicken casserole for you, dear,' she said. 'There's enough for Mum and Dad as well if they come home tonight. I know you won't feel like cooking.'

Laura was amazed and touched by the kindness shown to the family at this time.

Within a week, Gerry and Denny, the young man with head injuries, were transferred to Walton Hospital, Anne and John had returned from Birmingham and everything was almost back to normal.

Laura had been off work for three days and on the evening of the second day Sean had telephoned her. He had met Mary and been told of Gerry's accident and he sounded warm and concerned as he inquired about Gerry and how she was coping with the shock.

'I know you won't feel like going out at present,' he said. 'But I'll keep in touch and we'll have a good night out when things settle down.'

Something patronising in his tone and perhaps the memory of Peter Cunliffe's frequent phone calls to Julie made her say curtly, 'I cancelled a night out with Mary and I won't be going out with the office crowd for Colette's birthday but I'm sure I'll enjoy a night out soon. Everyone has been kind, calling to see us.'

There was silence for a moment then Sean said stiffly, 'Mary didn't mention that. Take care. I'll keep in touch.'

I should have said I haven't got an infectious disease, she thought indignantly. He practically passes the gate on his way home but I suppose he has too much on to call in. Mary had called and so had a man from the office who lived locally, as well as some of Julie's friends and their grandparents and other relatives.

Later she thought of Sean's warm and loving tone when she had answered the phone and reminded herself that he had only heard of the accident a few hours previously. Perhaps I'm being unreasonable, she thought yet again, but I'll wait and see.

On Wednesday evening she and Julie were able to see Gerry, now installed in Walton Hospital, and found him very subdued. He told them that the fifth member of the group had been discharged from hospital and taken to Sheffield by his brother.

'He was asleep in the back of the van, well wrapped up,' Gerry said. 'That probably saved him. He only had cuts and bruises.'

The doctor had warned them not to talk about the two friends who had died and they left Gerry after a few minutes as he seemed drowsy. 'He seemed so different,' Julie said. 'Will he ever get over it, I wonder.'

'Yes, of course he will. He'll bounce back,' Laura said but privately she had doubts. I don't feel certain about anything any more, she thought.

Gerry was still in hospital for Christmas although his foot had improved but Denny stayed in intensive care. Laura had returned to work and had met Sean on the station platform on the first day. He was solicitous in his questions about Gerry and the accident and arranged to see her on the Friday evening.

'You won't feel like going to a club but we could go to the pictures,' he said and Laura agreed.

Laura refused to go to the baths, saying that the weather was too bad, but Sean arranged to go out with her on four occasions the following week and Laura would have been completely happy, revelling in his loving efforts to comfort her, if a small voice had not suggested that it was because she had planned to go out with others.

Sean's sudden attentiveness made it difficult to carry out her plan of letting the affair fade away and also made her mother believe that all was well between them.

The family visited Gerry every evening during the visiting hour six thirty to seven thirty and other relatives and friends often called for a brief visit. One evening Anne and John had to attend a meeting at Julie's school about A levels and Anne suggested that Sean might accompany Laura to the hospital.

'He could come here for his meal from the station and you could go together to the hospital,' she said.

Laura was non-committal. Sean had never suggested visiting Gerry and one night he had wrinkled his nose when she stood beside him in a cinema queue after visiting the hospital. 'I can smell that hospital smell on you,' he exclaimed. 'God, I hate hospitals.'

'Thanks,' Laura said huffily. 'I hope you never have to go in one then.'

She moved away but he flung his arm round her and pulled her to him. 'Only joking,' he said and kissed her.

Now she decided not to ask him outright but to tell him what her mother had suggested.

'Sorry,' he said hastily. 'I've got a squash court booked with Owen,' and she said no more.

She told her mother that Sean was unable to come for the meal. Anne made no comment and when John looked up from his newspaper and exclaimed, 'But—' she hastily interrupted him to ask him to be sure to be home early for the visit to the school.

Laura went alone to the hospital and found her cousin Dilly and her boyfriend Andy there. Andy was a cheerful extrovert and his account of trying to house-train a puppy brought a rare smile to Gerry's face. Soon afterwards Dilly's elder sister Moira arrived with her fiancé and the jokes came thick and fast.

'Thanks, Andy,' Gerry said as they prepared to leave. 'You're a tonic. You've all made me feel better.'

'It's my face,' Andy said. 'It cheers people up to know that theirs isn't like it.'

Laura had laughed as heartily as the others at the jokes but when they left and she bent over Gerry to say goodbye, he suddenly held her fiercely with his good arm and kissed her. 'Take care of yourself, kid,' he said softly. 'You're worth the very best.'

Laura felt her eyes fill with tears as she whispered, 'You too, Ged,' using their old childish name for him.

Her cousins were waiting for her but she was quiet and thoughtful as they drove her home. Why had Gerry said that? Was it because he sensed her unhappiness and saw her alone among the other happy couples? The old Gerry would never have noticed but now perhaps he had been made more perceptive by his own suffering and misery. And was he, too, hinting at doubts about Sean by telling her that she was worth the very best?

She waited for her parents and Julie to return from the meeting and told them briefly about Dilly and Moira and their boyfriends being at the hospital and that Gerry was much more cheerful. Then she went to bed, saying that she had a headache.

She woke suddenly in the early hours of the morning to find the room flooded with moonlight. She went to the window and stood looking out at the moon through the bare branches of the trees and the familiar shapes in the garden made unfamiliar by moonlight and thought over the past months.

I've been a fool, she thought. Ever since our party I've been bending myself out of shape trying to change. Stopping myself from saying what I think to Sean and dithering about trying to decide whether I loved him or not. From now on I'll just be myself and I'll tell him straight as soon as I see him that it's time we packed in.

Feeling relieved and calm, she went back to bed and immediately fell asleep.

She slept late and caught a later train than Sean in the morning but she saw him among the homegoing crowds flooding into Exchange Station after work. He looked furtive and she realised that he was hoping to avoid her but she grasped his arm firmly and drew him aside.

'I want to get this train,' he protested. 'I've got five-a-side tonight.'

'You can spare me a few minutes,' she said and he looked alarmed. 'Don't worry, I only want to say that it's time we called it a day. It doesn't suit either of us and we each need to be free to do what we want.'

He gaped at her. 'What? Why?' he spluttered. 'What's brought this on?' Then he looked at her with narrowed eyes, suddenly suspicious. 'Have you met someone else?' he demanded.

'Of course not,' Laura said. 'It's just that you've got other things to do like your squash and football.'

'So that's it,' he said triumphantly, before she could say that she also had other interests. 'I knew it. You've got a weed on because I can't see you every night but the teams *need* me.'

Laura suddenly lost her temper. 'They could manage without you when you suddenly wanted to see me nearly every night because I was going out, having a life of my own. You couldn't stand that, could you, big-head? You're just a dog in the manger.'

Sean's face was red with anger and he snarled at her, 'I gave up matches to take you out but you never came to watch me on Saturdays or came out with the lads at night. You want things all your own way.'

'*I* do?' Laura exclaimed. 'You've got a cheek. I didn't go because I didn't like to hear what they said about you but you're too thick-skinned and conceited to realise it.'

'Don't you criticise me,' Sean snapped. 'You never appreciated me. Plenty of girls would be glad to go out with me.'

'Those who like immature morons,' Laura said. 'Selfish to the bone. I wish them joy.'

She turned away but Sean gripped her sleeve. 'Don't you be telling people you chucked me,' he said, '*I* finished with *you*.'

Laura pulled her sleeve out of his grasp and looked at him with contempt. 'Childish too,' she said and went towards the train.

The next train was in and filling rapidly and Laura and Sean pushed on but in separate carriages and when the train drew in to Blundell-sands station, Laura walked home without a backward glance.

I've done it, she thought with relief then smiled to herself as she thought over the conversation. I was going to be so dignified, too, she thought ruefully, and part as friends, but once Sean started spouting I couldn't resist telling him what I thought of him. Might do him some good anyway, make him less big-headed.

There was the usual rush to get to the hospital and no opportunity to see her mother alone until late evening, but as she helped Anne to prepare supper she told her quietly that she had finished with Sean. 'For good?' Anne asked.

Laura grinned as she thought of her comments to Sean but she only said lightly, 'Definitely for good, Mum.'

'I can't say I'm sorry, love,' Anne said. 'But won't it be awkward so near Christmas? Only ten days to go. Have you got his present?'

'No, I hadn't realised it was so close. Everything seems so upside down lately. But I had to do it now, Mum. It's dragged on too long as it is.'

'I don't think you were really suited,' Anne said diplomatically. 'You'll know when you meet the right one.'

"'Across a crowded room,'" Laura quoted, but her mother was relieved to see how heartily she laughed and how unconcerned she seemed about the parting.

If I ever do meet anyone else, thought Laura, I won't make the same mistake. I won't try to change myself to suit them. I'll just be myself, say what I think, do what I like and if they don't like it they can lump it. She hummed cheerfully as she carried the tray to the table.

Chapter Fifteen

Although Laura appeared cheerful she still had bad moments remembering the early days when she believed that Sean truly loved her and she had loved him without reservation. She had given Julie an edited version of their parting and Julie insisted that Sean did love Laura but was too immature to realise it.

'I can't wait around for him to grow up,' Laura joked but in her heart she knew that Sean loved no one but himself.

Peter Cunliffe had travelled home with David to spend some time with Julie before going to his widowed mother in Manchester for Christmas and Julie tried to conceal her happiness from Laura. She thought it would make Laura feel even more unhappy about Sean but Laura assured her that she felt only relief at finishing with him.

'Don't be spoiling your time with Peter for my sake, Ju,' she said. 'It's a different situation altogether. You two were made for each other and I'm very happy for you.' She was amazed sometimes at how close she had grown to Julie since Gerry's accident. A few months ago I couldn't have imagined talking to her like this, she thought.

Everyone in the family tried to make Christmas a cheerful time but in spite of their efforts there was a shadow over it and everyone was relieved when it was all over.

Gerry was still in hospital and suffering a lot of pain from his injured foot and the other casualty Denny was not responding to treatment.

Maureen came to stay for Christmas and the family were shocked at the change in her. They had visited her frequently and found her serene and happy, with little change physically, but now the disease seemed to have made a leap forward in its inexorable progress. She was as loving and resigned as ever but it was a grief to all the family to see how restricted her movements had become and the hesitation in her speech.

Sarah and Joe had another worry too. Rosa had not returned to the College of Art after her return from hospital but drooped about the house showing no interest in anything. She still refused to answer telephone calls although the faithful Neil still persisted and her mother now flatly refused to tell anybody that Rosa was out. 'I'm telling no more lies for you,' she declared. 'You can tell them yourself,' but Rosa refused to be provoked.

When David returned from Cambridge with Peter Cunliffe, Sarah hoped that Rosa would rouse herself and take some trouble with her appearance. 'I'm sick of seeing you in that dressing gown,' she told Rosa. 'I hope you'll get dressed while the lads are home and do something with your hair. It's a disgrace.' Rosa only retired to her bedroom and stayed there while David and Peter were in the house.

She was still keeping to her bedroom on New Year's Eve when the rest of the family gathered at her grandmother's house. 'I'm not sorry to see the end of this year,' Sarah said. 'And we thought life was going to be so good when we first moved to our new houses.'

'It will be, love,' her mother said. 'It usually happens that troubles come all together then there's a long spell with everything going smoothly.'

'It's been an eventful year,' Greg said. 'All the trouble in Ireland and the investiture of the Prince of Wales and then men on the moon! I never thought that would happen in my lifetime.'

'It's hard to take in,' Anne said. 'We stood in the garden, didn't we, John, looking up at the moon and trying to realise that two men were actually on it.'

'I don't agree with it,' John declared. 'There's plenty to be sorted out on this planet before we start meddling with others. The money it cost could be put to better use.'

'It's still a wonderful achievement,' his father said mildly. 'And some progress has been made here, John. The abolition of the death penalty and the barricades coming down in Belfast and the Peace Line instead. And the Soviet Union and America have ratified the Nuclear Non-proliferation Treaty. That should please you.'

'And don't forget votes for eighteen-year-olds,' Cathy said.

'Did you campaign for that, Nana?' asked Laura and Cathy laughed. 'No. Someone else must have done that,' she said. 'We only fought for votes for women and now half of them don't use them.'

'I'll certainly use mine,' Laura declared. 'When I've made up my mind.'

She winked at her mother who said firmly, 'Now don't start a political argument on New Year's Eve, Laura.'

'I suppose all these things are important,' Sarah said, 'but when things go wrong for our kids, they don't matter at all by comparison. I can honestly say that's the most miserable Christmas I've ever had.'

'The thought of those two poor lads that died and their families threw a shadow over everyone, apart from all the other troubles,' Cathy said. 'It was a pity Mick and Gerda could only stay for Christmas Day. He might have cheered us up.'

'Why did he have to go back?' asked Helen.

'Something had gone wrong with one of the processes,' Cathy said. 'He was as near to being worried as I've ever seen him. I think it could be quite dangerous.'

'Never mind,' Greg said, giving her a hug. 'We've nearly finished with nineteen sixty-nine now, love. Next year has got to be better.'

For the first few weeks of the new year everything seemed unchanged then suddenly everyone had cause to feel happier. Gerry's broken arm had healed and there was so much improvement in his foot that he was due to be discharged to attend as an outpatient twice a week. An operation was decided on for Denny which was completely successful, so he too was discharged from hospital.

The new term had started at the College of Art but Rosa was still drooping about the house, much to her mother's disgust. She had obtained a few commissions for illustrations for greeting cards and calendars before the episode with Ricky and her father fixed up a garden shed as a studio for her, hoping to encourage her to work again, but she was not interested.

It was a phone call from a man who liked some work that she had left with him months earlier that roused her from her lethargy.

'I never saw anything like it,' Sarah told Anne. 'One minute she was lying on the sofa like a dying duck and the next she was round the house like a whirlwind. I thought we'd need an operation to get that dressing gown off her but she was into the bathroom like a flash then came down looking like a fashion plate.'

'I suppose the truth is it came at the right time,' Anne said. 'She was ready to start again, just needed a trigger.'

'She knew I'd had enough too,' Sarah said. 'I made her take the calls from Neil and the others even if she hung up on them and I'd told her what I thought of her the night before. This call saved her face.'

Ricky seemed to be forgotten but her experience with him seemed to have made her more mature. She went back to the college to gain her diploma and worked hard in her shed/studio to fulfil her commissions for cards, calendars and labels. She avoided the wilder spirits at the college now and made new friends. They were amazed at her success and frankly envious, and Rosa seemed blissfully unaware that her looks and charm had a lot to do with her success and opened many doors to her which were closed to other people.

Her dates soon became as frequent and as varied as in the past and one was with a guitarist in a popular Liverpool group. Before long she was occasionally singing with the group. Her voice was light and pleasant and she sang songs like 'Those were the days' and 'Yesterday' and she was an immediate success.

Her parents were pleased and proud and Laura, who was enjoying life herself now, felt no envy for Rosa's success, only for her ability to shrug off unpleasantness and live for the moment. With all her many boyfriends Rosa's own heart was never involved and she lacked the imagination to realise the suffering of those who loved her fruitlessly.

Rosa's return to college coincided with a new direction in Sarah's life too. She had been promised a new lease of life after the successful heart operation and she had been determined to make the most of it. She had always been interested in floristry and had taken a course at a further education college. Now she began full-time work at a city florist's.

Anne wanted to find a job too and she and Sarah had long talks about it. Sarah advised her to work part-time at first after being at home so long to get used to regular hours. 'You'll find it strange being told what to do at first,' she said, 'after arranging your day to suit yourself but if you don't like it you can always pack it in and try something else.'

John had not been aware of Anne's plans, not because she concealed them from him deliberately but he was out so much that he was never there when she discussed them with Sarah. The shock of Gerry's accident drove thoughts of everything else from their minds and it was not until an evening in Sarah's house that John heard anything about Anne's intentions.

They had finished their meal and were relaxing before walking to the parish club when Sarah said casually, 'I think I've seen just the job for you, Anne. Vernon's want people for three evenings a week, six till ten, in Long Lane.'

'But I've never worked in the pools,' Anne said.

'It's all right. You'll be trained and it's easy,' said Sarah.

John suddenly found his voice. 'What's this about a job? You don't need a job,' he said.

'I do. I want to get out. Meet people,' Anne said.

'You don't have to work for the pools for that,' John said. 'You can go to town, go and see your friends. Mum and Dad are always pleased to see you.'

'It's not the same. I'd just like to do something different.' She laughed. 'Widen my horizons.'

She was trying to soothe John by making a joke but he sneered, 'Filling pools envelopes? Very life enhancing.'

Joe and Sarah were irritated by his tone and Joe said quietly, 'I think it's Anne's choice.'

'Of course it is,' Sarah said. 'I really enjoy my job and our Eileen says she can't imagine not working. All the younger women among her friends have jobs. Good jobs too.'

'What's that to me?' John snorted. 'Anne doesn't need a job. I can keep my wife as I said I would when we got married.' His face was red with anger and his voice loud. Joe's face also grew red and his lips tightened.

Before he could speak, Anne said quickly, 'What's that got to do with it? Joe can keep Sarah and Martin can keep our Eileen but they can still enjoy having a job.'

John realised too late the implications of what he had said and used Anne's intervention to cool his temper and say gruffly, 'I'm just old-fashioned, I suppose.'

'Old-fashioned? You're prehistoric, John,' Sarah exclaimed, laughing, and John managed to smile at his sister.

None of them wanted an open quarrel and when Joe suggested another drink before they went to the club they accepted and were careful not to mention the subject of Anne's job for the rest of the evening.

As soon as Anne and John reached home the quarrel was resumed. John seemed to regard it as an insult and a disgrace to him that Anne felt she needed to earn and Anne found it impossible to explain why she wanted to work outside her home.

'Going out to work for a few shillings as though I can't provide all you want,' John raged. 'What are people going to think?'

'They'll think I should be working anyway,' Anne retorted. 'Most women do when their children are grown up and they haven't got so much to do.'

'Yes, if they need the money,' John said. 'But you don't. What do you want that I can't give you?'

'I want a bit of independence,' Anne said wearily. 'Can't you understand?'

'No, I can't,' John snapped. 'The kids might be grown up but they still need you. They need meals cooked for them and the house cleaned and the clothes washed. I think you've got more than enough to keep you occupied.'

'And waiting on you,' Anne said. 'Don't worry, I'll still be the family skivvy. You won't suffer.'

'That's uncalled for,' John said angrily. 'Even thinking about a flaming job has changed you. Anyway, it's a daft idea and you can forget it.'

Anne drew in her breath with anger and disbelief. 'Now I will get a job,' she declared. 'I wasn't completely decided before but I'm not

192

going to be dictated to by you. Like over the driving lessons. I'll earn some money and I'll take them.'

'Earn some money?' John echoed. 'The money was there for driving lessons if you wanted it.'

'Yes, but you didn't want me to take lessons, did you? What did you say when I suggested it? You needed the car for work and after that you could always drive me wherever I wanted to go. The truth was you didn't want me to be independent or to drive your precious car.'

'But it wasn't the money,' John said. 'You're making out now I begrudged the money, saying you'll earn your own. You know the money was there if you wanted to take the damned lessons.'

'Yes, but it was your money and I wouldn't take it knowing you didn't want me to have the lessons,' Anne said. 'If it's my own money I can please myself.'

'What do you mean, my money?' John roared. 'When have we ever had mine and thine with money? You did your share by looking after the family and I did mine by earning the money but it was always *ours*. What's got into you?'

'You don't understand,' Anne cried. 'You're too thick to see what I mean.' She was sorry that she had mentioned the driving lessons and surprised herself by her bitterness about them. She had not even realised that she felt a grievance until the quarrel had brought it out, but now, in the way of quarrels, many old grievances came to the surface.

'It was going to Ireland on your own that's put these ideas into your head,' John said. 'Going off without me like that. I should have known what would happen once all the Fitzgeralds got their heads together. I'd be the monster that wasn't good enough for their dear baby sister.'

'We had more important things than you to talk about,' Anne said. 'But you think you're always the centre of attention, don't you?'

'I know what your family think about me. They've never forgiven me for the bad time you had after Julie was born.'

'Don't talk rubbish,' Anne said. 'That's only your guilty conscience. There was a medical reason for that. It was an illness. And what about you? The way you tried to make our Joe look small tonight.'

'I didn't,' John said. 'I only said I could keep my wife and that's the truth. Nothing for him to take the huff about.'

'You made out that Sarah had to work,' Anne said hotly. 'But you're always the same, blundering in saying what *you* think, never mind if it hurts other people.'

'That's not true. I'm very tactful. That's why I'm a good negotiator.'

'Tactful!' Anne exclaimed. 'Were you tactful with Peggy Burns years ago, sounding off that we shouldn't have bombed the Japanese when you knew the way Michael Burns had come home from the Jap prison camp? Four and a half stone and destroyed in mind as well as body. No wonder she went for you.'

John stared at her in astonishment. 'But that was years ago,' he said. 'Good God, Gerry was only a baby.'

'Yes, and you haven't changed,' Anne said, swiftly changing ground. 'I could think of lots of examples. You're always sure that you're right and everyone else is wrong and you have to be in charge.'

John's temper reached boiling point and he jumped to his feet and banged on the table. 'There's no arguing with you,' he shouted. 'I *was* right about the atom bomb. You know I was. You said it yourself.' Neither of them had heard the door open but Laura suddenly arrived in the kitchen. She was horrified to see her father leaning over her mother, shouting and banging on the table while her mother looked up at him.

'Leave her alone!' she yelled, dashing over to put her arm round her mother.

'Mind your own bloody business,' John shouted back and Anne twisted away from Laura's arm.

'It is my business,' Laura retorted. 'She's my mother. I'm not going to let you bully her.'

'Don't interfere, Laura,' Anne said. 'This is between me and your father. Go and make a pot of tea – and shut the scullery door after you.' Laura looked at her with disbelief and reproach but she went into the scullery and shut the door.

John said bitterly, 'I'm even treated with contempt by my own children and we know whose fault that is, don't we?'

'Yes, your own,' Anne said swiftly.

'You have to have the last word, don't you?' John said savagely and as Anne simply looked at him with raised eyebrows he suddenly flung away. 'To hell with it,' he muttered. 'I'm going to bed.' He went out without saying goodnight and slammed the door behind him.

Laura was standing in the scullery struggling against giving way to tears. She was angry with her father but even more she felt bitterly hurt by her mother's rejection of her. She heard the slammed door then silence and she peeped cautiously into the kitchen.

Her mother was sitting at the table, her chin cupped in her hand, and Laura was unable to see her face. Resentment at being rejected by her mother struggled with her feeling of protective love for her and love won. She went to stand beside her and touched her gently on the shoulder. 'Are you all right, Mum?' she asked.

Anne turned her head and smiled at her. 'Yes, love. I'm sorry you walked in on that. It's rare for Dad and me to quarrel like that.'

'Yes, because you always give in to keep the peace,' Laura said indignantly but her mother shook her head.

'You've got it all wrong, love.' Anne stood up. 'Did you make the tea?'

'Oh no. I forgot,' Laura exclaimed and they went into the scullery together in complete accord.

Chapter Sixteen

John was amazed by the quarrel and the bitterness Anne had shown. All the following day he brooded on it and was brusque and short-tempered with his colleagues. What's got into her? he wondered. We never disagree. But then he thought uneasily of Anne's comments about Peggy Burns and the driving lessons. He felt that Anne had been as surprised as he was when her comments suddenly erupted but she must have been brooding on these things for years and said nothing about them.

Women, he thought in disgust. She goes on one holiday without me and suddenly she's full of talk about wanting to be independent. And the cheek of our Sarah looking for a job for Anne and then Joe putting in his penn'orth about it being Anne's choice. I'm glad I said that about being able to keep my own wife because it's the truth. I know teachers are paid peanuts and Sarah needed to work but Anne doesn't.

Laura was delighted that her mother had stood up for herself, as she saw it, and hoped she would soon find a job. She's given in to him for too many years just to keep the peace, she thought, unaware how often Anne had humoured her to avoid conflict.

John confidently expected that Anne would drop the idea of a job now that she knew how he felt about it and he arrived home at six o'clock prepared to behave as though the quarrel had never happened. Gerry, now walking with a stick, arrived home at the same time but only Julie was in the house.

She took a meat and potato pie from the oven and served three portions. 'Laura's working late and Mum's gone out,' she explained. 'She's gone with Auntie Sarah to Vernon's in Long Lane.'

Gerry saved John from having to ask by saying, 'Vernon's? Why have they gone there?'

'Part-time jobs have been advertised,' Julie said. 'Mum's gone to apply and Aunt Sarah's gone for moral support.'

She laughed and Gerry said without surprise, 'Good on her. I hope she gets it.'

'It's only three evenings a week, six till ten,' Julie said, 'but it'll sort of ease Mum in gently to working again.'

John had been silent but now he said sharply, 'Your mum has never stopped working. How do you think this house has run so smoothly?'

'I know, Dad,' Gerry said. 'But she must get bored rigid stuck here on her own all day. She'll enjoy having a job as long as she doesn't take too much on.'

John was glad that neither Anne nor Laura was present to hear the conversation but he was fuming. For Anne to go off to apply for the job without a word to him, knowing how he felt, convinced him that it was a deliberate insult.

She's done this to defy me and I'm not having it, he thought angrily, but when Anne and Sarah returned excited and happy because Anne had been accepted it was impossible for him to say anything.

'They were only taking a small number of inexperienced people,' Anne said, 'and I was the last one. There were crowds of women in the entrance hall and I left Sarah and went over to a little group to ask what we had to do.

'Suddenly this woman swooped down on us. She was as thin as a lath with jangling bracelets but she was very nice. She called to the commissionaire, "No more inexperienced ladies, Mr Hanley, after this. Only experienced. Come along, darlings." I was swept off with the others into a room and we were given forms to fill in.'

'I was still standing by the door like one of Lewis's and suddenly she was gone,' laughed Sarah. 'It was like a madhouse.'

'But what a laugh,' said Anne. 'There were six of us and they just left us to fill in the forms. I answered the questions truthfully but the woman next to me seemed to make up her answers as she went along. She asked me to check her form and according to the dates on it she'd started work when she was five years old. When I told her, she said she was just trying to knock a few years off.'

'Tell them about the woman and the carrots,' Sarah said. 'I tell you, Anne, you'll see life if you go there to work.'

'We were all looking at each other's forms and one woman had said that she had six children. Someone said she shouldn't have put that down because they'd think she would often be off and she was quite indignant. "I'm not denying my children for no job," she said. "If these don't want me I'll go and clean carrots in Hartley's but I'm not denying my kids."'

They were all laughing and Anne looked so happy, her cheeks flushed and her eyes sparkling, that for a moment John felt a twinge of doubt about his opposition to the job. The next moment wounded pride made him say harshly, 'And what about you? If this falls through, will *you* go and scrape carrots? Anything for a job, I suppose.'

Everyone except Anne began to speak at once. Gerry said indignantly, 'Hold on, Dad.'

Julie was saying, 'But Mum's *got* the job.'

Sarah was glaring at John. 'It's only twelve hours a week, for God's sake,' she said angrily. 'I don't know what all the fuss is about.'

'It's the thin end of the wedge,' John declared.

Anne ignored him and when Gerry asked about the pay, she told him it was twelve shillings a night, three shillings an hour. 'But don't forget they'll have to train me,' she said.

'And no matter how little it is, it's something you've earned yourself,' said Sarah. 'It's a toe in the door, too. You'll enjoy it, Anne.'

'I'm sure I will. I really liked those women tonight and the Vernon's people were so nice.'

John could bear no more and banged out into the hall but no one seemed to notice that he was going. Laura was coming in the front door and he said savagely, 'I hope you've brought champagne. Your mother's celebrating earning twelve shillings a night.' He rushed up the stairs while Laura stared after him open-mouthed.

She went into the kitchen and said, 'Hi. What's happened? Why all the hilarity?'

'Mum's got the job in Vernon's,' Julie said eagerly. 'Isn't it fab?'

Laura kissed her mother and said with delight, 'Congratulations, Mum. I'm made up. When do you start?'

'Next Tuesday. I seem to be making a lot of fuss. It's only twelve hours a week, three shillings an hour.'

'Of course you're not making too much fuss,' Sarah said stoutly. 'It's the first job you've applied for and you've got it. Think of all those other women there who didn't.'

Laura said nothing about her father's comment but later she said to Gerry, 'How did dear Papa take this?'

'Didn't seem too pleased,' he told her cheerfully. 'I think it was the pay he didn't like. He'll probably be outside there with a banner next week.' He laughed heartily.

Laura smiled but said seriously, 'Three bob an hour's not bad for a clean, light job and she'll be sitting down.'

'Twelve bob a night. It'd buy six pints and a packet of fags. Not bad at all,' said Gerry with a grin.

'Anyway, the money doesn't matter,' said Laura. 'What matters is that Mum is doing what *she* wants to do for a change instead of running after everyone else and fitting in with them.'

Although the family decided that the pay was unimportant, to John it added to his sense of injury. He had stayed upstairs nursing his grievance until Sarah had gone home but when he and Anne were alone later he burst out, 'I can't understand you. You'll leave your home and fall out with me for thirty-six shillings a week. Good God, are you mad? I'm earning a thousand pounds a year and it's there for you in our joint account. You've only got to draw it as you need it.'

'It's not the money. I just want to see if I can do a job. Can't you see that, John?' She spoke mildly but John refused to be placated.

'No, I can't see it. I blame our Sarah. Getting you to neglect your family for a few shillings and some mad idea of independence. I've always been proud that I could provide for my family.'

Anne suddenly lost her temper. 'That's the rub, isn't it? For once I'm doing what I want to do, not what suits your image of yourself. And saying I'm neglecting my family! You're the one who's mad. I'm going out for a few hours in the evening when my work here is done. I'm entitled to that, aren't I? You're out often enough. I could have done it without telling you and you'd never have noticed. Anyway, I'm not going to discuss it any more.'

'I go out for good reason, to do things that need to be done,' John exclaimed. 'Don't compare my work with this crazy idea.'

Anne turned her head and looked at him with weary contempt. 'I can see I'm wasting my time,' she said. 'You're too selfish and conceited to be able to see anyone's view that doesn't agree with your own.'

John was taken aback. 'This isn't the last word on this and don't think it is,' he blustered but Anne walked into the scullery, leaving him fuming. The way she looked at me, he raged silently. It's gone far enough. I'll have to put a stop to it but he was at a loss to know how.

The subject was not mentioned again while John was at home and he still hoped that Anne would 'see sense', as he thought of it. There was a strained atmosphere while he was at home and he and Anne only spoke to each other when necessary. He knew that Anne hated discord and in the past she had always been willing to concede an argument to avoid it so he hoped that this would happen now.

Anne had no intention of giving way this time. On Sunday they were all at the grandparents' home for tea except John who had gone to the union headquarters for a meeting and Anne told Cathy and Greg about the new job. They were delighted because she was so pleased about it. Sarah and her family were also there, and although Anne had only said laughingly, 'John thinks I'm mad,' Sarah told them more about John's opposition.

Anne had confided to Sarah that she had had another row with John after she left but had not given her any details and now she was glad as Sarah declared that John was completely unreasonable. 'He had a cob on just because Anne wanted a few hours for herself,' she told her parents. 'You know, the great "I am – I can keep my family".'

'I think he lives in the past,' Cathy said apologetically to Anne.

'He had too much of his own way when he was young,' Sarah said. 'You spoiled him, Mum.'

Anne said nothing. She felt that his mother and sister were entitled to criticise John but the more they said, the more protective she felt towards him. Is it worth falling out with him over this? she wondered but when she recalled some of John's comments she felt fresh indignation.

'That last pay rise did it,' Sarah declared. 'It went to his head being on a thousand a year.'

Cathy said quietly, 'He's done very well but Mick has been very successful and it hasn't made him throw his weight about.'

Anne was grateful to her father-in-law when he said, 'Let's be fair. Until the war married women were not employed in most jobs and professions. Women were expected to leave work when they married and stay at home with their families and most were happy to do so. John just hasn't moved with the times.'

'But, Dad, this is nineteen seventy,' Sarah protested. 'And anyway, the point here is that this is what Anne wants to do and John thinks he has the right to veto it.'

'Remind John that I went to work when the children were young, Anne,' Cathy said, smiling. 'I went as a waitress for functions and I enjoyed every minute of it. The characters I met! And his father didn't object, in fact I got the VIP treatment when I came home. The cup of tea and the footstool for my feet, didn't I, Greg?'

'I remember,' Sarah said. 'And you used to bring home cake and sweets and little pots of jam. I remember some of the tales you used to tell too.'

'Mum told us some tales even from just the interview,' Laura said. 'I'm sure you'll enjoy it, Mum.'

Anne smiled but said nothing and Greg tactfully changed the subject and talked about Gerry's prospects. He had been told at the hospital that he would be able to discard the stick within a few weeks as the foot was almost completely healed and he had applied for an office job.

'I'll still do the odd gig, filling in for someone,' he said. 'But I've had enough of the travelling around, roughing it. This will suit me better.' He said nothing about the physiotherapist with whom he had been out several times but Anne knew about her and smiled at him. She had not met the girl but liked what Gerry had told her about Margaret and hoped that they would settle down together.

Anne went to Long Lane to the office of the pools company at five thirty to be in good time and was nearly swept off her feet by hundreds of girls pouring from the building.

Laura had arrived home early to accompany her, saying that she was well in hand with her flexitime and it would be an ordeal for her mother to travel alone. Without her there, Anne might have lost her courage and decided to go home but Laura held her arm firmly and battled through the crowds to the gate.

'I didn't realise the day workers would still be here,' she said breathlessly. 'But never mind, Mum, you'll be all right now.'

Anne wondered briefly whether Laura had come less for her sake than to be sure that her father was not triumphant, but she thrust the thought away as Laura stopped another woman who hovered nearby and asked if she was starting on the evening shift.

'Yes, but I'm dead nervous,' the woman said. 'I haven't been out to work for eighteen years.'

'It's longer than that for me,' Anne said eagerly. 'Should we go in together?'

The woman agreed and Laura said bracingly, 'You'll be all right, Mum. There'll probably be others like you too. I'll go. Good luck. See you later.'

She kissed Anne and left and the woman said, 'Your daughter? It was good of her to come with you wasn't it?' Anne agreed, feeling ashamed of her earlier doubts about Laura's motives.

The woman said her name was Daisy and Anne introduced herself, then they went timidly into the big office. They were placed near each other at long desks at which the women sat facing each other. The system seemed to be that experienced clerks were alternated with the inexperienced women.

The woman next to Anne ignored her but said to a woman on the other side of the desk, 'I think they've got a cheek putting women who haven't a clue with us. Why should we train them when we're only getting the same money?'

The other woman smiled apologetically at Anne. 'Hi,' she said. 'My name's Bernie. What's yours?'

'Anne. Anne Redmond.'

Bernie said cheerfully, 'Don't take any notice of Janet. Someone had to train her but she likes a moan. Don't you?' she said to Janet.

Janet smiled at Anne. 'Nothing personal like,' she said. 'I just don't like to be put on.'

The supervisor walked up behind them. 'What's up?' she asked. 'Who's putting on you?'

'I'm just saying we shouldn't have to train the new ones. Nothing personal,' Janet said.

'It's manners to wait to be asked,' the supervisor said sharply. 'How long since you worked here anyway?'

'Seven years,' Janet told her, 'but before that I worked here since I left school.'

'You'll probably be a bit rusty then,' the supervisor said. 'You won't have time to train anyone. You'll be too busy keeping up.'

There were piles of coupons and envelopes stacked on each desk and the supervisor, who said her name was Audrey, bent over Anne. 'I'll show you what to do, love,' she said. 'Put these rubber thumbs on.' She showed Anne how to pick up the coupons and the envelope and place the coupon inside the envelope with smooth, quick movements.

Anne was naturally dextrous and soon managed the process. Audrey moved away to help others.

Anne was concentrating hard and her pile was going down but she was alarmed to see how swiftly the woman on her left worked. 'Don't worry,' she said, seeing Anne glance at her pile. 'I only left two years ago to have a baby. I'm hoping to come back full-time but this will keep my hand in.'

Audrey walked along checking the envelopes while another girl replenished the stacks of coupons and envelopes. The experienced women seemed able to talk without slowing down in their work but Janet had her head down working without speaking. 'Here,' she called breathlessly for more coupons but she had to go to the end of the desk for string.

Bernie leaned forward and winked at Anne. 'I bet she's never worked so hard in her life,' she chuckled. 'She's afraid you'll beat her.'

Daisy was almost opposite Anne and she seemed to be having a lot of trouble. She gave little screams at intervals as her coupons and envelopes flew into the air from her hands or her piles toppled over but Audrey was kind and reassuring. 'Take your time until you get into it, love,' she said. 'Don't worry what anyone else is doing. It's like riding a bike. Once you've done it you can always get back into it.'

Anne was torn. She knew that Daisy was looking at her piles diminishing, knowing that Anne was new too, and she wanted to slow down to encourage her but on the other hand she wanted to alarm Janet.

Before she had decided what to do, a voice over the tannoy told them that a break for fifteen minutes was starting. Everyone produced flasks of tea or bottles of orange juice and sandwiches. Anne was thankful that she had been advised to bring something by Sarah and she took out her flask and sandwiches.

Bernie stood up and stretched and Anne was surprised to see that she was plump although her face was thin.

'I'm on a diet,' she announced, taking a packet from her bag. It contained two Ryvita biscuits which parted with a loud sucking sound.

'In the name of God, what have you got in them?' someone asked.

'Nothing. I only buttered them,' Bernie said. 'I told you, I'm on a diet.' The women fell about laughing.

'Only buttered them – with half a pound of butter,' someone laughed but Bernie took their teasing in good part.

Bernie and Janet had known each other slightly years ago but all the other women were strangers to each other yet Anne felt that by the end of the fifteen minutes they were all friends. Towards ten o'clock Audrey walked around with a small box handing each woman a wage packet containing twelve shillings.

'Why are we being paid nightly?' Janet asked.

'I don't know. They were just sent down,' Audrey replied.

'I don't like the sound of this,' Janet said as soon as she had moved away. 'I know this is only temporary but paid by the night! Doesn't look as if it'll last long.'

'Well, I'm not grumbling. I'm glad of it,' the woman on Anne's left said. 'My little girl lost one of her sandals in school and I had to use my family allowance for another pair for her. This'll get me through tomorrow. I'm made up.'

'I still think it's a bad sign,' Janet said.

'We'll just have to make the most of it while we've got it,' Bernie said. 'They wouldn't go through all this taking people on and making arrangements just for a couple of nights.'

Anne walked out with Daisy at ten o'clock feeling that if she enjoyed the other nights as much as this one, she would be happy. Daisy was not as cheerful. 'I couldn't get into that filling and one of them said we might be sorting and filling tomorrow. God, I'll be hopeless at that.'

'You don't know till you try,' Anne said. 'That one next to me, Janet, seems to think it'll finish any minute anyway.'

'I don't care if it does,' Daisy groaned but Anne thought privately that she would be very disappointed.

When she reached home John and Gerry were both out but she was warmly welcomed by the two girls. Julie made tea while Laura put a footstool for her mother's feet. 'You must have the VIP treatment like Nana,' she joked. 'How did it go?'

Anne displayed her wage packet and told the girls of some of the incidents. Then John arrived home. He and Anne were still stiff and monosyllabic with each other but he said quietly, 'Are you all right?'

'Yes, thanks,' Anne said briefly but she smiled at him.

Laura said quickly and defiantly, 'Mum enjoyed it, didn't you, Mum? You liked the women and the work was easy, wasn't it? Although that woman Janet sounds a bit of a moaner but I suppose she's harmless.'

She intended to make her father feel excluded and she was unintentionally abetted by Julie who brought John a cup of tea and said cheerfully, 'We kept up the family tradition, Dad. The footstool for Mum like Nana used to have after work.'

John had been about to respond to Anne's smile by asking about her evening but he turned away and picked up the *Echo*.

Anne, always sensitive to his moods, talked of other matters but when they were in their bedroom preparing for bed she told him about Daisy's difficulty with the work. 'If it had been like that for me,

I'd have given up, John, but I could keep up with the other women and I felt really proud of that. I know it must sound daft to you when I was only filling envelopes but when you're at home for a long time you lose your confidence and I just want to know that I *can* do it.'

John put his arms round her and kissed her. 'I still think it's wrong as a matter of principle,' he said. 'And I can't really understand what you mean but I can see it's important to you, love. I don't want us to fall out about it.'

Anne laughed. 'You know what you are? You're a dinosaur,' she teased him.

Anne again met Daisy at the gates on the next work night and as they went in Daisy said that she dreaded the evening. 'Sorting and filing,' she groaned but Anne assured her that it would be easy, as much to convince herself as Daisy.

'Bernie said if you can use the phone book you can do it,' she said.

'We haven't got a phone,' Daisy said.

Anne was relieved to find that she found the work easy after it had been explained to her by Audrey and even Janet said grudgingly, 'You done them all right.' Daisy was immediately in difficulties and Audrey returned to her time and again until even her patience grew thin. 'Don't you know your alphabet?' she exclaimed.

'It's a long time since I was at school,' Daisy said defensively.

The women on either side helped her too but when she went off to the toilet at the break, one of them said, 'God help the day girl on that desk. She's not even trying, just shoving them in anywhere.'

'Our friend here's doing well,' Bernie said, nodding at Anne.

Becca who sat on her left said encouragingly, 'Yes, and you're quick too. Have you done filling before?'

'No, never,' Anne said feeling a rush of confidence and pleasure. The fears that the job would soon end proved unfounded and, as the weeks went on, Anne found that the work came easily to her and she enjoyed it more and more. She also enjoyed the company of the other women and found their conversation endlessly interesting and sometimes very illuminating.

Daisy had not returned after the second evening and she had been replaced by a talkative young woman named Lorraine. 'Do youse have any trouble with your fellers about coming here?' she asked one night.

Anne thought with amazement that other men must agree with John until Becca on her left said, 'No, mine's very good. As long as the baby's fed and down and the other kids are in bed, he doesn't mind. And I make sure our dishes are washed up but he'll take his dinner out of the oven and even put his dishes in the sink.'

Anne listened astounded, wondering whether Becca was being sarcastic, but she realised that she was sincere when her story was capped by other women boasting of how good their men were to serve their own meal left prepared for them and even make their own tea.

God, what a selfish shower, Anne thought, realising how different were John's objections and counting her blessings when she thought of the treatment she received after work.

'I done a twilight shift at the factory near us before I come here,' Lorraine said. 'My feller had to stay in with the kids but I got home at ten past ten and he was right down to the club. I give him the money for a pint but a couple of nights me mam came to sit in and he still wanted his beer money off me. He's not getting none of this though. I told him. I spend it on food for his belly so he's not getting beer money as well.'

'So we might see you with a black eye one of these nights,' Bernie joked.

Lorraine said seriously, 'It wouldn't be the first one he's given me.'

John was the only one at home when Anne returned that evening and when he brought her a cup of tea, she told him about the conversation about husbands. 'So you see, this job has had one good effect, John,' she said laughing. 'It's made me count my blessings.'

He smiled. 'I always said you didn't appreciate me,' he joked but then more seriously he said, 'I think I was wrong about this, Anne. I can see you enjoy it and people seem to think it's all right for women to work. I don't. I think a stable society needs the woman as the homemaker and the man as the provider and it's greed to want more than the man can provide. I don't mean you,' he added hastily. 'Our family are grown up now but in general.'

'I see what you mean,' Anne said. 'But practically all of the women there are working because they need the money. I told you about the woman whose child had lost her sandal. Some of them are using it to ease them back to full-time work.'

'But why?' John said. 'Our Sarah worked but only for a few hours while her children were at school, but some women with very young families are working full-time. At one time people expected less. Everyone lived on what their husbands earned so no one had much more than anyone else and they were content.'

'I think some families couldn't have survived without the mothers working,' Anne said. 'But where a man had a decent job, his wife didn't work because she was looking after the family, but I think you hit the nail on the head about expectations.'

'It's a fact, Anne,' said John. 'Look at Moira. I was horrified when Tony told me the size of the mortgage they're taking on. I know they've both got good jobs but it means they'll both have to work to pay for that house and furnish it. And what if she has a baby? Will she let someone else bring it up?'

'All the young ones have the same idea, though,' Anne said. 'That's what I mean. Women below a certain poverty level have always worked just to keep their children fed, but now even if the man earns plenty they still want more and you can understand it. The jobs are there and all their friends have the same high standard of living.'

'Yes, but we're sowing the wind and we'll reap the whirlwind, Anne,' John said. 'How are children to grow up with no stable background, pushed from pillar to post, brought up by anybody but their mothers? A proper home is more important to kids than expensive toys and foreign holidays and it will be too late when people realise that.'

Anne looked thoughtful. 'We've had our cake and eaten it, I think, love,' she said. 'I was at home when the children were young because we could afford to live like that and now I've got a job I enjoy. I had the choice but there'll always be women who *need* to work, John.'

'I know,' he agreed. 'At the council meeting last night I was talking to an old fellow who's been on the council for years and we talked about women working. He said it's a political thing really. Well, not even that. Government policy under any party.'

'I don't understand,' said Anne, looking puzzled.

'He said many women worked for the first time during the First World War and some of them would have liked to carry on working but it didn't suit the government. There were so few jobs for men they couldn't afford to let women work. They made it a rule that women left work on marriage and where they couldn't enforce that they made it seem socially unacceptable to work. Manipulated people.'

'Including you,' Anne said dryly, but John chose to ignore her comment.

'Now there's full employment and women are needed, they're encouraged to work,' he said.

'Dear God and we think we make our own choices,' Anne exclaimed. 'We're just pawns in the game.'

Laura came through the room on her way to the scullery and John picked up some papers and went out into the hall.

'Did I interrupt something?' Laura said aggressively as she returned carrying hot milk, but Anne laughed.

'No, we were only talking politics,' she said. 'About the council and people who are on it with your dad.'

'I suppose he'll want to stand as an MP next,' Laura said.

'No, you have to compromise to become an MP and that Dad will never do.' She smiled and touched Laura's cheek. 'Any more than you will,' she said teasingly.

Chapter Seventeen

Moira's wedding was planned for early May and there was great excitement when the uncles in Canada decided that they would return home for the wedding and a visit to the family.

Eileen and Martin and their two sons were coming from Dublin and Maureen would also attend the wedding so it would be a reunion for the Fitzgerald family. It was arranged that Maureen and the unmarried brother from Canada, Terry, would stay with Anne and John, and the other brother Stephen and his wife Margaret and their two daughters with Sarah and Joe.

'The first time we'll all have been together since my dad died,' Anne said to Laura. 'It'll be better for Terry to stay here because he was engaged to Sarah at one time. They parted as friends when she decided to marry Joe so don't mention it to anyone, will you?'

'Of course not,' Laura said, flattered that her mother talked freely to her. 'Does Dad know?'

'Of course,' said Anne. 'We were all young together and Sarah is his sister.'

'And Uncle Joe's your brother,' Laura said. 'It seems strange, doesn't it? Brother and sister married to brother and sister. I could never work it out when I was little.'

'I don't see anything strange about it,' Anne said. 'Sarah and I worked together and we were friends so we knew each other's families.'

Cathy and Greg had offered hospitality to Eileen and her family, but a week before the wedding Cathy fell down stone steps and broke her ankle, so Eileen and Martin and their two boys went to stay with a relation of Martin's who lived in Seaforth.

Anne and Sarah booked a large room in a local hotel for the family reunion two nights before the wedding, with a buffet supper provided by the hotel. John collected Maureen earlier in the day and they were all relieved to see that she was not much worse than at Christmas.

Terry had also arrived and there was an emotional reunion between him and Maureen and Anne. Laura watched him curiously. He was a tall, muscular man, very tanned, with receding dark, curly hair and she thought he looked more like her Uncle Tony than her mother and Maureen and Joe.

Anne's hair was still dark and her face unlined but Maureen's face was marked with suffering and her hair grey. Terry hugged her, visibly upset, saying, 'Oh Mo, you look so like Mum.' He hugged Anne too and said, 'And you're like Mum as she used to be when we were little.' Laura thought he was tactless but his sisters were not offended. Maureen only smiled and said as she drew away and wiped her eyes, 'Wait till you see Anne's youngest, Terry. She's the image of what Mum must have been in her youth, in every way.'

Julie appeared at that moment and Terry stared then exclaimed, 'I can see what you mean, Mo.'

Julie smiled shyly and Laura stood by, ignored but feeling that she should be used to feeling excluded.

It was Maureen who finally noticed her and said gently, 'And don't you think that Laura's like John, Terry?'

Terry agreed and Maureen said with a smile, 'You young people will be fed up with us. It'll be nothing but matching up when we all meet again after all these years.'

She was quite right. At the gathering in the hotel the main topic was the likeness of the younger people to various members of the family. 'I feel as though I'm in the ring in the cattle market,' Laura muttered to Gerry.

'Cheer up. They'll have to finish with the topic sometime,' he murmured. 'Look at Dad. He's suffering as much as us.'

'I know. That's all that helps me to bear it,' Laura said and Gerry glanced sharply at her, uncertain whether she was making a joke or not.

Julie was the centre of attention as everyone commented on her likeness to their mother and soon it became too much for Julie. She whispered to Laura, 'I'm going to find the Ladies. Are you coming?'

They slipped away and as they went into the Ladies' Toilet they were confronted by a full-length mirror.

'Gosh, I'm glad to get away for a while,' Julie said but Laura said nothing. She was gazing, fascinated, at the reflections of herself and her sister.

'I didn't realise I look such a big horse beside you,' she exclaimed.

'Don't be daft. It's me that's small, not you that's big,' Julie said.

'But I look huge, and the size of my hands and feet compared to yours.' Laura went closer to the mirror and looked with disfavour at her tall figure and with envy at Julie's petite form and her small features with large brown eyes reflected there.

Julie's straight dark hair was long and thick, worn with a centre parting, and Laura fingered her own dark curls with disgust. 'Trust me to have curly hair when straight hair is all the fashion,' she said. 'And to be so hefty when people like Twiggy are fashionable.'

'You're not hefty. You're normal,' Julie insisted. 'I'm the freak. Size three shoes! I'll never be able to get fashionable shoes. You're just tall but you've got a lovely figure and normal size hands and feet.'

She went into a cubicle but Laura remained staring at her reflection, examining her face critically. Her skin was good and her dark blue eyes were large and fringed with dark lashes but she thought her high-bridged nose looked too large. With that and her determined chin she could see why Sean had said that she looked arrogant and sure of herself. Other people had hinted the same to her.

If they only knew, she thought. Inside I'm just jelly. Julie is much more confident than I am although she looks so timid.

The door opened and one of the Canadian cousins came in as Julie came out of the cubicle and began to wash her hands.

'Hi,' the girl said. She looked at Julie. 'I can tell you're a Fitzgerald – the Spanish look – but where do you come in?' looking past her to Laura.

'I'm the daughter of Anne, the youngest Fitzgerald, and this is my sister,' Laura said. 'Our name is Redmond.'

'I'm Rilla,' the girl said and grimaced. 'Called after Marilla the aunt in *Anne of Green Gables,* would you believe it? Stephen's my father.'

'I love that book,' Julie and Laura said together and they all laughed.

'Yeah, but I hate my name,' Rilla said. 'You don't look like sisters. Is your father called John?' and when Laura nodded, she said triumphantly, 'I thought so. I guessed because you're so like him.'

That's all I need, Laura thought, escaping into a cubicle. She wished that David or Rosa had come to the party but David was now into his finals and Rosa, though she had promised to come, had not arrived. She had left home a few months earlier to live in what she called an artists' colony near Lark Lane in the south end of Liverpool, much to her parents' distress.

'Her sensible phase didn't last long,' Sarah said to Anne. 'Now it's all flower power, make love not war.'

'Nothing wrong with those sentiments,' Anne said. 'But I can't see why she needs to leave home.'

'I'm afraid of what she'll get up to,' Sarah confessed. 'She's so easily influenced.'

'Never mind, she'll settle down one of these days,' Anne consoled her but Sarah said it was what would take place before that happened that worried her.

Only Moira's fiancé was at the party in addition to the family until late in the evening when Rosa appeared with a man. There was a stunned silence as they entered, Rosa in a long, handwoven kaftan with ropes of beads about her neck, flowers in her hair and hanging from her ears, and bare feet. She was completely at ease and said gaily, 'Hi, everyone. This is Naughton. He's American.'

Naughton raised his hand. 'Hi,' he said. His wild hair cascaded down his back and a luxurious growth covered his face so that he seemed to peer out as from undergrowth. He, too, wore a handwoven garment and a flower in his hair and his feet were bare.

Rilla waved an arm and said, 'Hi, babes.'

Sarah and Anne were the first to recover among the older people and went forward to greet the couple. Sarah tried to introduce them but Rosa only smiled vaguely at everyone and Naughton's attention seemed to be on the long tables of food at the back of the room.

Anne took them over to the food but Rosa dismissed the meat pies, ham rolls, spare ribs and chicken patties.

'We don't eat flesh,' she said grandly so Anne offered egg mayonnaise and salmon sandwiches or cheese. Rosa hesitated but Naughton was already filling his plate so Anne left them to help themselves.

'I think Naughton would have had all the meat stuff as well if he'd been alone,' Anne said to Sarah.

'Rosa's always fanatical about everything while the craze lasts,' she responded wearily. 'The state of her, Anne! I feel ashamed.'

'Why? She still looks fantastically pretty even in that get-up,' Anne said laughing.

John was looking at Rosa and Naughton with disgust. 'What the hell is it?' he said to Tony and he laughed.

'A caveman maybe, who doesn't believe in carrying a club.' Although Tony found them amusing John was outraged, particularly by Rosa.

'Just look at her. Bare feet! When I think that my grandfather Lawrie Ward, her great-grandfather, fought all his life so that there would be no barefoot children on the streets of Liverpool. And there's a girl from a good home with plenty of shoes walking around like that.'

'But that's the point, John. They're doing it from choice. The kids you're talking about were barefoot through poverty,' said Tony.

'It still annoys me. I'm glad my grandfather didn't live to see it,' John said stubbornly.

'Who's that?' Rilla asked Laura.

'My cousin Rosaleen. Your cousin too because her father is Joe Fitzgerald,' Laura said. 'She's a case. We were best friends when we were kids but I don't see so much of her now. She moved out to live in what she calls an artists' colony a few months ago.'

'Is she into flower power?' asked Rilla. 'There's a hippie commune near where we live full of people like that weirdo she's got in tow. All into free love. Is she?'

'I don't know,' said Laura, 'but her crazes never last. I think her mother was hoping she'd be back to normal before the wedding so she's been keeping quiet about this.'

'What are they like, her parents?'

'Couldn't be more conventional. They had family prayers until a few years ago. Their son's at Cambridge, a very quiet, clever fellow, David.'

'Sounds like a drip,' Rilla observed.

'No, he's not,' Laura said indignantly. 'He's all right. A good skin.'

'I guess that's why Rosaleen is way out. She's rebelling against them,' Rilla said and Laura laughed.

'No, it's just because she doesn't give a damn. She never has done. She does whatever takes her fancy at the time and she could get away with murder. And she *is* an artist. She sells her stuff and she went to the College of Art.'

Rilla seemed to lose interest in Rosa and was gazing about the room and Laura tried to edge away. I've had enough of this one she thought, with her opinions on everything and everybody, but Rilla was now looking at Julie who was talking to aunt Maureen.

'Proper little ray of sunshine, isn't she?' Rilla sneered. 'Like my flaming sister. They called her Joy and she thinks she has to live up to it. Real pain, she is. I suppose yours is the same.'

'No, she's not. We get on all right, Julie and I. My brother had an accident a while ago and we got much more matey while we were worried about him.'

'I can't stand my sister,' Rilla said frankly. 'Can't wait to see the back of her. Is that your brother over there, the fair fellow? What sort of an accident did he have?'

'He was the drummer in a group and they were coming back from a gig when they crashed the van. Two of them were killed and Gerry and another fellow badly injured but he's OK now.'

'He played in a group? Like the Beatles?' Rilla said, round-eyed.

'Not quite,' Laura said but Rilla insisted that Laura should introduce her to Gerry. She stayed with him, bombarding him with questions when she found that he knew members of groups like Gerry and the Pacemakers, the Moody Blues and Faron and the Flamingos.

Laura thankfully slipped away from them. A little of her would go a long way, she decided. Criticising everyone and *hating* her own sister!

Helen nervously spoke to Rosa before the end of the evening, asking her to look more conventional for the wedding. 'Twin set and pearls?' Rosa joked but Helen was unable to smile.

'Please, Rosa,' she said gently. 'It's Moira's day. You don't want to take all the attention away from her, do you?'

'I couldn't. She's the bride,' Rosa said, looking surprised, but she was fond of her quiet little aunt and could see that she had nerved herself to make the request so she said cheerfully, 'OK, Aunt Helen. I'll melt into the background. Promise.'

'You'd never do that, love. You're too pretty,' Helen said. 'But just a bit less – striking.'

Rosa's laughter pealed out. 'I'd better get rid of hairy Dan from Dingle too.' She looked down at her feet and said ruefully, 'I'll even wear shoes just for one day.'

Helen reached up and kissed her. 'I hope you didn't mind my asking. You're a good girl, Rosa.'

Rosa laughed again. 'Don't say that, Aunt Helen. You'll get me a bad name.'

Naughton was eating his way steadily through all the non-meat food on the buffet, including the sweets. Rilla had attached herself to Laura again and commented that Naughton behaved as though he had not seen food for a month. 'It's a wonder he can find his mouth through all that hair,' she said. Laura said nothing. She was determined not to agree with Rilla or to criticise the guests.

Helen told Sarah that Rosa had agreed to dress more conventionally for the wedding and even wear shoes. 'She was very good,' Helen said. 'Didn't mind at all that I asked her.'

'Thank God for that,' Sarah exclaimed. 'She always puts us in the wrong. This business of not eating meat or using leather. She makes us feel like heartless cannibals but I'm not depriving Joe of his roast dinner for her or anyone else.' She sounded so indignant and determined that Helen smiled.

'I didn't realise that was the reason for the bare feet. I suppose her principles are good.'

'Yes, but there are never any half measures,' Sarah said. 'We hoped she'd settle down after that Ricky business, but it didn't last.'

'It's her artistic temperament,' Helen consoled her.

The wedding morning was bright and sunny as the Redmond family prepared to leave for the church. Peter Cunliffe had arrived with David from Cambridge so he was with Julie while Terry was escorting Maureen. Gerry and Margaret and Anne and John paired off as they walked down the aisle of the church. Laura followed, feeling alone and conspicuous and sure that everyone was looking pityingly at her.

Only David and Laura of their generation were unattached. The Canadian girls were understood to have boyfriends at home and the Irish boys were too young. It doesn't matter for David, Laura thought bitterly. Everyone assumes that it's a man's own choice but I suppose I've been written off as an old maid.

There was a stir as Rosa appeared, drifting demurely down the aisle in a dress of floating green chiffon with a broad band of green chiffon in her auburn hair, but the main surprise was her escort. Neil walked self-consciously behind her wearing a dark suit and tie and followed her into the pew beside David.

Laura could see that David's shoulders were shaking with laughter and everyone was smiling broadly but suddenly the organ, which had been playing quietly, burst into the strains of 'Here Comes the Bride'.

Moira appeared wearing white lace and carrying roses, her plain face transfigured with happiness, followed by Dilly, and Jack's sister wearing blue taffeta. Jack stepped out to meet her, an adoring smile on his face, and they moved together to stand before the priest.

As the Nuptial Mass proceeded, Laura knelt, her hands gripped tightly together and her mind full of bitterness and envy. Will I ever kneel on the altar as a bride? she wondered. It was unlikely, she thought. She watched Moira and her new husband and looked around the church at other couples. Dilly glancing over at Andy and his beaming smile back, Margaret looking up at Gerry, Julie in a blissful dream as she knelt close to Peter. Even the older couples were smiling at each other drawn close by the words of the marriage service and the obvious happiness of the bride and groom. The other guests, friends of Moira and Jack, all seemed to be in pairs and Laura felt that she was the only one in the church who was unloved and unwanted.

I'm not jealous of Julie, she told herself, and I don't begrudge her or Moira their happiness but why is life so easy for some people and so hard for others? She glanced along the row at her father who knelt with his head flung back and his lips firmly closed. Why couldn't I have been born looking like Julie, she thought, with her easy nature, instead of being like *him*, with his Roman nose and his jaw and his talent for saying the wrong thing?

The congregation rose to their feet and with a sudden change of mood Laura thought defiantly, I don't care. At least I'm honest and I say what I think and what I know is the truth. If people don't like it, I can't help that.

The organist broke into the triumphant sound of the Wedding March as Moira and Jack began to walk down the aisle. Laura glanced behind her and saw David who winked at her and gave her a grin and suddenly she felt more cheerful. At least there was one person who understood her and liked her.

She had determined that she would avoid her cousin Rilla at the reception but she found it impossible. She was sure that Rilla would have attached herself to Gerry if Margaret had not been with him, and that she herself was only a substitute, but it was impossible to shake Rilla off.

She was still freely offering her opinion on everyone she met and annoying Laura by finding something derisive to say about everyone, including her hosts, Sarah and Joe. 'Makes me suspicious when people are so gushing,' she said, 'bending over backwards to welcome you. Makes you wonder what they're saying behind your back.'

'Would you rather they didn't welcome you?' Laura said sharply. 'And I can tell you neither of them are the sort to talk behind your back.'

'Ma and Pa and dear little Joy are lapping it up,' Rilla sneered. 'But me, I guess I've got a suspicious nature.'

'You've made that very clear,' Laura snapped.

Rilla was obviously annoyed. 'Yeah but I look at Sarah and Joe always so correct and *good* and I think, you're not all you seem. I know something about them.'

'What?'

'Terry, who's staying with you, he fancied Sarah when they were young, God knows why. They were engaged but he was taken prisoner of war and while he was away Joe moved in and Sarah sent Terry a "Dear John" letter. That's why Terry came out to Canada. So you see, Sarah and Joe are not so good after all.'

Laura was white with temper and she grabbed Rilla's arm and pulled her to a quiet corner. 'Listen,' she said. 'You've got the wrong end of the stick and I don't suppose it's the first time. It was a casual thing with Sarah and Terry, just a few dates before he was taken prisoner. It was Sarah and Joe that really fell for each other but Terry was writing to Sarah and she was writing back so everyone thought they were engaged. My mother told me about it.'

'But Joe still moved in while his brother's back was turned,' Rilla said.

'No, he didn't,' Laura said hotly. 'He wouldn't. My mum said they would have been married early in the war but Sarah and Joe waited all those years until Terry came home and they could sort it out with him. It turned out that he didn't really want to get married either. He wanted to go to Canada with a fellow he met in the prison camp.'

'Sounds a bit iffy to me,' Rilla said, unconvinced. 'People are not like that.'

'Joe and Sarah are but I wouldn't expect *you* to understand that,' Laura said but Rilla failed to rise to the challenge.

'Terry came over with a fellow from the camp, did he?' she said thoughtfully. 'I've often wondered about him. Why he never married.' She laughed. 'Now I've seen Sarah I know it wasn't because he was still carrying a torch for *her.*'

Laura felt that she could stand no more of her cousin and with an abrupt, 'See you,' she turned and stalked away. She was storming through a side room when her elbow was gripped and she turned to see her Uncle Terry laughing down at her. 'Hi. Why the thunder-clouds?' he said.

'It's that Rilla. She's got a tongue like a viper,' Laura exploded. 'She says Sarah and Joe—' She stopped, suddenly realising that Terry was involved too.

'Go on. What about Sarah and Joe?' Terry asked.

Laura said recklessly, 'If you want to know, she said Joe did the dirty on you with Sarah while you were a prisoner and she wouldn't believe me when I told her she was wrong.'

'You knew all about it then?'

'Mum told me when you were coming to stay with us so I wouldn't put my foot in it with you.' She smiled ruefully. 'It's a habit I have.'

'Let's sit down here,' Terry suggested, 'and you can tell me what Anne said.'

'She said that you and Sarah were just friends before you were taken prisoner but on your last leave you took Sarah's photo back with you and everyone linked you together. Mum said she was Sarah's best friend and she should have known she was really in love with Joe but they didn't tell anyone. Only your mother guessed and she told Sarah not to hurt you.'

Laura stopped because Terry was sitting with his head bent and his hand over his eyes, but he said huskily, 'It's all right, kid. Just thinking about my mum. Go on.'

'Mum said Maureen knew but she never said anything and the rest of the family only knew when you came home and you wanted to go to Canada with your friend.'

'Your mum seems to have explained it very well,' Terry said. 'You know, when I was young, everything was a laugh with me, even with Sarah. I liked her, I even fancied her, but it was kid's stuff. Getting engaged or married was something far in the future and we thought we had all the time in the world to sort ourselves out. It all changed with the war, although I didn't change much at first. It was all a big laugh proposing and Sarah told me to get up and stop being daft.'

'Sarah didn't take it seriously then either?' Laura said.

'Lord, no. It was her mum really who gave me the photo when I went in to say goodbye to her. She was a smashing woman, Mrs Redmond.'

'She still is. She's my nana,' Laura said. 'She would have been here today if she hadn't broken her ankle.'

'Of course. I must go and see her before we go back,' Terry said. He grinned. 'I fancied her for a mother-in-law.'

'So you didn't fall out with Sarah and Joe when you came home?'

'No. It was funny really. I thought I should marry Sarah because she'd waited so long but I really wanted to go to Canada with my mate Frank. Sarah and I soon sorted it out. I went to Canada and Sarah married Joe and it suited all of us. I tell you though, kid, I respect them for keeping quiet like they did.'

'Mum said that everyone was surprised and yet not surprised in a way because Sarah and Joe seemed so right together. Your dad was upset at first about Sarah but Maureen told him your mum knew before she died and gave them her blessing so he was happy about it then. He was very fond of Sarah.'

'Mo,' Terry said sadly. 'She held up the house for all of us. I can't bear to see the way she is.'

'But she accepts it,' Laura said. 'She sees it as another way of helping those poor refugees by offering up her pain for them.'

Terry hugged her. 'I thought you said you were tactless but you've said all the right things to me and none better than that.' He kissed her and pulled her to her feet. 'Come on, kid. We'll get a drink and find Maureen.'

As they walked out of the room, they came face to face with Rilla and Terry said cheerfully, 'I believe you've been discussing ancient history with Laura. It's like she told you. It was a misunderstanding that was easily cleared up and Joe and Sarah behaved very honourably.' He nodded to Rilla and they walked on. 'I couldn't resist that,' he said with a laugh. 'Hope I haven't dropped you in it, kid.'

'Don't worry. I'll see as little of her as possible from now on,' Laura said.

In spite of her determination to avoid Rilla, she found that she was engaged to take her round the clubs with Gerry one evening. 'Can't Margaret go with you?' she asked Gerry but he said she had an evening clinic.

'Anyway, she's our relation, worse luck,' he said.

'I don't know how she managed this. You're too soft, Gerry.'

'She's a strong-minded woman,' Gerry grinned. 'Believes in equality, Burns her bra, all that sort of thing. Something like you.'

'Me?' Laura exclaimed. 'I don't believe in all that.' She laughed. 'I agree with Grandma. She used to say the man wasn't born who was *her* equal, or like Miss Jenkyns in *Cranford* who felt the same.'

'I'll take your word for that,' Gerry said with a grin. 'But you'll come, won't you, Lol? I can't get out of it and I couldn't cope with her on my own.'

Laura agreed cheerfully. She felt much happier since talking to Terry and felt that in him she had made a friend.

When Joy found out about the visit to the clubs she demanded to be included, and as it annoyed Rilla, Laura readily agreed. In the course of the tour round pubs and clubs, Gerry met many musicians he knew who willingly chatted up the Canadian girls and gave them their autographs. After the clubs closed, Gerry took them to a cafe in Dale Street where many of the groups went for a meal and there they met Peter Taylor, now lead singer with a famous group.

'We formed a group called the Merrymen,' Peter told the girls. 'We had some good laughs, didn't we, Gerry?'

'Yeah, those rehearsals in your cellar,' Gerry laughed. 'Good job the house was solid.'

Peter introduced them to a friend of his. 'Phil Casey, the quiet man,' he said.

The Canadians lost interest in Phil when they heard that he was only a bank clerk, but Laura was anxious to disassociate herself from them and stood aside from the group to talk to him.

'I'm sorry, we've interrupted your meal,' she said to him. 'I feel ashamed. They're so pushy but being relations we've got to stick with them.'

'They're all right. Just young and new to this scene,' he said quietly. 'Don't worry. Any more of that curry and we'd have flames coming out of our mouths.'

Gerry had unwisely told Rilla that Peter's parents lived in the house in Magdalen Street where the Fitzgeralds had lived and that was where the Merrymen had practised.

'Do you still live there?' Rilla demanded.

Peter said easily, 'No. I'm living in sin in Princes Park but my parents are still there.'

'And you're still in touch with them?' Joy asked.

He said that he was and the girls immediately began to press him to arrange for them to be shown round the house. 'My dad and Terry are never done talking about it,' Rilla declared. 'Gee, we can't come to Liverpool and not go over it. This meeting was fate.'

Laura was cringing with embarrassment and she muttered to Phil, 'Oh, why didn't Gerry keep his mouth shut? He knows what they're like.'

'No harm done,' Phil said. 'Peter won't mind and his parents might enjoy showing someone from your family round the house, especially relations from Canada.' He smiled at her. 'Don't worry so much.'

Peter promised to arrange the visit and his parents extended the offer to all the visitors from Canada. Terry, Stephen, Margaret and the two girls were shown round the house and given tea by Peter's mother and they returned full of praise for the Taylor family.

'They've hardly made any changes,' Terry said. 'And they told us that the basement that Dad fixed up as an air-raid shelter was used by Peter and his group to practise down there and it was so solid that they hardly heard them.'

'We made some noise too,' Gerry said with a grin. 'They were very good to us, Pete's mum and dad. Mrs Taylor used to bring us coffee and sandwiches and Mr Taylor drove us about in his van to gigs until Peter got his licence.'

Laura said nothing. She thought of Phil Casey's comments and decided that he was right. She worried too much.

One evening Terry came out to the garden where Laura was weeding, carrying drinks for both of them. They had become very friendly since the wedding and Laura felt that she would miss him – the visitors were due to leave within a week – although she would be pleased to see Rilla and Joy go.

'Come and sit down and have a break,' Terry said and they sat together on the garden bench. 'I'm glad I came home,' he told her. 'It's been great to see my brothers and sisters and get to know the younger generation, especially you, Lol.'

'Thanks,' Laura said gruffly. 'I'm glad to know you. You were just names to me before.'

'I'll have a lot to think about when I get back but I love Canada. God's own country, as far as I'm concerned.' Terry said reflectively. 'I was glad to see Maureen particularly and now I've seen more of her I agree with you. She's accepted the illness and she's very happy where she is. Her religion always meant a lot to her – too much, I sometimes thought.'

Laura looked at him in surprise and he said, 'I used to think it ruined her life but I don't know. She was in love with a fellow for years and he was with her but he'd been tricked into a marriage when he was young, so as far as they were concerned he was a married man and out of bounds.'

'But if he was tricked into marriage?'

'They didn't see it like that,' Terry said. 'To them he'd made a solemn vow before God, till death us do part.'

'So they parted?' Laura said.

'Oh no. They tried to but they cared too much for each other. They saw each other but they never lived together. It'd be hard for your generation to believe, I know. They were truly in love all those years but they never, er, it was never consummated, as they say.'

'What happened?' Laura asked.

'He died. His wife was living with another woman and never even came to the funeral. And Mo ruined her life for a marriage like that,' he said bitterly.

They were both silent for a while, until Laura said quietly, 'It would be the only way for Maureen though. She's very strong where her principles are concerned, and if the man was the same, they wouldn't have been happy living any other way.'

'I can see that now,' Terry said. 'But it seems such a waste. They were really and truly in love. Like Sarah and Joe. We made the right decision there after the war.' He smiled. 'I suppose Rilla told you I was a queer.'

Laura's head jerked back involuntarily and Terry said, 'I can see she has but it's not true, kid. Frank was a good friend to me in the camp and I don't think I'd have got through without him. I was wet behind the ears and he'd knocked about the world and knew the ropes.'

'I didn't believe her,' Laura protested.

Terry nodded and went on, 'He'd lived in Canada and wanted to go back after the war. We often talked about it and I wanted to go there too but I didn't know how Sarah would take the idea. I still thought she might want to get married, you see.'

'But didn't you write to each other?' Laura asked. 'Couldn't you have sorted it out by letter?'

'It wasn't as simple as that. We were only allowed one small letter and we had to crowd a lot into it. And then it went through several hands before Sarah got it. Try baring your soul on a postcard.' He laughed. 'Of course at first some of my letters went to Mum with just messages for Sarah and when she wrote to me it all had to be family news and everything in the garden was lovely. Keeping my spirits up, she thought, I suppose.'

'But you sorted it out to suit everyone in the end,' Laura said. Terry nodded and they sat in companionable silence until he said abruptly, 'I'll tell you something, kid, that I've never told anyone else. I suppose people think it's strange that I never married.'

'*I* don't,' Laura said. 'I don't think everyone who doesn't marry is a queer.'

Terry grinned. 'Well said, kid. I've never married because of Maureen and Chris and Sarah and Joe really. They showed me what it can be like when two people really love each other and I'm not going to settle for less. I've never met anyone I feel like that about and who feels the same about me and until I do I'll stay single.'

The light was fading and as they sat together in the dusk confidences seem to come easily and Laura said softly, 'I feel the same as you. Even if we never meet the right one, I don't think we should marry anyone just to be married.'

'No. I want a wife and family as much as any man and you'd make a good wife for the right man. Nothing like a happy marriage,' Terry said, 'but a bad one can be hell on earth. Better stay single all our lives than that, kid, and perhaps drag children down with us.'

With the darkness a chill breeze had sprung up and they stood up stiffly and collected Laura's tools. 'I stopped the weeding all right, kid,' Terry said and Laura smiled.

225

She remained in the same dreamy state for the rest of the evening although visitors came and went and when she was finally alone in her bedroom she was able to think over her conversation with Terry. I didn't even know I felt like that about marriage until we talked, she thought wonderingly, but it's true.

Another thought struck her. Terry had talked about Sarah and Joe's happy marriage and Maureen's love affair but he had said nothing about her parents' marriage. Could it be that he saw theirs as one of the bad marriages? Her common sense told her that unless her parents were keeping up a false front for the sake of their children their marriage could not be described as hell on earth. But it was a mistake and they should never have married, she decided.

Chapter Eighteen

Eileen, Martin and their sons went back to Dublin at the end of the week and a few days later the Canadian relatives left. Anne was upset to see her family go and Laura parted from Terry with regret. She promised to write to him but she flatly refused to correspond with Rilla.

'I can't see the point,' she said bluntly. 'It's not as if we have anything in common.'

'But you could send me news about what's happening in the Liverpool clubs. Tell me about all the groups,' Rilla said.

'And then she could brag to all her friends,' Joy said slyly.

Rilla turned on her but before she could speak Anne said hastily, 'Laura's not much of a letter writer but Julie'll write to you, won't you, Julie?'

Julie looked startled but she agreed and Joy said indignantly, 'Julie should write to *me*. We're the same age.'

Gerry had come in to say goodbye to the visitors and Rilla grabbed his arm. 'You'll write to me, won't you, Gerry? Tell me all about all those friends of yours we met. If you give me Peter Taylor's address I'll write to him too.'

'He's, erm, he's moving,' Gerry said but Rilla was undeterred.

'I'll write to his mother's house then,' she declared. 'She can send it on.'

Her parents had heard the last few words and Stephen said mildly, 'Don't be pestering people to write to you, Rilla.'

Her mother added, 'You know it always ends in tears.'

Rilla immediately threw such a tantrum that they were all relieved when Tony arrived. Joe had driven them over to Anne's house and

227

soon the Canadian relations were all packed into the two cars with their luggage and driven off to the airport by Joe and Tony.

'Strewth, what a performance,' Gerry said as they all went back into the house after waving them off. 'Do you think that girl's a ha'penny short of a bob? She doesn't behave like a girl of twenty.'

'No, she's just thick-skinned and fond of her own way,' Laura said contemptuously.

'You might have promised to write to her, Laura,' her mother said reproachfully. 'She is family, after all.'

'And now Gerry's got let in for it,' John said.

'And me with Joy,' Julie added.

'You could both have refused like I did,' Laura said. 'Why should we write to them? She knows I don't like her and she can't stand me either. She was just trying to use me. Mind you, I haven't found anyone she has a good word for anyway.'

'I have,' Gerry said with a grin. 'Peter Taylor. I'd better warn him because his girlfriend is mad jealous. She'll tear his head off if letters start coming for him.'

'It was lovely to see our Stephen and Margaret,' Anne said, wiping away a tear. 'Although they deserve better children than those two. And our Terry! He hasn't changed a bit. I'll miss him out of the house.'

The evening pools work had finished before the visitors came and with a glance at her father Laura said, 'You'll have to find a day job, Mum, to take your mind off it.'

'I intend to,' Anne said, smiling.

John ignored Laura's challenging glance and only said, 'Terry seems to have done well, even after splitting up with Frank. He said they parted good friends. It was just that Frank got itchy feet, he said, and he didn't want to leave Ontario.'

'I should think he'd be glad to see the back of Frank from what I remember of him,' Anne said. 'I'll never forget when Terry came home. He'd been a prisoner of war for five years and we couldn't wait to see him and this Frank arrived with him. He wasn't the retiring sort either. He pushed in, introducing himself and trying to take over.'

'But who was he?' Julie asked.

'A friend of Terry's from the camp. His father had been killed in the Blitz and he had no home so Terry brought him to ours,' Anne said. 'He was a pain. Eileen couldn't be civil to him, he annoyed her so much, but he was thick-skinned. Now if *he* was Rilla's father I could understand it.'

Laura hugged the knowledge to herself that Terry had told her all about his business and his partner Frank in their frequent conversations, although they had never again talked as intimately as on that evening in the garden.

Cathy's foot had been slow to heal and Laura visited her frequently. Even to her grandparents, though, she never talked of Terry's disclosures.

Letters arrived for Julie and Gerry and were replied to briefly and soon the memory of Moira's wedding and their visitors faded as other events crowded upon them.

Laura had been taking driving lessons, helped by Gerry who often took her out for practice, and her test was due in August. She could think of nothing else and snapped at John when he told her not to worry – she could always take it again.

'Thanks for the vote of confidence,' she said. 'You seem quite sure I'll fail.'

'Don't be so unreasonable,' Anne said. 'Dad was only trying to make you feel better,' but John had slammed out of the room.

Laura was shaking with nerves when the day of the test came and as she drove out of the test centre the front wheel of the car touched the kerb. She felt quite despairing. Her father was right, she thought. She had failed and he would probably gloat and say, 'I told you so.' She drove without a care, anxious only to complete the test and escape. She was astounded when the examiner told her that she had passed.

'But I touched the kerb,' she stammered.

'I know you did but you're an excellent driver,' the examiner said calmly.

There was great jubilation in the family at the news and Anne and John told Laura something which they had been keeping as a surprise.

She would be twenty-one in September and had refused a party which her parents had offered but they told her now that they had heard of a second-hand Mini for sale, which was in very good condition, and if she liked it they would buy it for her twenty-first birthday present.

'A car!' Laura gasped. 'I thought I might get a wristwatch. What colour is it?'

'Typical woman's question, that,' John said but he was smiling. 'It's red. What colour would you like?'

'Red,' Laura said promptly.

'We haven't done anything final about it until you see it and we know you like it,' Anne said.

'And until you knew I'd passed my test,' Laura said.

'That too,' John said dryly. 'Otherwise you might think we were trying to rub salt in the wound.'

Laura flushed, feeling that her father might well be right, although he appeared to be making a joke. She felt ashamed and decided that from now on she would be a much nicer person.

Laura fell in love with her little car as soon as she saw it and it brought her endless pleasure. Even more than the car itself, the fact that her parents had stretched their resources and put so much thought into the gift for her made her feel for the first time that she was as important to them as Gerry and Julie.

She kept all this to herself and as she found it so hard to show emotion Anne and John had no idea how delighted she was and felt vaguely disappointed by her response.

John had an important meeting on the night of the actual birthday and had booked for the family to have dinner at the Adelphi Hotel on the following Saturday but Anne worried that Laura might be offended at this arrangement.

She said nothing to John but told Gerry and he told her that Laura would probably be celebrating with people from the office on her birthday. 'Saturday's much better for the family dinner,' he said. 'Even Laura couldn't be narked about that.'

'She's so prickly though, Gerry,' Anne sighed, 'especially about anything with Dad. I know she can't help her nature and I make allowances but Dad gets annoyed with her.'

'They just rub each other the wrong way,' Gerry said easily. Don't worry about it, Mum. Just let them work it out for themselves.'

'I suppose I do worry too much,' Anne agreed. 'I'm on pins when they're together in case a row blows up out of nothing.' She laughed. 'I should be like Miss Dillon who comes to empty the Mission box. She lives with a difficult sister but she says, "When Maud has an awkward mood on, I just leave her alone and let her soak, and she comes round."'

'Good advice,' Gerry said laughing. 'And Laura's all right. She just calls a spade a spade.'

'You can say that again.'

Laura made no objection to the arrangements. The tradition in the office was that the birthday person bought cakes for the tea break, and sometimes went for a drink after work, and as this was a special birthday, everyone in the office went to Rigby's for drinks after work.

One of the girls produced a birthday cake and Laura was plied with drinks, some of them unfamiliar to her, but after the first few she was willing to try anything. Late in the evening she was taken home by taxi with one of the girls and Anne opened the door to find Laura on the step supported by Olive from the office on one side and the taxi driver on the other.

'Good God, is she drunk?' Anne exclaimed in horror.

Olive said, 'No, only merry.'

'It's the day for it, isn't it, Ma?' the taxi driver said. 'Not every day you're twenty-one and at least she's had a good time.'

Anne invited them in but the taxi driver said he had to get on and Olive said she would keep the taxi to go home so after profuse thanks from Anne they left.

Anne steered Laura, still smiling foolishly, upstairs to the bathroom and then to her bedroom. With some difficulty she got her into bed, helped by Julie who had already been in bed.

Julie was giggling so much that she was not much help and Anne, although laughing herself, said, 'It's not funny. She'll have a terrible head in the morning. I wonder what she's been drinking.'

When John returned she told him about Laura, playing it down a little. John smiled but he said seriously, 'I hope this is a one-off, Anne.

I hate to hear of young girls drinking. There are so many bad lots about and a girl that's drunk is very vulnerable.'

'Of course it's a one-off,' Anne said. 'As the taxi driver said, it's not every day you're twenty-one.'

Laura woke during the night and staggered to the bathroom. Anne heard her vomiting and came to see to her. Laura groaned, 'Oh Mum, never again. I feel like death.' She tottered back to bed and Anne brought her aspirins and a fruit drink.

'I won't wake you for work if you're asleep,' she said.

Laura moaned, 'Don't, Mum, I've got plenty of flexi.'

Anne went back to bed relieved that Laura, although suffering, was at least coherent and there was no danger that she would choke.

Laura had to endure a lot of teasing at the office but she took it in good part, appreciating the way her colleagues had made her birthday special.

She still went to work by train but she made full use of her Mini in the evenings and at weekends. Soon after her birthday she arranged to drive to a club in Southport with Claire, the granddaughter of their next-door neighbours, and John took the opportunity to lecture her on the dangers of drinking and driving.

'I know there's drink served in these clubs,' he said. 'You may think you'll just have one then be tempted to have another, but it's not worth it, Laura. Think how you'd feel if you were responsible for the death of a child because you were a drunk driver, like that fellow from Childwall. He's got to live with it all his life, that he deprived that child of the life she should have had and caused the family so much grief.'

Laura listened impatiently and as soon as he stopped she said angrily, 'I wouldn't dream of drinking if I was driving. Just because I had a few on my birthday doesn't mean I'm an alcoholic. You're more likely to drink and drive than I am.'

'Me?' John exclaimed. 'I would never drink and drive. I feel very strongly about it. Everybody knows I do.'

'And I feel strongly about it too so there's no need to lecture me about it.'

'I'm telling you for your own good. You're only young and you're new to driving so I'm just warning you. But of course nobody can tell *you* anything. You know it all,' John said angrily.

'I know the dangers of drink driving and you wouldn't have said anything if I hadn't got drunk on my birthday,' Laura muttered. John made an impatient gesture and turned away.

Laura told Mary about it during their lunch hour the following day. 'He never misses a chance to get at me,' she said. 'He's going to take all the good out of giving me the car if I have to have a lecture every time I go out.' She stopped in dismay, feeling that she had been tactless. It had been Mary's twenty-first birthday the previous week and although she had been taken out to dinner and given a gold watch by Danny there had been no celebration in her family.

'I'm sorry,' she said.

Mary shrugged. 'I didn't expect anything so I wasn't disappointed. They didn't do anything for the others so why should they for me? I tell you what though, Lol, I really appreciated that Blue Grass perfume and the glam nightie. You must have second sight.'

'What do you mean?' asked Laura.

'I mean I'm moving in with Danny. Without benefit of clergy, as they say,' she said flippantly. 'So I'll use the nightie.'

Laura was silent for a moment. She knew that this was happening frequently but no one in her immediate circle had yet defied convention and she was at a loss for words.

'Are you shocked?' Mary asked.

'No, no, of course not,' Laura said hurriedly. 'I don't know how you've stuck it so long, but where will you live?'

'We've got a flat in Bootle Village,' Mary said. 'Danny said we won't have any trouble with the landlady because she's been living over the brush herself for years.'

'Have you told your parents yet?' Laura asked.

Mary said she would simply leave without any goodbyes. 'They won't care,' she said bitterly. 'Except for the loss of my housekeeping money. He can't do anything though. I'm over twenty-one and I always said that was when I'd go. When are you going to take the plunge?'

'I won't go without my mother,' Laura said. 'I don't need to worry about Julie now but one day I'll take my mum away from his tantrums and really cosset her.'

'I think you might have it wrong about them,' Mary said tentatively. 'He never hits her, does he?'

'No, I haven't got it wrong,' Laura said angrily. 'I know what goes on. It's mental cruelty. She can't have any life of her own and he does just what he likes. Putting himself about being the big fellow at all these committees and Mum at home just a skivvy for him.'

Mary abandoned the subject and began to talk of her plans for the flat. 'I'll still go out at night, Lol, the clubs and that,' she said. 'Danny's determined to pass as an accountant so he'll be studying nearly every night.'

'He won't mind you going out when you're living together?' Laura asked.

'No. It won't be that sort of relationship. We'll both do our own thing,' Mary said.

Laura was relieved to hear it. She had made friends in the office and sometimes went out with Claire but Mary was her only real friend. She was reserved with other people but she felt that she could talk freely to Mary as Mary did to her and they understood each other. She had feared that Danny might be a threat to their relationship, although she had been pleased for her friend.

'I'm surprised your Gerry's settled back at home,' Mary said. 'People don't usually like to lose their freedom after they've tried living away from home.'

'He had to come home after the hospital and, knowing Gerry, he's just drifted on,' Laura said. 'Anyway, as far as freedom goes, he just does what he likes anyway. He can't do wrong as far as my father's concerned.'

Gerry confirmed this when she spoke to him about it. 'It's not all it's cracked up to be, living away from home, especially a home like this where we can please ourselves pretty well. It was a shock to my system when I first left home, I can tell you.'

'How do you mean?' asked Laura.

'There was nothing there when you wanted it. No toothpaste when you went to brush your teeth, no sticking plaster if you cut yourself, no cotton or needles or buttons if you had to mend a shirt. No scissors, no shoe polish.' He laughed. 'It was dead funny. We had a clothes line but no one had thought of pegs so we hung shirts and things over the line and the damn things blew away all over the place.'

'You took enough dishes and towels and pans and things from here.'

'I know, but it's the other things, the details that you take for granted,' Gerry said. 'No. I'm staying put. I know when I'm well off.'

'And you can do what you like. Dad would never stop you from doing anything you wanted to,' Laura said resentfully.

'I haven't noticed you being restricted. What do you want to do? Hold orgies?'

'No, you fool,' Laura said, laughing and giving him a push. 'I'm just interested because Mary Morgan has left home.'

'I know, to move in with Danny. I saw him at evening class and he told me.'

'At evening class? I didn't know you'd started that. What are you taking?'

'The things I should have taken at school,' Gerry said ruefully. 'More O levels, then I'll go on to A levels. I want to get into teacher training.'

'I didn't know,' Laura said in surprise.

Gerry shrugged. 'I like kids and I've thought about it for ages but Margaret got me to join this session and start to do something about it. You know me. I'd just have been thinking about it for ever.'

'I'm very glad, Ged,' Laura said warmly. 'I think you'll make a good teacher. I wouldn't. I'm too bad-tempered.'

Rather to her chagrin Gerry made no protest but only said, 'Margaret thinks I've got the temperament for it.'

'Everybody seems to be making changes except me. I'm just going along in the same old rut.'

'If you're happy in it, why change? I thought you were having a good time, enjoying yourself, especially with your Mini.'

235

'I am,' Laura said hastily. 'I'm made up with my car and I like the crowd at work.'

'There you are then,' Gerry said breezily, 'If it ain't broke, why mend it?' and went to the phone.

Laura eyed him thoughtfully. It looked as though there was another influence in Gerry's life now and it would be interesting to see what happened if Margaret's ideas for him clashed with his father's.

Laura had felt much happier since Moira's wedding. Talking to Terry had helped her to see things more clearly and now she could tell herself that the reason she was alone was that she was more choosy than most people and prepared to wait for the right man, or stay single.

Not for the first time, she wondered whether Rosa was into free love, as the awful Rilla had assumed, and thought she probably was.

I'm probably the only one who isn't, she thought. All the girls in the office seemed to be on the pill. Some got it from their family doctors and some from the family planning clinic in Old Hall Street but all took it. They wouldn't need it unless they were having sex, she thought. They know I'm not and probably think that chance would be a fine thing as far as I'm concerned, although after the usual discussion during the tea break Olive had said to her, 'You must be shocked by us, Laura. You still go to church every Sunday, don't you?'

Laura had agreed that she did and only later thought that she should have said that she was not shocked. I was too eager to grab at Olive's theory of why I'm not on the pill, she thought ruefully.

The house was empty apart from herself and Gerry, who was still on the phone. Anne had earlier gone with Sarah to see an old friend who was ill and had not yet returned. 'Probably having a few jars somewhere now she's a liberated woman,' Gerry had laughed. Julie was out with Peter and their father was at the Labour Club.

'I don't know why Dad needs to be fussing down at the club,' Laura said when Gerry came back into the room. 'Labour'll get in again, won't they?' A general election had been called by the Labour leader Harold Wilson for 16 June.

'If there's any justice they will,' Gerry said. 'When you think of the economic mess the country was in after thirteen years in office by the Tories, Harold Wilson has done wonders. The balance of payments was so much in the red and he's got it right again and brought in reforms in housing and education and social services. *And* abolished hanging and made divorce easier.'

'Good Lord, Gerry, you sound like Dad,' Laura exclaimed. 'Maybe you should be down there with him tub thumping.'

'No. I agree with him and I'll vote Labour,' Gerry said seriously, 'but I don't want to get involved in local politics.' He tapped a pile of books on the sideboard. 'This is how I'll repay Dad, by getting my head together and making a good teacher.'

'You're very serious all of a sudden. Is this the influence of a *good woman*,' she mocked.

Gerry smiled and said quietly, 'No. I realise what I've put Dad through and how good he's been to me and I want to repay him. I've been a disappointment to him up to now.'

'I don't know where you get that idea,' Laura said. 'He was made up when you were playing in the groups, bragging about you to everyone.'

'In the early days with the Merrymen perhaps,' Gerry said. 'Don't get me wrong. I don't regret anything I've done for my own sake, I've had a bloody good time and made some fantastic mates, but I know I've caused Dad a lot of worry in the last few years, yet he's always stuck by me. I was very flip when I talked about the advantages of living at home, but believe me, Lol, I was damn lucky Dad welcomed me back after the way I'd treated him.'

'And what about Mum?' Laura demanded. 'You keep going on about Dad but Mum was the one who worried about you and looked after you, especially that first time with the drugs.'

'Mum too,' Gerry agreed. 'But you don't know the half of what Dad has done for me.'

'I know how Mum has worried about you and nursed you but you seem to take all that for granted,' Laura said indignantly. 'I suppose you're like Dad and think that's all she's good for.'

'Don't talk through the back of your neck,' Gerry advised her. 'I'm talking about Dad travelling miles to see me and then finding me stoned and being bawled out and humiliated by me but still leaving me money and trying to keep in touch. Not once but over and over again.'

'I didn't know you were back on the drugs,' Laura said.

'We all were. It was the only way to keep going,' Gerry said. 'The last time Dad came wasn't long before the accident and the way I treated him, I couldn't have blamed him if he'd washed his hands of me completely after that.'

'Do you think Mum would have let him?' Laura demanded.

Gerry shrugged. 'I suppose not but it was for her sake that Dad came that time. He told me she was worried but I was mad because I thought he showed me up with the lads and I said some unforgivable things to him.'

'They evidently weren't. Unforgivable,' Laura commented dryly.

'Anyone but Dad would have said I'd got what I deserved in that crash and refused to get involved,' Gerry said. 'Dad didn't – or Mum,' he added hastily as he saw Laura's face. 'I realise now what I put them through and I'm going to make a success as a teacher for his sake. To try to repay Dad for his faith in me.' He sounded so earnest that Laura looked at him in amazement and began to laugh.

'Must be the knock on the head,' she said flippantly. 'Where's the scatterbrain we know and love?'

Gerry grinned but said no more and Laura went into the garden feeling disturbed and uncertain. This new Gerry was so different to her happy-go-lucky brother that she felt she had lost a companion, especially as he now had such warm feelings for their father. John had always doted on Gerry but on Gerry's part there had never been any deep feelings; he had sailed through life on good terms with everyone and a dear friend to Laura. They could always have a laugh and a joke together.

The father that Gerry had talked about had not fitted her image of John as a selfish, domineering father and a bullying husband. I know what he is and I know how he's treated Mum, she thought stubbornly. It's Gerry who has got hold of the wrong end of the stick, probably because of the drugs, yet she still felt troubled.

She stood for a while letting the peace of the garden soothe her as it always did until she heard her mother's voice and went back into the house.

Chapter Nineteen

Laura had not seen Rosa since Moira's wedding but after leaving Mary one lunchtime, she came face to face with her cousin who was with two other girls.

'Rosa, you look filthy,' Laura exclaimed but Rosa and her friends only laughed.

'I know, darling,' Rosa drawled. 'The poxy landlord cut off the water and electricity in our grotty flat.' Her usually shining hair was lank and greasy and her face and feet were grubby as well as her clothes.

Her two friends, who wore outlandish clothes and jangling bracelets, looked even dirtier and the one nearest to Laura had numerous flea bites on her arms and neck.

Laura was distressed to see her cousin, usually so fastidious, in such a state and she said indignantly, 'There's no need for you to be dirty, Rosa. You know you can always go home for a bath.'

'We're starting a new fashion,' the flea-bitten girl screeched. 'The great unwashed,' and they all fell about cackling with laughter. Laura looked at them with disgust.

'Come home, Ros,' she said quietly to Rosa. 'I'll smuggle you into our house if you don't want to be seen till you're clean.'

Rosa smiled at her with affection. 'It's all right, Lol,' she said. 'We're moving into a squat in Princes Park. The guys are fixing it up now. There's water laid on and one of the guys can fix the electricity there. He couldn't in the flat because the poxy landlord was always about. Come with us and see it now.'

'I can't. I've got to get back to the office,' Laura said. 'But I could come at five o'clock. What's the address?'

Rosa gave it and Laura left them feeling seriously worried. How could Rosa have got into that state in such a short time? She recalled her at Moira's wedding, bandbox fresh and beautiful, chatting demurely with relations with Neil standing quietly beside her. Playing the part of the dutiful daughter, Laura thought, and suddenly she felt more cheerful. Rosa might just be playing yet another part now, the great unwashed, as that horrible girl had said. Probably making a virtue of necessity because of the conditions she was living in, thought Laura.

She went to the address in Princes Park after buying scented soap and bath salts in George Henry Lee's and a large fruit cake from Reece's. Rosa saw her from a window and called her down the side of the house to a kitchen door.

The fruit cake was immediately seized on and devoured by the six people who shared the squat, and although a piece was cut for Rosa, none was offered to Laura. Rosa put the soap and the bath salts into the large pockets of a quilted jacket she wore, winking at Laura although the others seemed too busy with the cake to notice.

'Rosa, are you *hungry*?' Laura whispered in dismay but Rosa laughed cheerfully.

'No, this lot are always like that,' she said. 'Comes from communal living. Everyone wants to make sure of his share.'

She took Laura on a tour of the house, a large, detached mansion which had evidently been unoccupied for some time. Mattresses had been laid on the floor of several of the large bare rooms and cardboard and straw stuffed into the elegant fireplaces.

'Boosey says it looks like professional packers have packed the stuff, probably for storage, which is a good sign. They've left some kitchen stuff which is very handy, a table and a couple of chairs and some cracked dishes,' Rosa informed her.

Laura said nothing. She felt uneasy, feeling that the rightful owners or the police would appear at any moment, and she wondered how the squatters could be so relaxed. I hope this phase doesn't last long with Rosa, she thought.

Before she left she asked Rosa diffidently if she needed money but Rosa told her she had money to collect as soon as she had cleaned herself up.

'Not that I'd have minded going there unwashed but there's a stuffy elderly man at the gallery. I wouldn't want to give him a heart attack,' she said gaily.

'It's a good thing your mum can't see you,' Laura told her bluntly. 'You'd give her a heart attack all right.'

Rosa suddenly looked more serious. 'Is she all right? Mum?' she asked.

'Yes. I suppose she worries about you but she doesn't say anything. She was proud of you at the wedding, I think. Have you seen Neil since?'

'Neil?' Rosa said in a surprised tone. 'Oh no.'

They rejoined the others and Laura wondered how the four girls and two men were attached, if at all. I'll bet if they do pair off at all one of the men will be Rosa's, Laura thought grimly as she left, and although she hasn't seen Neil she only has to whistle and he'll come.

She said nothing at home about seeing Rosa but she told Mary the next day. 'You've got to admire her,' Mary said. 'She has the courage to try out her wild ideas and stick some discomfort for them. She's a case, isn't she?'

'Yes, she is, but she's sound, you know, Mary. I'm determined I'll keep in touch with her now.'

'I had an encounter too last night,' Mary said. 'I met Monica.'

'Monica!' Laura exclaimed. 'I haven't seen her for ages and I don't care if I never see her again. We used to think she was just tactless but you know, Mary, when she put her foot in it, she never said anything to harm or embarrass herself only other people. Because she said poisonous things in such a dozy voice we thought she was just thick but I realise now she was vicious.'

'Yes, and never more so than when she thought that Denis might be interested in another girl. Not that he was ever interested in *her*. She was the one who clung on like a leech, and cultivated Bert because he was Denis's friend, or so we always thought.'

'Thick and Thin,' Laura said with a laugh. 'Remember when Monica started going round with them and someone said they should be called Thin, Thick and Thicker?'

'Yes, but wait till I tell you,' Mary said. 'She's getting married!'

'Married?' Laura echoed. 'So she caught Denis at last.'

'No. She's marrying Bert and you only had to look at her to see why. She's about five months pregnant.'

'Bert? I can't believe it,' Laura said.

'I know. I rang Cathy Gillespie last night because she's still friendly with that crowd and she said they were all stunned. She told me Denis was just the same, still poncing about being the ladykiller, and he'd made a few dates but Monica always managed to break it up and hung on to him everywhere they went. Bert was still like the spare part.'

'Then how come they're getting married?' asked Laura.

'Cathy said Monica suddenly started making up to Bert a few months ago and they all thought it was a laugh. Dave Snell couldn't stand Monica because he said she nearly broke things up between him and his girlfriend, with her tactless remarks. He said he was made up for Denis that he'd got rid of her. He thought he'd have to buy Denis a packet of slug killer before he could get shut.'

They both laughed and Laura said, 'I see what Dave means. She reminds me of a slug. But when's the wedding if she's five months already?'

'She said August but she didn't mention invitations,' said Mary. 'I wonder if Denis will be best man.'

'I pity any poor child born to that creature,' Laura said, remembering Monica at their house-warming party.

'So do I,' Mary said. 'I wasn't going to repeat this. Danny told me to put it out of my head and forget it but I can't. Do you know what she said when I told her about me and Danny? "Danny Roberts! Well, I suppose it's not as though you're marrying him, and anyone would do, really, to get you away from home."'

'The bitch!' Laura said forcefully. 'She's only jealous, Mary, because Danny's such a nice fellow. That creep she's marrying must be half-witted as well as thick-skinned if he can't see through her. Do as Danny says and forget it. In fact, why are we wasting time even talking about her on such a lovely day?' They said no more about Monica and soon it was time to return to work.

The day was warm and sunny but Laura worked late to build up her flexitime so that she could have a day off. Two others were also working late and one of them said he was going on the river later.

'I'm looking forward to watering the garden,' Laura said. 'Everything is really dry.'

'I'm not surprised. It was the warmest night for a hundred years last night, at least for the fourth of June,' the man said. 'Do you really enjoy watering?'

'Yes. You can almost hear the plants drinking it in,' Laura said and he laughed and told her that it was her motherly instincts which made her enjoy supplying what they needed.

Laura was amazed when she arrived home to find that the front garden had been watered and she hurried round to the back garden. That, too, had been watered and she stormed into the house.

'Who watered my garden?' she demanded.

Her mother told her that her father had done it. 'He's taking a night off and he did it to save you having to do it.'

'To save me?' Laura said angrily. 'I've been looking forward to it. You know how I like watering.'

Their raised voices brought her father in from the front room, demanding to know what was wrong.

'You watered my garden,' Laura said angrily.

'What are you making a fuss about *now*?' John said irritably. 'If it wasn't done you'd be moaning that everything was left to you.'

'No, I wouldn't. I never complain about doing anything in my garden and I enjoy watering.'

'So do I and it's *my* garden if it comes to that,' John said. 'I've let you have a free hand out there but you haven't got a monopoly, you know.'

Anne could see that Laura was near to tears and also on the brink of saying something she would afterwards regret. Before she could tell John to keep his garden and do all the work himself, Anne said quickly, 'We all enjoy sitting in the garden although we don't do any of the work. You have a flair for it, Laura. Must be inherited from your father, John, or maybe from your grandfather. He had an allotment and grew lots of vegetables, didn't he?'

Her lengthy speech gave Laura and John time to cool down a little and John said stiffly, 'I did it very thoroughly. Thought I'd better before they start banning the use of hosepipes.'

'That'll be the next thing, I suppose,' Laura said gruffly, 'A couple of fine days and it's panic stations.'

John returned to the other room and Laura ate her meal quickly.

Her pride would not allow her to go into the garden so she told her mother that she intended to go for a run in her car.

'That's good,' said Anne. 'A pity to waste such a lovely evening. Will you pick up Mary?'

'No. She's out with Danny.'

'And Claire's not visiting next door,' Anne said. 'It's a pity Rosa's moved away. She'd be company for you.'

'I don't need company,' Laura said curtly, taking her car keys and going out to drive to the esplanade in Waterloo. She parked near the gardens which lay close to the river and walked through them, her head bent and her hands in her pockets.

The scent of the flowers in the gardens was wafted by the warm breeze off the river and the wide sky was filled with the rosy afterglow of the sunset. The evening star had appeared in a sky of delicate translucent green but Laura strode on, oblivious of the beauty around her.

She knew that her mother had not intended to hurt her but her words had made her realise how lonely she was. Other people were strolling round the gardens but all were in couples or small groups. Only she was alone and she thought with nostalgia of her teenage years when she had been one of a crowd of friends. Now everyone seemed to have paired off or moved away and she thought that if they had been real friends she would have stayed in touch with them. She probably had few friends but many acquaintances even then, just as she did now.

She liked the people in the office, and they went out together usually on Friday nights for drinks after work, but most of them were married or settled with steady partners. Her nights out had occurred less and less often.

Only the previous week her mother had urged her to spend less time in the garden and to go out and enjoy herself. 'And don't depend on Mary so much, love. Make other friends like yourself. Go out more with Claire from next door.'

I know what she was really saying, Laura thought. She meant I should go out with someone who was unattached so I'd have more chance of tapping off. Mary's settled with Danny and not interested in anyone else so we are like a pair of old married women when we go out but I enjoy Mary's company so I don't mind.

And Claire! I could have told Mum that Claire isn't so keen on going out with me. I cramp her style. Laura recalled the last time that she and Claire had driven to Southport to a club. They had danced with two young men who had afterwards bought drinks for them in the bar. Claire was delighted with them but Laura had told her that she considered the one who attached himself to her pushy and uncouth and Claire's young man a flashy poser.

This was when she and Claire had visited the Ladies and they had come as near as possible to quarrelling. 'Do you *have* to be so rude to every fellow we meet?' Claire said. 'You won't wait to see how things go. Just condemn them right away.'

'I don't need time to see through these two,' Laura retorted. 'Boris and Jason! They couldn't even give their real names and saying that they were airline pilots! Must think we're soft.'

'It's all part of the game,' Claire protested. 'But that's the trouble with you, Laura, you won't go along with anything. You want everything black and white.'

'If you mean I won't tell lies,' Laura began but Claire interrupted her.

'It's not telling lies. It's just technique. Knowing when to encourage a fellow and when to play hard to get. You only know about choking them off.' She laughed as she said it but Laura knew that she meant what she said.

'If you mean those two, I can tell you they don't need any encouragement. It's plain what they're after and I can tell *Boris* now he's not on,' Laura said bluntly. 'If he thinks that chatting me up and buying a few drinks means he'll have sex with me, he's got another think coming.'

Claire had obviously been offended by her plain speaking although she had only said that she was going back to Jason and to the dance floor. Laura had avoided Boris and after a while he had decided to cut his losses and she saw him with another girl.

Later Claire said that she would probably stay in Southport instead of going back to her grandmother's house. 'Jason will give me a lift,' she said, not meeting Laura's eyes, so Laura had driven home alone. She had wondered what was happening with Claire and Jason but decided that Claire could look after herself.

Now as she walked through the gardens she thought that she and Claire would probably remain friends on the surface but the night-clubbing in Southport had ended.

Dusk was falling and she went back to her car, feeling depressed and lonely, then she thought defiantly that she had one true friend in Mary who was worth six of Claire. Her cousin David had always been a good friend too and they were on the same wavelength; Terry had singled her out and seemed to like her best of the relations he had met for the first time. She drove home feeling much more cheerful.

Her mother was alone watching television when she arrived home but she turned the sound down.

'Hello, love. I'll make a cup of tea,' she said brightly.

Laura said, 'I'll make it. Watch your programme.'

'It's rubbish anyway. I was only watching to pass the time,' Anne said, standing up and following Laura into the kitchen. 'Did you meet anyone you knew?' she asked.

'I didn't go out to meet anyone,' Laura snapped then felt ashamed as she saw her mother's face. 'I'm sorry, Mum. I didn't mean to snap.'

'I only thought you might have met some of your friends. People from the church perhaps or other friends getting some fresh air. It's such a lovely evening. Did you go to the shore?'

'Yes. To the gardens. You should have come with me, Mum. It was lovely down there.'

'I should,' Anne agreed. 'Better than sitting indoors watching rubbish. Dad's been catching up on his paperwork and he's gone to bed. Having an early night for once.'

Laura smiled but she knew that her mother would not have gone with her in case she spoiled her chances of meeting an eligible young man, or friends who might lead to such a meeting. I can't understand her, she thought. I'd expect her to be warning me off marriage after her own experience, not to be trying to marry me off as soon as possible. Perhaps she just wants to be sure that I marry someone very different from Dad and I'll be happy.

They talked together companionably for a while then Laura went to bed but she felt too restless to sleep. She tried to read but she was unable to concentrate so she sat by the open window looking at the white flowers glimmering in the borders and scenting the soft night air which flowed through the window but nothing soothed her troubled mind.

The train of thought started by her mother's innocent words made her question all that was happening in her life and her attitude to other people. Was she really always out of step with everyone else and narrow-minded and intolerant too?

She and Julie had joined the Young Christian Workers at their local church soon after their arrival in the parish and Julie had made many friends there but Laura was often involved in arguments with other members. It was a time of change in the Catholic Church and there were many discussions which quickly became acrimonious when Laura joined in.

She thought about that now and remembered that she had stopped attending the meetings after someone told her she had a closed mind. But it isn't true, she thought indignantly. I just thought the changes were too many and too sweeping and should have been introduced gradually and I had the courage to state my views. I'm sure many of them agreed with me but weren't honest enough to say so.

It was the same at work. She was sure that she was not the only one who found parts of the programme *That Was The Week That Was* obscene and sacrilegious but no one had the courage to agree with her. They were afraid to be thought old-fashioned or fuddy-duddy, she thought. Today they'd been discussing easier divorce and living together before marriage and about a famous actress who had announced the birth of her 'love child'.

'Life's better for everyone now,' a girl named Barbara had announced. 'People are more broad-minded and anything goes.' She looked at Laura and laughed. 'Except for people like Laura. You'd never move in with a feller, would you, Laura?'

Laura's reply had been a curt 'No'. She was not going to tell this crowd that she would never leave her mother and was saving hard to provide a home for her and take her away from her bullying husband.

She had gone on to tell them that a lot of these changes in attitude were all talk. Arty people in London might behave like that but if any of the office staff had a baby outside marriage they would find that attitudes had not really changed. Anyway even in her grandmother's and great-grandmother's time some people were tolerant and helpful to girls in that situation.

'I remember when I was only a child, my nana and grandma were making baby clothes for a neighbour's daughter who was having a baby and wasn't married. My grandma's old friend said she shouldn't encourage the girl because she was bad and my grandma said, "Bad girls don't have babies, Peggy. They know what to do about them",' Laura told them.

Olive had only said that some people had been like that but Barbara seemed angry. 'We're all on the pill,' she said, 'so how would your grandma class us?'

Break was over before Laura could think of a reply but she felt that the other girls had treated her coolly for the rest of the day.

I was only speaking the truth, she thought now and I'm not going to stop doing that no matter who it offends. That's my way and if people don't like it, they can lump it. She went back to bed and soon fell asleep.

Unknown to Laura, her mother had confided her worries about her to Gerry and a few weeks later he produced tickets for the Cabaret Club in Litherland. 'Pete Taylor's group is on and he gave me these complimentary tickets. Margaret and I can't go but will you and Mary use them? Should be a good night,' he said.

Mary and Laura were pleased to accept the tickets and, on the night, they were met in the entrance foyer by Peter's quiet friend, Phil Casey. He took them to join a large group of people, introducing them to Peter's girlfriend Gail, the wife of the group's drummer and the road manager.

Two other girls paused briefly to speak to Gail and then said that they must go back to their own crowd. 'Rhoda from our place is getting married next week and her feller's out on a stag night tonight so we're having a hen night for Rhoda. Fair's fair,' one girl said.

There was another couple at the table and Phil introduced them. 'Maurice and, er...'

'Brenda. Hi,' the girl volunteered then neither of them spoke again either to each other or to anyone else.

Gail was related to Danny, Mary's boyfriend, and she and Mary began to talk about Danny's studies. Laura told Phil that Gerry was unable to come because he was enrolling for another course that night.

'He wants to train as a teacher,' she explained. 'He's a changed man since that accident or perhaps it's since he started going out with Margaret. I think she suggested the teacher training.'

'Good on him anyway,' Phil said. 'He's such a good drummer though. It's a shame he didn't get into a good group like Pete.'

'He still does the odd gig,' Laura said, 'so he's got the best of both worlds.'

She found Phil very easy to talk to and discovered that he, too, was studying, in his case for banking examinations, and had recently been promoted. 'It nearly always means a move though,' he said ruefully. 'I thought I might have to leave Liverpool but luckily I was only moved to the Allerton Branch. It suits me because I'm living in Woolton.'

'At home?' Laura asked and Phil told her that his family lived in Bebington on the other side of the Mersey. 'I share a house with three other fellows and a girl.'

Gail and Mary had been listening to their conversation and Mary said she supposed that the girl did all the cooking and washing up.

'You must be joking!' Phil exclaimed.

'You haven't seen her,' Gail laughed. 'Six foot tall and a real women's libber. They're all terrified of her.'

'We're not,' Phil protested. 'Jody's all right but she won't stand any messing. She drew up a rota and she sees that we stick to it. Only fair anyhow.'

The road manager had stood up and Gail turned to him and began to talk urgently. Under cover of this Phil said quietly to Laura, 'Do you hear from your Canadian cousins?'

'No. I refused to write to Rilla. We've got nothing in common. She asked for Peter's address but we didn't give it to her.'

'Good job,' Phil said with a heartfelt sigh. 'She's been writing to Pete at his mum's house but luckily Gail doesn't know. She'd kill her if she did, as well as giving Pete a hard time.'

'Does he answer the letters?' Laura asked.

'No. He asked his mum to burn them. He's hoping she'll get fed up if he doesn't answer.'

'She's a pain,' Laura began but Gail had turned back to them and dropped into the empty seat on the other side of Phil.

'I want Decco to ask Peter to come and see me but I know he won't,' she said. 'Will you go and tell him, Phil?'

'They must be getting ready to come on if Decco's gone backstage,' Phil said. 'Leave it till later, Gail.'

Gail's eyes were glittering and her cheeks red with temper. 'You all think I can be pushed around. Well, I'm not having it,' she snapped. 'I'll go backstage myself.'

'*Don't*, Gail,' the drummer's wife urged. 'They'll be all hyped up to come on. You'll upset everything,' but Gail seemed determined.

'All right. I'll go,' Phil said and went off.

Gail stayed in the same seat with Phil's empty chair on her right, glowering at the stage, and the drummer's wife whispered to Mary, 'She wants him out here so everyone knows he's hers before he comes on stage.'

Laura could have spoken across the empty chair to Gail, but decided if she wanted to sulk, she could, and turned to Mary.

Within a few minutes Phil came back with Peter who said angrily to Gail, 'What's up? What's so important?'

'I wanted to give you a kiss before you went on,' she said, flinging her arms round his neck and her lips on his.

He pulled away and said brusquely, 'OK, I've got to go. See you later,' and dashed away but Gail settled back with a satisfied smile and a complacent glance round the audience.

The silent Maurice spoke at last to suggest that they moved to fill the road manager's chair so that all would have a good view of the stage, and by some adroit manoeuvring on Gail's part, Laura found that Phil was at the end, Gail on his right, Laura next to Gail and Mary next to Laura.

'That was crafty,' Mary whispered to Laura but the cabaret began and they all watched the stage.

When Peter's group came on there were squeals from a group of girls who were near the stage and some of them threw flowers and packets of sweets on to the stage.

Gail was obviously furious but Laura leaned forward and said curtly, 'For God's sake, Gail, you know it goes with the job. If you don't like it, you'd better find a fellow who doesn't have to get up on a stage for his living.'

'You'd like that, wouldn't you?' Gail said angrily. 'I suppose you've got your eye on Peter.' She spoke loudly and people were looking towards their group.

Nell the drummer's wife hissed, 'Look. Can we *listen* to them?' and Laura and Gail said no more.

When the cabaret was over the lights went up and people began to move around. A group of young men, obviously celebrating, passed their table. Two of them paused. 'Hi, Phil,' they said and Phil waved to them.

'Drinking mates from the Elephant in Woolton,' he explained but the two men lingered and he was forced to introduce them. 'Nick and Dave,' he said and to the men, 'Mary and Laura. Gail and Brenda and Maurice you know.'

Nick held out his hand to Laura. 'Nick Clegg,' he said, then shook hands with Mary, and Dave shook hands with both girls.

Nick was a tall, dark man with a beaky nose and a determined chin but Dave was as fair as Phil, with the same blue eyes.

'Bit far from the Elephant tonight, aren't you?' Phil said. 'What brings you here?'

'Celebrating a birthday. Owen's twenty-first. A crowd of us from Christ's and this was his choice,' said Dave, while Nick stood looking at Laura. 'He's going home to Wales at the weekend,' Dave went on while Nick still silently stared at Laura. 'They're all teetotal there so all he wants tonight is drink and plenty of it. Isn't that right, Nick?'

Nick only nodded and Laura was silent but Mary said brightly, 'Is it Christ's College Woolton you're at? The teacher training place?'

Dave said it was.

'That's where Gerry's hoping to go, isn't it Laura?' Phil asked.

'Yes, but he's not qualified yet,' Laura said.

Nick spoke at last. 'Who's Gerry?' he asked.

'My brother,' Laura said.

Phil added, 'Gerry Redmond who was the drummer in the Merrymen when Pete Taylor played with them. Remember him?'

The lights dimmed again and dancing began. Gail grabbed Phil's arm. 'Ooh, come on, Phil, I love this,' she cried, and they all moved to the dance floor, Mary with Dave and Laura with Nick.

'A strong silent type you've got there,' Mary whispered to Laura, giggling, and Laura felt that she was right.

She could see Mary chattering away to Dave but Nick made only monosyllabic replies to her efforts at conversation so she said no more. When they returned to the table, Phil and Gail were already there with Peter and Gail and Peter seemed to be having a heated argument. It seemed that Peter's group were going on to another gig at Burscough and Gail wanted to go with them but there was no room for her.

Peter looked harassed and Gail tearful and as she was quickly becoming hysterical Peter seemed desperate. He turned to Phil. 'Could you bring her in your car, Phil? I know it's a lot to ask but there's no way we could fit her in. Please mate.' He was gripping Phil's arm.

Phil nodded and said quietly, 'OK, Pete.'

Gail's tears dried as though by magic and Peter said gratefully, 'Thanks, Phil. It's a good way off, means you'll have to stay to bring her home as well.'

Phil only said, 'That's all right.'

'Thanks, pal,' Peter said again. 'I'll owe you.' He went backstage and Gail went off for her coat.

Mary said to Phil, 'Where's Burscough exactly? Quite a long drive isn't it?'

'I think so,' Phil said. 'I've got maps and an A to Z in the car.'

'Rather you than me,' Dave said frankly. 'I don't know why Pete puts up with her tantrums.'

Phil only shrugged and the next moment Gail returned but before they left Phil said to Laura, 'Nice to see you again. I hope things work out for Gerry. I'm really sorry to go now.'

Laura smiled at him. 'Yes, Peter's luckier in his friend than in his girlfriend. I'll give your message to Gerry.'

He went off with Gail who was waiting impatiently and Mary exclaimed, 'Laura! I'm sure she heard you.'

'I don't care if she did. It's the truth.'

'She's bad news,' Dave said. 'We see her and Pete occasionally in the Elephant and she can be very fetching, looks quite tasty, but it must be like sitting on a powder keg for Pete.'

'Maybe that's the attraction,' Laura said.

'Probably,' Nick agreed.

'He speaks! He speaks!' Dave said, pretending to fall back in amazement but Nick only grinned and suggested drinks.

While the men were at the bar, Mary told Laura that Dave had said he was engaged to a girl in his home town of Morecombe. 'I don't know what the score is with Nick,' she went on. 'But I can't imagine he'd say enough to propose to anyone. I'm sorry, you seem to have drawn the short straw with him but they'll probably be going on somewhere with their mates so we'll be shut of them.'

'He's all right. Just very silent,' Laura said, laughing.

'And how!' Mary exclaimed.

Dave and Nick came back accompanied by Owen who was trying to persuade them to go to another club in Liverpool.

'Bring the girls,' he cried waving his arms and nearly overbalancing.

Mary said quickly, 'Oh no, we have to go soon, but you go with him, lads. It is his birthday.'

'No way,' Nick said suddenly. 'Take Owen back to the gang, Dave.' He looked at Laura. 'Have you got time for another dance?' he asked.

Laura went with him to the dance floor, looking back to see Mary leaning back in her chair helpless with laughter. She soon joined them on the dance floor with Dave. 'He found his tongue when it mattered,' she murmured to Laura. 'Maybe he's all right after all. Do you want to stay?'

Laura shook her head and as they went back to the table she said quietly, 'Tell them we've got to go because of Danny and they can go on with their friends.'

Dave made no protest when Mary told him and she said to Laura, 'I'll go for our coats. I've got the tickets.'

Dave went with her and Nick said abruptly to Laura, 'I'd planned to take you home. Is there any reason why I can't?'

'Only that I don't want you to,' Laura said sharply, irritated by his tone.

He looked startled but persisted, 'Then can I see you again? You're not married or anything, are you?'

Laura was about to make a cutting reply when she thought of Claire's words – 'You only know how to choke them off – and she said instead, 'No, I'm not.'

'Then could we meet in town and do a film or could I ring you?' he asked urgently.

'All right. I'll meet you in town,' Laura said and it was quickly arranged.

She told Mary about the date as they left the club and Mary was pleased. 'Dave says Nick's all right. Very straight. He says he's not usually so quiet. He says what he thinks,' she laughed, 'so you two should get on well.'

'I can't make him out. I don't know whether he's shy or moody or what but if I don't like him I don't have to see him again. That's why I said I'd meet him in town.'

'And if you go to the pictures, he won't have to talk,' Mary said with a chuckle.

'Don't tell anyone about this, Mary, will you? I'm not saying anything at home,' and Mary agreed.

Chapter Twenty

Laura was determined to say nothing about Nick to her mother, dreading to see her look overjoyed because she had at last made a date, and when Gerry asked whether she had enjoyed the night she said only that the show was good.

'Did Pete's group go down well?' Gerry asked.

'Oh yes. They were fantastic,' said Laura. 'That girlfriend of Peter's is a pain though, isn't she?'

'Yeah, I don't know why she acts the way she does,' Gerry said. 'It's not as if he ever gave her any cause for jealousy. He can't help the groupies following them round and squealing at him.'

'He's such a nice lad too,' Anne said. 'I always liked Peter. He deserves to be happy.'

'Gail's all right, except for the jealousy. It's like a disease with her.'

'Do you know Rilla's been writing to him at his mother's?' Laura said. 'Good job Gail doesn't know about that.'

Gerry laughed. 'And it's a good job she's safe in Canada if Gail ever finds out. Gail's got a temper to match her red hair.'

'That reminds me, Laura. Have you seen Rosa lately?' Anne asked. 'Aunt Sarah's worried because they haven't heard from her for a while. She always keeps in touch.'

'I saw her a couple of weeks ago,' Laura said. 'But we only waved. We were in the Moonstone, the crowd from the office, because someone was leaving.'

'Who was Rosa with?'

Laura shrugged. 'I didn't know him. She's left the squat, you know, and moved into a flat.'

'It wasn't that Ricky Hewlett?' Anne asked. 'Uncle Joe heard from that policeman friend of his that Hewlett was seen in Liverpool.'

'Good Lord, no,' Laura said. 'He was only a young fellow, quite dishy. Way-out gear but then Rosa looked like Earth Mother too.'

Laura kept to her resolve not to mention Nick or her date to the family and only told her mother on Monday night that she would go to the cinema straight from work the next day and would have something to eat in town.

'That'll be a nice change,' Anne said and Laura felt a pang of guilt. Her mother was so unselfish, never complaining about her own life and only anxious for her children to be happy. At least she worries about me now, as well as Julie, she thought.

She wore a suede mini skirt and a skinny rib jumper to work on Tuesday and carried a fringed suede waistcoat in a bag which she concealed in her desk drawer. She worked until six thirty, then in the deserted washroom she was able to wash and make up her face at her leisure. Her short hair needed little styling and she had just donned the waistcoat when a cleaner came in.

'Jeez, you don't half look smart, queen,' she exclaimed. 'Gorra date?'

'Yes. We're going to the Odeon,' said Laura.

'Back row, eh?' the woman said, winking at Laura. 'Enjoy yourself, girl, but don't do nothing I wouldn't do.' She cackled with laughter and Laura went out smiling and for the first time enjoying the feeling that she was out on a date.

I don't know why I've been so secretive about it, she thought. I think everyone's been watching me and pitying me but I suppose the truth is they couldn't care less. They're only thinking about what concerns themselves.

Nick was waiting on the corner of London Road outside the Legs of Man pub where they had arranged to meet and Laura felt proud to claim him and walk up to the cinema with him. He was so tall and dark and although not strictly handsome she decided that he looked a real man.

There was little time for conversation before the film began but at the intermission Nick was almost the first to be served at the bar and carried the drinks to where Laura sat at a small table in the corner.

She found that it was easy to talk to him and told him that she had come on from work as she lived in Crosby and worked in town. He asked about her family and she told him that she lived at home with her parents and brother and sister and he told her that his family lived in Ormskirk in Lancashire and he shared a flat with two other men near Christ's College.

'I'm in my last year now,' he said. 'I'm going to like teaching. I did some teaching practice in a Kirkby school and I enjoyed it.'

'Kirkby!' Laura said. 'Thrown in at the deep end, weren't you?'

'No. I took fourteen-year-olds and they were no different to fourteen-year-old boys anywhere,' Nick said forcefully. 'It's a case of give a dog a bad name.'

'No, it's not,' Laura said, annoyed by his tone. 'Not with me anyway. I know someone who did supply teaching there. He said on his first morning the kids asked whether he supported Everton or Liverpool and he thought whichever he said half of the class would tear him limb from limb so he said he played rugby. They decided he was a divi and he got nowhere with them.'

Nick laughed heartily. 'Like a religion in this city, isn't it? I was all right. I qualified as an FA coach last year so I coached the school teams and I was home and dry with the kids. Anyway, forget that. I want to talk about you.'

'But I don't,' Laura said curtly. She was still annoyed by his response to her innocent remark about Kirkby. I didn't come here to be preached at, she thought, but the bell for the end of the intermission stopped any further conversation.

'Blast,' Nick muttered and they joined the crowds returning to their seats. After the film was over they walked to Exchange Station and Laura decided to say goodbye to Nick there as they lived in opposite directions but he refused.

'I'm not letting you travel home alone,' he said masterfully.

'But I live a few minutes' walk from the station,' Laura protested. 'And you live as far as Crosby the other way from here,' but much to her own surprise she was overruled.

There were few people on the train and they talked amicably all the way home, mostly about the people at the Cabaret Club and about

Mary. Laura told Nick where she worked and that she met Mary for lunch every day and he told her that he knew Phil Casey fairly well because he often met him in the Elephant on Sundays and had met Peter and Gail there occasionally.

'It's a pity Gail's so jealous and without any reason,' Laura said. 'Must spoil things for them.'

Nick shrugged. 'I can understand her.' He glanced at Laura. 'I'm a bit that way myself. What's mine is mine, you know.'

'You've put your finger on it,' Laura said triumphantly. '"What's mine is mine." Nobody owns another person. Jealousy is an insult because it means you don't trust the other person.'

'Of course it doesn't. It means you love them and don't want anyone else butting in.'

'I don't agree,' said Laura. 'I wonder why Peter Taylor puts up with it. I wouldn't.' They sat in silence for a moment then Nick said he had not been in the north end of the city before.

'Quite near the river, aren't you?' he said, obviously changing the subject, and Laura answered in the same tone.

As she and Nick stepped off the train, Sean passed with another man.

'Hi,' he said casually.

And Laura as casually said, 'Hi.'

'Who's that?' Nick asked.

Laura said briefly, 'An old friend. I see him occasionally on the train.'

She was annoyed with herself for explaining and smiled brightly at the young ticket collector to show her independence.

'Hello there,' he said. 'Thought you'd be deserting us now you've got wheels. Smashing little cars, those Minis, aren't they?'

'Yes, I'm made up with mine,' Laura said. 'But I still need the train.' She looked at Nick, daring him to comment, but he said nothing.

When they reached the corner of her road, she stopped in the shade of a horse chestnut tree in a nearby garden. 'I'll say goodbye here,' she said. 'There should be a train due in a few minutes.'

'When can I see you again?' he asked.

Laura hesitated. She had enjoyed the evening and liked Nick's company, except when he was airing his views, she thought, but perhaps I can cure him of that so she smiled at him and suggested meeting on Saturday night.

She had been undecided whether to say anything to her mother about her date but the matter was decided for her when Mrs Barret from next door passed with her dog and said good evening. No way, Laura thought, would she let her mother be told by anyone else.

She stood stiffly within Nick's arms at first as he kissed her, then relaxed and responded but when his kisses became too urgent, she drew away. Nick released her immediately. 'I'm just an old-fashioned girl,' she said, laughing breathlessly.

Nick held her hands and smiled into her eyes. 'I like old-fashioned girls.'

'Do you know many?' she asked flippantly.

'There's only one I want to know.'

Laura was smiling when they parted. I do like him, she thought, and I admire him for sticking up for the kids from Kirkby, too. He might have only been joking about jealousy and I took it too seriously.

She was looking forward to telling her mother about Nick but when she went into the living room her father and Gerry were sitting with her mother and all looked serious. 'Julie?' Laura said in alarm.

Her mother said quickly, 'No, she's out with Peter. Nobody's ill. But Mr and Mrs Taylor have been here.'

'Why?' exclaimed Laura.

Gerry said grimly, 'That nut job. That Rilla is expecting a baby and says it's Peter's.'

'*Peter's?*' gasped Laura. 'No way. He couldn't stand her. At least he was polite to her for our sake but no way could that have happened. He only saw her the night we went round the clubs and then at his parents' house.'

'And he left there soon after we arrived, after he'd introduced us to his parents,' Gerry said.

'That's when she says he made a date with her,' Anne said. 'Can you remember what happened the next night? She says she went out with him. I've been racking my brains trying to remember.'

'I don't remember, Mum,' Laura said. 'I only know I wasn't with her because I avoided her after that night at the clubs.'

'Why did you say Peter couldn't stand her, Laura?' her father asked suddenly. 'He seems to have scarcely seen her.'

'It was that night we went round the clubs with them,' Laura said. 'We went to a cafe in Dale Street and met Peter there. When we were coming away she flung her arms round his neck and kissed him and he had to pull her arms away. He said to Phil Casey he thought he'd been attacked by an octopus, then he saw me there and said he was sorry. I told him I couldn't stand her either.'

'Doesn't sound as though he fancied her, does it?' John said to Anne and her eyes filled with tears.

'I feel so ashamed,' she said. 'Poor Mr and Mrs Taylor. What a return for their kindness.'

'Does Peter know?' Laura asked.

Her father said grimly, 'Yes. Stephen wrote to them and said Peter wasn't answering Rilla's letters. Mr Taylor told us Peter asked them to burn them when they came. Mr Taylor rang Peter to tell him and apparently Peter just kept saying, "No way, Dad", over and over. Mr Taylor thinks Peter's girlfriend was in the room with him and he couldn't speak freely but he's coming to see them tomorrow.'

'We've had a letter from Stephen and Margaret too,' Anne said. 'They're terribly upset. They say Rilla wouldn't admit she was pregnant at first, then she wouldn't say who the father was, but then she suddenly broke down and told them it was Peter but he wouldn't answer her letters.'

'That's what worries me,' John said. 'Why did he ask his mother to burn them unread?'

'You sound as though you doubt him,' Laura said hotly. 'It was because his girlfriend's so jealous, that's all.'

'Can't they do tests or something?' Gerry asked. 'Anyone could say something like this, couldn't they?'

'Not until the baby's born,' Anne said. 'Margaret says she's about six months so the dates fit. I wanted to phone them but we thought we'd see if you or Gerry could remember anything that would help. I don't believe it for a minute. I think that girl's just making it up about Peter.'

'I think she's cracked,' Gerry said bluntly. 'Mrs Taylor says Peter gets fan mail sometimes at their house but she just passes them on to someone at the group who deals with them. He only said about the Canadian ones to burn them because the first one was so crazy and she was a relation of mine so he didn't want anyone else to see them. And this is his thanks.'

'Well, there's nothing we can do tonight,' John said. 'We might as well go to bed. Perhaps you two could think back to that time and try to remember what happened the night after you went to the Taylors' house.'

'I'll wait for Julie,' Anne said. 'Does anyone want tea?'

All declined and went up to bed. Julie arrived a few minutes later and she and her mother soon followed the rest of the family. Anne said nothing to Julie about the events of the evening, she felt unable to go through the whole sorry tale again.

Laura had planned a peaceful, happy time before she slept, going over the evening in her mind and thinking about Nick, but she found it impossible to think of anything but her cousin Rilla and Peter.

I know she's making it all up, she thought indignantly. Perhaps she's not even really pregnant, just having one of those phantom pregnancies. Certainly there was nothing between her and Peter Taylor, except that she had a stupid crush on him. But how to prove it?

Even if it could be proved that Peter was not the father after the baby was born so much harm could be done before that, not only in his private life with Gail but also to his career. Laura tried desperately to remember those few days after Rilla had met Peter but her mind was still blank when she fell asleep.

The next morning her mother looked at her hopefully. 'Did you remember anything, love?' she asked but Laura could only shake her head.

'Gerry couldn't either,' Anne said with a sigh. 'He feels terrible about it. Wishes he had never let that faggot talk him into taking her round the clubs and particularly to the Taylors'.'

'Nothing we can do about that now, Mum,' Laura said, hugging her mother. 'Don't worry. We know it's a lie and truth will out, as Grandma used to say.'

'I hope you're right,' her mother said as Laura bolted some toast and drank a cup of tea. 'I'm going to ring round the family and see if anyone can remember anything useful. I'm so upset about the Taylors.'

Laura was halfway to the station before she remembered that she had said nothing to her mother about Nick and hoped that she heard nothing from Mrs Barret.

As soon as she walked in the office, Brenda called to her. 'All right, dark horse. Who was the tall, dark, handsome man you were in the Odeon bar with last night? And don't say he was your brother or your cousin.'

'I wasn't going to,' Laura protested.

Brenda said laughing, 'Good job. No brother or cousin should be looking at you the way he was. What's his name?'

'Nick. Nick Clegg,' Laura said, blushing. 'I didn't see you there, Brenda.'

'No wonder.' Brenda grinned and began to sing, 'I only have eyes for youhoo.'

'Come on, tell us more,' Olive demanded and Laura told them that he was a friend of a man she knew and that she was seeing him again on Saturday night.

'Where did you meet him?' Olive asked and when Laura told her that it was the Cabaret Club she said indignantly, 'And you never let on yesterday?'

'I was undecided whether to keep the date,' Laura said and was thankful that the chief clerk walked through the office at that moment and they all dispersed to their desks.

Laura tried at intervals during the day to cast her mind back to the days when her Canadian cousins were in Liverpool, particularly the time immediately after Rilla's meeting with Peter Taylor, but she was unable to remember the evenings in detail.

When she reached home, her mother told her that she had telephoned her brother Stephen in Canada. 'Your dad said he was going to so I did it now. Dad's so annoyed he might say too much to Stephen.'

'What did Stephen say? Do they still believe Rilla?' Laura added eagerly.

'Yes. Stephen got quite ratty with me. I told him it was completely out of character for Peter and told him what you said about the octopus and he was really huffy. He said, "My little girl's highly strung but she's not a liar. If she says it's him, it's him." I asked him what Terry said about it but he said he's in Ottawa on business and then he put the phone down on me. I was upset at first but now I don't care if they do fall out with us.'

'I don't think they've told Terry anything about it,' Laura said. 'He's never mentioned it in his letters to me.'

Anne's eyes had filled with tears but she wiped them away. 'I went round to Sarah's this afternoon and told her about it and she was furious. You know she and Joe never say anything nasty about anyone but I think they'd had more than enough of those girls when they stayed there. The things she told me about what went on with them! She said Margaret and Stephen had no control over them at all and they did what they liked. The were absolutely spoiled and unprincipled.'

'That's a thought!' Laura exclaimed. 'What about Joy? She wouldn't back Rilla up in her lies because they hate each other.'

'Not unless it suited her,' Anne said grimly. 'Who knows with that pair. Stephen didn't mention her and I never thought about her.'

Julie, who was now a librarian, was on late duty but John and Gerry arrived home from work and Anne told them about her phone call to Canada. 'I wish you'd left it to me, Anne,' John said. 'I'd have demanded more details from him to get this sorted out.'

Laura expected her mother to tell him why she had made the call but she only said that she had been to see Sarah and that she had told her a lot about the two Canadian girls.

They had just finished their meal when Sarah and Joe arrived and Joe told them that he had phoned Stephen in Canada.

'So did I,' Anne exclaimed. 'What did he say to you? That his little girl didn't tell lies?'

'I told him his own common sense should tell him that it was all fantasy,' Joe said grimly. 'I reminded him about the way she carried on about the Beatles and all the rest of them. If she'd had a date with Peter

Taylor she'd have been shouting it from the rooftops but he said Peter had asked her to keep quiet about it because of his girlfriend.'

'The crafty bitch!' Laura exclaimed.

'She's dangerous, mixing fact with fiction,' Gerry said.

Joe went on, 'I advised him to find out who was really the father. Obviously someone she doesn't want them to know about and probably someone near home. I said she probably named Peter because she lived in a fantasy world and she thought he was so far away it wouldn't matter but these groups are plagued by hysterical girls and they have lawyers to deal with them so he'd better be careful. They could find themselves in a lot of trouble.'

'That was clever, Joe,' Anne said admiringly. 'What did Stephen say?'

'Not much. He seemed a bit stunned. I think it's given him something to think about. Don't worry any more about it, Anne. It'll be sorted out.'

'I'm just so upset about the Taylors,' Anne said. 'Ashamed that our family should have brought this trouble on them. If only we could remember what happened that night she was supposed to be with Peter.'

'Has anyone talked to Peter?' Joe asked.

'No. Mr Taylor told him over the phone and Peter just said it wasn't true but he was seeing his parents today to talk about it,' said Anne.

'Perhaps it can be done the other way,' Joe said. 'Peter may be able to prove where he was at the time she says he was with her.'

Gerry jumped to his feet. 'I'll go to the Taylors,' he said. 'Tell them what we've done and see what Peter's told them. I won't be long,' and he dashed out.

'It's going to be difficult to prove he wasn't with her at some time,' John said. 'I mean,' he hesitated and glanced at Laura then he went on, 'it doesn't take long and if she's saying it was a furtive meeting...'

Does he think I don't know the facts of life? Laura thought angrily but then she thought he expected her to say he was making a point in favour of Rilla's claim. I know he's not and it's a good point, she thought honestly, but she said nothing and went out to the garden.

I still haven't told Mum about Nick, she thought. Trust me to have my pleasure spoiled by something like this coming up, then she felt ashamed as she thought of the real trouble other people were experiencing.

She knew that Terry was due back from Ottawa the next week and she decided to write to him and tell him the whole story. Rilla would wriggle out of any evidence they offered that she was not with Peter when she said she was. As her father said, a furtive coupling need only take a short time and Rilla was quite capable of twisting her story to make it sound plausible. Laura felt disgusted as she thought of a decent man like Peter facing such an accusation. Phil Casey will go mad, she thought. Terry was on the spot and he could make Rilla tell the truth.

Unlike her parents, he could see her in her true colours and he would not hesitate to cross-examine her. It offered much more hope than anything that could be done at this end, she thought. Then we can forget the whole messy business.

When Gerry returned he told them that Peter and Gail had consulted the solicitor who acted for the group, who had asked to see Stephen's letter. He had advised them not to answer it but to leave matters with him. He had given Peter a copy of a rough draft of a letter he intended to send.

'I couldn't get over it,' Gerry said. 'It warned them that they were making a serious accusation which could damage his client's reputation and career and cause much mental distress to him and to his family. I can't remember all of it but there was something about Peter categorically denying the accusation and that groups were subject to these claims from hysterical girls, which always proved to be unfounded, and sometimes professional help from a psychiatrist was needed. It was brilliant.'

'Pretty much what our Joe said to Stephen,' Anne said. 'He's got a good brain, our Joe. I'm sorry they've gone home.'

'People don't realise how clever he is because he's so quiet,' Laura said, glancing at her father. 'But he can run rings round others who make a lot of noise.'

'Mrs Taylor felt much happier about the whole thing, Mum,' Gerry said hastily. 'But she was worried about upsetting you.'

'I hope you told her I've been worried about her,' Anne said. 'But it looks as though it can all be sorted out now.'

'And Gail was with Peter?' Laura was astonished. 'I thought he'd have to hide it from her.'

'Mrs Taylor said Peter was so upset last night he had to tell her. He thought she'd blow her top but she was great. It was her idea to go to the solicitor.'

'Just shows you should never judge people too hastily,' Anne said but she sighed. 'I can't help worrying about Margaret and Stephen. To be told the girl is unbalanced on top of everything else. I don't know how they'll bear it.'

'Don't waste sympathy on them,' John said brusquely. 'They're only reaping what they've sowed. Anyway, there's been enough fuss about this business. Forget it, Anne. Put it right out of your head and let them sort it out themselves.'

'That's easier said than done,' Laura snapped. She put her arm round her mother and said quietly, 'Don't worry, Mum. When it's sorted out they'll probably decide that Rilla was upset and confused because of her condition. They'll find some way of excusing her, you'll see.'

Gerry took books from the sideboard and went into the other room to study and John waited until Laura moved away from her mother then went to Anne and kissed her.

'I'm going to the Labour Club for an hour, love,' he said. 'Someone I want to see but I won't be long.'

'Yes, all right.' Anne smiled at him. 'Don't forget, I'll do those envelopes for them.'

'OK. It'll be a great help,' John said, smiling back at her.

Laura watched them with disgust. Why doesn't she snarl back at him when he speaks to her like that, she thought, instead of being so meek with him?

John went and Laura and her mother were alone in the living room. 'I wish you wouldn't pick your dad up so sharply, Laura,' Anne said. 'He only wants what's best for us but he can't say anything right as far as you're concerned.'

Laura was astounded and gaped at her mother, too surprised to think of a reply.

266

Anne went on firmly, 'I know you're not very happy at present, love, but you shouldn't take it out on other people. Dad has had his own disappointment with Labour losing the election in June and all his worries about what this Heath fellow is doing. Try to control your temper, Laura, and watch your tongue.'

Laura felt as though something had burst in her head and she faced her mother trembling with anger. 'You tell *me* to watch my tongue. What about him? The way he speaks to you and when I try to defend you, you pick on me. It's always me who's in the wrong. Everyone knows he's a bully.'

'*Laura!*' Anne said sharply. 'Don't you speak like that about your dad. Show some respect. I know you pride yourself on speaking your mind but you go too far.' She, too, was red-faced with anger and hearing the raised voices Gerry came from the back room.

'Hey, hey, what's going on?' he said. 'Sounds as though you need a referee.' Laura pulled away and stormed out into the garden although it was already dark.

The light from the window made shadows and her feet scuffled through fallen leaves as she rushed to the apple tree at the bottom of the garden and leaned against it, tears of shock and outrage pouring down her face. If her mother had suddenly bitten her she could not have been more surprised.

The way I've tried to defend her, she thought wretchedly, and now she turns on me and takes his part. Blames me for being bad-tempered when I've only shouted at him when he's been bullying her. And that crack about me being unhappy. She means because the other two are settled and I'm on my own. Laura had just decided that wild horses would not make her tell her mother about Nick when Gerry came into the garden.

'Lol,' he called then came close to her. 'There you are,' he said. 'Come in. It's too cold and damp out here and Mum's upset about you.'

'Do you think I'm not after what she said to me?' Laura said, keeping her tear-stained face averted from him.

Gerry put his arm round her and said gently, 'We're all on edge with this business, Lol. Mum would never have flown off the handle like that if she hadn't been all strung up about this business with Rilla, blast her.'

They began to walk slowly back to the house but Laura said with a sniff, 'It's unfair, Gerry. Mum blaming me and sticking up for him when I was only complaining about the way he spoke to her. Telling her to put it out of her mind in that tone as though she was fussing about nothing.'

'Yeah, well, I don't think it was just that. You and Dad do get across each other, don't you? And Mum's pig in the middle trying to keep the peace. I think she'd suddenly had enough on top of this other business. The trouble is you and Dad are too alike.'

'*Gerry*,' Laura exclaimed. 'How can you say that? We're not alike at all.'

Gerry still had his arm round her and he gave her a hug. 'Of course you are,' he said. 'Both strong-minded. The irresistible force meeting the immovable object.' He laughed. 'Come on. My feet are freezing.'

Anne came to Laura as they went in the house and kissed her. 'I'm sorry I upset you, love,' she said.

Laura thought that her mother had not admitted that she was wrong but she said nothing and gratefully accepted a steaming cup of tea.

Gerry decided to abandon his studies and stayed in the living room with his tea so there was no opportunity for Laura to tell her mother privately about Nick. She went up to bed as soon as she had finished the tea, not sorry to defer telling her mother. Worn out by her emotion, she fell asleep immediately.

Chapter Twenty-One

Although the quarrel between Laura and her mother had been brief, it affected Laura deeply. She felt that it opened her eyes to many things to which she had been blind.

Her mother had never criticised their father to the children but Laura had seen that as misguided loyalty and a desire to keep the family together. She believed that, for the same reason, her mother had never argued or resisted. Laura had always viewed her as a victim of her husband's selfishness and bullying, needing protection until the day came when she could leave him and live in peace with her loving daughter.

Now Laura suddenly saw that long-held dream for what it was, a childhood fantasy, a fairy story that could never come true. Her mother would never leave her father. Whether it was because she had been brainwashed, dominated for too long, as Laura suspected, or because of her strong sense of duty, she would stay with him until parted by death.

Laura's outrage at her mother's defence of her father and criticism of herself returned but she thought sadly that in spite of that she could never leave her mother. I'll just have to stay and look after her, she thought, whether she appreciates me or not.

She had still said nothing to her mother about Nick but when Saturday morning came and they were alone in the kitchen, she said abruptly, 'I won't be here to eat tonight. I'm going out for a meal and to a singing pub.'

'That'll be a nice change,' Anne said. 'With Mary?'

'No, with a fellow I met at the Cabaret Club. Nick Clegg,' Laura said. Her mother looked round in surprise and Laura added quickly,

'He knows Peter Taylor and his friend Phil Casey. They all drink in the Elephant in Woolton.'

'So he lives in Woolton?' Anne said.

Laura told her that he was from Ormskirk but was at Christ's College in Woolton.

'That's where Gerry's hoping to go,' her mother exclaimed.

'Yes. There was a crowd of them at the club celebrating a twenty-first. Phil introduced us to some of them. I went to the pictures with Nick on Tuesday night.'

She expected her mother to ask reproachfully why she had said nothing at the time but instead Anne put her arm round her shoulders. 'And you walked into all that hassle about that Rilla,' she exclaimed. 'I'm sorry, love, I hope it didn't spoil your night.'

Laura laughed. 'No, of course not,' she said. 'Have you heard any more about that business?'

'No. We'll just have to wait now, I suppose,' Anne said. She longed to ask for details about Nick but since the night of the quarrel a gulf seemed to have opened between herself and Laura. It was nothing really, only a few words, Anne thought, yet it seems to have altered things so much between us. She felt that she had to watch her words carefully now, yet no matter how difficult Laura had been with other people in the past she had always been a loving daughter to her and had never spoken sharply to her.

Laura enjoyed the night out with Nick although it started with an argument. She knew that students' grants were small and few of them had any other income so she told Nick that she would go Dutch. He looked at her with such surprise that she explained, 'I mean we'll go half on expenses tonight and any time I go out with you.'

'No, you won't,' he said angrily. 'If I ask a girl out I don't let her pay for herself.'

Laura picked up her bag and scarf. 'All right. Ta-ra,' she said, pushing back her chair

Nick gripped her arm. 'What do you think you're doing?' he said furiously.

'I'm going,' she said. 'Everybody does this now. Why should you be different? If you won't let me pay my share, I'm not staying.'

'You're making that up. Everybody doesn't go Dutch, as you call it. You're just saying that because you think I'm destitute as I'm on a grant.'

'Don't be daft. I don't know anything about your circumstances. I only know I earn a good salary so I don't have to be the little woman. I have my pride too, you know.' Nick sat looking at her, uncertain whether he should be offended, and Laura began to laugh. 'Well, are we on?' she demanded. 'Or do I have to go?'

Nick laughed too. 'I thought you said you were old-fashioned,' he said. 'You sound like New Woman to me.' But Laura had her way and they shared expenses.

Nick suggested going to the Elephant on Sunday when many of his friends would be there but Laura refused. She liked him but felt that she would rather wait to be more sure before appearing as his official girlfriend.

She looked forward to telling Mary all about it on Monday but when they met at lunchtime Mary was bursting with news which she began to tell before they even went into the cafe. 'What do you think?' she began. 'Monica had a baby girl on Thursday and Cathy and Joanne went to see her on Sunday. It's the image of Denis!'

'*Denis*?' Laura exclaimed. 'But what about – she's married to Bert. I thought it was his.'

'So did he,' Mary said. 'Still does because crafty Monica said to the girls that the baby was the image of her Aunt Madge who lives in London. They said there's no doubt though, no matter what she says. The child is the dead spit of Denis.'

'But the Aunt Madge – is it like her too?'

'Who knows? Nobody's seen her for years. She didn't come for their wedding but then not many people did. No wonder it was such a quiet affair and rushed through the way it was. Bert's been taken for a sucker all right.'

'Poor Bert,' Laura said. 'I hope he never finds out. Has Denis been to see the baby?'

'No. Cathy said she couldn't resist asking about him but Monica said he had been very tactful. He'd told them that he realised that newlyweds wanted to be on their own. That two was company and three a crowd and he was working away at present anyway.'

'No flies on Monica,' Laura commented.

'No. Cathy said it'd make your flesh creep to see her holding Bert's hand and the soft fool drooling over her and the baby,' Mary said.

'Do you know, that's made me think. I wonder what Rilla's baby will look like?'

'It won't look like Peter Taylor, that's for sure,' said Mary grimly. 'But what about Gail? Who'd have imagined she'd be so calm about it? I thought she'd have been on the first plane to Canada to tear Rilla's head off.'

They both laughed but Laura said thoughtfully, 'Just shows. You can never tell with people, can you?'

The lunch hour was nearly over before she was able to talk about Nick, although she knew Mary was interested in him.

'Is he still as silent?' Mary asked. 'Or was he just struck dumb by your beauty that night?'

No matter how Mary joked, Laura knew that there was no malice in her comments and she told her that Nick had plenty to say when they were out. 'Too much, sometimes,' she said. 'He's a bit opinionated at times.'

'Speaks his mind?' Mary gave her a sidelong glance and when Laura agreed, she said laughing, 'You two should have some interesting conversations. Both with strong opinions on most things.'

'We've come near to a few bust-ups already,' Laura admitted. She told Mary about the argument about sharing expenses and Mary said she thought it was only fair in the circumstances.

'I earned more than Danny so we always went fifty–fifty when we went out. Still do, though it's more like seventy–thirty now because Dan can't work overtime while he's studying and he has to buy a lot of books and stuff for the course. When he qualifies, things will be different, of course.'

'Our generation is more sensible about things like that,' Laura said. 'When I think about the way my father bullied my mother just because she wanted to take a job! Mind you, she got her own way in the end.'

'Is she still working for the pools?' asked Mary.

'Yes, but only temporary work, and they are only called back for such short periods. She's applied for a post as school secretary though,' said Laura.

'My mother wouldn't have had the spirit to even suggest taking a job to my father,' Mary said scornfully. 'But times are changing.'

'They certainly are,' said Laura. She was silent for a moment thinking of the tale Terry had told her about Maureen and the married man she loved. Should Maureen and Chris have lived together like Mary and Danny? Would they have been happy or would Maureen's scruples have spoiled their life together? Too late now anyway, she thought sadly.

All the family were worried about Maureen. The remission of the disease had been short and when Sarah and Joe had visited her the previous Sunday they had found her in the infirmary of the rest home. The nun who was caring for her explained that Maureen was now unable to hold a cup or to manage cutlery and in the infirmary there would always be someone on hand to help her.

Anne and John had decided to visit her on Wednesday and Laura had arranged her flexitime so that she could accompany them. Julie and Gerry were unable to arrange time off but they sent flowers and loving messages to their aunt who had always been special to her nephews and nieces.

Maureen was propped up on a pile of pillows and was very happy to see them. She was in a six-bed ward with two empty beds and she told them that the three other patients had much more to bear than she had. The woman in the bed opposite had a cage-like arrangement supporting her bedclothes and Maureen said that her arthritis was so painful that she was unable to bear the weight of the bedclothes on her legs.

'She never complains,' Maureen said, 'although she is in so much pain.' She told them that another patient was in the terminal stage of cancer and the other was in for a rest because she suffered from angina.

They were shocked to see how much weaker Maureen seemed to be and John urged her not to talk and tire herself. She smiled at him. 'It won't make much difference, John,' she said gently. 'I love to see people, especially the family, and talk to them,' but she seemed breathless.

Anne took Maureen's hand and leaned her face against it and they all talked quietly until presently a nun came with a feeding cup for Maureen and lifted her higher on her pillows. The curtains were drawn round the bed and her visitors retreated to the bottom of the bed. John went off to smoke and Anne talked to the arthritis sufferer.

Another nun came carrying a magnificent bouquet to the patient. 'More flowers, Mrs Hunt,' she said. 'Aren't they all very good to you?' and then to Anne, 'Mrs Hunt has four grand, clever sons. All very important men in different parts of the world but sure they never forget their mother. The flowers and the baskets of fruit!'

Anne smiled at the woman as the nun carried the flowers away to find vases and Mrs Hunt said in a weak voice, 'Sometimes I wish they weren't so clever. Even one or two of them near home so they could visit me. I envy Maureen her visitors.'

'We were such a big family, you see,' Anne said quickly. 'I was the youngest of eight and Maureen was the second eldest. She was like a mother to me.'

'Aye. She's a lovely woman,' said Mrs Hunt. 'I think they're ready for you now.'

The curtains had been pulled back and Maureen was sitting up on her pillows looking fresh and comfortable but they were alarmed to see that an oxygen cylinder had been put in place by her bed and that she held the mask in her left hand.

'It's all right, Anne,' Maureen said quickly. 'Sister put it there in case I need it. They're wonderful, you know. You never have to ask for anything. It's always there before you even know you need it. Now tell me, Laura, are you enjoying your car?'

'Oh yes,' Laura said eagerly and told her aunt about her expeditions in the car and then about her dates with Nick. She stopped when Maureen lifted the oxygen mask to her face but Maureen took it away briefly and said, 'Go on talking, love. I can take this while you talk. I'm enjoying hearing all this,' so Laura told her that Nick was at Christ's College and of his teaching practice in Kirkby. Anne then talked to her about Julie and Peter and Gerry and Margaret, while Maureen took more oxygen. Finally she put the mask aside and smiled at them.

'That's better,' she said. She took Anne's hand. 'I'm so happy, love, to see you settled with a good man and such good children. You were always my little pet. Such a happy little girl, you were, and you made everyone around you feel happy. Remember Uncle Fred's name for you? Happy Annie.'

Laura could see that her mother was struggling with tears but she said steadily, 'Ah yes. Happy days. Those parties at Uncle Fred's when we were all young and Mum and Dad still with us. They were great.'

Maureen smiled. 'Theresa and Jim came to see me with their youngest child last week. Did you know they have seven children now, including two sets of twins?'

'Yes, and Theresa looks after Aunt Carrie as well and takes it all in her stride,' Anne said. She turned to Laura. 'These are the relations in Runcorn. Aunt Carrie is my mother's sister and Fred was her husband. Theresa is their daughter.'

'She's a case,' Maureen said. 'She said one of her older girls was going out at nearly eleven o'clock and when she was telling her off, Aunt Carrie said, "Leave her alone and let her enjoy herself. She's only young once." Theresa was so indignant. She said, "You know, Maureen, Mam would have knocked me from here to next week if I'd come home at that time, never mind going out."' The oxygen seemed to have helped Maureen and she breathed easily even after talking.

Anne said happily, 'Theresa was always a good laugh. She and our Eileen were a right pair. The tricks they played on the lads they went out with!'

'Aunt Eileen in Dublin?' Laura said in surprise and Anne laughed.

'Yes. We weren't always the sedate old people we are now, you know. Eileen and Theresa between them went out with half the lads in Liverpool.'

'But it was all very innocent,' Maureen said. She seemed breathless again and lifted the oxygen mask to her face.

Anne stood up. 'We'll go now, Mo, and let you rest,' she said gently. 'But we'll come again soon.'

Maureen took the mask away and said, 'Thanks for coming, love. I feel so much better for seeing you, and you, Laura pet.' They both kissed her and John, who had appeared in the doorway, came to the bed.

'I knew you'd want to talk to Anne,' he said, kissing Maureen. 'Take care now.' Maureen held his hand and murmured something to him and he said quietly, 'I will, Mo. Don't fret.'

Laura wondered what had been said but her father volunteered no information. Her mother had missed the exchange as she was saying goodbye to the other patients. Anne smiled cheerfully as she waved to Maureen from the doorway of the ward but as soon as they were out of Maureen's sight she wept without restraint. Laura put her arm round her, weeping herself but trying to comfort her mother.

John had paused to speak to a nun who had emerged from a nearby room and Anne and Laura had almost reached the car when he joined them. 'Oh John, doesn't Mo look ill?' Anne said tearfully. 'What did Sister say?'

John said evasively, 'I was only thanking her for looking after Mo so well. Being so kind to her. Did you notice the oxygen cylinder was placed on her left because she has some power in her left hand and can manage the mask herself. She's getting the best of care, Anne.'

'Yes, I know,' Anne said in a muffled voice but Laura knew that she was not comforted.

Sarah and Joe arrived soon after they reached home and Anne told them about the oxygen and Maureen's weakness but said that she was still cheerful. Laura told them about Maureen's visit from Theresa but John said nothing.

No one noticed when he slipped away but when Laura went into the hall later he was using the telephone and waved at her furiously to close the door into the living room. Then she heard him say, 'That's the position, Eileen. I thought you should know but I don't know how you're placed for coming over. You know you're very welcome to stay here if you come.'

Laura went up to the bathroom feeling as though there was a heavy weight on her chest. Was Maureen so ill then? But she had been ill for so long and recovered on other occasions. Surely her father was just being alarmist. She wondered what the nun had really said to him and why Maureen had whispered to him.

When she came out of the bathroom she saw that her Uncle Joe was also in the hall and as she descended the stairs she heard him say, 'Thanks, John. It had to be done but you've saved me doing a job I dreaded.'

'They were both upset but they knew it had to come. You're never really prepared for it, though, are you?'

They looked up and saw Laura and Joe said hurriedly, 'I'd better go back. They'll wonder where we are.' Laura was about to follow him but her father took her arm and drew her into the front room.

'You saw how ill Maureen was today,' he said. 'I've just rung Eileen and Terry and they'll both come to see her. Stephen and Margaret can't leave Rilla at present.'

'But Dad, is she really going to *die*?' Laura gasped.

'I'm afraid so, love,' her father said gravely. 'The sister told me that it can't be long now. Her heart is failing. She said we must be prepared. Maureen herself knows.'

'You mean they've told her?' Laura said indignantly.

'They don't need to. Maureen knows how ill she is but she is quite happy and prepared for death. She whispered to me to try to make it easy for Mum. That's why I'm telling you, Lol. Mum and Maureen have always been so close that she'll be heartbroken. We'll all have to try to soften the blow for her.'

Laura was crying bitterly and he put his arms round her and held her close. After a few minutes she raised her head from his shoulder and drew away, wiping her eyes and saying resolutely, 'I'm all right now, Dad. I'll run upstairs and bathe my eyes before I go back. Are you going to tell Mum?'

'Not in so many words,' he said. 'I don't think I'll need to. I'll tell her I've sent for Terry and Eileen – but I'll choose the right moment.'

'And I'll be here with her. I can take time off. I've got holidays in hand,' Laura said eagerly.

'No. Save them. You might need them later to help Mum,' John said.

It seemed to Laura that she and her father had never been as close as they were at this time. They were united in their tender care for Anne in her grief for her beloved sister and Laura felt no jealousy when Anne turned to John and John never resented but rather encouraged Anne's clinging to Laura.

Sarah and Joe's grief was made worse by worry about Rosa who seemed to have disappeared but during Maureen's last days a phone call from David brought them comfort. He said that Rosa was safe and was staying with him and they would both travel to Liverpool together. He would tell them more when they arrived.

'I don't care what made her stay away from us,' Sarah said to Anne. 'I'm just so relieved that she's safe.'

Terry and Eileen and Martin arrived within a few days, Terry staying with Anne and John, and Eileen and Martin with Tony and Helen as David and Rosa were home with their parents.

Terry's presence was a comfort to Laura, although there was little opportunity for private conversation. All their minds were filled with thoughts of Maureen.

Eileen had planned to travel alone but Martin told Tony that he thought she would be too upset to make the journey alone. 'She worried about me leaving the business again so soon but our Kathleen's husband is a grand man. He'll keep an eye to the business for me and our two lads are staying with him and Kathleen,' he said.

Tony said seriously, 'I'm glad, Martin. She'll need you, especially going back. You're a good man yourself.'

When David and Rosa arrived Rosa flung herself at her parents, weeping and telling them that she was sorry that they had worried about her. 'I just didn't notice the time passing,' she said. 'I hadn't realised it was so long since I'd seen you until David told me off about it.'

David told them later that Rosa had become attached to an actor in a repertory company and had travelled about with him. She had quarrelled with and parted from the man when she was near Cambridge and had come to him.

'She didn't intend to worry you,' David said. 'She just lives in a world of her own.'

278

All the family were able to visit Maureen during the last days of her life and all were comforted by her serenity and happiness. On the last day they were all gathered about her bed when the Irish sister who had chiefly cared for her brought water to moisten Maureen's lips.

Some could not restrain their tears but the sister said softly, 'Don't fret now. Sure, isn't it only a step she's taking from the ones she loves here to the loved ones who are waiting for her in heaven. Won't you all be together in God's good time?'

Maureen smiled round at them then her eyes closed, her breathing so soft that it was hard for them to realise when it ceased.

At her Requiem Mass the family were comforted by the feeling that it was less an occasion for mourning than a celebration of a good life. Many representatives were there from the charities with which Maureen had worked at home and abroad and many tributes were paid to her, but it was the words of an old priest who had known Maureen all her life that meant most to the family, and which were long remembered by them.

He said, 'The world is richer for Maureen. In her own quiet way she did so much good for so many people without thought for herself but now she has gone to her reward. We thank God for her and have all been enriched by knowing her. Our grief now is for ourselves who will miss her but all who love her will know that she has entered into happiness and rejoice for her. She never complained but used her suffering for others and her strong faith sustained and comforted her to the end. We thank God for Maureen.'

Friends and relations came back to Anne's house after the funeral, many of them unknown to Laura. A stout women came to her and Gerry and introduced herself. 'You don't remember me, do you? Monica, Bridie's daughter. I used to look after you when you were little when your mum was ill.'

'Monica?' Laura said doubtfully. 'I think so but you were very thin then.'

Monica laughed heartily. 'And now I'm very fat. You're your da's daughter all right. He always came right out with things.' She seemed unoffended but Laura was furious. The cheek of her, she thought. I'm nothing like my *da*, as she calls him.

Gerry said easily, 'Monica, yes, I remember you. Didn't you go to be a nursery nurse?'

'For a while,' Monica said. 'Then I went on to ordinary nursing. I'm a theatre sister now.' Gerry introduced Margaret and said that she was a physiotherapist and they were soon deep in conversation. Laura moved away. If I ever have a daughter I won't call her Monica, she decided.

Terry had told Laura by letter that on his return from Ottawa he had tried to make Stephen 'see sense' and thought that he had succeeded. Now he told her briefly not to worry about Rilla's accusations. It was all being sorted out.

Later, when only the immediate family were left, the subject of Rilla was discussed by them for the first time.

'What's happening, Terry?' Joe asked. 'We haven't heard any more from Stephen.'

Terry shrugged. 'She hasn't admitted she told lies about Peter Taylor but Stephen and Margaret know it was just fantasy,' he said. 'They've written to the Taylors and apologised. Told them the doctor says she is unbalanced at present and can't tell fact from fiction. Peter and his parents have been very understanding, Margaret told me.'

'And has she been treated by a doctor – for her mind, I mean?' asked Tony.

'She's been in hospital,' said Terry, 'but they're saying as little as possible to me. I'm just annoyed that I was away and couldn't stop Stephen going off half-cocked like that.'

'The more I think about it, the more I wonder at him and Margaret,' Anne said. 'A few things they said here made me think they'd had trouble before with that girl. Not like this, of course.'

'Remember Rilla going on about writing to people just when they were leaving?' Gerry said. 'Her mother said something then about pestering people and it always ends in tears.'

'I don't blame Margaret so much,' Terry said. 'She tries to be firm with those girls but Stephen undermines her and spoils them.'

'You know what he said to me, Terry, when I phoned them about this?' said Anne. 'He said, "My little girl is highly strung but she's not a liar" but evidently she is.'

'Stephen was always a fool,' John said bluntly. 'Look at the girls he went out with, even got engaged to. They could tell him anything, twist him round their little fingers, and he was too thick to see through them.'

'He was always gullible,' Tony agreed. 'He was lucky to escape from some of the harpies he got mixed up with. I know we were all relieved when he settled with Margaret.'

'I'm sorry for Margaret,' Terry said. 'When they've had trouble with the girls, especially Rilla, Margaret has all the worry. Stephen just won't face facts.'

'He'll have to face them now,' said Joe. 'When is the baby due exactly?'

'About a month, I think,' said Terry. 'I'll let you know as soon as it happens.'

Terry and Eileen and Martin all planned to leave the following day so they said goodbye to their relatives that evening.

'At least Rilla's affairs have taken our minds off our loss for a few hours,' Terry said as Sarah and Joe left.

'And put things in perspective,' Sarah said. 'Death makes everything else seem so trivial, doesn't it? Nothing else is worth worrying about.'

Chapter Twenty-Two

Laura had made no arrangements to go out either with Nick or Mary from the time of her father's warning until Maureen's death and for several days after the funeral. It was only when Anne and John arranged to visit Helen and Tony, and her mother urged her to go out, that Laura made a date with Nick.

She had explained to Mary during their lunchtime meetings that her mother had not asked her to stay with her. 'It isn't that she needs me because my father is at home more now and there's always either Julie or Gerry or one of my other relations there but I want to be with her. And I'm not in the mood for going out anyway.'

Mary had understood and said Laura should do whatever she wanted. She would know when she was ready to go out again but Nick grumbled several times when he phoned and she refused to go out.

She arranged to meet him in town and go for a drink with him and when they first met he was sympathetic but severely practical. 'I know you were upset but be reasonable, Laura,' he said. 'There was no cure possible so it could only mean more and more disablement and pain for your aunt as time passed. An early death was the best solution.'

'I know that,' Laura said angrily. 'But it doesn't stop us from grieving for her. My mother's heartbroken.'

'But for selfish reasons,' Nick said. 'You're thinking of yourselves, not your aunt.'

The fact that he was right made Laura even more angry and she said furiously, 'I suppose you think I'm making too much fuss.'

'It's a bit excessive, I think,' Nick admitted. 'After all, she's not a member of your immediate family is she?'

'She was my mother's sister and in our family that is *close*,' Laura said angrily. 'I don't know what your family's like but everyone matters in ours. When my grandma died it was the worst thing that had ever happened to me. She was my great-grandmother really and I go to see my nana and grandad every Tuesday after work. I love them.'

'Of course we hear this in psychology lectures that children often relate better to an older relative than to their own parents,' Nick said pompously.

Laura glared at him. 'Don't talk to me about bloody psychology,' she hissed. 'I'm talking about ordinary family feelings. About people caring about each other.'

'I wouldn't call that ordinary family feelings,' Nick said. 'It all sounds a bit extreme to me. A bit unhealthy.'

They were sitting at a small table near the window in the bar and Laura turned away from him. If I say anything I'll say too much, she thought. I don't want to make a show of myself, but she longed to scream at Nick and scratch his face.

He spoke to her several times but she kept her shoulder obstinately turned against him so he stood up and went to the bar.

He realised that he had offended her and meant to give her time to cool down but she could see him in a facing mirror chatting to the barman and laughing at something the man said. That was enough for Laura and she picked up her coat and handbag and left.

As soon as Nick realised she had gone, he left the bar and rushed after her but she ran through the side streets to the station. Nick was close behind her but a train was in and Laura stepped on to it just before the doors closed.

Nick came dashing down the platform and Laura could see his angry face through the train window as she was borne away but she was unrepentant. I've had enough, she told herself. I don't care if I never see him again.

Shortly after she left the station at Blundellsands she met her cousin David and he greeted her cheerfully. 'Hi. I've just been to your house to say goodbye because I go back to Cambridge tomorrow but only Julie was in. She didn't think you'd be back until late.'

'I didn't intend to be,' she said. 'But I couldn't stand that big-head any longer.' She had talked at length to David about Nick and Anne had also spoken approvingly about him so David was surprised.

'I thought he was OK,' he said. 'What happened?'

Laura poured out all the comments by Nick which had annoyed her so much and told David that she had walked out on him. 'Or run rather,' she said. 'He came flying down the platform just as the train moved off.'

'So he had to run after you?' David said thoughtfully. 'It doesn't sound as though he intended to hurt you.'

'But he implied there was something wrong with us because we were so upset about Maureen,' Laura said indignantly. 'That's more than tactless. He said we were extreme. Do you think we are, David?'

'No, but then I'm family,' he said with a grin. 'Perhaps we're a bit unusual in this day and age. They say family ties are loosening and the end of the seventies might mean the end of the family as a unit.'

'Not our family,' Laura declared. 'Anyway, I'm not going to be lectured by him about psychology as though I was a backward child or an hysterical female. I'm finished with him.'

David tucked her arm in his and walked back with her slowly. 'Don't be too hasty, Laura,' he said. 'I think we're all a bit on edge at present, a bit touchy. I thought Nick sounded a decent fellow. You've enjoyed going out with him, haven't you?'

'Yes, he can be good company,' Laura admitted. 'But he can be very opinionated too and I'm not putting up with being lectured.'

'You know best,' David said mildly, 'but nobody's perfect, you know, Lol. I think it's a question of finding someone with the sort of faults that you can tolerate. I could never stand anyone who was mean or selfish.'

'Nick hasn't got those faults,' Laura said swiftly. They had reached the gate of her house and David said he would say goodnight.

'I'd think about Nick's good points,' he said. 'Make quite sure it's what you want before you give him the chop, Lol.'

'I think I've already done that,' Laura said but she spoke ruefully.

It was a long time before Laura slept. Her mind was too active, at one moment recalling the comments by Nick which made her angry again and determined to finish with him and at another thinking of the good times they had spent together and the good points that David had advised her to look for.

She fell asleep eventually but woke feeling unrefreshed and thinking that it was pointless for her to think whether she should finish with Nick or not. She remembered his face as she had last seen him on the station platform and felt that the matter was already decided. He would never forgive the blow to his pride.

She said nothing about the quarrel either at home or at work and as it was the day when Mary went to the hairdresser's in her lunch hour she was unable to confide in her. Thoughts went round and round in her head and made it difficult for her to concentrate on her work and it seemed malign fate that a long document had to be prepared which kept her nearly an hour late in leaving the office.

Her father had been home and had left again but her mother and Julie chatted to her as she ate her meal. The telephone rang twice but both times her mother answered it, although Laura had jumped to her feet. 'Eat your meal, love,' Anne said. 'I'll answer it. It'll only be more messages for Dad. It's worse than ever now he's on the Council. The phone hasn't stopped tonight, has it, Julie?'

Julie agreed and when it rang a third time she went into the hall to answer it. They heard her say 'Hi' in a pleased tone then she stayed there talking and laughing, it seemed to Laura, for hours.

She was fuming as she drank a cup of tea and tried to answer her mother rationally when she asked about her day at the office but all the time she was wondering whether Nick was trying to phone to speak to her. Perhaps he had tried several times if the telephone had been engaged so much with messages for her father and now with Julie's marathon conversation.

On the other hand, it was quite possible, even probable, that he did not want to speak to her ever again, she thought with one of her sudden swings of mood. I don't care anyway, she thought defiantly, but she was relieved when Julie at last put down the phone and came back to the kitchen.

'Peter?' her mother said smiling at her and Julie blushed.

'Yes, he's sent off the application form for that post in the prep school.'

'Where is it?' asked Laura.

'On the Wirral,' said Julie. 'He thinks he'd like teaching younger boys and if he gets a housemaster's post I'd like it better with younger boys.'

Laura and her mother looked at each other in amazement and Julie said hastily, 'We're just looking ahead, of course, but this is the best time for Peter to decide.'

'Of course, of course,' her mother murmured but it was plain that Julie's plans had been a shock to her.

Julie turned to Laura. 'You haven't forgotten the Spanish, Lol, have you?'

Laura had indeed forgotten that she had arranged to enrol for Spanish lessons at evening classes with Julie but she said quickly, 'No, but it's a bit late tonight, isn't it? They're enrolling for three nights, aren't they?'

'Yes, we can go tomorrow night,' Julie said.

Their mother said placidly, 'Tomorrow the weather might be better. Just listen to that wind.' Neither she nor Julie commented on the fact that Laura had both nights free or asked any questions about Nick.

As the hours passed without a phone call from Nick, Laura realised how much she had secretly been expecting him to phone and apologise and how much she had wanted it to happen. Her pride prevented her from trying to call him although she made excuses to herself. It was impossible to reach him at the college and if she phoned his house she would probably get one of the other men. If Nick had told them about the quarrel she would feel humiliated, she told herself.

She went up to the bathroom and was plucking her eyebrows when the phone rang again and she threw down the tweezers and started out of the door but her mother had already picked up the phone. 'Hello? Hello, hello,' she kept saying and as Laura looked over the banisters she saw her mother flip over the pad by the phone and heard her say, 'A pen, quick.'

Julie put the pen in her hand and Anne said, 'Six o'clock this morning. Seven pounds, two ounces. Black hair.' She was scribbling furiously then she said, 'And both well? I'm so glad, Stephen.'

Then she wrote again. 'Margaret Stephanie.' She interrupted the babble from the phone to say, 'Congratulations to you and Margaret. Your first grandchild, and to Rilla too. I'm sure the baby will bring you a lot of happiness.' There was a little more excited speech down the phone then she said goodbye.

Laura came downstairs and her mother turned to her and Julie. 'Did you hear that, girls? Rilla had a daughter this morning.' She glanced at the pad in her hand. 'Stephen was so excited I had to jot things down. He was just tumbling it all out.'

Julie looked over her shoulder. 'Seven pounds, two ounces. Is that the baby's weight?'

'Yes. He said she's got a tuft of black hair but she opened her eyes when he looked at her and he thinks she knew him. He said she didn't just look blankly at him.'

'He didn't say it looked like Peter Taylor?' Laura asked.

Her mother said impatiently, 'Oh no. They've put all that nonsense behind them. They're going to call the baby Margaret Stephanie.' Laura was about to say more but Julie winked at her and shook her head. As they went back to the living room, Julie said in a low voice to Laura, 'Mum's made up. As much because the rift with the Canadians has been healed as about the baby,' and Laura was relieved that she had said nothing to spoil her mother's pleasure.

'I must tell Joe and Tony,' Anne said and immediately went to telephone but Joe's line was engaged. 'I spoke to Helen and she was pleased that Stephen let us know,' she said. 'I think I'll walk round to see Sarah and Joe, girls, because I couldn't get through to them.'

'I'll come with you,' Laura said. It was after ten o'clock and too late, she thought, for Nick to ring, yet she was relieved when Julie decided not to come with them. She would be at home to take any calls.

Laura hoped to see Rosa who was still staying at her parents' house but she was out when they arrived there.

287

Sarah and Joe were pleased to hear about Rilla's baby and Joe asked if Anne thought the Taylors should be told. 'I don't know,' she said doubtfully. 'Strictly speaking, it has nothing to do with them, does it? I don't want them to think that we think it has.'

'Mm, least said, soonest mended, I suppose,' said Joe.

'Gerry said Mr and Mrs Taylor were willing to let it drop,' Anne told them, 'although Gail thought Peter should sue them. The solicitor advised them that as Rilla and Stephen have apologised and Rilla has withdrawn the accusation they should let it drop. He says only the family know of it now and it's better to keep it like that.'

'Yes, there'd always be people who'd say there was no smoke without fire and that sort of thing,' Joe said. 'I think that was good advice.'

'I'm just sorry that there's been all this trouble because of our family. I think the Taylors have been very generous.'

'And if Rilla wants to come here again I'll be away from home,' Laura said.

Her mother nodded. 'Yes, and I'll come with you.'

When they returned home Julie said she had heard the phone while she was in the bath but it had stopped ringing before she could reach it.

'Probably yet another message for Dad,' Anne said. 'I think he'll have to install a secretary.'

Laura wondered whether it could have been Nick but decided that if he intended to get in touch he would have phoned earlier. If he was ringing so late it could only be because drink had given him Dutch courage.

A letter to Laura from Terry told more about the baby and Rilla. He wrote that the baby was small but healthy and, in his opinion, remarkably ugly. Very red and wrinkled with a tuft of dark hair like an Indian, but of course he had to admire it.

'I believe Rilla pinbrain told the nurses that its father was a famous pop star but they had been warned to ignore her fantasies. The important news is that a young man has turned up claiming to be the father. He says that he and Rilla have been meeting regularly, although she managed to conceal this from her parents and even from Joy. He is a clerk in a grocery store and apparently believes that Rilla is an heiress! They seem well matched but not much hope for the child.'

When John had returned home on the evening of Stephen's phone call, he showed little interest, seeming far more interested in a box of leaflets he carried, which he wanted the family to distribute, but when Laura read Terry's letter aloud he was annoyed.

'Have as little as possible to do with them, Anne,' he said. 'They haven't seen the last of their troubles with that girl but don't get involved. I know you want to keep in touch with Stephen but let them keep Rilla's antics in Canada. Don't invite them here.'

Laura expected her mother to argue but she only said mildly, 'Don't worry. I've had enough,' and seemed unperturbed.

The hours and days seemed to drag past as Laura waited to hear from Nick.

'No word from Nick yet?' Mary asked her over lunch. Laura shook her head and Mary went on, 'I think you should contact him, you know. After all, you were the one who ran out on him.'

'With good reason,' Laura flared. 'Anyway I don't care. I'm well rid of such a pig-headed fellow.'

'I thought he had a lot going for him. But you know best.' She glanced at her watch and stood up. 'I'll have to fly. Doesn't this hour go quickly?'

Laura agreed but thought that for her no hour went quickly. In spite of her defiant words to Mary, she longed to see Nick and would have snatched at the slightest move on his part to show regret for their quarrel but she felt unable to make the move herself.

The previous night she had gone with Julie to enrol for the Spanish classes and they had stayed talking to friends they met there who were enrolling for various courses. Better than sitting about waiting for the phone to ring, she told herself, but deep down she was wondering all the time whether there was a call from Nick.

As soon as they arrived home she looked hopefully at the message pad beside the phone but it was blank except for the indentations made by her mother's excited scribbling the previous night.

Now as she returned to the office she decided that she was going to stop hoping to hear from him and forget him. If he really cared for me he would be only too anxious to make up, she thought. After all, the quarrel was his fault although I was the one who actually left.

She was expected at her grandmother's house for the evening meal and she decided that she would stay there for the whole evening. I'll have to be careful to keep the conversation away from Nick though, she thought; she had said nothing at home about breaking with him.

She found it was easy to do this. Over the meal the conversation was all about gardening as her grandfather had grown the Brussels sprouts and the potatoes that they were eating. Afterwards he went to his study and Laura sat close to her grandmother as they talked about Maureen.

'I dread Christmas, Nana,' Laura said. 'It will be so strange without Aunt Maureen.'

Cathy sighed. 'I know, love. It's times like Christmas and birthdays that you feel it most, yet in a way they're the times you feel closest to the ones who have gone.'

'I still miss Grandma, but I know you and Grandad must miss her even more because she was always here with you.'

'Yes. I relied on her so much. On her good sense. She was always a tower of strength to all the people in the neighbourhood where we lived when I was young. You only knew her as an old lady, Laura, but she did so much for other people all her life.'

'There were a lot of people at her funeral,' Laura said. 'I remember an old man said to someone, "By God, there were plenty round us who would have foundered without Sally and Lawrie Ward." I thought that was lovely. To be remembered like that.'

'It was,' agreed Cathy. 'Before the welfare state, you know, Laura, people had no one to turn to except people like my mum and dad. When we were children we were quite used to hearing a knock at the door or a stone thrown at the window in the middle of the night and Mum would go out to help. Dad would go with her. They must have been at hundreds of deathbeds and at births too.'

'Grandma must have been very clever if so many people relied on her.'

'She was very sensible and experienced. She had her own remedies that she made herself and she was always so calm in an emergency.

Sometimes if she was just *there*, it helped. I remember a woman saying after some sort of accident, "People were screaming and we were all frantic then someone said Sally Ward's here and everyone calmed down."'

'I wish I could be remembered like that,' Laura said wistfully. She smiled. 'I'll probably be remembered for my big mouth.'

'Don't run yourself down, love. Anyway let's hope it's a long, long time before you need think about being remembered. You've got all your life ahead of you. We live in a different world and Grandma's skills aren't needed now with such a good health service.'

'"Security from the cradle to the grave,"' Laura quoted with a smile.

'Yes, it's my dad's dream come true. Mam always said that she did what was next to her hand but Dad worked on a bigger scale. Mind you, he did a lot to help neighbours in a practical way, stuff from his allotment and that sort of thing, but he'd tackle anyone. Go right to the top if necessary to get justice for poor people.'

'No wonder they were remembered as good people.'

'Yes, but they weren't thinking of being remembered when they did these things, love,' said Cathy. 'Just did them because they needed doing. Just like your dad does now as a councillor.'

Laura's head jerked round. 'My dad?' she exclaimed. 'I don't think it's the same at all. He's not a councillor for unselfish reasons. He enjoys the power it gives him.'

'I think you're too hard on him, Laura. He does an awful lot of good and he really tries to help people. You know he was always very close to my father and they talked about my dad's ideals even when John was only a little lad. He's tried all his life to live up to his grandad.'

'He has a funny way of doing it,' Laura muttered, fiddling with the braid on the arm of the chair. 'He rubs everyone up the wrong way and he's always causing rows among the committees because he argues about everything they propose.'

'That's his way of getting things done, I suppose,' said Cathy. 'People can't help the nature they were born with or inherited. My mother's father Matthew Palin had strong views and spoke out about them even if it got him into trouble, according to my mother.' She paused. Laura said nothing and kept her head down, still fiddling with the braid.

Cathy went on gently, 'You, if anyone, should understand him, Laura. He may be outspoken and offend people but he has a very kind heart and he really tries to help those who can't help themselves.'

Laura was uncertain about how to reply. She felt that she had hurt or annoyed her grandmother so she said no more about her father. 'Heredity is a strange thing, isn't it, Nan? The three of us have the same parents, brought up the same way yet we are all different, and Rosa and David couldn't be more different yet the same applies to them.'

'Sometimes you have to go further back, the same as with John,' said Cathy. 'Rosa may not be like our Sarah or like Joe but she puts me in mind of my own sister Mary. She was beautiful, too, and with that same red-gold hair and lots of boyfriends. She charmed everyone, Mary did, and she could twist my dad round her little finger, although our mam was strict with her. She was afraid Mary was too beautiful for her own good. I was like a little mouse beside her.'

Greg had come back into the room and he said quietly, 'Your nana's too modest, Laura. She was beautiful too but in a less flamboyant way than Mary and she had a lovely character to match her looks.' Cathy blushed and they smiled at each other. 'She hasn't changed, either,' Greg added.

To Laura it was like the thrust of a knife. They were old, really old, she thought, over seventy, yet they could still look at each other like that. Will I ever meet anyone who could love me like that, she wondered, or who I could love?

She thought of her unsatisfactory affair with Sean, her dates which never led anywhere and now Nick. She felt the familiar fear that she was unloveable as she compared herself with Rosa and Julie.

She stood up. 'Speaking about Rosa reminds me. I'd better get back. I've hardly seen Rosa since she came home and she might be at ours now.' Even to herself she could not acknowledge that she was anxious to see if there was a message from Nick.

Her grandfather insisted that he would drive her home. He seemed to think that she might have been upset by Cathy's words about Mary and Rosa and as soon as they were in the car he said quietly, 'Rosa has only been once to see us since she came home. I'm afraid she is like Mary unfortunately. Hard-hearted and selfish. Not like you, love.'

'Rosa's all right, Grandad,' Laura protested. 'She's not *really* selfish. She just gets mixed up with the wrong people but she's got a lovely character really.'

'Mary had some good points too,' Greg said, 'but she also mixed with the wrong people and was influenced by them. She brought a lot of grief to her parents and family, just as Rosa has done.'

They said nothing for a moment then Laura laughed. 'You were lucky that you married the right sister then, weren't you, Grandad?'

'I was indeed,' Greg said gravely. 'I hope you will be as happy as we are when you marry, Laura. It's not just luck, you know, love. You have to work at a marriage to make it a success. Give and take. That's the secret.' He glanced at her. 'Even when you're courting that applies. Cathy and I disagreed about several things when we were courting but a bit of give and take and we soon sorted them out.'

Laura felt that he understood more than she had realised about Nick and was trying to give her good advice. I suppose they wonder why I can never keep a boyfriend, she thought miserably, but they had reached her home so it was not necessary for her to reply.

Greg came in with her and they found Anne alone. Julie was out with Peter and Gerry with Margaret, she told them, and John had just sat down to his meal when he was called out to settle a dispute with a landlord. 'The woman was in floods of tears so he left his meal and went off with her, swearing vengeance on the landlord,' Anne said.

'He must be sorry sometimes that he's on the housing committee,' Greg said but Anne laughed.

'No, I think he enjoys a good fight, especially with someone who's trying to take advantage of a widow. How is Nana?'

'Very well,' Greg told her. 'She always enjoys a visit from Laura and Gerda and Mick are coming for the weekend.'

'We were talking about Grandma. All the good she did before the welfare state,' said Laura. 'It's hard to picture the lives women lived then, especially before the war. Grandma was badly needed.'

'Yes, she was a woman of her time,' Greg said. 'And very wise and tolerant too, although she was a woman of strong principles in her own life.'

A woman of her time. Laura repeated the phrase to herself, thinking that no one would ever apply it to her. I'm out of step with nearly everybody of my own generation. Even Nick, she thought suddenly.

She recalled on their second date Nick's casual question, 'Are *you* on the pill?' and her own swift reply: 'No, I don't need to be. I told you, I'm old-fashioned.' He had laughed and it had all seemed light-hearted but now she wondered. Perhaps he wanted to know where he stood and their quarrel had been fortuitous. It had given him the excuse to finish with her and find someone more 'with it' and less uncompromising about sex.

She was unaware that she was scowling until her grandfather touched her arm and said quietly, 'I'm off now love,' then even more quietly, 'Cheer up. Everything works out in the end.' He kissed her and said goodbye to Anne.

Laura went into the other room. She needed time to consider her unwelcome thoughts about Nick's motives before she spoke to anyone, and anyway, nobody here either knew or cared how she felt. None of them had even mentioned Nick to her, she thought bitterly.

Chapter Twenty-Three

Anne had watched Laura's scowling face with dismay. Whatever's upset her now? she thought. Laura's moods were so unpredictable and now she had disappeared into the back room to brood on something. She was so short-tempered that everyone was afraid to provoke her by asking any questions but Anne felt that Laura was the one who suffered most.

If only she'd tell me, talk to me, she thought. I can't help her when she bottles everything up like this. I know something has gone wrong between her and Nick but I can't ask her outright when she obviously doesn't want to talk about it.

She heard a car draw up and a moment later Julie and Peter Cunliffe came in. 'I've just come to say hello and goodbye, Mrs Redmond,' Peter said cheerfully. 'I've got to get off right away.'

'No time for a cup of tea?' Anne asked.

'Oh no, thanks all the same.'

Julie went to the door with him and came back smiling. 'We've had a lovely evening,' she said. 'We went out to a carvery in Aughton and then on to a pub where there was a fab group playing.'

Anne smiled at her. Thank God for Julie, she thought. Happy, uncomplicated Julie, then she felt guilty as she thought of Laura's unhappiness, which was surely the cause of her moods and short temper.

'Where's Dad?' asked Julie.

Anne told her about the weeping woman. 'He must be following it up tonight because he hasn't come back. He didn't have a mouthful of his tea either.'

'Never mind. He'll get something somewhere. Laura not back either?'

'Yes, Laura's back.' Anne looked meaningfully at Julie and jerked her head towards the other room. 'Grandad came in with her.'

'Something wrong?' Julie whispered.

'Not that I know of,' Anne whispered back. 'She seemed all right when they came in.'

They heard a noise in the hall and Laura looked in. 'Hi, Julie,' she said. 'Anyone want the bathroom? I'm going up for a bath.'

'No, no,' Anne said hurriedly. As Laura went upstairs, she said in a low voice, 'Oh Julie, I hope she didn't hear us talking about her.'

'She couldn't have done,' Julie assured her. 'And anyway, we weren't saying anything nasty about her.'

A little later Laura came down in her dressing gown and Julie made tea for all of them. A moment later they heard voices and Gerry came in at the back door with Phil Casey. Both were soaked, their hair plastered to their heads by the rain and their hands filthy.

Phil looked flushed and uncomfortable and he said diffidently, 'I'm sorry. It's so late. I could have driven straight home.'

'All the way to Woolton?' Gerry exclaimed boisterously. 'No way. I had a burst tyre and luckily Phil saw me and stopped to help. Is the bathroom clear, Mum?'

'Yes. There are plenty of towels in the airing cupboard,' Anne said, smiling at Phil.

Gerry led the way to the bathroom followed by Phil who smiled at Laura as he passed her. She nodded curtly, uneasily conscious of her faded candlewick dressing gown and her damp hair and shiny face.

'Gerry's an idiot,' she exclaimed as soon as the young men had gone upstairs. 'Barging in with him without any warning. Look at the state of me.'

'You're quite respectable,' Anne assured her.

Julie said mischievously, 'And nice and clean.'

'I'll cut some of that ham for sandwiches,' Anne said and both girls helped her. When Gerry and Phil returned with clean hands and dry hair the table had been laid for supper. Anne took Phil's wet jacket and hung it near the Aga to dry. He seemed bewildered and said nothing but Anne pressed him to eat and Laura poured tea for him.

Her dark mood seemed to have lifted and she joined cheerfully in the conversation.

The talk turned to Rilla. 'Did you know that they know the real father now, Phil?' Laura asked.

He nodded. 'Yes, Gerry told me. I'm glad the baby's all right.'

'Yes, a little girl,' Anne said. 'My brother and his wife are thrilled with her. Mr and Mrs Taylor were very good about it.'

'They're nice people,' Phil said.

'Have you known them long?' asked Anne.

'Since I was about eleven. I was at school with Peter. We lived in Prospect Vale then and we were both at St Edward's. Two years before Gerry.'

'I don't remember you at all at school,' Gerry said. 'I knew Pete but only because of the skiffle groups.' He laughed. 'We were beneath the notice of most of the older fellows.'

'Two years makes a big difference when you're at school,' Phil agreed.

'And you never got mixed up with the pop groups?' Anne asked him.

'I don't play an instrument and I can't sing,' Phil said. 'But Pete and I have always been good mates. When I started school I was a right shrimp but Peter was always a big strong lad and he sort of looked after me.'

'Not much of a shrimp about you now,' Anne said laughing and looking at his tall, broad-shouldered figure.

'I was glad of your strength tonight, I can tell you,' Gerry exclaimed. 'I was never so glad to see anyone. Those damn nuts were jammed fast and I'd never have managed without you.'

'Lucky you met,' Anne commented.

'We were all together in Southport,' Gerry explained, 'and I'd taken Margaret home and was coming here. Phil was on his way home.'

'The others were in the van,' Phil said. 'I'd left just before them and I saw Gerry broken down.' He looked at the clock and said he must go.

Anne examined his coat. It was nearly dry and he put it on. He glanced at Laura. 'It's nice to see you at home.'

'In all the glory of my tatty dressing gown,' Laura retorted. 'Gerry should have had more sense than to barge in like that with you.' She regretted the words as soon as they were spoken. I made it sound as though he was unwelcome, she thought, and saw with dismay the tide of red which suffused his face, his fair skin making it even more noticeable.

Anne and Julie seemed to notice nothing and Julie offered to lend him an umbrella as the rain still poured down. 'His car's just outside. You won't melt, will you, Phil?' Gerry laughed and went to the door with him.'

When he returned, Anne said thoughtfully, 'He seems a nice lad. Mrs Taylor thinks a lot of him.'

'Yes, he is,' said Gerry. 'Awful quiet though. I've never heard him talk so much. Must be your ham sandwiches, Ma.'

'It's just Mum,' Julie said. 'She can get anyone talking.'

Laura said nothing, still cursing herself for her tactless remark, but the next moment John arrived home, full of indignation about the landlord and satisfaction with what he had done about him.

'A right damn Rachman, he was,' he declared. 'But I've clipped his wings. He'll frighten no more women.'

'I hope you were careful,' Anne said anxiously. 'These people can be dangerous, you know.'

'I just made some people get off their fat backsides and earn their big salaries,' he chuckled. 'I got one fellow out of a Masonic dinner. He wasn't very pleased.'

Anne looked at Gerry and sighed then she brought John a plate of ham and tomatoes. 'Your dinner's ruined,' she said. 'Dried to a crisp,' but John declared that ham and tomatoes was fine.

Anne went and brought the pad from beside the phone. 'There were several messages for you,' she said.

John glanced at the pad and said that he had seen two of the callers. 'I'll see the other fellow tomorrow.'

They used small blocks of offcuts for messages and Laura picked up the pad to replace it on her way to bed. She was about to put it on the telephone table when she dropped it and realised that there was writing on both sides of the pad.

The top pages carried tonight's messages but on the underside, written in her father's sprawling handwriting, was a message. 'Laura, Nick rang. No message but will you ring him back on this number when you get in from work.'

She stood holding the pad feeling a mixture of relief that Nick had phoned and anger that he had left it so long, then a growing doubt about the message. How long had it been there?

She marched back into the living room and thrust the pad before her father's eyes. 'When was this written?' she demanded.

'Last night – no, Monday night,' he said. 'Why?'

'Why didn't you mention it?'

'Because I was out when you came in probably,' he said impatiently. 'It's clear enough, God knows. There's even a phone number I took down.'

'What is it? Is it important?' her mother asked.

Laura ripped off the page and said curtly, 'No. Goodnight again,' and left the room.

She flung the pad on the telephone table but carried the message up to her bedroom, to sit looking at it and thinking. Monday. He had rung on Monday and had probably been waiting for a phone call from her ever since, but how had she missed the message? She thought back to Monday evening.

She had come in late from the office, after her father had gone out. She remembered the phone calls she had attempted to answer but which had been answered by Julie or her mother, and Julie's long conversation with Peter, and the other call while she was in the bathroom. A vivid memory rose in her mind of leaning over the banister and seeing her mother flip over the pad and call for a pen to take down the details of the call from Canada.

If anyone was to blame it was her mother for turning over the pad, but the top page had been filled by her father's writing and she needed a clean sheet. I can't blame Dad except for not telling me and there was so much going on when he came in, with the fuss about Rilla's baby, it's no wonder he didn't think of it.

She stood up and moved restlessly about the room. She knew that she was thinking about the message to avoid thinking about Nick and what she should do.

Was she pleased that he had phoned or angry that he had made no further effort to contact her? He's bloody arrogant she thought, yet he *had* phoned soon after the quarrel and perhaps when there was no return call he assumed she wanted to finish with him. She thought of all the explanations needed if she phoned him now but then she realised with relief that it was too late to call him now anyway.

I can just put it all out of my mind until tomorrow, she decided as she slipped into bed, yet she found that it was impossible. She sat up and took two aspirins to help her to sleep but her mind was still too active.

I should be pleased that he phoned, she thought, remembering how anxious she had been to hear from him, yet she recalled the original quarrel and his comments about her family's grief. Do I want to make it up? She tried to think of Nick's good points. His care of her when they were out together, his sense of humour, the things he said which made her feel confident and happy.

I do care for him, she told herself, and crushed down a less worthy thought that she enjoyed being one of a couple and had no wish to be a pitied single again. She still felt too excited to sleep and she got up and sat by the open window, breathing in the damp, salty November air. Gradually she felt calmer and could think more objectively.

Nothing had really changed. She knew now that Nick had phoned, but he knew only that he had phoned and she had not replied. It might already be too late to make up the quarrel but she decided that she would ring the following evening and they would know where they stood.

The decision made, she got into bed again and deliberately turned her thoughts to the earlier part of the evening. Her conversation with her grandparents and memories of her beloved Grandma, then Gerry coming in with Phil Casey. She recalled Phil's painful blush at her brusque reply to his remark about seeing her at home and later Gerry talking about him being usually so quiet and diffident but speaking freely to her mother.

Her mother had a gift for making people feel at home and drawing them out to talk about themselves, she thought, and I have a gift for shutting them up. Suddenly it occurred to her that if she had said it to Nick he wouldn't have reacted like that. He'd have taken offence and said something to hurt her in return.

The following morning her mother asked about the message that had been overlooked. 'Are you sure it wasn't important?' she asked but Laura shook her head.

'Not at all,' she said. She drained her coffee cup and jumped to her feet. 'Sorry I can't finish that toast, Mum. I'll miss the train. 'Bye,' and she dashed out.

She was too busy to brood much during working hours and was not meeting Mary at lunchtime but on the way home she kept changing her mind about whether or not to ring Nick, then as she stepped off the train she thought impatiently, I'm sure other people don't pick over everything the way I do. The ins and outs of Muldoon's cat, as Grandma used to say. I'm just going to make up my mind and stick to it.

As soon as she reached home she shut herself in the hall and dialled the number. Fortunately it was Nick who answered and he said, 'Laura!' in a delighted voice, then his voice cooled and he said stiffly, 'You got my message then?'

'Only last night,' she said and explained.

'I wondered why you didn't ring back,' was his only comment.

His tone annoyed Laura and she said tartly, 'You were quite sure that I would then?'

'I think common courtesy would demand it,' he snapped, then in a more placatory voice, 'There was a misunderstanding at the Moonstone. I didn't mean to offend you.'

'I was hasty too, I suppose,' Laura said grudgingly and Nick seemed to think the matter was closed.

'Are you free tomorrow night?' he asked.

Laura still felt annoyed and she said that she had made arrangements for Friday night but she agreed to meet him on Saturday, for a visit to the Odeon cinema. I'll see how he behaves then she thought as she replaced the receiver, then picked it up again immediately and dialled the number of her Uncle Joe's house.

Rosa answered and Laura asked her if she would be in the next evening. She felt that she should make arrangements so that she had not lied to Nick but Rosa said immediately, 'I was going to go to yours tonight but can you come here instead? Mum and Dad have gone to a hotpot supper so we'd have the house to ourselves. I want to talk to you.'

Laura agreed and went immediately after her meal. Rosa looked as beautiful as ever but more conventional in a pale green trouser suit and green eyeshadow with her red-gold hair piled on top of her head. 'I like that hairstyle,' Laura commented. 'Makes your neck look even longer.'

Rosa grimaced. 'Not much of an asset,' she said, 'except for the guillotine or for a wife of Henry the Eighth,' and Laura laughed and pretended to shudder.

They went into a small sitting room where a bright fire burned and music was playing softly on the record player. 'The Righteous Brothers!' Laura exclaimed. 'I used to love this record.'

Rosa softly sang along with 'You've Lost That Loving Feeling' as she poured drinks then they curled up in armchairs before the fire.

'It's ages since we had a proper talk,' Laura said. 'I thought you might be off again before we got the chance.'

'No danger,' Rosa said briefly. 'I'm staying at home now.'

Laura felt relaxed and happy. Even if I don't see Ros for months, she thought, it's always as though we've never been apart when we meet again. We shared so much when we were kids and teenagers.

The room was warm and cosy, softly lit by the pink-shaded standard lamp and the bright fire, the only sound rain beating on the windows and the plaintive music of their earlier years. It was easy to exchange confidences and when Rosa asked about Nick, Laura told her all that had transpired between them.

'I lay awake for hours last night trying to decide whether I liked him or hated him,' she said. 'I'm still not sure whether I should have agreed to see him again on Saturday.'

'But you must have liked him at first,' Rosa pointed out. 'Otherwise you'd never have gone out with him.'

'I did,' Laura admitted. 'Mind you, he'd been very silent that night for some reason.'

Rosa laughed. 'And that's how you like him – silent?' Then more seriously, 'But did you enjoy being with him, Lol?'

'I did,' said Laura. 'He's good to go out with. I know some girls sound off about equality and all that. Don't want fellows to open doors for them or look after them generally but I like good manners and I liked the way Nick treated me when we were out. He was good company, too, and we had a laugh together. I wasn't ashamed to be seen with him either.'

'So what have you got against him?' Rosa asked.

'Just his arrogance. Honestly, Ros, he had an opinion on everything and was always sure he was right. No wonder we were always arguing.'

Rosa looked across at her cousin and smiled. 'I thought you liked plain speaking. I can see how you would fall out.'

'Yes, plain speaking, but what he said that night in the Moonstone was just offensive. It was the first time I'd seen him since Maureen died too. To say that about us grieving for her – that it was extreme. He couldn't really care for me, could he?'

'I think he could and still say that. After all, there's usually a hidden agenda in any quarrel.'

'What do you mean?' Laura asked, looking puzzled.

'I mean that what you seem to row about isn't really what's biting you,' Rosa explained. 'Why wasn't Nick at Maureen's funeral?'

'It was for family and friends. He didn't know her.'

'Neither did Peter Cunliffe or Margaret Norton really,' said Rosa, 'but they were there for Julie and Gerry's sake. Nick should have been there for yours to comfort you.'

'I didn't ask him,' Laura admitted. 'In fact, I didn't go out with him after Dad told me it was near the end until a few weeks after the funeral. He rang but I just wasn't ready to go out.'

'But if you really cared for each other you should have wanted him there. Did it ever occur to you that he might be hurt at being excluded and that was the real reason for his remarks that night?'

'This hidden agenda thing, you mean,' said Laura. 'No, I think he was airing his views as usual, not stopping to think about my feelings.'

Rosa looked at her and seemed about to say something but instead she stood up and poured fresh drinks. 'I think you have to decide whether you miss Nick for himself or whether you just miss going out with him.'

'A bit of both, I suppose,' Laura said honestly.

Rosa sank gracefully into the armchair again. 'It seems to me, Lol, that Nick cares more for you than you do for him. He came after you when you quarrelled and he was the one to ring up to try to make up. I imagine that he's as stiff-necked as you so it must have been an effort for him.'

'What do you mean? Stiff-necked like me?'

'All right then. Obstinate, outspoken, proud. Take your pick.'

Laura sipped her drink reflectively. 'You think I should make allowances because I offend people sometimes without intending to,' she said. 'I know I do, Ros. Even last night…' She stopped but as Rosa said nothing she told her about Phil Casey. 'I wouldn't have deliberately said anything to embarrass him. He's a real nice fellow but a bit shy. Not very confident.'

'You know him well then?' Rosa asked and Laura explained that she had known him for some time but they only met occasionally.

'Anyway, I think Nick has tried to make up and you should meet him halfway,' Rosa said. 'If you go out with him on Saturday, make a fresh start and don't be raking over old rows. I think he has a lot going for him.'

'So you think I should keep the date?'

'Of course. If you don't you'll never know how you really feel about him and in a few years' time he'll have a halo. Or perhaps he won't, knowing you.' Rosa laughed. 'Anyway, give it a go. He sounds a decent fellow and there aren't many of them around.'

The Righteous Brothers record had been replaced by 'Goodbye My Love' by the Searchers and now another record dropped on to the turntable, 'If You've Gotta Go, Go Now' by Manfred Mann. Laura looked over at Rosa. She was curled up in the armchair holding her drink close to her, looking pensive and rather sad, and Laura said carefully, 'I didn't know you had these records, Ros. They remind me of the youth club.'

'Mum and Dad bought them for me when I was in my teens,' Rosa said. 'I was more into the Kinks and the Rolling Stones, but this is nostalgia time.' She sighed.

'But these are all sad. All about parting and regret.' Laura hesitated then said quietly, 'How is your love life going, Ros?'

Rosa shrugged and smiled at her cousin, knowing that Laura was trying to be tactful. 'It's non-existent. That's why I wanted to talk to you, Lol. I haven't told Mum and Dad yet but I'm pregnant.'

Laura choked on her drink then coughed and recovered. 'How did that happen?'

Rosa said flippantly, 'The usual way,' but Laura could see the shine of tears in her eyes and she impulsively jumped to her feet and embraced Rosa.

'Don't worry, Ros. Everything will be fine. I'm so happy for you. Are you pleased?'

'Yes, I am,' Rosa said. 'I wasn't at first but now I feel all broody when I see photos of babies and mine seems a real person to me. I wish I knew whether it was a boy or a girl.'

'You soon will,' Laura said. 'And either will be very welcome in the family.'

Laura asked no questions but Rosa told her that the baby's father was Lex Mountford, the actor with whom she had been living. 'I'm not going to tell him about the baby though,' she said.

'You don't think he has a right to know?'

'No, I don't,' Rosa said forcefully. 'He wouldn't welcome the news anyway and anyone who doesn't welcome my baby can piss off.' She smiled at Laura's expression. 'I've shocked you saying that yet you weren't shocked about the baby.'

'I wasn't shocked,' Laura said sturdily. 'I've heard that expression before. I was just surprised to hear you use it. Have you finished with Lex then?'

'Yes. Oh Lol, I can't tell you crazy I felt about him at first. I've never felt like that before, as though I couldn't bear to be away from him, and I thought he felt the same about me. I was so proud when he was on stage and when he came off we spent every possible minute together.'

'I suppose that appealed to you too. The romantic bit about him being an actor.'

'Yes, it was all wonderful to me. Even touring, with the dirty backstage of theatres and grotty digs and the waiting around and sitting through boring rehearsals. Just being with Lex made it wonderful.'

'And when did it wear off?'

Rosa laughed aloud, the musical laugh that was part of her charm. 'Oh Lol, you're so down to earth,' she said. She sat looking into the fire and Laura waited, saying nothing.

Finally Rosa said in a low voice, 'It *was* wonderful, Lol. We were truly in love and at least I know that this baby was conceived in love. It was as though no one else existed for either of us but then Lex began to get involved again with all the feuding and bitching that went on in the company. Then a new actress, only a kid really, made a play for him. Flung herself at him just to get a better part but he fell for it.'

'Oh Ros, and you'd started with the baby?'

'I didn't know I had. I was just so disgusted that he could fall for such obvious tricks. I despised him for it and I just left. I went to David because they were playing Cambridge and David sorted me out.'

Laura had sat down at Rosa's feet and looked up into her face. 'So David knows about the baby?'

'No. I suspected while I was with him but I didn't *know* until I was here at home. You're the only one who knows,' said Rosa.

Laura knelt up and put her arms round her cousin. 'Don't worry, Ros. Everything will be fine. Do you want me to tell them?'

Rosa hugged her but shook her head. 'No, thanks, but I hope everyone will be like you about it. Thanks, Lol. I'll have to pick my time to tell Mum so it's not too much of a shock. With her heart, I mean.'

'Tell her and your dad together,' Laura advised. 'Anyway, nobody thinks anything of it now. We were only talking about that in work the other day, the way attitudes have changed, although I said Grandma was never narrow-minded, even though most people were in her day.'

'I'm glad I didn't live then,' said Rosa. 'I couldn't have stood all that hypocrisy and the restrictions. I think we have a much more truly moral outlook now although we're more relaxed about sex. People are more compassionate and generous and kinder in every way. I think flower power will bring an end to war eventually, if we stop hating foreigners and being greedy. Love one another. It will be a better world for my baby.'

Laura smiled at her. 'You've changed already, Ros. I've never heard you talk like that. I didn't know you ever bothered to think about things like that. You're not just a pretty face any more.'

They were silent for a while. Laura was thinking that the old Rosaleen, beautiful and charming, had sailed along on the surface of life, not even noticing when she hurt people and caring for no one but herself. Now the real Rosa, the one she had instinctively known was there, had emerged and she felt that she loved and respected her.

Rosa, too, was thinking over her conversation with Laura. It had always been a joke in the family that Laura could silence a roomful of people with one of her uncompromising comments and that she was naturally tactless but sublimely unaware of it. Even when they were very young Rosa had always defended Laura when she had offended someone, knowing instinctively that anyone who acted as compassionately as Laura could never intend to hurt with speech.

Now she realised that under Laura's shell there was a sensitive and vulnerable human being who knew that her blunt comments offended and regretted it but was unable to change her nature.

Laura was still sitting at her feet and Rosa impulsively leaned forward and put her arms round her. 'Oh Lol, I'm glad I've got you,' she exclaimed. 'You're always so understanding and you've helped me so much. I can face everyone now.'

Laura embraced her. 'You've helped me too, Ros,' she said. 'Thanks for the good advice. I'll tell you how I get on with Nick on Saturday.' She glanced at her watch. 'Lord, is that the time? I'd better go before your mum and dad come back in case you have a chance to tell them tonight.' Rosa knew that it was not necessary to ask Laura to say nothing about her confidences.

As she walked home, Laura thought about Rosa's baby and how the news would be received by the family. She had no doubts that they would close round Rosa, no matter what she decided to do about telling the baby's father, and smiled as she thought of how all the knitting needles would soon be busy with small jackets and bootees.

When she arrived home her mother and Julie greeted her with smiling faces. 'You've just missed Margaret and Gerry,' her mother said. 'They'd been to see Margaret's parents. They're engaged, Laura!'

'Going for the ring tomorrow,' Julie added joyfully.

Laura was able to say without a pang, 'Great. I'm so pleased for them. Sorry I missed them.'

'They would have waited to see you,' her mother said apologetically, 'but Margaret is on duty so early tomorrow.'

'I'll see them tomorrow night when they've got the ring,' Laura said and Anne looked at Julie and seemed to give a sigh of relief but Laura noticed nothing.

The next day she told Mary about Margaret and Gerry's engagement but said nothing about Rosa's baby, although all day she wondered whether Rosa had been able to tell her parents the previous night. She cut the usual Friday night drinks with her colleagues and hurried home, but though her Aunt Sarah and Uncle Joe called to congratulate Gerry and Margaret, they said nothing about Rosa.

Greatly to her mother's relief, Laura had told her that she was going out with Nick on Saturday night so it was not necessary to consider Laura's feelings when Margaret's engagement ring was handed round. She had chosen a solitaire diamond ring.

'I'd like a solitaire for mine, wouldn't you?' Julie said as she took the ring from her finger and passed it to Laura to try on. Laura slipped the ring on her finger then took it off and handed it to Margaret.

'I don't think so,' she said. 'Everybody seems to choose them now.'

There was a stunned silence then everyone spoke at once. Laura cringed inwardly. I've done it again, she thought, but she had only spoken the truth. The numerous engaged girls in the office had almost all chosen solitaire diamonds for their rings.

Margaret did not seem offended. 'Strange how fashions change, isn't it?' she said calmly. 'My gran had five stones, a half hoop of diamonds, but Mum's is three diamonds on a twist like yours, Mrs Redmond.'

'And mine,' Sarah said and the moment passed.

'I just hope you have as happy a marriage as Sarah and I have had,' Anne smiled at Margaret.

'Yes indeed, and I'm sure you will, love,' Sarah said. 'You and Gerry are so well-suited and you've both been brought up in happy homes so you'll be able to create your own.'

Laura listened in amazement. Were they trying to pretend to Margaret or did her aunt and her mother really delude themselves that her mother's marriage had been happy? Surely her mother didn't really believe it and her aunt, she knew, was not blind to her brother's faults. In fact, she had often told him about them. I give up, Laura thought. I'll never understand their generation.

Chapter Twenty-Four

Laura had arranged to meet Nick at the station and she felt a leap of pleasure as the train drew in and she saw his tall figure waiting for her. She wore a mini skirt in a pale stone-coloured leather, and matching boots in soft leather to above her knees, and a fur jacket.

'You look fantastic, Laura,' Nick exclaimed as he rushed to meet her.

'Best rabbit,' she shrugged, glancing down disparagingly at her jacket, although she had dressed very carefully for the date.

At first conversation between them was stilted but neither of them mentioned the quarrel and soon they were joking together and exchanging news. Both were careful to avoid anything controversial so it was a happy and harmonious evening. They enjoyed the film and linked arms and held hands throughout.

When they went to the bar in the interval, Nick told Laura that he had forgotten his house key. He could only see her on to the train and then he'd have to go straight home to be sure of getting in. And the following day he had to go home to Ormskirk as it was his mother's birthday but could he see Laura at lunchtime for a drink?

'At the Elephant, you mean?' Laura said, knowing that he usually went there on Sunday lunchtimes.

'No, not in Woolton,' he said hurriedly. 'I thought somewhere near you in Crosby.'

'Yes, all right. There are a few good watering holes near us, the Royal or the Blundellsands Hotel, and lots of others. You can get a bus to Ormskirk from Crosby as well,' Laura agreed cheerfully.

The only hint of discord between them came as they left the cinema to walk to the station. As they strolled along, Laura talked about Gerry's burst tyre and how Phil Casey had helped him.

'They came in like drowned rats,' she laughed, 'their hair plastered to their heads by the rain and their hands filthy. Mum had to dry Phil's coat by the fire while they got cleaned up and had some supper.'

'I didn't know Phil Casey was so well in with your family,' Nick commented jealously. 'It sounds as though he's really got his feet under the table in your house. Just shows. You can't trust these quiet ones.'

'What do you mean?' snapped Laura. 'It's the first time he's been. Gerry was damn glad of his help, especially on such a night.'

'And he'd jump at the chance of seeing you again,' Nick said. He laughed disagreeably. '*Seeing* would be the word. He's dumb in every sense of the word but I saw how he stared at you at the Cabaret Club.'

He was holding Laura's arm but she snatched it away. 'If I remember right, Phil had more to say than you at the Cabaret Club. *You* were the dumb one,' she said angrily.

Nick seemed to realise that he had said too much and tried to take her hand again. 'I *did* keep my mouth shut that night,' he admitted. 'I was trying to avoid saying the wrong thing,' but Laura refused to be mollified.

'Pity it didn't last,' she retorted. They had reached the station and as they stood arguing, the Southport train slowly moved out of the station. 'Now look what you've done,' Laura exclaimed. 'I've missed my train.'

'That settles it. I'm coming with you,' Nick announced. 'I'm not letting you travel home alone at this hour.'

'Don't be a fool,' Laura said. 'You won't be able to get in your house and I'm all right. This isn't Chicago or New York. I'm safe enough.'

'I'm coming with you,' Nick repeated stubbornly and declared that if his own landlord didn't open the door he would knock up one of his friends and beg a bed. 'It won't be the first time I'll have slept on someone's floor,' he added with a grin.

He said no more about Phil Casey and Laura decided to ignore the quarrel that had been developing.

On the train she told him that she had mentioned Chicago and New York because of a frightening story she had read a few nights earlier. It concerned a girl who had boarded an underground train in one of those cities, she was not sure which, and found three men in the compartment.

'She thought the middle man was drunk,' Laura said, 'because the other two men were holding him upright and he was staring straight ahead but she felt frightened. Another man got in and pretended to know her and bundled her out at the next stop. He told her the two men were gangsters and the man in the middle was dead. If she had stayed on to the end of the line they would have killed her.'

'And you'd still have got the train on your own,' Nick exclaimed. 'Honestly, Laura, sometimes you're too independent for your own good.'

The train had reached Blundellsands station and Nick insisted on walking with Laura to her house.

'I was going to ask you to come round one night,' Laura said. 'But perhaps I'd better not as you seem to think it means so much.'

'I don't understand.'

'Well, you said Phil had his knees under the table because he came in to get dry,' she said.

Nick laughed sheepishly. 'I talk out of the back of my neck sometimes. The old green monster gets to me. I know I don't really have to worry about a drip like him.'

Laura was about to make an angry retort in defence of Phil but instead she said curtly, 'You'd better get going or you'll miss the last train.'

'Did you mean that about me coming here?' Nick asked.

'Yes, we can go to a local cinema and come back for supper or stay in and play records. See what the weather's like.'

Nick kissed her and went off smiling confidently but his words about Phil Casey had an unexpected effect on Laura. She had liked Phil from their first meeting but until Nick showed jealousy towards him she had thought of him only as a friend. She had never had any romantic ideas about him or thought that he had about her. He was so quiet and self-effacing and had never seemed to try to single her out. Now, however, she thought of the way she had often glanced up to find him looking at her and she recalled how he had always been on hand to help her with her coat or in other ways. She found him easy to talk to and at the Cabaret Club they seemed to be getting to know each other better until Nick appeared on the scene.

She thought of the evening he had come home with Gerry and tried to remember the exact words he had used as he said goodbye to her. Something about being nice to see her at home but she had snubbed him. I should have realised how hard it was for a shy fellow like Phil to say that but all I could think of was my shabby dressing gown, she thought ruefully. Yet even that showed that I cared about what he thought.

She was surprised when she heard the clock strike two o'clock and realised that she had been thinking about Phil all the time and scarcely given a thought to Nick, except to feel indignant that he had described Phil as a drip. He's *not* a drip, she thought resentfully, just a quiet type, the opposite of a self-confident loudmouth like Nick.

In the cold light of day she decided that she was mistaken about Phil being attracted to her. I'm not like Rosa with everyone falling for me, she thought as she examined her face in the bathroom mirror. If I'm going to get ideas about everyone Nick's jealous of I'll be making a right fool of myself.

Julie appeared at the bathroom door and Laura said, 'OK, I'm finished. I'm sorry I looked in the mirror. I was awake until after two o'clock and I look a wreck.'

'It's that mirror,' said Julie. 'I avoid looking in it, especially in the morning. Spoils my confidence for the day if I do. Must be the way the light falls or something.'

'I don't think I'll see much difference in any mirror,' Laura groaned.

She and Julie went with their parents to ten o'clock Mass and saw Rosa there with her parents. Laura wondered whether she had found an opportunity to tell her parents about the baby. When they all met outside the church she looked inquiringly at Rosa but she shook her head, unnoticed by everyone else.

Sarah was saying to Anne, 'You're not going to Nana's today, are you? What time are Margaret's parents coming to you?'

'Just for tea,' Anne said. 'I'd have asked all the family to meet them but Mr Norton's an invalid so it'll be easier for him with just us,' and Sarah agreed.

Later, over the leisurely Sunday breakfast, Laura told her mother that she had invited Nick on Thursday night. 'That all right?'

Anne smiled. 'Of course. I'll be pleased to meet him.'

It seemed like fate that Gerry said immediately, 'Phil Casey was impressed by your hospitality, Mum. He couldn't get over the way you welcomed him at that hour and rustled up such a nice supper.'

'It was the least I could do,' said Anne, 'after he'd helped you, and on such a night. I thought he was a really nice fellow.'

'Yes, he's a good skin,' Gerry agreed and went on to talk of other things, but Laura's mind wandered back to Phil. Everyone seems to like him, she thought.

Later she walked to the station and met Nick as he came off the train at Blundellsands. The weather was bright and dry although very cold and they decided against the large hotel opposite the station and instead walked along to the Brooke Hotel.

It was crowded with young people and Laura saw several friends from the church and the Spanish class, including one who was with a young man who had been at school with Nick. He worked in a local bank and had a flat nearby, he told Nick, and Nick ordered drinks for the couple when he ordered for himself and Laura.

The volume of noise was rising as more and more people arrived but they managed to find a table for four in a quiet corner. The couple had been introduced as Tricia and Nigel and as soon as they sat down Nigel announced that they planned to marry in the following September.

'You've got to plan long-term,' Tricia said to Laura. 'I was telling your Julie. The Blundellsands is booked two years ahead for wedding receptions. We were lucky. We got a cancellation for September.'

'What about you, Nick?' said Nigel, who seemed a brash young man. 'Any sign of wedding bells for you?' He looked at Nick but it was Laura who answered.

'Oh no,' she said emphatically. 'We've only just met.'

'Come off it, Laura,' Nick protested. 'We've known each other for months.'

Tricia said diplomatically, 'It just seems a short time to Laura. Time flies when you're enjoying yourself.' They all laughed, even Laura though unwillingly, and Nick explained that he had not yet finished teacher training.

'Will you settle round here when you qualify?' Tricia asked.

'It depends where I get a job,' Nick said vaguely.

'Some good schools in this area,' Nigel said. 'Unless you're like Tricia's cousin. He got a first-class honours degree, could have taken his pick of schools, but he chose to teach at some awful sink school in the East End of London. You wouldn't do that, would you?'

'Not likely,' Nick said decidedly. 'Perhaps he can afford to be an idealist. I can't. I intend to do what's best for Nick Clegg. Look after number one, I say.'

'Following in the family tradition,' Nigel said slyly. 'How are they, anyway?'

'All right,' Nick answered curtly.

Laura added, 'It's Nick's mother's birthday today. He's on his way there now to see her.' She was anxious to correct the cynical impression she felt that Nick had given but Nigel laughed.

'The dutiful son, eh?' he said. 'That's a new one, Nick.'

'She's fifty and wants a parade of family unity at the Conservative Club so the old man summoned us.'

'Derek as well? Will he turn up?' asked Nigel.

Nick laughed disagreeably. 'He will if he knows I'm going. He's got to protect his interests, although the old man has no hold over him, as he has over me. He didn't exactly say I'd have to manage on my grant if I didn't turn up but the hints were heavy.'

They were all laughing except Laura. She listened with dismay. This was a Nick she had never suspected but perhaps it was all a joke and she was failing to see the point.

She was glad when Nick glanced at his watch and decided that it was time to go, and she could say goodbye to Tricia and Nigel, hoping that she would never see them again. She thought that Nick would feel as she did but he seemed to have enjoyed meeting his old friend.

'I didn't expect to see old Nigel in this neck of the woods,' he said. 'We've been friends since we were about five but I've lost touch with him over the last few years.'

'You didn't mean that? The way you talked about your family?' Laura asked. 'You've never talked about them to me.'

He shrugged. 'Not much to say. We don't live in each other's pockets. We're reserved people, not emotional like your family seem to be.' Laura's head jerked round and he said hastily, 'I don't mean either way is better than the other, just different.'

'But you are going to see your mother because it's her birthday?' Laura insisted.

Nick simply nodded but then as Laura seemed to expect him to say more he added, 'My parents live full lives. My mother is very involved with the local Conservative Party, and my old man with business and Masonic dinners and so forth, and of course he gets hauled in for Conservative functions too. They don't *need* the company of my brother or me. In fact they'd find it hard to fit us in.' He laughed.

'So your family are Conservatives then?' Laura tried to imagine a meeting between them and her father.

'Of course. Aren't yours?' Nick said in surprise.

'No, my father's a Labour councillor.'

'Good God. That's unusual in our class,' Nick exclaimed.

'What do you mean, our class?' Laura said belligerently. 'I'm working class and proud of it.' Even as she spoke she knew she was simply being contrary. She held no strong views about politics and at one time had considered joining the Conservative Party just to annoy her father, but she was irritated by Nick's arrogance and by the side of his nature he had shown while talking to Nigel.

Nick seemed angry. 'Don't be ridiculous, Laura,' he snapped. 'You're no more working class than I am.'

'How do you define working class then?' Laura asked in a tone which should have warned him.

'Uncouth, illiterate, full of grievances but without any sense of responsibility,' he blundered on. 'Like the men my grandfather employed. Always wanting to form a union or shorter hours, more pay, and too stupid to see they were cutting their own throats until it was too late and his business failed.'

His face was flushed and Laura could see that she had touched a nerve but they had reached the bus stop. She only said quietly, *My* grandfather says no one should argue about politics or religion. He says it's only an accident of birth that forms our ideas about either so we should respect other people's views.'

'He's right,' said Nick with one of his sudden changes of mood. He put his arms round her and kissed her. 'I'm sorry we wasted time talking about such things. Forgive me?' The bus arrived so she nodded and smiled as he boarded the bus and was borne away but as she walked home her thoughts were not pleasant.

She was not concerned about Nick's politics but she felt that he had sounded like an intolerant snob. Was that his real self? She would have to think deeply about this before she saw him again.

There was little time to ponder as the whole family was caught up in Anne's preparations for their visitors, in spite of Gerry's protests that it was all unnecessary.

Margaret's parents were very pleasant and friendly. Mrs Norton was very like Margaret, with the same air of cheerful common sense; Mr Norton, who suffered from Parkinson's disease, seemed very frail. Anne was pleased to see Gerry's gentle care for him.

'Gerry's like a son to us,' Mr Norton said quietly to Anne later. 'We always wanted a son. It's a relief to me to know that there'll be such a good, sensible lad as Gerry to look after Margaret and her mother when I'm gone.'

'Please God that won't be for a long time,' Anne said gently. 'Gerry was very happy-go-lucky when he was a young lad but Margaret's been a good influence on him. He's grown up since he met her.'

'Ah well, youth is the time to be carefree. But he's still a happy lad. Like a breath of fresh air when he comes in but sensitive and reliable too. You must be very proud of him.'

'We are,' Anne exclaimed fervently, near to tears as she remembered the worries of the past. 'I'm glad you're as happy about the engagement as we are. It's a good start for them.'

Later, while Julie and Laura washed up after the meal, the others moved to the sitting room where Gerry pushed a sofa close to the fire for Margaret's parents and he and Margaret, Anne and John grouped themselves around them.

After commenting on the comfortable room, Mrs Norton took her husband's hand and said directly, 'Father would like the wedding to be soon if everyone's agreeable.'

'We are, certainly,' John said immediately.

Gerry smiled at Margaret. 'Can't be too soon for me.'

Mr Norton seemed tired, leaning back against the sofa cushions, but he said in a weak voice, 'There'll be no problems. Margaret is our only one so everything we have will be hers. Tell them about the house, Mother.' He closed his eyes.

Mrs Norton said briskly, 'Gerry and Margaret know about this. When we bought our house my mother was a widow and not very strong so we had a little bungalow built on so she could be independent but near to us if she needed help.'

Mr Norton opened his eyes. 'Granny flats, they call them now,' he said.

Mrs Norton pressed his hand. 'My mother died fifteen years ago and we've suggested that we move in there and Gerry and Margaret can have our house.'

'That's very generous of you,' John exclaimed.

Gerry said that he and Margaret felt that they should go in the bungalow and Mr and Mrs Norton stay in the house. 'You've lived there so long,' he said to Margaret's mother. 'And you've got all your own things about you there. You shouldn't have that upheaval.'

'That's thoughtful of you, Gerry, but really we'll be happy to move to the bungalow. Father drew up the plans for it very carefully to make life easier for my mother so it will be perfect for him now.'

'The house is too big for us. Too much for us,' Mr Norton said. His wife added, 'My mother's furniture is still there so we'll do some swapping and changing between the house and the bungalow. We'll be happy there and I hope you young people will be happy in the house.'

The trembling of Mr Norton's hands and head had become more marked and a glance passed between Mrs Norton and Gerry. He stood up immediately. 'I'll get your coats,' he said.

Julie and Laura had come into the room and Margaret's mother said how happy she had been to meet them. Julie made an appropriate reply and Anne said anxiously, 'I hope we haven't overtired you, Mr Norton.'

'No, no, I've enjoyed myself,' he assured her. 'And we've got things settled.'

'It's been very nice to meet you,' John said heartily. 'Of course we expected to like anyone who had a daughter like Margaret.'

'Yes indeed,' Anne concurred.

'And we've enjoyed meeting you,' Mrs Norton said. 'Believe me, you've got a son to be proud of.' She slipped her hand through Gerry's arm and looked up at him affectionately. 'I couldn't find a better man for a son-in-law if I knitted him myself.'

They all laughed but Mr Norton said reprovingly, 'You're embarrassing the lad, Mother.'

'No, don't stop her. I can take any amount of that,' Gerry laughed as he helped the older man with his coat.

Later Laura commented to Julie, 'What came over Dad? I've never heard him so amiable – effusive even. I thought he'd resent them claiming his darling son.'

'I think Dad liked hearing Gerry praised and so did Mum. After all, they've taken a few knocks about him during the past few years. It's nice for them to know he's appreciated.'

'He's certainly that,' Laura laughed. 'He'll have a head like a football with all the praise.'

'I don't think so,' Julie said seriously. 'He's gone through a lot himself too and worried about letting Mum and Dad down. This is just what he needs, I think.'

Laura felt ashamed of her comments and said quietly, 'I'm sure you're right, Jul, and he will be a good help to Margaret's parents. That's a terrible thing, Parkinson's disease, isn't it?'

'At least it hasn't altered Mr Norton's character. A man who used to work in the library has got it and he's changed completely. Of course he's much younger.'

It was still early evening and Anne rang Sarah to tell her about the visit. She came back into the living room saying, 'Sarah, Joe and Rosa are coming over for an hour.'

Laura immediately wondered whether Rosa had told them about the baby.

As soon as they arrived, Anne launched into a description of Mr and Mrs Norton's visit. 'They're really nice,' she said. 'And very fond of Gerry but the poor man seems so ill. I think that's why he wants Gerry and Margaret to marry quite soon.'

'So you said on the phone,' Sarah commented vaguely.

Joe added quickly, 'If they have somewhere to live, there's no reason for them to wait, is there?'

Gerry had not returned but when the rest of the family were settled with the inevitable cups of tea Sarah said abruptly, 'We have some news too. Rosa is going to have a baby in June.'

For a moment there was a stunned silence then Anne hugged Sarah and John leaned forward and put his hand over Rosa's. 'I'll tell you something, love,' he said. 'No baby could come to a home where it would be better loved.'

Anne and Julie said together, 'That's very true,' and both kissed Rosa.

Laura said nothing. She was staring at her father in amazement, wondering how someone she thought so lacking in sensitivity could so quickly find the right words to say, but just as she began to feel more warmly towards him he asked roughly, 'What's wrong with you, Laura, sitting there saying nothing?'

'Laura's known since Thursday, haven't you, love?' Sarah interjected quickly.

Laura said in a low voice, 'I didn't know whether you knew that Ros had told me. I thought you might mind.'

'Not at all.' Sarah said. 'I'm glad Rosa was able to talk it over with you and get things clear in her mind.'

Joe added, 'We appreciate your keeping it to yourself until Rosa told us, Lol.'

'Rosa told us after Mass so we were able to tell Nana and Grandad,' said Sarah. 'We thought it might be a shock to them but they were delighted at the idea of a new baby in the family.'

'I'll bet Nana's already rooting out patterns for bootees and matinee coats,' Julie laughed. She stood up. 'Should I make more tea, Mum?' she asked but John jumped to his feet.

'No. This calls for a drink.' He went out and returned with bottles of sparkling wine. Glasses were quickly found and John raised his glass of wine. 'To Rosa's baby. Welcome,' he said and Julie and Rosa burst into tears.

'We'll drink ours in the other room,' Laura said, ushering the weeping girls out, but not before Rosa had kissed John.

'Thanks, Uncle John,' she murmured.

They soon calmed down and Rosa said as she dried her eyes, 'Your dad has the knack of saying the right thing, doesn't he?'

Laura laughed aloud so heartily that the others smiled. 'I'll bet that's the first time anything like that has been said about him. I'd have said he had a reputation for saying the wrong thing.'

Julie agreed that their father was often tactless but when the occasion demanded he could find the right words.

'He has a compassionate heart, as Nana would say,' said Rosa. 'And at times like this he shows it, but then everyone has taken the news very well.'

'Why shouldn't they?' Laura demanded. 'A baby should always be welcomed. As you told me, Ros, this baby was conceived in love and it'll be surrounded with love from all of us. I wish I knew whether it was a boy or a girl. I don't like saying "it".'

'I don't mind which it is,' Rosa said dreamily. 'I'd like a girl for some reasons and a boy for others. I hope it's not like me though. I couldn't stand the hassle,' and they all laughed.

In the living room no one had mentioned the father of the child until Joe announced quietly, 'The actor fellow Rosa was living with is the father but Rosa doesn't want him to be involved.'

Sarah said, 'I'm glad she doesn't want to marry him. We never liked what we heard about him and Rosa doesn't need him.'

'He just seemed to bewitch Rosa, didn't he?' Anne remarked. 'She'd always kept in touch with you no matter where she went until she met him.'

'I wouldn't like to go through that time again,' Sarah sighed. 'Not knowing where she was or how she was.'

'Not even knowing if she was still alive,' said Joe. 'That friend of mine from the police has told us he feared the worst. He was keeping an eye on all reports of assaults or murders in case Rosa was among them. Good job we didn't know at the time, although I must admit sometimes in the small hours of the morning I thought of the possibility but you know how it is. I pushed the thought away.'

John nodded. 'I know. We think it doesn't happen to people like us but I suppose everyone thinks that.'

'She'll never be as thoughtless again,' said Anne. 'Not now she's going to be a mother herself.'

'Yes, it's made a difference already,' Sarah agreed. 'I'm glad she was able to talk to Laura about it. We knew she was worried about something, didn't we, Joe?'

'Yes, but we thought she was fretting for that fellow. She's seemed so much happier since Thursday and of course now we know why. She'd been able to talk to Laura and get things straight in her mind. Laura's a good, kind girl and very sensible. She's always been a good influence on Rosa.'

'They'll be able to see more of each other now that Rosa'll be at home,' Anne said. 'Laura's missed Rosa. They've always been such good friends.' She sighed. 'Perhaps she'll be less moody when she can talk to Rosa. We never know where we are with her, especially since she's been going out with this Nick. She tells me nothing and I'm afraid to ask when she's got a mood on.'

'Don't you like Nick?' asked Sarah.

Anne shrugged, 'I haven't met him yet but he's coming here on Thursday. But they seem to do nothing but fall out. It's off and on all the time as far as I can make out.'

'They're a worry, aren't they?' Sarah said. 'I'm sure our parents didn't go through all this with us, Anne.'

'I don't know,' said John. 'I can remember you wanting your own way and defying Mum and Dad when you were a kid, Sarah, and I don't doubt Anne was the same. Isn't that right, Joe?'

Joe laughed. 'Anne didn't have to struggle for it. Being the beloved youngest we all wanted her to have whatever she wanted but this is a different world, John. Young people have a lot more in material things but they don't have the sense of security that we had and God knows they have temptations we never even knew.'

'Yes, life was simpler for us,' said Anne. 'For one thing we never went very far from home. All our spare time we spent with the family or friends we'd known all our lives, dancing and cycling and that sort of thing. We were never tempted to do wild things because no one we knew did them, and as for drugs! We thought it was an American name for medicine – at least I did.'

'Yes,' agreed Sarah. 'We knew exactly how far we could go and we kept to the rules without realising it.'

'Without thinking, you mean,' said John. 'That was the trouble with us. We didn't *think*. We accepted the status quo because we were all right but at least this generation thinks for itself. If it makes mistakes, well, that's the price and they don't mind paying it.'

'Good God, John, when did you ever accept the status quo?' Joe laughed. 'What about going off to fight in Spain and carrying on your grandad's battle where he left off? Don't kid yourself, mate.'

Anne stood up. 'This is getting very heavy, as the young ones would say. I'll make another cup of tea and a sandwich.'

'And then we'll have to be on our way,' Sarah said. 'Look at the time!' She followed Anne into the kitchen and Joe and John lit fresh cigarettes.

'That was a good thing you said to Rosa, about the baby being loved,' Joe said quietly. 'I didn't really expect condemnation from the family but I'm surprised how well everyone has taken the news. It was a shock to us when Rosa told us. With all her wildness we never really expected this to happen.'

'We all love Rosa and it's true what I said, Joe. Everyone will love the baby. Anyway, we've got two girls ourselves. Who knows what'll happen with them? Nothing's sure these days.'

'I don't think you need worry,' Joe said. 'That reminds me. We haven't told Tony and Helen yet. Their girls have never given them any worry and Moira's settled now and Dilly engaged. I don't know how they'll feel about our news.'

'*I* do,' John told him robustly. 'Helen will hug and kiss everyone, especially Rosa, then she'll knit enough to fit out triplets and Tony'll make a cradle in his workshop.'

They were laughing when Sarah and Anne came from the kitchen and the girls came through from the back room and shortly afterwards Sarah, Joe and Rosa left.

Chapter Twenty-Five

Laura had deliberately avoided thinking about Nick during the day, pushing thoughts of him away to be considered when she was alone in bed, but tired by the emotions of the day she fell asleep immediately.

It was only two weeks to Christmas and she was so busy at work and at home that there was little time for thinking. Still confused by the facet of his character she had seen on Sunday, she was glad to push away any thoughts of him that intruded and concentrate on Christmas preparations.

She was able to avoid any discussion with Mary too as they spent their lunch hours rushing round the shops for gifts and clothes.

Nick phoned her on Monday night but their conversation was brief and on his part breezy and confident as they made arrangements for Thursday night. He seemed unaware of having raised any doubts in Laura's mind.

On Thursday he came to the house and was introduced to Laura's mother and to Julie. Gerry had just left and her father was out, Anne explained. Laura hoped that he would still be out when they returned for supper after the cinema.

Nick seemed to make a good impression on Anne and Julie and Laura felt proud of him in spite of her secret misgivings. She had still not thought deeply about his behaviour on Sunday and was uncertain whether she could understand and accept it.

As they left the house they met David coming in the gate. 'Oh, are you off out?' he exclaimed in disappointment and Nick's face was thunderous until Laura introduced David as her cousin and said that her mother and Julie were in the house.

'I'll catch you again then, Lol,' David said, and to Nick, 'Good to meet you.'

'Did you know he was coming?' Nick asked as they walked on.

'I knew he had just come home,' Laura said. 'He's at Cambridge and he'd stayed on to do some research.'

'And he drops in without invitation?' Nick said.

'He's my *cousin* and a good friend too. They only live round the corner,' Laura told him angrily. Then as much to her own surprise as Nick's, something made her add, 'And of course he's a member of the uncouth working class. He knows no better.'

'That's nonsense and you know it,' Nick snapped. 'It was a simple remark but you make everything an excuse for a row.'

They walked on in offended silence, in Laura's case with difficulty as numerous retorts rose in her mind but were suppressed. If I hadn't invited him back for supper I'd walk away from him, she thought, but I'm stuck with him for tonight now.

She saw several girls she knew in the queue for the cinema and in spite of herself she softened towards Nick when she saw the approving glances they gave him. When they were in their seats and he slipped his arm round her and took her hand, she sat stiffly upright for a moment then relaxed into his arm.

When they came out, the tiff was forgotten and as they strolled home Nick was gentle and loving, telling Laura how much he loved her and longed to be with her all the time. As they stood on the corner of the road before going into the house, Laura responded fiercely to his kisses and he crushed her close to him.

'I wish we didn't have to go in,' she whispered.

Nick murmured, 'Or that the house was empty.'

Laura drew away from him with a sigh. 'We must though,' she said and they went into the house hand in hand.

David had gone but to Laura's dismay her father was at home and was introduced to Nick. At first the conversation over the supper table was general but John had been at a meeting of the housing committee and before long his indignation burst forth.

'This fellow Heath – what does he think he's playing at, selling council houses?' he demanded. The family were used to his outbursts and rarely argued with him but Nick seemed to think that the question was addressed to him.

'People have the right to own their own homes,' he said belligerently.

'Of course, but *council* houses,' said John. 'They were built to rehouse people who had been living in slums and there are still thousands in that position. We've got a waiting list as long as your arm and they want to sell off our housing stock. What's going to happen to those people?'

'You can build houses for them with the money from the sales, can't you?' said Anne.

'That's just the point. We don't know yet what's going to happen to the money from the sales. It seems the government want to freeze it – maybe use it for something else.'

'But they couldn't do that, Dad,' Julie exclaimed.

'They can and they will,' John declared. 'They just don't care about people at this end of the scale. And *they* don't have to face people living in two rat-infested rooms and tell them that there's no hope of anything better for them ever, like I'll have to do.'

Laura had been signalling to her mother and Anne said cheerfully, 'Well, I think that's for the housing committee,' giving John a warning glance. 'I believe you met David on your way out, Nick. He only got home last night so he came round to see us.'

John had subsided and Nick asked, 'Is he your sister's son?'

'No, he's John's sister's son and my brother's son.' Nick looked mystified and she explained, 'Sarah and I were friends when we were young and I married her brother and she married my brother Joe.'

'So it's an exceptionally close relationship,' Nick commented. 'Such cousins couldn't marry each other.'

'No, but fortunately they wouldn't want to,' Anne laughed, 'although they're all good friends. Our families have always been so close that they've grown up together. More like brothers and sisters.'

'David's very clever,' Julie said. 'He got first-class honours and now he's doing research but you'd never know it. He's so quiet and unassuming.'

Anne had been pressing food on Nick but finally he told her that it was impossible for him to eat any more. 'I don't think I'll need any more food for several days,' he said smiling and Laura glowed with pride when she saw how much the family seemed to like him. Even her father talked to him about the teacher-training course.

The only jarring note came when Anne asked whether he lived in the college or in lodgings. Nick glanced at Laura and said awkwardly, 'Er, I shared a flat with two other men but I've moved into a bedsit.'

'When did this happen? I thought you were settled there,' Laura exclaimed.

Nick said briefly, 'On Monday. I moved into the bedsit last night.'

'But why?' Laura demanded.

Her mother said swiftly, 'You haven't much longer at the college, Laura tells us. This is your final year, isn't it?'

He agreed and Anne began to tell him of Gerry's hopes of starting soon at Christ's College. They finished the meal and moved into the sitting room and a short time later Gerry and Margaret arrived.

Laura introduced Nick and Gerry said he thought they had met. 'Don't you drink at the Elephant in Woolton?' he asked. 'I might have seen you there. We often go to meet up with Pete Taylor and Phil Casey on Sunday lunchtimes.'

Laura saw Nick's face when Phil Casey's name was mentioned and suddenly wondered if he was the reason why Nick had wanted to meet her in Crosby on Sunday but she pushed the thought away with other disagreeable memories of that day.

Before long Nick made his goodbyes as he was catching the last train and was warmly invited to come again by Anne. Gerry shook hands with him. 'Perhaps we'll see you at the Elephant,' he said. 'We'll be going on Sunday.'

Nick smiled non-committally and Laura went to the door with him to see him off. She longed to ask him about his move to the bedsit and why he had not told her but there was no time and she returned to the sitting room with mixed feelings about the evening.

As soon as she returned, Gerry took Margaret's hand. 'We've got something to tell you,' he said excitedly. 'We've fixed the date for the wedding. First Saturday in March.'

There were exclamations and congratulations and Anne said, 'I'm made up, Margaret, but it's short notice for your mother. You know that we'll do everything we can to help.'

'Thanks. Mum will appreciate that,' Margaret said but a shadow came over her face. 'I just hope Dad will be all right. That's all that really matters.'

'He will,' Gerry said. 'He told me that he's determined to give you away.' He turned to his mother. 'We've fixed up the Nuptial Mass. The parish priest called to see Mr Norton this evening and we settled it there and then.'

'We thought we'd do the same as Moira for the reception,' Margaret said. 'Book the hall and hire caterers. It'll be much easier at such short notice.'

'Yes, the BS is booked up two years ahead,' said Julie and Laura remembered the conversation the previous Sunday. It seemed as though everything was conspiring to remind her of the revealing conversation with Tricia and Nigel in the Brooke but she determinedly thrust the thoughts away.

John said suddenly, 'I hope you're not thinking of inviting that shower from Canada for the wedding. We can do without them, Gerry.'

'Terry should be invited,' Laura protested.

Anne said quietly, 'We won't talk about invitations for anyone until Margaret's mum and I have had a talk. She might want it very quiet because of Mr Norton's health.'

Margaret smiled. 'Don't worry about that, Mrs Redmond. We have only a very small family but we'd like all your family there. Dad says he wants it to be a proper do.'

Everyone smiled and Anne said only, 'We'll see.'

Laura watched them enviously. Why were things so complicated for her and Nick and so straightforward for other people? she wondered. Gerry and Margaret never seemed to quarrel and it was the same with Julie and Peter Cunliffe, although Laura suspected that that was because Julie allowed Peter to make all the decisions.

She said as much to Julie when they were washing up together in the scullery and Julie gazed at her wide-eyed. 'But we discuss things,' she said. 'Perhaps it does seem as though Peter makes all the plans for us but he's very sensible, you know, Laura, and I know he only wants what's best for me.'

'But there must be things you don't agree with,' Laura said force-fully. 'Don't you ever tell him what you want and see that you get it?'

'But I get what I want,' Julie insisted. 'It just happens to be the same as what Peter wants. Do you mean about the job he's applied for?' She looked puzzled and Laura found it hard to explain.

'That's an example,' she said finally. 'He seems to just assume that you want to be a housemaster's wife and you're expected to go along with it.'

'But we discussed it. We discuss everything,' Julie repeated. 'If that's Peter's job, I have to be prepared to do the wife's part. Like a vicar's wife or a doctor's wife. I don't mind, honestly, Lol. I'll enjoy it.'

'I can't make you see what I mean,' Laura said. 'Nick and I – we keep falling out and there's always a good reason, yet that doesn't happen with you and with Gerry.'

'Gerry and Margaret have had a few rows but they didn't last,' Julie said cheerfully. 'And with me and Peter, up to now we've been apart most of the time so we couldn't waste time not speaking when we were together. We'll probably have rows now.'

Laura laughed. 'Just to oblige me, you mean. Do you never have any doubts, Ju? You've never been out with any other fellow. How can you be so sure?'

'I just am,' Julie said simply. 'And so is Peter. We think we were just lucky to meet each other when we did.'

'I didn't know that Nick had changed digs,' Laura said. 'We'll probably fall out when I tackle him about that.'

'But do you need to?' asked Julie. 'What does it matter? It isn't as if he's moved in with another girl.'

'But it *does* matter,' Laura cried angrily. 'He decided on Monday and moved last night and never said a word to me. I'm his girlfriend, not some casual acquaintance.'

'But don't start bawling him out until he's had a chance to explain,' Julie advised and Laura laughed.

'How well you know me,' she said. She hung up the tea towel and they went back into the living room.

She had arranged to meet Nick in town on Saturday night and she determined to take Julie's advice and wait for him to explain why he had said nothing about his move. He met her at the station and as they left to walk to the cinema they met Margaret and Gerry.

'Hi,' Gerry called. 'We were just talking about you two. Are you going to the Elephant tomorrow lunchtime?'

'I don't know. Why?' Laura said and Margaret explained that they planned to go and could give Laura a lift if she wished. Nick said nothing.

Laura was sure that Nick was reluctant to go because of Phil Casey so she deliberately forced the issue by saying, 'Thanks. That'll be handy, won't it Nick?' and he could only agree.

He said nothing about his change of address as they walked to the cinema and neither did Laura, but her manner towards him was cool. It was only when they were in the bar of the cinema at the interval that Nick said awkwardly, 'That move. It was only on the spur of the moment. Those fellows. I couldn't stand them any longer. Had a blazing row and moved out.'

'But where did you sleep?' asked Laura.

'On Dave's floor Monday and Tuesday but I'd fixed up the bedsit,' he said.

'It seems a shame when you've only got another few months,' Laura said. 'After being with them all this time.'

'I've only been there for five months,' said Nick. 'Everybody moves around.'

Laura was surprised but decided to say no more about the move, feeling that she was making a mountain out of a molehill if it was all so casual.

On Sunday Nick was waiting outside the Elephant as she drove up with Margaret and Gerry and Gerry dropped them while he parked the car. 'My turn for the fruit juice today,' Margaret said cheerfully. 'I'll be driving home.'

'Load of bloody nonsense,' Nick growled. 'Bloody Barbara Castle. She's spoiled everyone's enjoyment.'

It was clear that he was in a bad mood but Margaret said with spirit, 'I think she was right. I believe in the Breathalyser. I've seen too much of the results of drunken driving not to think it should be curbed.'

'Nonsense,' Nick said. 'I drive better after a few drinks.'

'Don't be daft,' Laura exclaimed. 'You know Margaret's right and so was Barbara Castle. It's only men who think they drive better after drinking.'

'That's why it took a woman to push through the Road and Safety Act,' Margaret said, winking at Laura.

Gerry returned, complaining about the difficulty in parking, and there was no opportunity for Nick to reply to the girls. They went into the bar and greeted friends there. Laura saw Phil Casey immediately, standing with Peter Taylor and Gail and another man, and smiled across at him. Gerry began to push through the crowd towards them, greeting friends boisterously, followed by Margaret and Laura.

Nick walked behind Laura scowling and nodding curtly to various acquaintances and his scowl deepened when he reached the group and saw that Phil was smiling at Laura. Gerry immediately began to talk about his wedding plans but the man who stood beside Phil said quietly to Nick, 'I hear you've had another bust-up. I met Kevin Cosgrove in Lark Lane.'

'I suppose he gave you his version,' Nick replied venomously. 'I walked out. Couldn't stand them any longer.'

'And where are you now?'

'A bedsit in Smithdown Road. Very handy.'

'On your own? Well, I suppose it's better,' the man said.

Nick, realising that Laura was close to Phil, put his arm round her. 'You haven't met my girlfriend, have you?' he said to the man. 'Alec Gibson, Laura Redmond.'

Gail had been eagerly questioning Margaret and now she said to Laura, 'And you're going to be a bridesmaid, Laura. What are you wearing?'

'It hasn't been decided.'

Margaret said quickly, 'But you liked the idea of blue velvet, didn't you, Laura?'

'Then it's decided,' Gerry laughed.

'But what about Julie and Margaret's friend? They're bridesmaids too,' said Laura.

'Yes, but you know our Julie'll go along with anything and Amy's easygoing too, isn't she, Margaret? No, as long as Laura agrees, you're home and dry.' Gerry laughed again.

'Are you making out that Laura's awkward?' Nick said belligerently.

Gerry chose to treat the remark as a joke. 'Now would I say a thing like that about me darling sister?' he chuckled, leaning forward to pat Laura's cheek. 'She knows me better than that.' Everyone laughed but there was a moment of strain and Phil Casey looked at Nick with dislike.

Laura longed to say something but could think of nothing. Phil seemed to realise this and said gently, 'This will help your mum and the rest of the family to get through Christmas without your aunt. Planning for the wedding, I mean.'

'Yes, it will,' Laura agreed eagerly. 'Everyone is so pleased about it too. Not just us because we like Margaret so much but her family because they like Gerry.'

Nick's arm tightened round her waist. 'Her father's a very sick man though, isn't he?' he said, determined to be included in the conversation.

Laura turned to him and said irritably, 'Yes, but keep your voice down. You don't want Margaret to hear you.'

She was annoyed, feeling that Nick seemed to be showing himself in a bad light, and he was aware of this. 'Let's break away from this crowd. I'd rather be on our own,' he whispered.

She shook her head. 'We can't do that, not yet.'

More people joined the group then some began to break away and Nick urged Laura to sit at one of the tables. 'Come on. Let's sit by ourselves.' He urged her towards a table in the window but Laura resisted. She touched Margaret and suggested a visit to the Ladies.

Margaret agreed and Laura pulled away from Nick's encircling arm.

When they returned, Nick was with a group from Christ's College and the girls joined Gerry, Peter and Gail, Phil and Alec Gibson.

'I see Nick's had another row and upped sticks from his flat,' Peter said to Laura, laughing. 'He's a dab hand at making enemies, isn't he?

But he's a good skin,' he added hastily as he saw the expression on Laura's face.

She was silent and Alec Gibson said, 'The trouble is he's so right wing and most of the fellows lean to the left. He won't compromise or keep quiet about it either.'

This time Laura reacted. 'Why should he keep quiet if that's what he believes in?' she said aggressively.

Alec Gibson hastily agreed and Gerry changed the subject by asking if anyone knew where to buy drink cheaply.

Although Laura was annoyed with Nick she resented any criticism of him by others and when Phil tried to talk quietly to her she gave him no encouragement.

Nick joined her and this time she smiled up at him and readily agreed to go to a small table with him.

'My feet are killing me,' she joked to Margaret but as they walked away she heard Alec Gibson say in a parody of Greta Garbo, 'I vunt to be alone.' She felt that she had made an enemy and later in the crush near their table she saw a young man glance at them and say something to Alec Gibson.

'They deserve each other,' she heard Gibson say, loudly enough to be heard by them and a few others. Nick started from his seat but Laura gripped his arm.

'*Sit down*,' she hissed. 'Don't give him the satisfaction.'

Gerry and Peter had also heard and as Nick subsided in his seat they drifted over and stood by the table. 'I'll be starting at Christ's just as you finish, Nick,' Gerry said. 'I'll have to pick your brains.'

'Feel free,' Nick said. 'And you're welcome to any books. I'll be glad to be finished with them.'

'Any idea where you're going to teach?' Peter asked.

Nick shrugged. 'I've sent off a few applications. I'll have to wait and see.'

Phil had not joined them but Laura was conscious of his eyes fixed on her and felt a sensation of warm happiness. I wish I could talk to him, she thought, but she knew any attempt to do so would provoke an outburst from Nick.

Before long Margaret glanced at her watch and decided that it was time to go. Nick leaned close to Laura. 'I've got a lot of studying to do but I'll drive you home,' he murmured. Laura insisted that there was no point.

'I can travel back with Meg and Gerry,' she said, 'and you can make good use of the time.' Margaret and Gerry backed her up and Nick decided that he would leave with her and return to his bedsit.

'I must say goodbye to Gail.' Laura went to where Gail stood with another girl, with Phil standing leaning against the wall nearby.

'We're off now, Gail,' Laura said and as someone spoke to the other girl she added in a low voice, 'I'm sorry about all that hassle with my crazy cousin. Do you know she's had the baby and the father's turned up? She's been having psychiatric treatment.'

'Good job she was in Canada or I'd have scrambled her brains a bit more,' Gail answered. 'But I knew it wasn't true.'

'So did everyone except her doting father,' Laura said. 'I'm really sorry though.'

'Not your fault. Peter was worried about your family but it's all over now. Goodbye, Laura.'

Phil had been looking at Laura and now he leaned forward. 'Goodbye for now, Laura,' he said quietly but in such a warm and loving tone that Laura's eyes widened in surprise and she blushed deeply.

She felt a sensation of weakness but she swallowed and said, 'Goodbye for now, Phil.'

Nick dashed up and took her arm. 'Come on, darling,' he said. 'Gerry and Margaret are waiting.' She allowed herself to be bustled away, still feeling bemused, yet reflecting cynically that Nick had never called her darling before.

The car was outside with Margaret at the wheel and Nick kissed her passionately before opening the car door. 'I'll ring, make arrangements,' he said, leaning into the car, but she could only nod and smile at him.

'Are you OK?' Gerry asked.

She croaked, 'Yes, thanks,' but they were travelling along the dock road before she could rouse herself from her dream to talk to them.

'Sorry I kept you waiting,' she said. 'I went to say goodbye to Gail. Apologised and told her about Rilla's baby and the father turning up.'

'What did she say?' asked Gerry.

'She said she'd have scrambled Rilla's brains a bit more if she'd been able to get her hands on her.'

They all laughed and Gerry said grimly, 'Might have been what she needed, the stupid bitch.'

'That Phil Casey is a nice fellow, isn't he?' said Margaret casually. 'Is he courting?'

'No. He's had a few dates. He's not bent and Peter reckons he's carrying a torch for someone. You'd never find out from Phil though. A clam's got nothing on him.' He and Margaret laughed and Laura bent her head, hoping that they were unable to see her face in the driving mirror. She knew that Margaret suspected nothing and had spoken only out of casual interest, yet she felt as though something momentous had occurred in the past hour.

Gerry and Margaret went on to discuss various people who had been in the Elephant, but Laura's mind was filled with thoughts of Phil and memories of his voice all the way home.

Chapter Twenty-Six

As though they had been conjured up by the conversation about Rilla the previous day, two letters from Canada arrived on Monday morning. One was from Margaret and Stephen and was for the family and Terry had written to Laura.

Both letters gave the same news that Rilla was to be married to the father of the baby, Ellis Juniper. 'We plan only a quiet wedding,' Margaret wrote, 'so I am not sending out invitations but I know you will wish the young couple well. We will tell you about it in our next letter. The wedding is on January 10th.'

'January the tenth!' exclaimed Anne. 'We couldn't have gone if we wanted to.'

'I've no intention of ever going there or having them here,' John declared. 'Whenever I see that girl it'll be too soon for me. I hope you've got more sense than to get mixed up with them again, Anne.'

'Of course I wouldn't have gone there and I don't want to see Rilla,' said Anne. 'But Stephen's still my brother and I'm not going to lose touch with him.'

Laura slipped her letter in her pocket and left for work. On the train she read the letter and smiled to herself. Terry wrote that the bridegroom's full name was Ellis George Juniper.

> *'Quite a mouthful isn't it? Especially for such a miserable little wimp. Just between us, Lol, I don't agree with this marriage at all and I think Margaret has her doubts. Rilla has no thought of giving the baby a name, she just wants a ring on her finger and to be called Mrs Juniper and she has romantic dreams of floating down the aisle in a white dress and being the centre of attention. Also, Joy is courting and talking about an engagement,*

337

but Stephen sees none of this. He has rushed into action and got it all set up but I see no future for the marriage. However, I say nothing.

'On a pleasanter note. I think Nick sounds a nice guy and I hope it works out for you, Lol. I wouldn't worry about him speaking his mind. Shows he's honest and you know yourself sometimes remarks sound quite different to what you intended to say.'

Laura folded the thin sheets and stuffed them back in the envelope, smiling to herself. I wonder what Terry would say if I told him about Phil, she thought, then remembered that there was really nothing to tell. A few remarks, the way Phil looked at her and the shock of the loving, caressing tone of his voice on Sunday. Yet she knew in her heart that there *was* a bond between herself and Phil and it was growing deeper and stronger. But what about Nick? What she felt for Nick and for Phil was so different. Could she really be in love with either of them or was it possible to love two people at the same time? Suddenly she felt that she was being ridiculous, thinking like this and jumped to her feet as the train drew in to the station.

She tried to think of more practical matters as she walked to the office but thoughts of Nick and Phil refused to go away. She thought again about the way Phil had looked at her and spoken to her on Sunday and felt how romantic it was to feel his gaze on her all the time. Like Mr Darcy in *Pride and Prejudice,* she thought, then told herself not to be a fool. If Phil cared for her why didn't he do something about it?

Fortunately the office was not busy and she sat at her desk still deep in thought and still confused about her feelings. Being with Nick was so exciting, even when they were quarrelling, and when he kissed her she felt weak with love and a strange passion that she had never felt with anyone else.

She was adamantly opposed to sex before marriage but when she was with Nick she was strongly tempted to break her own rules and she could more easily understand those who did. Yet away from him she sometimes felt that she didn't even like him. The more she knew of his character, the more she realised that his standards and outlook on life were totally different to her own, yet who was right?

Everything was changing so fast, yet someone had told her that she was in a time warp. Maybe I am, she thought, but so is my family and plenty of others. Even the Catholic Church seems to be changing, although fundamentally it's still the same. Like me, she thought wryly.

She felt a touch on her arm and Olive from the next desk leaned over. 'You should know that by heart,' she joked. 'You've been staring at that Certificate of Origin for twenty minutes. Where are you?'

'Miles away,' Laura confessed. 'Have you finished your Christmas shopping?' Olive was easily diverted and asked no questions about Laura's thoughts and Laura began to work with determination. She and Mary spent their usual hectic lunch hour shopping and spoke only briefly about how they had spent the weekend.

Soon after she arrived home on Monday evening there was a phone call from Nick. 'I was annoyed that I left you after the Elephant yesterday,' he said without preamble. 'I didn't get much work done anyway. Couldn't stop thinking about you.'

'I'm sorry about that,' Laura said, meaning that she was sorry that he had been unable to work.

'Not your fault,' he said magnanimously. 'I'm not blaming you.'

'Thanks a lot,' Laura exclaimed sarcastically.

'What about tomorrow night?' he went on. 'I can come to Crosby.'

'No, I go to Spanish class with Julie on Tuesdays. Anyway, I thought you had a lecture on Tuesdays.'

'I do but I'll cut it. And you can cut your class. It's not really important, is it?'

'It is to me,' Laura declared but she knew that if he had asked differently she would have missed the class without a qualm.

'If I'm willing to miss a lecture I'm sure you can miss a tinpot evening class,' Nick said angrily.

'Are you trying to annoy me?' Laura demanded. 'Because if so, you're succeeding.'

There was silence for a moment then Nick said in a different tone, 'I can't wait to see you again, Laura. I'd come tonight if I could. I love you.'

Laura's indignation vanished and she said softly, 'All right. Come to the house. I'll explain to Julie about the Spanish class.' It was only after she had replaced the receiver that she thought he might have expected her to say that she loved him in return. But I'm not sure it's true, she thought. I feel all mixed up.

She was tempted to go up to her room to think about Nick and Phil but she decided to forget them for the evening. I think I've done enough thinking about the pros and cons. I'll just take things as they come.

Nick rang again later to say that he had obtained tickets for a carol concert at one of the local churches and to fix a time for calling for her the following evening.

When he arrived he was carrying a plant bearing tiny orange globes. 'I thought it looked like a miniature orange tree,' he said. 'I suppose you know the name of it.'

'I do but I can't think of it at the moment,' Laura said. 'Thanks, Nick. It's lovely.'

He also produced a box of chocolates as they drove to the church and Laura remembered her conversation with David about him. He certainly isn't mean, she thought, and as David said I should be concentrating on his good points, not trying to find fault.

They spent a happy evening at the concert and when Nick held her close before he left and told her that he loved her, Laura could wholeheartedly return his kisses and tell him that she loved him too.

She was still in a happy glow when she went into the house. Her mother looked up and smiled. 'You didn't bring Nick in for supper?'

Laura said that he had borrowed a friend's car and had to get back. 'Just as well I didn't anyway,' she said, looking round the littered room.

Julie was sorting through a large box of Christmas decorations and laying them out on the sideboard and her mother was wrapping Christmas gifts. The ones to overseas relations had been sent off earlier but she was wrapping gifts for various old neighbours and people like the lady who emptied the Mission box and another old lady who delivered the parish magazine.

'Honestly Mum, your list gets longer every year,' Laura exclaimed in amusement. 'And you've still got to start on the family.'

'I know, love,' Anne said apologetically. 'But they are only little bits and they mean so much to people on their own. I just thank God for our family.'

Laura knew what she meant and went to make tea but when she returned Anne said, 'That reminds me. I wanted to ask you for ideas for Nick, for his present.'

A few hours earlier Laura would have told her not to bother but now she said she would think about it.

'I suppose he'll want to be with his family on Christmas Day,' Anne went on. 'But what about asking him for Boxing Day. Will he be free?'

'I'm not sure. We haven't talked about Christmas, about what we're doing. I'll ask him for Boxing Day.'

Julie looked round in surprise. 'Haven't you talked about Christmas at all?' she asked. 'Peter and I have been talking about it for weeks and making plans.' She blushed as she realised what she had said but Laura was unaware and her mother had carried her parcels into the other room.

'To tell you the truth,' Laura laughed, 'I don't plan too far ahead with Nick. We're always likely to have a bust-up before it comes off.'

'Oh *Laura*,' Julie said reproachfully. 'I thought you were settled with Nick now.'

'It's time I was, I suppose.' Laura smiled as she remembered Nick's kisses but then she thought of Phil. Would I even be thinking of Phil if I felt really sure about Nick? she wondered, then she firmly dismissed thoughts of either of them and when she went to bed she read until she fell asleep.

On Wednesday she was amazed to meet Phil as she left the office at lunchtime. 'Phil! What are you doing here?'

'I've got a few days off,' he said. 'I'm doing some Christmas shopping.' He turned and walked with Laura as she hurried along. She was about to ask what he expected to buy in the commercial centre of Liverpool but instead she told him that she was meeting Mary at a snack bar in Oldhall Street.

'We have a quick lunch and then dash round the shops,' she explained. 'I'll be glad when Christmas is over and we can have our meal in peace.'

'I used to know the best watering holes when I worked in town but a lot of them are gone,' Phil said. 'Er, do you mind if I join you for lunch? Or would Mary mind?'

'No, but you'll have to chew fast,' Laura laughed.

'Suits me.' Phil smiled at her and the next moment they met Mary by the steps down to the cafe.

'I met Phil outside the office,' Laura explained. 'He's working in Allerton but he's come in to shop.'

'Hi, Phil,' said Mary. 'That was lucky,' and Phil agreed, carefully omitting to say that he had been hanging around the office for more than an hour.

They rapidly ate sandwiches and drank coffee and the girls told Phil that they were dashing up to Blacklers and Lewis's to shop. 'I want some underwear for my nana,' Laura said, 'and Mary wants some for Danny's gran.'

Mary looked at Phil and said suddenly, 'I've got to be back in an hour but you could take longer, Lol. Why don't you take some flexi and help Phil with his shopping?'

Before Laura could speak, Phil said eagerly, 'That'd be great. Will you, Laura?'

Laura was about to refuse and say that Phil didn't need help but she looked up and into his eyes and said weakly, 'Yes. All right.' It was quickly arranged that Phil would meet Laura outside a shoe shop on the corner of Church Street and the two girls sped away.

'You're a dark horse, Laura Redmond,' Mary said mischievously as they slipped through the crowds. 'You must know he fancies you.'

'He's just a friend,' Laura protested.

They had arrived at the underwear counter in Blacklers and as they waited to be served, Mary said sceptically, 'Oh yes. And since when did a friend look at you like that? He's in love with you, Laura.'

'Have sense, Mary,' Laura scoffed. 'Just because he looks a bit moony. Probably looks like that at everyone,' but even as she spoke she felt that she was betraying the real feeling that she had for Phil and that she knew he felt for her.

A middle-aged assistant approached and Laura who knew her grandmother's size was quickly served. Mary was unsure about the measurements for Danny's gran but the assistant asked patiently, 'What build is she, dear? Is she like me or like that other assistant?'

'Like you,' said Mary.

The woman said placidly, 'Then she'll be an eighteen but if you keep the bill you can always change them if they're wrong.'

She bustled away and Laura commented, 'Aren't they patient? I'd tell people to get lost if they didn't know the measurements. No wonder my nana always shops in Blacklers.'

Mary's purchases were quickly completed and she smiled at Laura. 'All right. I can take a hint. You don't want to talk about Phil.' She glanced at her watch. 'I don't think I'll have enough time for Lewis's. I was late back yesterday. Should we start back?'

They began to make their way to Church Street and Laura said quickly, 'You're wrong, Mary. I wasn't trying to change the subject. There's just nothing to say about Phil.'

'I still say he's in love with you, Lol,' Mary insisted stubbornly. 'I thought there was something at the Cabaret Club but the Silent Man Nick moved in although it turned out he wasn't so silent.' She laughed.

'Then of course that cow Gail put her penn'orth in, but today I'm quite sure, Lol.'

'He'd say something, surely, if he felt like that.'

Mary disagreed. 'It's a bit awkward now that you and Nick are courting. Perhaps he thinks he's missed the boat or he's waiting for you and Nick to split up. I think he's a really nice fellow.'

'He is,' Laura agreed. 'But he's painfully shy. Strange, that, in a man, isn't it?'

'I like him,' Mary declared.

Laura, pretending to be joking, said, 'Better than Nick?'

She waited anxiously for Mary's opinion but she only said, 'I'll tell you after Saturday.' They had arranged to meet on Saturday for a Christmas meal, Mary and Danny and Laura and Nick, so that for the first time Mary would experience Nick's company.

They had stepped into a doorway to talk for a few minutes but they could see Phil waiting and made their way towards him.

Laura thought that she would feel self-conscious with Phil after Mary's words but they slipped easily into conversation. I always feel easy with Phil, Laura thought. I feel I can say anything and he'll understand.

He wanted presents for his parents and Laura questioned him about his mother's tastes. When she found that she liked Blue Grass perfume she took Phil to George Henry Lee's perfume counter. There they chose a large bottle of Blue Grass scent and found that they could buy a small case of soap, talcum powder and hand cream in Blue Grass scent for a nominal price because they had bought the perfume.

'I'm sure your mother will be pleased with that,' Laura said.

'I doubt it,' Phil muttered bitterly. Laura looked up at him in surprise and he went on hastily, 'I never get it right but this year with your help I'm sure she'll love this present.'

'She'll be hard to please if she doesn't,' Laura said bluntly but Phil said no more. They bought a cigar case for Phil's father then Laura said that she must return to the office.

'Thanks for your help,' Phil said as they walked back. 'I haven't a clue about scent. What's your favourite?'

'Oh, I've got expensive tastes,' Laura laughed. 'Gerry brought me Chanel No. 5 when he went to Lourdes with the school years ago. It was the only one he'd heard about and luckily he had enough money left to buy it in the duty-free shop on the way home. Since then my Uncle Mick gives me some for my birthday and I spread it out all year. He often goes abroad, you see.'

They stopped outside the office and Phil took her hand and looked into her eyes. 'I can't tell you how much I've enjoyed this, Laura,' he said quietly.

Laura, dismayed by the feelings aroused in her, blurted gruffly, 'Glad to help. Goodbye,' and fled into the office.

She went into the washroom before returning to her desk and was not surprised to see that her hands were trembling.

Whatever's wrong with me? she thought in dismay. I've always prided myself on being decisive and now I'm changing my mind every five minutes. She went to her desk and worked steadily, putting any thought of Nick or Phil firmly out of her mind.

After work she went straight to her grandparents' house for her meal and afterwards washed and set Cathy's hair. 'You've a real knack for that, love,' Cathy said admiringly as she looked at the result in the mirror and Greg laughed and said that if she ever lost her job she could open her own salon.

'Would you like that?' Cathy asked.

Laura shook her head. 'No, I'm happier working for someone else. I wouldn't like to have to make decisions. I can't make up my mind about anything lately.'

Cathy looked at her inquiringly but Laura did not elaborate so her grandmother changed the subject. 'Aunt Sarah was thinking of starting her own florist's shop but that was before they knew about Rosa. Now she's put her plans on hold. She'll probably work part-time after the baby's born so that Rosa can carry on with her art.'

'But that's a shame,' Laura said indignantly. 'Aunt Sarah's got her own life to live.'

'She doesn't mind. It's for Rosa,' Cathy said gently. 'You'll find that when you have children of your own, Laura. They come first.'

'Mine won't,' Laura declared. 'I don't think any woman should be a doormat for her husband or her family.'

'I'm sure Sarah'll enjoy looking after the baby,' Greg said, smiling.

Cathy asked about Laura's plans for Christmas but she was vague about them as she had not yet been able to ask Nick about Boxing Day and Cathy tactfully moved on to talk about Rosa's baby.

'Sarah told me what your dad said when he heard about the baby. That it couldn't come anywhere where it would be better loved. She was very touched.'

'It's true though, Nana,' Laura said. 'And Rosa was very much in love with Lex Mountford when the baby was conceived. It was only afterwards she was disillusioned with him.'

'Then it has a good start in life,' Cathy said comfortably and Laura hugged her impulsively. 'What's that for?' Cathy asked smiling.

Laura said gruffly, 'Just for being you.' The familiar wonder returned to her that Cathy and Greg could be the parents of a man like her father who selfishly trampled on other people's feelings but then she remembered his words to Rosa. He must be changing, she thought, not realising that it was her perception of him that had changed.

345

Laura had arranged to meet Nick after finishing work on Thursday and she reflected that she must be careful to say nothing about meeting Phil Casey. She knew how easily Nick's jealousy was aroused and she was anxious to be on good terms with him on Saturday night.

In the event they nearly quarrelled about something entirely different. Nick was waiting in the entrance to the offices and when she asked if he had waited long he told her that he had been in Liverpool all afternoon.

'Have you been off today then?' Laura asked.

'We finished last Friday for Christmas,' Nick told her.

Laura stared at him. 'So you didn't cut a lecture on Tuesday night then?' she said. 'The evening classes were closed for Christmas but I never thought about Christ's being closed.'

'So we tricked each other,' Nick laughed.

'But I didn't know or at least didn't remember until I told Julie I wasn't going,' Laura said. 'But you must have known. Why did you say that about cutting the lecture?'

'Just to twist your arm,' Nick grinned. 'What does it matter anyway? Neither of us missed anything and you enjoyed the carol concert, didn't you?'

'Yes, but—'

Nick leaned forward and kissed her so that she was unable to speak. What's the use? she thought. He just doesn't understand what I mean but the thought flashed through her mind – Phil wouldn't play a trick like that.

Before they parted, she told Nick about her mother's invitation to him for Boxing Day. 'We always have a family gathering on that day,' she said. 'It's usually good and you'll be able to meet the rest of the family. Unless your own family have plans, of course.'

'I'm sorry,' Nick said. 'I won't be here. Tell your mother thanks and I'm sorry to miss it but I'll be in the Lake District.'

'The Lake District?' Laura echoed. 'For *Christmas*?'

'Yes, I'm going with a couple of other fellows just for three days,' he said cheerfully, unaware of Laura's shock. 'I'll be back the day after Boxing Day.'

'But Christmas Day. Won't you be with your family? Laura said unable to hide her amazement.

'No, the parents will be abroad.' At the sight of her face, Nick laughed. 'Everyone doesn't make the fuss about these occasions that your family does,' he said.

'But *Christmas*,' Laura said, then more aggressively she asked, 'And when were you proposing to tell me about your plans?'

'I'll only be away for three days,' Nick said impatiently. 'I thought you'd be tied up with your family anyway. I know how you all gather for these occasions.'

'You speak as though we're some strange tribe with outlandish customs,' Laura exclaimed. '*We're* the ones who are normal, Christmas is special to everybody – well, almost everybody.'

'Don't be so damned intolerant, Laura,' Nick snapped. 'Everyone has the right to make their own arrangements. My parents celebrate with a holiday abroad but no doubt they'll have all the trimmings in the hotel and I prefer a walking holiday to overeating and overdrinking. What's wrong with that?'

Laura seized on his first words. 'Don't tell me not to be intolerant, Nick Clegg,' she said angrily. 'You know you're in the wrong, that I would expect us to spend Christmas together.'

'I just arranged this on impulse,' he admitted. 'If I'd realised how much it meant to you…' He tried to take her hand but Laura snatched it away.

'Don't flatter yourself. I don't need you to enjoy Christmas. Walk your legs off for all I care. I'll be enjoying myself.'

'Then what's all the fuss about?' Nick demanded.

Pride made Laura force a laugh and say airily, 'Nothing at all. I'll give Mum your message.'

He slipped his arm round her. 'Friends again?'

Laura reluctantly agreed, unwilling to spoil the plans for Saturday night. Nick seemed able to forget the disagreement immediately but for Laura it was a real struggle to overcome her anger. Only the thought of the night out with Mary and Danny made it possible.

She decided that she must warn Mary to say nothing about the meeting with Phil when she saw her the following day at lunchtime,

347

but the next day Mary rang to say that she would have to work through her lunch hour, so there was no opportunity. Mary now worked in the office of a firm of wine shippers and this was their busiest time.

Anne had been working in one of the retail shops of the same firm for several weeks, part-time. Her application for the post of school secretary had been unsuccessful and she had decided that she was not sorry. 'I don't think I'd have liked it,' she said. 'I like shop work. Meeting people,' and she had taken a few temporary jobs as part-time shop assistant.

John had been opposed to the job in the wine stores and his objections had grown as the shop became more and more busy in the run-up to Christmas.

'They coast along all year and make most of their money in these few weeks,' he said. 'And you're the muggins who is there for all the hard work.'

'I enjoy it, John,' Anne said mildly but John was not convinced.

'You're being exploited. Working for less money than those who've had it easy all year,' he told her.

Anne was on duty from four o'clock until ten on the last Saturday before Christmas and John was fuming. 'It'll be like a madhouse there and you know what your mother's like,' he said to Laura and Julie. 'She'll be working all out because people will be queuing waiting to be served.'

Laura was almost sorry that she had arranged to go out as Julie would also be out with Peter and friends.

'Don't start yelling at her when she comes home,' she told her father. 'She'll want a bit of peace when she comes in. I wish I hadn't arranged to go out.'

'Don't tell me what to do,' John yelled at her. 'I know how to look after her. I don't need you to tell me.'

Julie said quickly, 'It mightn't be as bad as you think, Dad. Mum said they've got extra staff on tonight,' and John and Laura calmed down.

Peter Cunliffe's application for the housemaster's position had also been unsuccessful but he had obtained another post in the same school which he hoped would lead to a housemaster's position in due

348

course. Julie and Peter had talked to Anne and John and visited Peter's widowed mother in Manchester the previous week and they planned to announce their engagement at Christmas. They had intended to keep their plans secret until Christmas Day but Julie could not resist telling Laura as they prepared for the evening festivities. 'I'm not telling anyone else,' she said. 'I want to surprise everyone but I wanted you to know, Lol.'

Laura hugged her. 'I'm made up and I know you and Peter will be happy together,' she said. 'But I don't think anyone will be surprised. They'll only be surprised that you didn't announce it sooner. There was never any doubt, was there?'

'No,' Julie admitted, looking a little crestfallen. 'But we didn't want to get engaged until we knew when we'd be married. We don't like long engagements.'

'So you've made your plans for marriage too?'

'Yes, on my twenty-first birthday in August,' Julie said shyly. 'Peter starts his new post in September so it will all fit in. We'll be able to have our honeymoon in the school holidays.'

Julie zipped up Laura's dress and Laura helped Julie with her hair as they talked and it came to Laura like a blow how much she would miss her quiet little sister. She kissed Julie and said softly, 'I can't tell you how happy I am for you, Ju. You'll make a lovely bride and I *know* you and Peter will be happy. If ever people were made for each other, it's you two.'

'Thanks, Lol. I hope it will be your turn next. You love Nick, don't you?'

'Sometimes I do and sometimes I don't,' Laura said honestly and they collapsed in giggles.

Mary and Danny were waiting in the foyer of the Adelphi Hotel when Laura and Nick arrived and Danny and Nick were introduced. 'I know some of your crowd,' Danny said. 'Gail Sugden is my cousin.' Nick looked puzzled and Danny explained, 'Peter Taylor's girlfriend. You know Peter and Phil Casey, don't you?'

'I've met them,' Nick said stiffly.

Laura waited in trepidation for Mary to mention the shopping expedition with Phil but she only said, 'We'd better leave our coats. I think our table's ready.'

They all enjoyed the evening. Danny was a cheerful, extrovert man with an easy conversational manner and a fund of stories. Laura thought she had never seen Nick so relaxed. The meal was excellent and the surroundings luxurious.

Mary looked round and said with a sigh, 'When I was a child I never thought I'd be dining here. So many doors were closed to us then.'

Danny laughed. 'Yes, but we've kicked them open. But hang around, girl. You ain't seen nothing yet, as the comedian said.' He raised his glass to her. 'You've had the hard times with me, but just wait, the good times are coming. We're going places, you and I, Mary.'

'Literally?' Nick asked. 'Will you leave Liverpool when you qualify, Dan?'

'No, not if I can help it,' Danny said. 'All my family are here and my friends and the same with Mary. I'm sure I'll get something here. I've had a few promises.'

'I've no family to worry about but I wouldn't like to leave either,' Mary said.

Nick looked at Laura with a quizzical expression. 'You don't feel that, do you, Laura? You'd be willing to spread your wings?'

'Not if there was any alternative,' Laura said. 'I don't really want to live anywhere but Liverpool.'

Nick looked thoughtful and Danny said cheerfully, 'The thing is, wherever you go in the world you'll always find a Liverpudlian. My brother's a seaman and he says that. He says when they hear the accent, the first thing they say is that they're exiled Scousers and the second is, "Which team do you support, Everton or Liverpool?"'

They all laughed and Nick pointed out, 'That proves that people do leave here in droves.'

'Yes, but not willingly,' Danny said. 'And they're still Liverpudlians until the day they die. They never lose their love for the city or their intention to come back when it's possible.'

'I think you'll find that you'll have to leave Liverpool if you really want to get on,' Nick said to Danny. 'I'm determined to go where the best chances of promotion are, no matter where. I'm sure you'll come round to my way of thinking, Laura.'

'Don't hold your breath,' Laura told him curtly. 'You might come round to mine.'

Mary and Danny pretended that it was all a joke but Laura knew that they realised as much as she did that something vital in her relationship with Nick had been asked and answered.

Chapter Twenty-Seven

Laura gave her mother Nick's message about Boxing Day, wondering how she would react, but Anne accepted it without comment. Her mind was so filled with last-minute plans for Christmas, thoughts of Julie's engagement and of Gerry's wedding, mingled with sorrowful memories of Maureen who would be absent from the family festivities, that she failed to realise Laura's distress.

She doesn't care, Laura thought bitterly. She doesn't even think that I might feel hurt and humiliated to be left alone for Christmas and I'm not going to spell it out for her. As always, she was disproportionately upset when it was her mother who failed her.

In the few days before Christmas Laura watched Julie who seemed incandescent with happiness and Peter who seemed to be constantly touching Julie and smiling at her. Margaret and Gerry, whenever she saw them, would sit close together and discuss plans for their wedding in March and Laura felt lonelier than ever.

They truly love each other, she thought, and the fear that she was unloveable returned. Nick said that he loved her but was it true? Actions speak louder than words, as Nana had often said. If he loves me he would want to be with me surely, especially at Christmastime. But then he had said that Christmas was not as important in his family as it had always been in hers and they obviously found it acceptable for him to spend Christmas walking with men he hardly knew.

I suppose he thinks those men might be useful to him, she thought cynically. He had told her that he cultivated people who might be useful in his career and when she protested he said it was quite usual. 'That's why boys are sent to public schools,' he said. 'Not for education but to make contacts which will be useful in later life. That's how people get on.'

He had also told her that was the reason he was active in his parish, to make sure that he was known to the parish priest. 'Priests are often chairmen of governors in Catholic schools and the word goes round. I'll be remembered as a good-living, hard-working Catholic layman when a headmastership comes up.' He had laughed as he said it and assured her that it was a joke when she seemed disgusted but she had an uneasy feeling that these were really his views.

Anyway, it means if that's the reason for the walking tour, I don't come first with him. His career does, so he can't really love me, she thought.

And what about Phil? Mary insisted that Phil fancied her but if he did, surely he would have done something about it. Perhaps Mary was just being kind because she could see that Nick was not loving and caring as Danny was with her. Laura had not seen Mary on either Monday or Tuesday lunchtimes as she was meeting Danny so there had been no opportunity to hear her opinion of Nick.

On Wednesday when Laura met Mary she said bluntly soon after they met, 'Well, what did you think of Nick?'

Mary laughed. 'He certainly had more to say than the other time I met him at the Cabaret Club. Danny liked him. He's good company, isn't he?'

'Yes he is,' Laura said, gratified. 'You know we're always falling out but in between we have good times. Danny's good company too. I've always liked Danny.'

'He's a smasher,' Mary agreed fondly. 'I should have all sorts of hang-ups after the childhood I had but Danny's put everything right for me. He's so good and so uncomplicated and he knows just how to sort me out. I feel safe with Danny.'

'You were lucky meeting him when you did,' Laura said and Mary agreed.

'His family are all the same too. Sound, as the fellows in our office say. There's one old aunt who gets a bit bitchy but his mother just says, "Now don't be at it, Marcella," and they all laugh.'

Laura felt the conversation was straying from the subject of Nick. 'Nick's family are not like that,' she said. 'They seem very cold with one another. His parents are going abroad for Christmas and I don't know what his brother's doing.'

'Oh, well, it takes all sorts,' Mary said tolerantly. 'And Nick's going on this walking tour? Be a bit cold, won't it?'

'Yes. Wouldn't suit me. I'm more for the fireside at this time of the year,' Laura said airily. Mary said nothing and Laura thought that she was not deceived.

They lit cigarettes then Mary said thoughtfully, 'I hope Nick wasn't right about needing to leave Liverpool to get a good job. Danny's sure he'll get fixed up here but perhaps it's different for teaching.'

'Not necessarily,' Laura said. 'I think they talk about it in the college and some of them talk a lot of hot air.'

'I hope he *can* get fixed up in Liverpool.' Mary touched Laura's hand. 'I'd miss you terribly if you went away, Lol.

For a moment Laura was unable to speak and she felt her eyes filling with tears but she bent her head and said gruffly, 'I'd miss you too,' then she blinked and said in her normal voice, 'Aren't we jumping the gun a bit here?' and they both laughed.

It was only just before she left Laura that Mary said casually, 'Seen any more of Phil Casey?'

'No, why should I?'

Mary shrugged and laughed.

The house was empty when Laura returned home but there was a note from her mother about her dinner. Anne was working until ten o'clock and Julie and Gerry were both out but her father returned at nine thirty and said he was going to the shop to pick up her mother.

'She's supposed to be working until ten o'clock,' he said. 'But you know what she's like. She'll be worrying if there are still customers there and staying to help the regular staff if I don't go for her.'

'Yes, she's too soft for her own good,' Laura commented ironically but although her father glanced sharply at her he said nothing.

Laura had cleaned the scullery thoroughly, after wrapping Christmas presents and writing last-minute cards, and now she prepared sandwiches and cut cake for her mother.

Anne looked exhausted when she came in and John was fuming. 'I knew it,' he told Laura. 'The shop was like a madhouse and the

354

so-called manageress off sick. Very convenient for her and muggins here run off her feet.'

'I was *swept* off my feet when Dad came in,' Anne said, smiling wearily. 'He came in like a whirlwind.'

'Just as well,' Laura said severely. She poured tea for her mother and urged her to eat but she seemed too tired. Perhaps Dad was right to try to block this job, Laura thought uneasily, but then she decided that her mother must make her own decisions.

Gerry came home a little later and handed a parcel to Laura. 'From Phil Casey,' he said. 'We all went back to the Taylors and went down to the cellar. You should have heard us! All our yesterdays as though we were all ninety. Mrs Taylor was asking about you, Mum.'

'I haven't seen her since we got so busy in the shop,' Anne said. 'But I'll be back to normal soon.' Anne and Mrs Taylor had become friendly after the meetings about Rilla and often spent an afternoon together to talk over a cup of tea.

'That's another thing you're missing with this damned job,' John said.

Julie had come in and urged Laura to open her parcel. Inside was a porcelain bottle with a dispenser containing Chanel No. 5 hand lotion. There was a card with it and Laura picked it up. 'Many thanks for your help with the presents. Love, Phil,' she read, then read it aloud, omitting the word love.

'I met him in town one day and helped him to choose presents for his parents,' she explained, annoyed to feel herself blushing.

'What did you choose?' asked Julie.

'Blue Grass scent for his mother and we were able to buy a case of soap and talc and stuff very cheaply with the scent and a cigar case for his father.'

'And did he know you liked Chanel No. 5 or was it just an inspired guess?' asked Julie.

'I told him,' said Laura. 'He asked my favourite and I told him about you bringing it home from Lourdes, Gerry, and Uncle Mick giving it to me for birthdays. I never thought of him doing anything like this or I'd never have said it.'

'He's a cracking fellow,' Gerry said. 'A real good skin. We seem to meet him everywhere we go lately. He was at that gig I did in Bootle and at the Ormskirk one.'

'With Peter and Gail?' Laura asked.

'No, on his own or with another mate. Margaret likes him. He's so quiet but you can always have a good laugh with him. We were with all the crowd tonight though.'

The conversation turned to other matters and soon Laura said goodnight and went up to bed, carrying her gift. She put the porcelain dispenser on her dressing table and sat looking at it and thinking of Phil.

What if it had been Phil who had been invited for Boxing Day? Would he have gone off doing his own thing and trying to further his career, leaving her alone among all the couples in the family? She was sure he would not. He'd want to be with me and do whatever made me happy, she thought, but perhaps Nick was trying to do something that would ultimately benefit both of them. She remembered the conversation about leaving Liverpool to improve career prospects. Even Mary had picked up the implication that she was involved in Nick's plans, as she had shown at lunchtime. Yet marriage had never been mentioned between herself and Nick. It's too soon anyway she thought, yet everyone, including Nick, regarded them as a steady couple. Nick had certainly assumed that if he left Liverpool she would be with him as his wife although nothing had formally been said.

I don't want him to ask me, she thought in sudden panic. I'm not sure what I want to do, then she comforted herself with the thought that Nick had only recently met her family and she had never met his. But she remembered her Aunt Sarah saying to her mother, 'And that's the first time you've met Nick after all these months?' and her mother's laughing reply, 'Oh, you know Laura, never does the conventional thing.' So that was no help.

Laura picked up the dispenser and squeezed some lotion on to her hand, thinking of Phil as she did so. He was another reason for her indecision but perhaps she was reading too much into a gift sent out of good manners. With a gesture of impatience, she switched off the light and slipped into bed.

The following day there was a note on her desk asking her to report to the Personnel Director's office at ten thirty. Her first thought was has there been a complaint about my work? And the second that her conscience was clear and she would not accept blame for anyone else's mistakes.

She went to the office with her chin in the air prepared to do battle but the Personnel Director received her politely and asked her to sit down.

He explained that changes would be made in the New Year. The growth in exports meant more documentation so they had decided to form a separate small office for it. 'We consider you reliable and conscientious, Miss Redmond,' he said, 'and very efficient so we have decided to offer you the position of Documentation Manager. You will have your own office and a staff of two and your salary will be increased by five hundred pounds per year, to be reviewed annually. Do you accept?'

Laura was too excited to work for the rest of the day and reflected that she would lose the job before she started if she went on like this. The rest of the staff were pleased for her, with only one or two exceptions, and suggested celebrating with a drink after work.

She explained that Nick was coming to her home early but arranged that the following day, Friday, they would have the celebration. It was Christmas Eve when they only worked until twelve o'clock.

The family were delighted with Laura's news and her father produced a bottle of sparkling wine to drink to her success. 'Do you keep a stock of wine for these occasions?' Laura asked, her face flushed with excitement and happiness.

'Well, you know what you used to say in the Guides, "Be prepared,"' John said laughing. 'I think I'll have to get a case in for all the celebrations that are coming up.'

Laura phoned Rosa to tell her the good news then handed the phone to her mother to talk to Sarah and ran upstairs to prepare for Nick's coming.

She wondered how he would react to the news about her promotion but she felt too happy to care. She was still bitterly hurt about his Christmas plans and although she tried to dismiss memories of the Sunday at the Brooke Hotel they often returned. She had been shocked by his comments about his family and about working-class men.

He sounded like a cynical snob, she thought, but he can be so different. I wish I could just forget things as though they'd never happened the way he can, although even that might be a sort of arrogance. He was satisfied so she must be. I'll have to have it out with him, she decided as she rapidly wound her hair onto Carmen rollers and made up her face. But not tonight she thought with a sudden uprush of happiness. Tonight I'm going to enjoy myself.

When Nick arrived he seemed pleased by her news but less excited than her family had been, although he congratulated her warmly. 'You look lovely tonight, Laura,' he murmured as he kissed her.

He had brought Christmas presents of a huge box of chocolates for her mother, a gaily wrapped box of fondants for Julie, a box of cigars for her father and aftershave for Gerry.

The family's presents for him were beneath the tree and Julie fetched them. 'Don't open them until Christmas Day,' she told him.

'He'll be halfway up a mountain on Christmas Day,' Laura said dryly. 'Better open them now, Nick.'

'I'm already wearing my mother's Christmas present,' he said, indicating his new leather jacket.

So you recognise Christmas enough to give gifts to each other she was about to say but she curbed her tongue and a little later she and Nick went into the back sitting room.

It was warm and comfortable, lit only by a shaded table lamp and the lights of the Christmas tree, and they sat close together on the sofa. 'I was relieved to hear you joke about my Christmas plans,' Nick said. 'I wish now I wasn't going away but I just accepted on impulse. I'm sorry now.'

Laura's feelings had been softened by the euphoria of her promotion and also by two glasses of wine and she leaned her head on his shoulder. 'Never mind,' she said softly. 'We'll enjoy New Year together.'

Nick held her close and kissed her tenderly. 'I love you,' he whispered, kissing her mouth and her throat and her eyes, as she clung to him. There was a sound in the hall and Laura pulled quickly away but it was only Peter arriving for Julie. The mood had been broken and Laura stood up and put on a record, Simon and Garfunkel singing 'Bridge Over Troubled Water', which Nick had brought.

Nick took a small parcel from his pocket. 'I didn't know what to get you, Lol. I hope you like this,' he said. Laura opened the jeweller's box to find a filigree bracelet set with garnets. 'It's lovely, Nick,' she exclaimed in genuine delight.

She kissed him warmly and gave him her present of a pair of gold cufflinks. 'I know they don't go with your usual rig of sweater and jeans,' she joked, 'but when you're dining at the top table you can wear them.'

'That might be sooner than you think,' Nick said. 'I'm going to make a success of my life, Laura. I'm determined. I made a bad start but I've got plenty of time.'

'What do you mean, you made a bad start?' Laura asked curiously.

Nick's face was grim as he said angrily, 'I had a lousy education. My father sent me to his old school as a weekly boarder and it was rubbish. He hadn't realised how it had deteriorated since his day. Then just as I left school he got into business difficulties and teacher training seemed my best option but it was a mistake.'

'I don't see why,' Laura said. 'You're doing well at Christ's, aren't you?'

'Yes, but a business career would have given me a better start. By the time I realised that I was halfway through a B. of Ed. degree and it was no use changing horses midstream.'

'But all this planning you're doing, getting well in with the parish priest and even going walking with these fellows. I thought that was all with the idea of getting a good teaching post.'

Laura failed to keep her distaste for his scheming from her voice, and Nick said, 'I know you don't approve of that, Laura, but it has to be done. I'll get the best possible teaching post but I don't intend to spend the rest of my life teaching.'

Laura looked at him thoughtfully. 'You're a bit of a Jekyll and Hyde, you know, Nick,' she said. 'I remember almost the first time I went out with you, you'd been doing teaching practice in Kirkby and you'd enjoyed it, and now you say you don't like teaching.'

'I didn't say that. I do like teaching but no one ever made a fortune teaching and that's what I intend to do. My great-grandfather did it and he started from scratch. I'll do the same, although I'll have a better start. In February I'll be twenty-one and I'll get five thousand pounds under my grandfather's will, and I'll get a good degree, I know. I've worked damned hard.' His face was flushed and he sat forward on the sofa, speaking rapidly and forcefully. He had never spoken so freely and with such passion before and Laura looked at him uncertainly. She stood up to change the record and Nick jumped to his feet and put his arms round her.

'Sorry. We shouldn't be wasting our evening talking about that,' he said, kissing her.

'No, go on, Nick. I'm interested. You've never talked about your ambitions before or about your family, for that matter. And I didn't know you were younger than me.'

'Very little,' Nick said. 'And I've nothing to hide about my family. It just hasn't come up.' He held her close and swayed to the music then he kissed her again and said exuberantly, 'Nineteen seventy-one will be our year, Laura. We'll be up, up and away and the world will be our oyster.'

'And I'll have my new job,' Laura said firmly. 'I'm going to make a success of that.'

She felt that Nick was going too fast for her and taking too much for granted but he only smiled. 'Oh, your job,' he said dismissively. 'Don't worry about that. We'll be far from here and your time will be fully occupied helping me before long.' He laughed. '"Being the hostess with the mostest."'

Laura pulled away from him. 'You're taking a lot for granted, aren't you? My job's important to me. What makes you think I'll drop everything and go off with you as your dogsbody?' Her face was flushed with anger but Nick chose to pretend that she was joking.

'Laura, you're a hoot,' he exclaimed. 'You'll be telling me next I have to go down on one knee and propose.'

'Anything but!' Laura said hastily. She was alarmed that he might think she was trying to force a marriage proposal from him and quickly changed the subject, although she wondered later if she had been manipulated as Nick boasted of manipulating others.

'Tell me more about your family and your great-grandfather,' she said. They sat down again and Nick slipped his arm around her and told her that his great-grandfather had opened a factory making industrial gloves. 'The First World War made him,' he said, 'but he still had to work on a shoestring. The men never complained though, too glad to have a job.' He went on to describe the conditions, unaware of Laura's horror. 'My grandfather took over a prosperous business in the thirties but he had endless trouble with the men. Bloody-minded. Always moaning about accidents and conditions and wages and making impossible demands and he was harassed by factory inspectors too.'

'Like wanting to form a union?' Laura said dryly.

But Nick went on, 'It was after the war that he really had trouble with the workmen. He had to keep the skilled men on although they were the most demanding but there was a constant turnover of unskilled. Nothing but strikes and rows and government inspectors interfering. He got fed up in the end and closed the place.'

'Why didn't he sell it?' asked Laura. She was enough of her father's daughter to think immediately of the men's jobs.

Nick said bitterly, 'He couldn't get a decent price but fortunately the firm next door wanted to expand so he sold the ground profitably. That's where my legacy came from. He died when I was three.'

Laura had moved to sit in a chair facing Nick and in the soft light she thought that, with his eyes narrowed, his beaky nose and his lips in a thin line, he looked like a bird of prey. The memories had aroused his anger again but he seemed to realise this. With an effort he laughed and said, 'But that's enough about the past. I just get annoyed when I think of what might have been. But I *will* succeed, Laura, I promise you.'

'If you're a good teacher, you'll succeed in my opinion,' she said. 'That's a lovely record, isn't it?' She stood up and turned it over but Nick was unable to leave the subject.

'I'll get a good teaching post but I'll succeed in business as well. I'm thinking of buying into a record company. It's only small at present but from little acorns, as they say.'

'But you won't be able to take any part in the business, will you?' said Laura. 'Teaching's a full-time job. It seems to fill my Uncle Joe's life anyway. There are so many after-school things, clubs for the kids and parents' meetings, and at the weekend he referees school football matches or takes boys away to Colemondy. That's apart from coaching boys who are falling behind.'

Nick snorted. 'You can forget that. I'll do what I'm required to do but I'll keep plenty of time for my business interests. I won't be teaching in a school like your uncle's anyway.'

'My Uncle Joe never begrudges his time to the kids,' Laura said hotly. 'And he's a happy man. He takes kids on field trips and one of his old pupils is studying botany at Oxford. That's what *I* call success.'

Nick came over to her and put his arms round her. 'I'm sure you're right,' he said easily, 'but we're wasting time.' He glanced at his watch. 'I'll have to go soon. Up at five tomorrow. Picked up at five thirty to drive to the Lakes.'

'Rather you than me,' Laura said.

'I wish now I wasn't going,' Nick repeated, 'or that you were coming with me. What about us having a weekend away together at Easter? It's time we had some time alone.'

Laura glanced at him wondering just what he meant but she only said quietly, 'I'll think about it.'

He seemed to have forgotten his anger and was loving and gentle, stroking her hair and murmuring endearments, but when his kisses became more passionate and his hands began to roam about her body Laura sat up and pushed him away.

'Come on, Laura,' he urged. 'Don't go prim on me now.'

'No. I told you the score when we first met.'

'But things have changed,' Nick coaxed. 'We're steady now. And you're not as narrow-minded as you make out. You've accepted Mary and Danny living together.'

'That's different,' Laura said. 'It doesn't mean *I'd* do it. My views haven't changed.'

'But you've got to move with the times. Get with it. Every girl I know is on the pill now.'

'I'm not and I don't intend to be,' Laura said stubbornly. Surprisingly, Nick laughed. 'God, you're a one-off. Prickly as a hedgehog and determined to have your own way, but I can wait, Laura. I know you want to as much as I do.'

'You'll wait a long time for me to change my mind,' Laura warned him but he laughed again and kissed her.

'Maybe that's why I love you, because you're so different. But don't push your luck.' He glanced again at his watch. 'This evening hasn't gone the way I intended at all,' he said. 'I wanted happy memories to take with me but we've done nothing but get heavy about my family and argue. And after your family tactfully leaving us alone all evening.'

'Not for what you seem to think,' Laura retorted. 'It hasn't turned out the way I expected either but I feel I know a lot more about you now.'

'Enough to know you'd be wise to hitch your waggon to my star?' Laura shrugged and said offhandedly, 'That's something else I'll have to think about.'

'I'll say goodbye and Happy Christmas now,' Nick said, kissing her again before they went into the front room.

Her mother was alone and Laura said calmly, 'Nick's going now, Mum. He has to be up at five o'clock.'

'That's an early start,' Anne said, smiling at him. 'Enjoy yourself anyway and Happy Christmas.'

'Happy Christmas to you, Mrs Redmond. Will you pass on my good wishes to the rest of the family?'

'I will,' Anne said and Laura accompanied Nick to the front door. 'I'm sorry about the weekend,' he said. 'But I'll be back on Monday and we can start afresh then, can't we?'

They said goodbye and Laura went back to her mother.

Anne was sitting with her swollen legs propped on a stool and Laura sat down near her. 'I'm sorry Nick won't be here for Christmas,' Anne said gently, expecting Laura to be instantly on the defensive.

'Yes,' Laura responded mildly. 'He's sorry himself but he accepted this invitation on an impulse and now he's committed. His parents have gone abroad for Christmas.'

'A lot of people do that but I wouldn't like it.'

Laura smiled. 'Some people think we're in a time warp, Mum.' The next moment they heard the front door open and John looked into the room. 'I forgot the presents,' he said and dashed upstairs.

'It's the old people's party at the luncheon club,' Anne explained as John came downstairs lugging a large sack.

'You look like Father Christmas,' Laura told him and Anne asked if the party was going well.

'Like a bomb,' John replied and looked at Laura. 'Where's Nick? Didn't he turn up?'

'Yes, but he had to go early,' Anne said swiftly before Laura could speak. 'I forgot to tell you, John. Nick's going on a walking tour in the Lake District for Christmas. He's being picked up very early tomorrow morning.'

John's face was a picture. 'A walking tour?' he said incredulously. 'So you'll be on your own for Christmas, Laura?'

'He'll be back on Monday.'

Her father exploded. 'Damn it, girl, have some sense. Get rid of him. He's no use to you.'

Laura was speechless.

'Oh John,' Anne said reproachfully and he suddenly put his arms round Laura.

'I'm sorry, Lol. I didn't mean to hurt you but it's true. You're worth better than him, love.'

Laura still said nothing and Anne urged him on his way. 'They're waiting for those presents, John.' He released Laura and touched her cheek and the next moment he was gone.

Laura stood looking down at her mother and thinking furiously. Suddenly all her doubts about Nick had crystallised and when her mother took her hand and said, 'Laura, pet, Dad didn't mean that,' she was able to smile wryly at her mother.

'He did, Mum, and perhaps he was right.' She sat down beside her mother and told her of the doubts which had been growing in her mind about Nick. 'I told him I didn't care about him going off tomorrow but it's not true. I was only saving my pride but if he really cared about me he'd want to be here, wouldn't he? And he's jealous and unreasonable sometimes and he has queer views about things. Sometimes I think I love him but I don't really like him.'

Anne was still holding Laura's hand and stroking it gently. She was torn between admitting her own doubts about Nick and comforting Laura. 'Some couples quarrel more than others but your rows with Nick, love, are they just about trivial things or are they, well, fundamental?'

'That's just it, Mum. He seems to be two people. He talked more about his family and his background tonight than he has ever done and I thought it would help me to understand him.'

'And did it?'

Laura smiled ruefully. 'Yes, but I don't think I liked what I found. He's bitter about things that have happened to his family and I think that's why he's so determined to be a success in life but I don't like his methods. He's absolutely ruthless and prepared to use anybody or do anything to get on and he doesn't see anything wrong in it.'

'But Laura, love, that worries me,' Anne said in dismay. 'You're too straight and honest to tolerate that. You've got to respect the person you marry – or am I going too fast. Has it got to that yet?'

'Nick *assumes* that it has,' said Laura, 'but he's never bothered to ask me about it. That's another thing. His arrogance. Although it suited me, Mum,' she added honestly, 'because I felt so undecided.'

'I think you should decide now before it goes any further,' Anne advised. 'In fairness to both of you if Nick thinks you'll marry him. Whatever you decide we'll accept, love. We just want you to be happy.'

'But you don't think I'd be happy married to Nick?'

Anne said quietly, 'I don't, love. Dad's right. You're worth better. Someone who appreciates you and truly loves you. Who puts you first all the time.'

Laura had never felt so close to her mother and impulsively she hugged her. 'Thanks, Mum, for helping me to make up my mind. I'm hopeless lately, dithering about. I'll do it. I'll finish with him on Monday.'

'I'm sure you'll be doing the right thing for both of you.'

Laura sat back and sighed. 'I know but I'll be sorry in some ways. We've had some good times together but I can see it wouldn't work. I'm glad I've finally decided.'

'So am I,' said Anne with unusual vehemence and they both laughed.

Chapter Twenty-Eight

Julie and Peter had gone to Manchester. His widowed mother was staying with her married daughter for Christmas and Peter and Julie went to spend the night and the following day, Christmas Eve, with them.

Gerry was at the Nortons' and John would be driving groups of pensioners home for some time so Laura made tea and she and her mother settled down for an uninterrupted talk.

She told her mother all that Nick had said of his family history. 'I think his family – I don't say they're any better than us – but I think they've had more money and moved in different circles. His mother is a leading light in the local Conservative Party and his father's a Mason. I don't know what they would think about Dad.'

'Because he's a Labour councillor?' Anne said. 'I don't think it would matter. Dad likes and respects some Conservative councillors more than some on his own side at times and I'm sure Nick's parents would be the same.'

'I told him Grandad says people shouldn't argue about religion or politics. The family you are born into decides how you worship or vote and we should respect other people's beliefs.'

'I hope everyone in this house does,' said Anne. 'That's how we tried to bring you up and anyway it's all chance, as Grandad says.'

Laura spoke again about Nick's account of his great-grandfather and his grandfather's factory and the trouble with the workmen. 'Reading between the lines, I think his grandfather was an old so and so. A bad employer or the factory inspectors wouldn't have been after him,' she said. 'But of course I couldn't say that to Nick. It's an old tale anyway. The factory closed down soon after the war. Nick admires his great-grandfather, thinks that what his ancestor did in his day, he can do now.'

'Perhaps he's got the same temperament as his great-grandfather,' Anne said. 'The same hunger for success.'

'Perhaps,' Laura agreed. 'He seemed all right but I didn't like what I heard about the grandfather. Apart from falling out with the workmen, he couldn't get on with his own son, Nick's father. Nick said they'd have split up but his mother kept in touch with the old man.'

Anne privately thought that she didn't like what she heard of any of them, including Nick, and was thankful that Laura had decided to finish with him but she only said, 'Let's hope Nick finds someone who suits him.' She sat sipping her tea and looking into the fire. 'Strange, isn't it?' she said reflectively. 'How circumstances can affect people, although I don't think they alter a person's basic character.'

'I've never really thought about it,' Laura admitted.

'I'm just thinking about the last time Mrs Taylor was here. We were talking about Phil Casey and she thinks his whole life was changed by his brother's death.'

'I didn't know he had a brother,' Laura exclaimed. 'He's never mentioned him.'

'He doesn't talk about him, apparently. Jonathan died of meningitis when he was sixteen and Phil was ten so it's quite a long time ago. He was at the college when he died. Had just taken O levels and done brilliantly.'

'I remember that,' Laura said. 'I remember the clever boy who died. There was a lot about him in the Catholic papers but I didn't know he was Phil's brother.'

'Mrs Taylor said the parents were devastated. He'd been a star pupil right through the school. Brilliant academically and at sports as well. He was Victor Ludorum at the last sports day before he died.'

'Poor Phil,' said Laura, 'trying to follow that.'

'That's what Mrs Taylor was talking about,' said Anne eagerly. 'She said some people manage to come to terms with grief, not that they feel less but they handle it better. Mr and Mrs Casey were just swamped by grief. It filled their whole lives. Poor Phil had his own sorrow to cope with because he idolised his brother but the parents just shut him out.'

'They should have controlled their grief. Thought about Phil,' Laura said indignantly.

'It's easy for us to say that, Laura. We haven't lived through a tragedy like that so we don't know what we'd do if it was us. Mrs Taylor said they're lovely people really.'

'And Phil was only ten, trying to cope on his own,' Laura said, still indignant.

'I think the Taylors were very good to him,' Anne went on. 'He started at the college and Peter palled up with him.'

'It's a good job he had someone,' Laura said.

'Yes, he was like another son to the Taylors. The masters at St Edward's were good too but he was always in his brother's shadow and his parents were in their own world, Mrs Taylor said. She reckons that's why Phil lost confidence in himself.'

'Why didn't someone speak to the parents? Tell them what they were doing?'

'Mr Taylor did try but it was no use. It was all very sad, Laura.'

'I know but Phil was the biggest loser, wasn't he?' insisted Laura.

'Yes. Phil told Peter that his mother cried when he took one of his reports home. She said why was it always the brightest and the best that are taken. Phil said to Peter that she thought the wrong brother had died.'

'But that was disgraceful,' Laura exclaimed, jumping up to make fresh tea. 'I don't care whether she was grieving or not, it was disgraceful. No wonder Phil is so quiet.'

'She probably didn't realise Phil heard,' Anne said. 'But that's what we were talking about. Circumstances affecting people. Mrs Taylor said she hoped Phil might be more confident now that he's been promoted and left home.'

'But he's not a weak character. Quite strong really, just quiet and shy. And no wonder,' Laura added darkly.

'She says he never makes dates but there's nothing queer about him. She thinks he might be in love with someone, a married woman perhaps,' said Anne.

Laura felt a stab of dismay, then she thought that Mrs Taylor was only guessing. She remembered the way Phil looked at her and the warm, loving tones of his voice. Perhaps… but her mother was talking. 'Don't mention this to anyone, will you, Laura? Mrs Taylor was speaking in confidence to me. She thinks the world of Phil.'

'Of course not. He'd go mad if he knew we were discussing him like this. But he's still on good terms with his parents, Mum. He chose their presents very carefully and I think he's going home for Christmas.'

'He is,' Anne said calmly, 'but he's coming here on Boxing Day.'

Laura almost dropped the teapot in surprise. 'Coming here?' she echoed.

'Yes. With Mr and Mrs Taylor. I know you said we were in a time warp but things *are* changing even here,' Anne chuckled. 'When we first had our Boxing Day parties all the family came except the ones in Ireland and Canada and all my Anderson cousins and my Aunt Carrie. It was all family.'

'I know. It was almost the only time we saw them. Dominic and Desmond and their families, and Carmel and her husband, and Theresa and Jim from Runcorn and their family and Great-Aunt Carrie. I can't remember the others.' Laura felt that she was gabbling still stunned by her mother's calm announcement that she had invited Phil.

Anne seemed to notice nothing and only said, 'You did well to remember all those but everything's different this year.'

'In what way?' asked Laura.

'Aunt Carrie's too frail to travel now so Theresa has a party in Runcorn for the Andersons so they can be with their mum. They haven't all been coming every year but it means a lot less are due this year and there are other people we need to ask now. Mr and Mrs Norton and Margaret's cousin Amy, the other bridesmaid, and Mrs Cunliffe and her daughter and son-in-law from Manchester. There'll still be the usual family and Moira's husband and Dilly's boyfriend as well.'

'But why Phil Casey?' Laura asked.

'Because I asked Mr and Mrs Taylor. Peter'll be working but Phil was going to spend the day with them so I asked him. I wonder who'll have their baby first, Rosa or Moira? They're both due about the same time.'

'It's going to be a bit awkward for me,' Laura said abruptly. 'I can't finish with Nick until I see him on Monday so I can't say anything about it on Boxing Day.'

'I wouldn't worry, love. Julie and Peter will be announcing their engagement. The Cunliffes will already know, of course, and we'll be celebrating it on Christmas Day but it will be the first time they see other people. Then there'll be all the excitement about the weddings and the babies. Just be vague if anyone says anything about Nick.'

Laura nodded. The only person she was concerned about telling was Phil but still she was glad that she would be seeing him on Boxing Day.

She yawned and stretched and her mother advised her to go to bed. 'Work in the morning and drinks when you finish at lunchtime,' she said. 'You can celebrate finishing with Nick as well as the new job, although you won't be able to say anything.'

Laura stumbled up to bed feeling suddenly exhausted.

John came in a few minutes later. 'Is Laura in bed?' he asked. 'Is she all right?'

'Yes, fine. She's decided to finish with that Nick.'

'Thank God she's seen sense,' John exclaimed. 'I've had my doubts about him from the start. I don't like the way he looks down his nose at everybody. An arrogant bloody so and so.'

'I've tried to like him for Laura's sake,' Anne said. 'But I never felt he was right for her.'

'She's worth better,' John said forcefully. 'This latest caper put the lid on it for me. Going off on his own at Christmas! Peter Cunliffe wouldn't do that or our Gerry, would they?'

'No,' Anne agreed then added slyly, 'but you would.'

John swung round, his mouth open to protest, then he saw that Anne was laughing. 'I know,' he admitted sheepishly. 'But only for something serious. A demo or something that you believed in as much as me. Not for my own pleasure.' He put his arms round Anne. 'And we'd both know it wasn't because I didn't love you. You've never had any reason to doubt that have you, love?'

Anne looked at him quizzically. 'No, and I must love you to have put up with you all these years,' she said, leaning her head on his shoulder.

'I know we've had our dust-ups over the years, but Laura and that fellow, they seemed to be always falling out. Fighting like cat and dog.'

'It would never have worked,' Anne said.

'No, because Laura's not like you. I know you keep us on an even keel, Anne. There's only room for one awkward cuss in a marriage.'

'It's more than the quarrels,' Anne said. 'Laura told me a lot tonight, more than she realised. I got the impression that he's absolutely ruthless and lacking in principle. He means to get on no matter who he treads on.'

'Thank God she's seen sense in time. I suppose you sorted her out.'

'No, it was you,' Anne said. 'I told her you didn't mean what you said when you rushed in but she said you might be right.'

'Well, that's a tum-up for the books for a start, her thinking I might be right about something. I hope to God she doesn't change her mind by Monday.'

'Does she ever? Once Laura makes up her mind it stays made up.' Laura would have been surprised to hear her mother, believing that she had been plagued by indecision all year.

John sighed with relief. 'Were you talking for long?'

'Not about Nick. I mentioned the Taylors to take her mind off him and then we just talked about Phil Casey and Boxing Day and Julie's engagement.'

'I'll have to get plenty in to celebrate the engagement,' John said. He stood up and pulled Anne to her feet. 'And then two weddings next year. We'll be paupers by next Christmas.'

'And two babies due in the family. Nineteen seventy-one will be an exciting year,' said Anne. 'But strange. We'll miss Julie and Gerry out of the house.'

'Never mind. They'll be in and out. Life will be different but still good, you'll see.'

There was very little work done in Laura's office the following day and several people grumbled that some other offices were closed on Christmas Eve but that was all forgotten when they left at twelve o'clock to celebrate.

Sleet was falling but everyone was in high spirits and in even higher spirits after they had celebrated Christmas and Laura's promotion for a couple of hours.

Mary had joined them and she and Laura left the others and went into the shopping centre for last-minute gifts. It was almost impossible to move but the crowd was good-tempered and the Christmas lights and the sound of carols made Laura feel almost light-headed with happiness.

When a shift in the crowd swept her and Mary into a secluded corner, she could not resist telling Mary that she was finishing with Nick. 'Don't tell anybody because I haven't told him yet,' she warned. 'I'll tell him on Monday.'

Mary was delighted. 'Great stuff,' she said joyfully. 'While you were paired off with him it was spoiling it for other fellows. I'm made up.'

The next moment they were swept back into the throng and although Mary had mentioned no names Laura knew who she was thinking of.

Christmas morning was dry but bitterly cold and Laura appreciated the midi coat and midi skirt which her grandparents had bought her for Christmas. Peter Cunliffe accompanied the family to Mass then to the grandparents' house to show them Julie's engagement ring. Sarah and Joe came with Rosa and David and there was great rejoicing but Laura's thoughts kept wandering to the party on Boxing Day when she would see Phil.

The Boxing Day party was a great success and no one mentioned Nick to Laura's relief. She thought they were being tactful until she realised that it was because there were so many other topics to discuss.

Only Phil, when he arrived with the Taylors, said quietly to her, 'I don't see Nick Clegg. Is he here?'

'No, walking in the Lake District,' Laura said briefly. Mick and Gerda arrived with her grandparents and she had to hurry away to greet them.

Mick and Gerda had given Laura the usual large bottle of Chanel No. 5 and Laura had applied it liberally as well as some of Phil's gift of hand cream.

Mick pretended to breathe deeply near Laura. 'Who is this who smells so sweetly?' he declaimed, striking a pose.

'The amateur dramatics have gone to his head,' Gerda said. 'I hope you still like Chanel, Laura. I thought we should ask you in case your tastes had changed.'

'Laura's tastes never change,' Rosa said. 'She'll stick with something even if she hates it because she won't admit she was wrong in the first place.'

They all laughed and Laura said in mock indignation, 'Do you mind? I'm always ready to admit it if I've made a mistake.'

Phil had drifted near them and her eyes met his before Rosa said gaily, 'Only joking,' and drew her away to talk to Moira.

Everyone mingled happily and the groups constantly changed but Laura was conscious all the time of Phil. She was anxious to avoid being alone with him while she was still trying to keep her decision to break with Nick secret but no matter where she was, greeting relations, being introduced to the Cunliffes by Julie or talking to Rosa or David, Phil was never far away.

She felt self-conscious about talking to the Taylors after her conversation with her mother but her father gave her drinks to carry to them and she felt that she had to sit down and talk to them. Phil had been talking to David but he left him and came to the Taylors.

'I'm just telling Laura how much we're enjoying ourselves, Phil,' Mrs Taylor said. 'Your mother has a gift for hospitality, Laura.'

'She's had plenty of practice with a family like ours,' Laura smiled.

'Mrs Redmond can do it at the drop of a hat too,' Phil said. 'I was very impressed that night I went to your house with Gerry after we'd changed the wheel. Your mother dried us off and provided supper of pea soup and ham sandwiches as though it was the most natural thing in the world at eleven o'clock at night.' They all laughed but Mrs Taylor looked thoughtfully at Phil.

'They were like drowned rats,' Laura told the Taylors, 'and I wasn't much better. I'd just had a very hot bath and I was in a tatty old dressing gown with my hair like rat's tails but nothing fazes Mum. She had them into the bathroom, Phil's coat drying and Julie and me making sandwiches and heating soup in no time.' She looked at Phil and felt satisfied that she had explained her brusque remark on that evening to him.

Margaret appeared beside them with Amy. 'Do you mind if I borrow Laura?' she asked. 'I don't often have my bridesmaids together to sort out details.'

Mrs Taylor agreed and Laura wondered whether she imagined an extra warmth in her manner as she said, 'I hope we can talk again later.'

Phil was often part of the same group as Laura but she managed to avoid talking privately to him for the rest of the evening. Even when the party broke up and people were leaving she frustrated Phil's efforts to talk to her alone.

I wish it was Monday, she thought. She longed to be free of Nick now that the decision was made yet she dreaded the encounter with him, partly because she was reluctant to hurt him. We've had good times together and often I thought that I loved him but I know I'm doing the right thing, she thought. Always some part of her had instinctively held back from total commitment to Nick and she felt that her instinct had been right.

The meeting with Nick was even worse than she feared. He came to the house by train on Monday and she suggested that they drove to Formby pinewoods in her car. Nick readily agreed, evidently thinking she wanted to be alone with him.

I do but not for the reason he thinks, thought Laura. All the way to Formby he talked about his weekend and how well he had kept up with the other men in spite of their longer training and experience. Laura scarcely spoke as she drove to the pinewoods but as soon as she stopped the car she turned to face him.

'I'm sorry, Nick,' she said without preamble. 'I've been thinking things over and I think we should finish. It's no use going on when we're not right for each other.'

He was at first incredulous then furiously angry and accused her of being childish and spiteful because he had been away for Christmas. Laura tried to deny this but he gave her no opportunity, going on to accuse her of finding someone who was a better prospect and of being sly and devious.

Laura was not the type to sit meekly while he accused her and she said things she had never intended to say. They were out of the car by now, shouting at each other across it, because Laura felt that he was so furious that he might attack her.

Finally the insults he was hurling at her family were too much for Laura and she shouted, 'Right. I'm going. I hope I never see you again,' and jumped back into the car.

He opened the passenger door and thrust his head in his face congested with anger. 'Don't worry, you won't, you slag. I'll make your name mud. You're the loser. I'm going to succeed and I'd have taken you with me away from all this. Remember that when I'm at the top and you're still in the gutter.'

He was almost gibbering with rage and Laura cringed away from him, then she turned the key in the car and the engine roared. He slammed the door and strode away and Laura managed to drive a short way before stopping the car and trying to compose herself. She was trembling with shock and it was some time before she felt able to drive home, but she scanned the road nervously in her driving mirror in case Nick appeared.

I can't tell them at home about this, she thought as she eventually drove home, but when she went in to the kitchen through the back door, her mother looked at her anxiously. 'Are you all right, love?' she asked. Laura burst into tears and dropped into a chair by the table.

Her mother drew a chair close to her and put her arm round her shoulder. 'What is it, love? What's happened?'

'He was horrible, Mum, horrible,' Laura sobbed. 'The things he said.'

Anne said soothingly, 'There, there, love, never mind. It's over now.' There was a bottle of brandy on the table and she poured some into a glass. 'Drink this,' she ordered.

The brandy helped Laura and she stopped shaking and sobbing.

'Where is he?' Anne asked.

'In the pinewoods. I left him there,' Laura said grimly.

'He'll be able to get a train.'

'I hope he turns the other way and walks into the sea,' Laura declared but the mood of defiance soon passed and she was weeping again. 'Oh Mum, I wouldn't have believed it,' she wept. 'He was absolutely wild. I was afraid of him. I thought he was going to attack me.'

'Never!' Anne exclaimed aghast. 'Oh Laura, thank God you're out of that.' She poured more brandy into the glass with a shaking hand and urged Laura to drink it.

Eventually Laura grew calmer. 'I was going to be so civilised about it,' she said. 'Stay friends with him. I was thinking this morning about the good times we've had together and that I'd be sorry in some ways to finish with him. I wanted to explain that we just weren't right for each other, to be reasonable.'

'But he didn't?'

'He flew off the handle right away. The things he said! I said nasty things too but it got really weird. He said horrible things about the family and just worked himself up into more and more of a rage.' Her lip trembled and she gulped at the brandy. 'I'd never have believed it, Mum. He called me a slag and said he'd make my name mud and that I'd be sorry when he was a big success and I was still in the gutter.'

'The gutter?' Anne exclaimed. 'The bloody cheek! And making your name mud. We'll see about that. He'll find he's gone too far. The family'll sort him out.'

'Don't tell Dad,' Laura begged. 'You know what he's like. He might get himself into trouble.'

'He probably would if he knew that fellow had upset you like this. God knows what he'd do to him but I'll be careful what I say to him. Never mind, love. It's over now.'

'I hope I never see him again. I'll never forgive him or forget the things he said.'

'Put it right out of your head,' Anne advised. 'Just be thankful you found out what he was really like in time. We had a friend when we were young who married a fellow like that. He seemed a decent man from a good family but he turned out a fiend, knocked her about, then he'd be all repentance and she'd give him another chance and it would happen again. She tried to get away from him but wherever she went he found her. That could have been you, love.'

'From what I saw today, it could,' Laura agreed.

'I suppose his pride was hurt,' Anne said. 'He was too big-headed to take rejection.'

'It certainly wasn't because he was upset about losing me,' Laura said grimly. 'All that guff about caring for me was just lies.'

'I don't think so,' said Anne. 'He probably loved you as much as he could love anyone, but people like him, they never really love anyone but themselves. Have some more brandy.'

Laura managed to smile. 'No thanks. I'll be tipsy and you'll have none left for your cooking. I'm all right now.'

'That's good. We'll have a cup of tea instead.'

'The cure for all evils,' Laura said wryly.

She left it to her mother to tell the family that she would not see Nick again, without too many details, and Julie responded by showing her even more affection.

'You've done the right thing,' she told Laura. 'He wasn't good enough for you.'

Gerry said the same to her and added, 'He's not liked, you know. Always throwing his weight about but creeping to people who might be useful to him. Even his mate Dave is cheesed off with him and there's no one more easygoing than Dave.'

Rosa and the rest of the family were informed and when Laura returned to work she told people at the office and within a few days it was general knowledge.

'People are hypocrites,' Laura said indignantly to her mother. 'Everyone seemed to like Nick when we were going out together and now they can't say a good word about him. They think I've had a lucky escape.'

'They were just being polite before,' said Anne. 'If he was your choice and you seemed happy, they couldn't very well say they disliked him.'

'I still think it was two-faced,' said Laura. '*I'd* have told the truth.'

Anne had been to tea with Mrs Taylor in the week between Christmas and New Year so Laura was fairly certain that Phil would know about her break with Nick. She wondered whether it would matter to him and what he would say if she met him again.

Her father's reaction surprised her. She had not seen him until they met in the hall the following day and he said gruffly, 'Glad you got rid of that fellow. Lifetime of misery ahead with him.' He thrust a paper bag into her hands. 'Russets,' he said. 'Saw them. Know you like them.'

'Er, thanks, Dad,' Laura stuttered, then as she looked into the bag she murmured, '"Comfort me with apples for I am sick of love."'

Her father was staring at her in amazement and she said, 'It just popped into my head. "The Song of Solomon."'

'That wasn't love,' her father said, still gruff. 'You'll find someone who will. You're a loveable girl.'

He bolted into the living room obviously embarrassed and Laura went up to her bedroom feeling warm and comforted. For the first time since the scene in the pinewoods she felt confident and happy.

A few days later she was clearing up loose ends before starting her new job when a call was put through from the switchboard. 'A Mr Philip Casey to speak to you Miss Redmond,' the girl announced. Laura said as formally, 'Put him through, please.'

'Laura?' said Phil. 'I'm in town. Any chance of meeting for a meal before you go home? Or is your mum expecting you home?'

'I'll ring her,' Laura said. 'I'll finish at five thirty. Can you come to the office?'

He was waiting in the foyer of the office block as she ran lightly downstairs and he took her hand and smiled down at her. Suddenly, without a word said, Laura felt a sensation of security and deep happiness which would never leave her.

The evening was bitterly cold and Phil took off his scarf and put it over Laura's head and round her neck. 'You lose most of your body heat through your head, you know,' he said and Laura stood meekly, thinking of another occasion when her Uncle Joe had done the same for his wife. The word cherish floated into her mind.

In the restaurant Laura asked Phil immediately if he knew that she had broken with Nick. 'Yes, Gerry told me and the other day I was at the Taylors and Mrs Taylor told me.' He hesitated then took

Laura's hand. 'She said she knew I was carrying a torch for someone and she thought it might be a married woman because I said nothing but she realised on Boxing Day it was you.'

Laura looked down at their clasped hands. 'I knew then that I wanted to end it with Nick but I couldn't say anything until I'd been able to tell him.' She shivered. 'It was awful. He made a terrible scene. Like a different person altogether. I've been a fool, Phil.'

'No, you haven't,' he comforted her. 'Clegg could be very charming when it suited him and he really fell for you. I was the fool to let him cut me out at the Cabaret Club because I knew then how I felt about you, that I love you, Laura.'

'I didn't know,' she said in a low voice. 'I always liked you, Phil, from when I first met you. I could always talk to you so easily.'

Their food arrived and they ate mechanically, smiling at each other, unaware of what they were eating.

'Coffee is served in the lounge, sir,' the waiter said when they had finished and they drifted to a secluded corner, still in a dream.

'I felt I couldn't butt in once you seemed fixed up with Nick,' Phil said as though their conversation had never been interrupted. 'I think now I was a fool. Do you think I'm a weed, Lol?'

'No, I think you're honourable,' she told him stoutly. 'You tried to play fair. Nick must have sensed something. He was mad jealous of you but then he was jealous of everybody.' She looked at Phil's expression and exclaimed, 'I'm sorry going on about him. I won't mention him again.'

Phil smiled at her. 'Then I certainly won't,' he said gravely and they laughed together.

'You've got dimples when you laugh,' he exclaimed. 'I've never noticed them before.' He leaned forward and kissed her. 'There's so much I want to know about you yet in a strange way I feel I know everything about you already.'

Laura smiled. 'That's exactly how I feel.'

The hours flew by as they talked over every detail of their meetings and it was only when the waiter had brought coffee twice and taken it away untasted that they returned to earth enough to set out for the station.

'Phil, it's late. What time will you get home to Woolton?' Laura asked when he went to the ticket office.

'That's all right. There's no one waiting up for me,' he said with a grin and in the train they sat close together, oblivious of other people.

Phil left her at the gate but arranged to meet her again at the office the following day. 'I'll be able to wait inside,' he said with a smile. 'I feel as though I know every brick of it. I've spent so many hours hanging about outside it, hoping to see you.'

'Why didn't you come in?'

'Because I had to pretend it was an accidental meeting.' Phil took her in his arms and kissed her tenderly. 'It's different now, isn't it?' he said softly. 'Do you feel it too, Lol, that this is the real thing? It is for me.'

'And for me,' Laura whispered.

Chapter Twenty-Nine

The weather after Christmas was atrocious. Snow, sleet rain and freezing fog followed in quick succession but Laura was too happy to care. She and Phil spent every available moment together but there never seemed enough time for all that they wanted to say to each other.

To add to her happiness, everyone liked and approved of Phil and he fitted in to the family as though he had always been part of it.

Phil had not spoken about his own family until a day early in January while they were still off work. They were in the kitchen with her mother when the window cleaner knocked for his pay and the cup of coffee Anne always provided for him.

He was a garrulous old man, proud of his knowledge of the family, and he said immediately, 'I suppose it was a sad Christmas for you, Mrs Redmond, missing your sister and that.'

Anne said nothing for a moment and he clapped his hand over his mouth. 'Oh, I shouldn't have mentioned her and reminded you.'

'Don't worry, Mr Tripp, I don't need Maureen's name mentioned to make me think of her,' Anne said with quiet dignity. 'She's always in my mind.' He looked abashed and she said quickly, 'We've lots of happy memories of her and we had a good Christmas. My younger daughter got engaged on Christmas Day.'

'Little Julie!' he exclaimed. 'It doesn't seem five minutes since she was a schoolgirl.'

'She'll be twenty-one in August,' Anne said.

'Fancy that.' Mr Tripp finished his coffee and picked up his cap. 'Thanks, Mrs Redmond, and all the best for the New Year to you and yours.'

He went out and Laura put her arm round her mother. 'Nosy old beggar,' she said indignantly. 'We haven't talked much about Maureen, Mum, but we've all been thinking of her.'

'Yes, love,' said Anne. 'But you know, Laura, I felt that she was here with us.'

'I felt that too,' said Laura. 'Especially on Christmas morning when we were toasting Julie's engagement. I thought how pleased Maureen would be if she knew and then I was sure she did know.'

'Yes, like Father O'Malley said. She left her body like a dress she had outgrown but her spirit, the real Maureen, lives on and she'll always be with us.' She wiped her eyes and gave Laura a quick kiss then she said briskly, 'Put the kettle on again, Lol. You'll need a hot drink before you go out. Poor Mr Tripp won't get many windows done today.'

Later Phil said quietly to Laura, 'Your mum's very brave, isn't she? She must have been dreading this Christmas without Maureen.'

'We all were,' said Laura, 'but everyone kept it to themselves for the sake of the others.' She glanced at Phil's face and said with rare tact, 'Of course we knew we shouldn't mourn Maureen's death because it was best for her. Life was getting so difficult for her. By the time she died she could scarcely move and she couldn't hold a cup. Even her sight was going.'

She slipped her hand into Phil's and he said quietly, 'We had a death in our family. My brother Jon. He was sixteen and he was only ill for two days. Meningitis. He was brilliant at everything, schoolwork, sports, everything.'

'None of that mattered, though, did it? The brilliance,' said Laura. 'It's losing a child and a brother. I don't know how people can bear it. I remember how we were when Gerry had that accident although he was all right, thank God.'

'My parents have never got over it. It shattered their lives,' said Phil. 'I miss him too. He was a smashing elder brother. Always had time for me although he had so much else on. We were real good pals and we were getting closer as we grew older.'

'At least your parents had you,' Laura said.

Phil shrugged. 'Yes, but I couldn't take Jon's place. I don't have his gifts, they couldn't be proud of me as they were of him.'

'But you're doing very well now, perhaps better than he would have done,' Laura said indignantly. 'It's not always the most brilliant who do best. A brilliant fellow started at Cambridge with David but he dropped out in his second year. I think your parents have got a lot to be proud of in you and I'm sure they know it.'

Phil smiled and squeezed her hand. 'But don't you think you might be just a bit biased?' he teased her.

'Maybe but I'm right too,' Laura insisted.

'I want to take you to meet my mum and dad,' he said. 'But I wanted to tell you about Jon first because my mum is bound to mention him. He still fills her life, you see. She's never got over his death. I don't think she ever will.'

'I'll be careful what I say,' Laura promised. 'I'll try not to put my foot in it, although I've got a bit of a talent for it,' she added ruefully.

'No, you haven't,' Phil said. 'You just speak the truth. Nowt wrong wi' that, lass.'

And in the same Lancashire dialect, Laura said, 'Eh, you'll do for me, lad.'

The family felt that happiness had smoothed many of Laura's jagged edges but she was still outspoken at times. Peter Cunliffe, who now saw her more frequently, was often amazed by her bluntness. He was even more amazed when Julie said innocently one day, 'You can tell Laura's really happy because she's so much more tactful and she never has black moods now.'

'Hell's bells, I don't know what she was like before, Jul,' he exclaimed, 'but she takes my breath away now. She certainly calls a spade a spade, doesn't she?'

'She's just straight, Peter,' said Julie. 'Absolutely honest. She might say something you don't expect but she'd never say anything about you behind your back. You can trust Laura absolutely.'

Julie was flushed and earnest and Peter said affectionately, 'I'm sure you're right,' and as the months passed he appreciated his future sister-in-law more and more.

Laura dreaded her visit to Phil's home in Bebington. She was prepared to dislike his parents for their treatment of Phil, and she was afraid that she would be unable to conceal her dislike and say something unforgivable, but she found that she liked them.

Hailstones fell as Phil drove up the drive to the house and they dashed through them from the car to the house. Mrs Casey had the front door open and drew Laura in and towards a fire in the hall. 'Oh, my dear, what a day,' she exclaimed and Phil's father fussed about Laura, taking her coat and brushing hailstones from her hair.

He was a tall, handsome man and Laura could see the resemblance between him and a large framed photograph of Jonathan which hung in the hall. Mrs Casey had blue eyes and fair hair like Phil but her hair was sprinkled with grey and her face was colourless and lined with suffering.

'Shall we have tea right away?' she suggested. 'It's a long drive from Crosby, isn't it?'

'Yes. As my mother would say we've passed twenty houses,' Laura said smiling. 'That's her yardstick for hospitality. I think it was her mother's too.'

She felt immediately at home with Phil's parents and her hostility towards them vanished. Even when they went from the dining room after the meal into another room which was like a shrine to their lost son, she still felt comfortable with them. Photographs of Jonathan were everywhere, Jon on the platform of the Philharmonic Hall receiving prizes, Jon holding cups or shields at sporting events, even Jon welcoming a famous person on behalf of the college. The only photographs of Phil were those taken with his brother. There were cabinets containing Jonathan's trophies and caps and the room was dominated by a large portrait in oils of him, which hung over the fireplace.

'My son Jonathan,' Mrs Casey said as Laura's eyes were drawn to it. 'It was painted from a photograph. He was a lovely boy. Such promise.' She wiped away a tear. 'Our lives were finished when he died.'

Laura felt a surge of love and pity for Phil. Although not usually demonstrative in public, she slipped her arm round his waist and kissed his cheek. 'Yes, I know Phil still misses him terribly,' she said. 'It must be awful to lose an only brother.'

Mrs Casey looked startled. 'Yes, indeed,' she murmured and looked at Phil, then at her husband.

Laura went on, 'My brother Gerry was in a bad car crash a while ago. Two boys were killed and Gerry and another lad were injured. I know how terrified we were until we knew he was safe and how awful it must have been for the other boys' parents.'

'Is this the brother who is getting married?' asked Mrs Casey. 'Mrs Taylor told me about your family but I don't think she knew about the crash.'

'Yes. I've only one brother and one sister,' Laura said. 'Gerry used to be a drummer in a group with Peter Taylor when they were young and he was always a scatterbrain but he's a changed man now. I don't know whether it was the crash or meeting Margaret. He starts teacher training in September.'

'Definitely meeting Margaret,' Phil said. 'The love of a good woman.'

They were all smiling now and Mrs Casey's melancholy was forgotten. Jonathan was not mentioned again.

Laura enjoyed her visit and when she left Phil's parents urged her to come again. As they drove home Laura told Phil how much she liked his parents. 'I'm sure I'd have liked your brother too,' she said. 'He looked such a normal happy boy in spite of all the trophies.'

'He was,' said Phil. 'In fact we were just a normal happy family until it happened and that made it worse somehow. The contrast. My mum and dad really liked you, Laura. When we were getting the coats, Dad said, "She's a lovely girl, Phil. Make sure you don't lose her."'

Laura laughed happily. 'No danger,' she said. 'I'm going to stick to you like a leech.'

Laura saw Nick only once and very briefly as she and Phil drove through Woolton and only heard of him through Mrs Taylor.

The two families had become very friendly and Laura often saw Mrs Taylor. When they were alone one day she said, 'That fellow you used to go out with, Laura. That Nick. Peter tells me he's jumping out of his latitude. He's come into money and he doesn't want to know his old friends, only people he can use. You're much better off with Phil. He's pure gold.'

'I know,' said Laura but asked for no more details.

She and Phil were still spending every possible moment together but when decimal currency was introduced on 15 February Phil had to work at the bank for seven days straight, from nine in the morning until nine at night. They could only keep in touch with a brief phone call when Phil returned to his digs and Laura realised guiltily that she had neglected Rosa and her grandparents.

They seemed to understand and welcomed her warmly when she visited them. 'I'm sorry I haven't been except Sunday mornings,' she told her grandmother as she set her hair. 'I'll come again every Tuesday now and do your hair. I don't know where the time's gone.'

'I do,' Cathy said, smiling at her. 'But don't worry, love. We're all made up you've met the right one at last. Phil's a lovely lad.'

'What happened to the Spanish lessons?' her grandfather asked. 'Have they bitten the dust?'

'We didn't go back after Christmas,' Laura confessed. 'Julie and I had too much else to think about.'

'So I noticed,' Greg said dryly but he smiled at her fondly.

Rosa welcomed Laura too. 'Welcome back from Cloud Nine,' she said. 'You look fab. Love must be good for you.'

'You look great yourself,' Laura said sincerely. Rosa seemed even more beautiful. Her skin glowed and her blue eyes were bright and she still moved as gracefully as ever, her bulge concealed by the loose kaftan she wore.

'Everyone is supposed to look beautiful when they're pregnant,' Rosa told her.

'Moira doesn't,' Laura said bluntly. 'I saw her at Nana's and she looked plainer than ever.'

'I hope you didn't tell her so,' Rosa said gaily.

'Of course I didn't. What do you take me for?'

'A reformed character, evidently.' Rosa hugged Laura. '"What is this thing called love,"' she sang.

The plans for Margaret and Gerry's wedding were well advanced and the arrangements for the young couple taking over the house seemed to have given Mr Norton a new lease of life. Snow fell lightly on the Friday but by the wedding day, Saturday 7 March, it had disappeared. The wind was very cold and Laura told Julie that she was glad that their dresses were of velvet.

'Yes, and with long sleeves,' Julie said. 'I was thinking of copying Margaret and wearing longjohns under mine but the church will be warm and we won't be standing around long for photographs.'

'But I thought you *were* wearing them. Mum got some for you, didn't she?' said Laura.

'Yes but I'm as strong as a horse now. I just can't convince Mum.'

'You haven't convinced me either,' Laura said. 'I think you should wear them.' But Julie could be stubborn. Although she made no answer, Laura knew that the longjohns would remain in the drawer.

It was a very happy day, with Margaret and Gerry so obviously in love and everyone convinced that it was the start of a very happy marriage. Laura thought of her sadness at Moira's wedding and how differently she felt now. She kept stealing glances at Phil as he knelt with her family and wishing that it was her and Phil who knelt on the altar to be made man and wife.

Margaret's father had refused to attend the ceremony in a wheelchair and had managed to walk down the aisle unobtrusively supported by Margaret and stand at the altar to give her away.

Anne had been sad that her firstborn was finally leaving home but when she saw the improvement in Mr Norton, she could only rejoice.

'Gerry's as good as a tonic,' Mr Norton told her later. 'Having him there to talk to and knowing my girls will be looked after when I'm gone has done wonders for me. Such a weight off my mind.'

Julie and Peter had been planning their wedding since Christmas but as soon as Gerry's wedding was over the pace increased.

Anne looked more and more harassed. 'It's so awkward, Peter's mother being so far away in Manchester,' she said to Laura. 'There's so many things I want to discuss with her.'

'You can always phone,' Laura pointed out.

'No, it's not the same,' Anne said distractedly. 'We must have been mad. Less than six months between the weddings. I don't know why we didn't suggest a double wedding.'

'It wouldn't have worked,' Laura said. 'Margaret and Gerry had made their plans before we knew about Julie's and anyway, Mum,

Julie's set her heart on being married on her twenty-first birthday. It's lucky it falls on a Saturday, isn't it?'

'Yes,' Anne said, her mind obviously elsewhere. 'Laura, I can't remember whether I arranged about the stand for the cake. And what about the list of hymns for the organist?'

'I'll find out,' Laura soothed her. 'Listen, Mum, why don't we sit down and make a list then we can tick things off as we do them?'

'No wonder you're so good at your job,' Anne said as they sat down with paper and pencil. 'What would I do without you, Laura?'

Laura reflected that it was fortunate that her mother was unaware that Phil had suggested a double wedding, with her and himself as the other couple.

Laura had told Phil how she felt about sex before marriage on their first date and he had agreed with her. 'I'm glad you feel like that,' he said. 'I respect you for it, Lol. I feel it's too important for people just to go from one to another as though it means nothing.'

'Oh Phil, that's *exactly* how I feel,' Laura exclaimed. 'People make you feel like a freak but why should we do what we feel is wrong just because everyone else is doing it? Not that I believe that everyone is but telly and magazines make out that's the way to live and some people just follow like sheep.'

'Everyone has to do what's right for *them*,' Phil said tolerantly. 'We're lucky that we agree on what's right for us.'

They had managed to keep to their principles but two nights earlier they had been sitting alone, closely entwined, as they listened to music when Phil had said suddenly, 'Oh God. I wish we were married, Lol. No wonder someone said, "Better to marry than burn."'

Laura, who was as tempted as Phil, sat up and drew away from him, averting her face.

Phil took her hand. 'I'm taking a lot for granted, aren't I?' he said but as Laura looked at him something vulnerable and insecure in his expression made her fling her arms round his neck.

'Oh Phil,' she said and he held her tightly in his arms.

'I love you so much, Lol,' he whispered. 'Will you marry me?'

'Of course I will,' she said, kissing him firmly.

He smiled and held her even more tightly. 'Hey, where's the maidenly coyness?' he teased her. 'Aren't you supposed to say, "This is so sudden. I'll have to think about it"?'

'To the devil with that,' Laura said and Phil laughed aloud.

'Oh Laura, I love you. I'll make you happy, I promise you.'

'I'm happy now,' Laura said. 'I couldn't be happier, Phil.'

He held her close and kissed her again and after a moment he said, 'There's no reason for us to wait, Lol. Why don't we make it a double wedding with Julie and Peter?'

'I'd love to,' said Laura, 'but we can't, Phil. I don't want to rush things like that and it wouldn't be fair to Mum. Three of us out of the house in six months! Anyway, I've promised to be Julie's bridesmaid and Mum needs me to help with the arrangements.'

Phil kissed her. 'I should have thought of that but I'm just impatient. You're a good daughter, Lol, so that means you'll be a good wife.'

'Does it?'

'Well, they say a good son makes a good husband so it must cut both ways. We won't wait too long, though, will we? I hate leaving you every night.'

'I'd like to enjoy being engaged though,' Laura said. 'Do things properly,' and after some discussion they decided to announce their engagement on Laura's birthday in September but to say nothing to anyone until then.

'I don't want to take any attention away from Julie on her wedding day,' Laura explained, 'and Mum's got enough to think about at the moment.'

In June two events occurred which could not be postponed until after Julie's wedding. Rosa and Moira's babies were born within a week of each other.

Rosa's daughter, christened Felicity Sarah, was born very easily, a small but healthy baby with neat features and a fluff of brown hair. She seemed a placid child who slept between feeds and rarely cried.

Moira's son Thomas was entirely different. It was a difficult birth. 'No wonder,' the midwife remarked. 'Look at those shoulders,' and another nurse said sourly, 'Nothing wrong with his lungs. He woke all the babies in the ward with his roars so I took him in the nursery and gave him a bottle. The next thing he was roaring again and waking all the nursery babies.'

'I'm sorry,' Moira apologised but she and Jack were delighted with their little son, even though once home he kept them both awake every night.

Laura reported to Rosa that Thomas looked almost square. 'He's so dark and has such a red face,' she said. 'His arms and legs are always flailing about and he looks ready to fight anyone. I'm sure he'll be a boxer or a rugby player.'

'Thank goodness I got the quiet one,' said Rosa, 'so that I can get on with my work and be independent.'

'Financially, maybe, but you'd be lost without your mum's help,' Laura said sharply. It still rankled with her that Sarah had given up her dreams of her own business for Rosa and it had never been acknowledged but she was too happy about the secret she shared with Phil to be angry for long.

They fixed on May for their wedding date. 'I love the month of May,' Laura said, then a thought struck her. 'It's not near Jon's anniversary is it?'

'No, that's in October. Twenty-eighth of October,' Phil said. 'I think May's a lovely month too.'

Laura had few secrets from Mary, whom she still met almost every lunchtime, and sometimes they made a foursome with Danny and Phil but even to Mary she said nothing about her engagement. She hugged it to herself, enjoying the feeling that only she and Phil shared this important secret.

The weather was bright and sunny and all Anne's problems had been solved and her worries dispersed when Julie's wedding day came. The reception had been arranged at the Adelphi Hotel and rooms booked for Peter's family and his many teaching colleagues and friends from Cambridge days.

David was Peter's best man and to everyone's surprise and delight he was accompanied by a slender dark-haired girl whom he introduced as Dr Hilary Speed.

'Are you a doctor of medicine?' asked Joe.

She said smilingly, 'No, of Philosophy. I'm an art historian.'

Sarah was a little in awe of her at first but Hilary and Joe were friends immediately and everyone liked the quiet, pleasant girl.

'You're a dark horse,' Laura said to David when they met in a quiet corner. 'How long has this been going on?'

'Some time now,' David said, smiling. 'I didn't want to bring her to meet the family until we had settled things between us. Do you approve?'

'I do indeed,' Laura said. 'I heard her telling Uncle Joe she was a musician too.'

'Yes, she plays several instruments,' David said proudly. 'But the violin is her first love.'

'You were made for each other,' Laura said. 'You'll be able to while away the long winter evenings playing duets.'

David pretended to punch her and Laura was struck by a sudden thought. 'Oh David, does this mean you'll announce your engagement? It might steal Julie's thunder.'

'Don't worry. Nothing would spoil this wedding for Julie,' he said. 'But we won't formally announce it. Just tell one or two people and wait for everyone to know by a sort of osmosis.'

Laura felt a sudden rush of affection for her cousin who had been her friend and companion for as long as she could remember. Always dependable, someone to whom she could confide her worries or her joys and know that he would understand and give her good advice. Her dear companion, more to her than a brother.

'Can you keep a secret, David?' she asked.

'You know I can but stop and think, Lol. Don't tell me something on impulse and then wish you hadn't.'

'No, I want to tell you. Phil and I are engaged but we don't want to say anything until after the wedding. Until my birthday in September.'

'I'm absolutely delighted!' David exclaimed, lifting her off her feet and whirling her round. 'I couldn't have heard better news. You're just perfect for each other, Lol.'

'Do I take it that you approve?' Laura said breathlessly, echoing his question, as he put her down and kissed her soundly.

'I do. Phil's one of the nicest fellows I know,' he said, 'and a perfect match for you.'

'But Phil's nothing like me,' Laura said and David laughed.

'That's what I mean.'

'I know you won't say anything, David. I haven't even said anything to Mum yet.'

'Silent as the grave,' he assured her, 'although I'll bet Aunt Anne has a shrewd idea how the wind is blowing.'

On the morning of the wedding Laura was awakened early by a shaft of sunlight falling across her face. She lay for a while torn between sadness and joy. She looked forward to the day ahead but there was a core of sadness when she thought that this was the day her sister would leave this house for ever and unite her life with someone else.

It was only in the past few months that she had fully realised how much Julie meant to her and how she would miss her quiet little sister. But Julie was making a good marriage and Laura was sure that she would be happy. Peter was a good man, she thought.

She rarely thought of Nick but now her thoughts turned to him briefly. He was a different breed to Peter Cunliffe. If he had been the one who would be with her today, she would have been worrying all the time in case he offended someone and afraid to speak to a male guest for fear of arousing his jealous rage.

Why did I stay with him for so long? she wondered. I must have been crazy. She sat up and looked at the clock and at a framed photograph of Phil which stood on her bedside table. Dear Phil. She picked up the photograph and studied it. She had taken it and Phil was smiling at her, all his love and tenderness for her showing as he looked directly at her. Thank God I got rid of that creep and met Phil, she thought, giving the photograph a quick kiss.

The sun shone for the rest of the day. Julie wore a full-skirted dress of white silk with a lace veil and carried a bouquet of red roses. She looked so beautiful that Laura felt near to tears as she gave the last touches to Julie's veil then set off for church, leaving her sister and her father alone together.

She knew that her father had also been struggling with his emotions but Julie was in her own world of happiness. John had recovered his composure when Julie floated serenely down the aisle on his arm, followed by Laura, her only bridesmaid.

Laura wore a dress of blue silk with a circlet of flowers on her dark hair and carried carnations and freesia. The church was full but she was only conscious of Phil who looked at her with loving pride. She smiled at him, feeling that she was as happy as Julie.

Later at the reception Phil whispered to her, 'You look fantastic, sweetheart, but you'll look even better in white.'

Some of Peter's colleagues and friends were meeting Julie for the first time and she greeted them with quiet dignity.

Laura saw how they responded to Julie's sweet smile and how Peter swelled with pride as he watched her and felt confident that Julie would fit easily and happily into her new world. She was amused when she heard one of Peter's friend say to another, 'Gorgeous girl. Is she Spanish?'

'Spanish descent,' the other man said knowledgeably and Laura smiled to herself. Yes, down several centuries she thought. From a sailor of the Spanish Armada washed up on the west coast of Ireland in the sixteenth century.

John's usual fluency failed him when he spoke as father of the bride but he raised a laugh when he said that Julie was a very considerate daughter. 'She decided to marry on her twenty-first birthday and save me the cost of another party,' he said.

When David spoke he recalled the night that Peter and Julie had met. 'It was at an impromptu party at Julie's home,' he said. 'The first time Julie had been allowed to stay up, I think. It was a great party and went on all night so I went to the Dock Road on my motorbike at seven o'clock to forage for bread and bacon. I little thought then that my young cousin and my best friend were making plans far beyond bacon butties.'

There was an extra warmth in David's manner as he proposed the toast to the bridesmaid and bent to kiss Laura and whisper, 'Your turn next.' She knew she had no need to fear jealousy from Phil and her pride in him increased as she saw how easily he mingled with the disparate groups of people. Yet he was always aware of her and at her side whenever possible.

He was still quiet and diffident at times with others but between them there was only a deep and loving certainty. She knew that Phil would always love and understand her and she would gradually heal the hurt which had destroyed his confidence after his brother's death.

We're right for each other, she thought exultantly, and ours will be the next marriage. Then we'll be together for ever.

Chapter Thirty

As the excitement of Julie's wedding began to die away Laura became impatient to announce her engagement.

'I don't think we need wait until my birthday,' she told Phil. 'It's less than a month away anyway.' She had told Phil that she had confided in David on the night before Julie's wedding and she said now, 'I know David won't say anything but I feel deceitful now about keeping it from Mum.'

'I should ask your parents' permission, really, if we're going to do things properly,' Phil said, smiling at her. 'The sooner the better as far as I'm concerned. I want to shout it from the housetops.'

'Oh Phil,' was all that Laura could say and she hugged him fiercely.

'My transfer has come just at the right time,' he said. 'We'll be able to tell your parents that you'll be living quite close to them.'

Because of reorganisation at the bank where Phil worked, he had been transferred to the Southport Branch which meant not only a slight increase in salary but that a house in Crosby was feasible. Laura could continue to travel to Liverpool by train and Phil could travel in the opposite direction from the same station up the coast to Southport. In both cases it was a short and swift journey.

Having decided to break the news, they went immediately to see Anne and John in the living room. They were watching television and filling envelopes with CND literature at the same time. When Phil diffidently told them that he and Laura wished to become engaged and formally asked their permission, Anne jumped to her feet and hugged first Phil then Laura.

'I couldn't be more pleased,' she exclaimed and John kissed Laura and shook hands with Phil.

'You had us worried with that last fellow,' he told Laura, 'but you're in safe harbour this time, girl.' To Phil he said, 'Look after her. She needs it.'

Phil took Laura's hand and smiled at her and Anne said brightly, 'Well, where's the Asti Spumanti, John?'

'Here,' he said triumphantly, taking a bottle and glasses from a cupboard. 'And never opened with more pleasure. I hope your parents will be as pleased as we are, Phil.'

'They will,' Phil said confidently. He and Laura had seen his parents often since their first visit. Occasionally his mother retreated into her own world while they were there but usually she was welcoming and affectionate towards Laura. Laura still felt that Phil was not appreciated enough by his parents but she said nothing to Phil of her feelings.

Anne had also been invited to visit Mrs Casey with Mrs Taylor and her soft heart had been touched by her grief. 'Poor woman,' she said when she returned home. 'Mrs Taylor said it's nearly eighteen years since Jonathan died and she should be getting over it but how can she?'

'I know, Mum,' Laura said curtly, 'but she should think about Phil and Mr Casey. I feel sorry for her while I'm with her but it makes me mad to see Phil treated as though he doesn't matter. She should be thankful she's still got Phil.'

'Don't be too hard on her, Lol,' her mother said. 'Just think if it had been Gerry.'

'If it had been you'd have been helping everyone else to cope, not just thinking of yourself,' Laura said fiercely.

'How do we know?' asked Anne. 'How do any of us know how we'll behave after a tragedy? Before this happened Mrs Casey seems to have been a normal, happy woman devoted to her family. Perhaps she thought she'd cope well with tragedy until it happened.'

Laura and Phil went to tell his parents of the engagement and both seemed pleased. 'I'm so happy, dear,' Mrs Casey murmured to Laura.

Phil's father kissed her and said, 'Delighted, delighted. You're a lucky man, Phil.'

Laura told them that her parents planned a combined birthday and engagement party for her and said her mother would be writing to ask them to come to it. 'Only a small party,' she said. 'Just the immediate family. They're all so pleased about the engagement and they'll look forward to meeting you.'

Mrs Casey seemed to shrink lower in her chair. 'Oh no, dear. I'm sorry. We couldn't,' she said.

'But it's for Phil's engagement,' Laura exclaimed.

'I know, dear, but we just haven't the heart for social functions now,' said Mrs Casey. 'I do wish you could have known Jonathan, dear, and you would understand. He was wonderful. There was never anyone like him nor ever could be. Our lives ended when he died.' She dabbed at her eyes with her handkerchief and Laura looked at Phil, at the hurt he was trying to conceal, and all her good resolutions about holding her tongue flew away.

'But what about Phil?' she burst out. '*He's* still alive. I know it was terrible to lose Jonathan but it was eighteen years ago! Even the Bible says, "To everything there is a season. A time to be born and a time to die. A time to weep and a time to laugh. A time to mourn and a time to dance." Jonathan loved Phil. He'd *want* you to rejoice with him.'

There was a stunned silence for a moment then Laura gasped, 'I'm sorry. I'll go. Goodbye, Mrs Casey.'

Still looking stunned, Mrs Casey murmured as though in a daze, 'Goodbye, dear.'

Phil put his arm round Laura and said quietly, 'Goodbye, Mum.' Again she murmured, 'Goodbye, dear.'

They went to the door and Phil's father followed them into the hall and held Laura's coat. 'I'm so sorry,' she said, near to tears.

He leaned forward and kissed her forehead. 'Don't be, my dear. You're a brave girl. Perhaps that should have been said long ago but no one had the courage. Come and see us again soon.' To Phil he said, 'Congratulations, son. I say it again, you're a lucky man.'

Laura managed to hold back her tears until she was in the car with Phil's arms round her then she wept bitterly. 'Oh Phil, I feel ashamed. I don't know what came over me. I couldn't help it. It all just gushed out.'

'Don't worry about it, love,' Phil comforted her. 'Dad was right. It should have been said a long time ago, as much for Mum's own sake as anybody else's, but none of us had the guts.'

'You were too kind, you mean,' Laura sobbed. 'You cared too much for your mum to hurt her but trust me with my big mouth.' She wept again but Phil held her close until the storm of weeping was over.

He said teasingly, 'I didn't know you knew the Bible so well.'

'I don't,' Laura confessed, 'but I often read through a book of quotations.'

By a mixture of cuddling and teasing, Phil managed to comfort Laura and restore her to calmness. When they eventually returned to the Redmond house she said nothing about her outburst to her mother.

'How did it go?' Anne asked. 'Were Phil's parents pleased?'

'Yes. Mrs Casey said she was and Phil's dad said he was a lucky man.'

'That's nice,' said Anne and went on to tell her that Julie and Peter had called earlier. Then she said casually, 'I sent off the invitation to Phil's parents. Julie took it to post.'

'That's good,' was all that Laura said but she wondered what Mrs Casey's reaction would be.

Laura had visited the house in Allerton which Phil shared with one girl, Jody, and three other men several times and they were pleased when Phil told them of his engagement. They all congratulated him and Jody said gruffly, 'You've done well there, Phil. Straight as a die, that girl. That's what you want in marriage, someone you can trust.'

'I can certainly trust Laura,' Phil said proudly. He felt sorry that he was leaving to take a flat in Crosby but it would be convenient for his new posting to Southport and for seeing Laura and househunting. They were looking for a house which was within walking distance of her mother's house.

The reply to the invitation to Phil's parents came promptly, accepting it. They wrote that they were delighted by the engagement between their dear son Philip and Laura.

Laura was astounded but she only said to her mother that Mrs Casey might find the party an ordeal. 'She hasn't been out socially since Jonathan died,' she explained but Anne promised to make it easy for Mrs Casey.

Mrs Casey had also sent a note to Laura telling her that she appreciated her honesty and her concern for Philip and looked forward to seeing her on the night of the party. Laura showed the note to Phil and he kissed her and said proudly, 'You see, *everyone* appreciates your honesty, Lol.'

He had told her of Jody's remark but Laura only said ruefully, 'That's the polite way of putting it, Phil. They mean I've got a big mouth.'

When he protested she only laughed and said, 'I don't suppose I'll change now. I've been like this all my life.'

Although Laura was still outspoken and had already ruffled a few feathers among the senior management in her new position as Documentation Manager, she was different with Phil. She had read somewhere that "love is the cross word withheld" and she was determined that she would say nothing that might hurt Phil or destroy his growing confidence. Her deep love for him made it easy for her.

On the night of the party she and Anne were both watching out for Phil's car, as he was bringing his parents, and they went forward to greet them as soon as they arrived. Mrs Casey looked pale and nervous but Laura saw that she had been to a hairdresser and was wearing a new outfit. Her husband held her arm protectively but he stepped back with a smile as Anne impulsively hugged and kissed her.

Phil had kissed Laura then she, too, kissed his mother, while Anne shook hands with Mr Casey. 'We can't keep calling you Mr and Mrs Casey,' she exclaimed. 'I'm Anne and this is my husband John,' as John appeared in the doorway.

'Kathleen and Will,' Mr Casey replied and they all went into the house.

Anne introduced them to Cathy and Greg first, then to the rest of the family. No one mentioned Jonathan but there was an extra gentleness in their greeting of Mrs Casey. Laura and Phil stayed close to her but John bore Will away to where Tony, Joe and Gerry stood talking.

Mrs Casey seemed fascinated by the two babies, Felicity who lay placidly in Sarah's arms and Thomas who lay on a rug on the carpet with wildly waving arms and legs. Cathy had drawn her down to sit beside her and asked if she might call her Kathleen and Phil's mother said admiringly, 'So you have two great-grandchildren?'

'No, only one. Sarah is my daughter and Rosa her daughter is Felicity's mother, but Thomas is the grandchild of Sarah's husband's brother Tony and his wife Helen.'

'Everyone in the room is related in some way,' Mrs Casey said wonderingly. 'My husband and I are both only children. It might have been easier…'

Cathy pressed her hand and said quietly, 'Yes, a big family can close round you in joy or sorrow. Greg and I are like you, with few relatives, but two of our children married into the Fitzgerald clan.' She laughed. 'I'm always thankful for it except when it comes to presents.'

Mary and Danny were kneeling beside Thomas who had grasped a handful of Danny's curls and was shouting with joy. 'Mary and Danny aren't related. Mary is Laura's friend from her schooldays.'

'I can imagine that Laura would be a faithful friend,' Mrs Casey said. 'I'm very fond of her.'

'And so am I,' Cathy said. 'She's always been special to us. She comes to see us every Tuesday and she does my hair. Sometimes she speaks her mind and people don't like it but she's as honest as the day is long and a real loving, compassionate girl. She was my mother's favourite and brought her a lot of pleasure and comfort in her last years.'

'Yes, I think Phil has been very lucky.'

'And so has Laura,' Cathy said firmly. 'I liked Phil the minute I met him and I've liked him more the more I've known him. He's a lovely lad, everything that Greg and I hoped for Laura. The way we feel about her there's not many fellows we'd think were good enough for her but Phil's perfect. We think the world of him, don't we, Greg?'

'We do indeed,' said Greg. 'He must be well thought of at the bank too to be promoted so quickly. You must be very proud of him, Mrs Casey.'

Mrs Casey looked startled but she said hurriedly, 'Yes, yes, of course.' She looked thoughtfully at Phil and then at her husband who was laughing at something one of the men had said.

The party marked the beginning of Mrs Casey's recovery although she still often had black days when she was overwhelmed by grief for Jonathan. The difference now was that she made a determined effort to overcome her sorrow and gradually picked up the threads of old friendships and commitments. Most people were eager to meet her more than halfway and soon she and her husband were leading a much more normal life, not unlike the life they had lived before the death of Jonathan.

Laura and Phil came often and were always warmly welcomed. Laura's outburst had never been mentioned again but there was a definite change in his parents' attitude to Phil. Laura often wondered whether her angry words had caused it or because they had seen how he was valued by her family.

David, who was the only one in whom she confided, said that it was probably a little of both. 'And don't forget that Phil's their son and they loved him. It was just that the shock of Jonathan's death knocked them off balance and they couldn't see Phil because of their obsession with Jon.'

'But they hurt him so much, David,' Laura said. 'Destroyed his confidence in himself.'

'Not intentionally, I'm sure,' said David. 'They still loved Phil and perhaps your words made them see what was happening. Phil's a strong character. He'll bounce back even if it takes one of your piledrivers.' He laughed and Laura was not offended.

As the preparations for the wedding went forward Anne and Kathleen Casey became firm friends. Laura and Phil spent much of their free time viewing houses but it was not until March that they found just the right house.

It was a smaller, more modern house than Laura's home, with a big garden. There was a large cherry tree at the end of the garden and Phil teased Laura that this was the deciding factor for her. 'We had one just like that in the garden where I lived as a child,' she admitted. 'I've always wanted one like it.'

The sale went through quickly as money was not a problem. They had both been saving and Phil was entitled to a low-interest mortgage as a bank employee.

They were discussing this on a night out with Mary and Danny and Mary laughed. 'Bet you're glad you saved, Lol, although this wasn't what you had in mind, was it?'

'Why? What were you saving for?' asked Phil.

Laura said airily, 'Just a daft idea I had. Are we ready for coffee?' It was obvious that she was unwilling to talk about it and Phil said no more.

The house was within easy walking distance of Laura's present home and of her Aunt Sarah and Uncle Joe's house where Rosa still lived with her baby Felicity. The faithful Neil was her escort when she needed one but Rosa seemed determined not to become seriously involved with any man.

Anne was delighted that Laura and Phil would be living so near to her. 'Everything has gone right for this wedding,' she said. 'Just like clockwork.'

'Practice makes perfect, Mum,' Laura laughed.

The day of the wedding was a beautiful May morning with blue skies and small fluffy white clouds and brilliant sunshine. The pews on the bride's side of the church were filled with Laura's numerous family and friends and the pews on Phil's side were filled too. His parents had renewed contact with so many distant relatives and friends during the past few months and all were pleased to attend the wedding and to see them looking happy again.

Laura wore a classically simple white satin dress and carried a sheaf of lilies and Phil looked at her adoringly as she came to stand beside him. He only said, 'Oh Laura,' but she knew all that he left unsaid. She wore a white satin Juliet cap on her dark hair so her face was not hidden by a veil and everyone could see the loving glances she exchanged with Phil.

'No doubt about this being a happy marriage,' Sarah whispered to Joe and he agreed.

'She deserves to be happy,' he said.

Later they said the same to David. 'She always had that way of holding her head back and looking at you with a sort of challenge,' said Sarah, 'but she's changed. Looks softer somehow.'

'She does but I think it's the real Laura showing now,' David said, then laughed. 'I don't doubt she'll still hand out a few home truths at times, though.'

Laura and Phil spent an idyllic honeymoon in the Isles of Scilly and returned to their house in Crosby where Laura was delighted to find the cherry tree in full bloom.

She had worried that her mother might feel lonely as her three children had left home within such a short time but Laura and Phil lived so close to her old home that she could spend much of her free time with her mother.

Three months after the wedding there was another cause for joy in the family. Margaret and Gerry's daughter was born and brought endless pleasure to Margaret's father for the last six months of his life.

After his death the baby Hannah was a consolation to Margaret and her mother and helped them to bear their loss. Gerry took charge and looked after Mrs Norton and Margaret, as Mr Norton had hoped he would.

'I feel ashamed,' Anne said to Laura. 'I miss Gerry out of the house so much and I envied Margaret's parents having him there all the time. I should have thought of the reason he was living with them and thanked God that Dad and I have good health and we have each other. Nothing matters but that.'

Laura looked at her in silence. She really means it, she thought. She really feels like that about Dad.

'I miss you and Julie too,' Anne went on, 'but it's lovely having you living so close. Makes it a lot easier for Dad and me.'

The cherry blossom had long since fallen to lie like drifts of snow about the garden until blown away by the wind but Laura loved everything about her house. The only drawback was having to leave it every morning to travel to work in Liverpool but she enjoyed her job and the challenge of running the busy office.

She was still forthright in her comments and was often involved in arguments in the office and very occasionally with Phil but he usually managed to defuse the situation and Laura was always eager to avoid an outright quarrel.

The only flaw in their happiness was that after two years of marriage there was still no sign of the baby they both longed for. Laura told Rosa that she had begun to dread visiting Phil's parents.

'She looks at me so hopefully and when I don't immediately announce that I'm pregnant her face falls,' she said. 'It's never mentioned so I can't tell her that Phil and I want a baby as much as she does – more, in fact.'

'That could be the reason you haven't had one,' Rosa suggested. 'You're worrying too much about it. Look at all the people who give up and decide to adopt, then start a baby right away.'

'You could be right,' Laura said doubtfully, 'but what can we do? It's too soon to think of adoption.'

'Just stop worrying, ignore Phil's mum,' Rosa advised. 'Tell yourself you'll work for a couple of years and then have a family.'

Laura smiled. 'You make it sound very easy,' she said. 'I had it all planned. I'd work until I was seven months, then stay at home with the baby for it's first few years. We could afford to do that. That's why it's so galling.'

They looked down the garden to where Phil was pushing Felicity on a swing. 'Phil's a natural father too,' Rosa said. 'He's the only one who can do anything with that little madam. She idolises him.' Felicity had grown into a self-willed and obstinate little girl and Rosa sighed. 'I was sorry for Moira at first,' she said, 'but I think I drew the short straw with Fliss. If she doesn't want to do a thing, nothing on earth will make her. You should have seen the three of us, Mum and Dad and myself, trying to make her take cough mixture last night but would she open her mouth? Would she hell.'

Laura laughed. 'Thomas is still wild though. I said to Moira that although he was mischievous, he was obedient, but she said he just goes and does something she hasn't thought of forbidding.'

'Maybe you're better off as you are, Lol,' Rosa said.

Laura could not agree. 'My only consolation is that Julie hasn't started a baby either. That sounds a selfish thing to say but Julie and Peter don't want a family yet anyway. We haven't given up hope yet and we're very happy otherwise so I shouldn't grumble.'

Although her father raged about the various troubles at home and abroad the strikes, the economic policy, the troubles in Northern Ireland and Watergate, Laura, cocooned in happiness, was oblivious of them. She ignored the news broadcasts and the newspapers and

Phil was too busy working to have time for them but inevitably both were affected by them at work.

The three-day week and the work to rule on the railways affected Laura's job most but Phil was harassed by the changes in economic policy and the rise in mortgage rate, with EEC regulations making his life more difficult, and he often had to work late at the bank. Both were consequently overtired, particularly Phil, and one morning when Laura snapped at him, he snapped back. She was unable to find her office keys and accused him of moving them.

Phil said angrily, 'Why is it always someone else's fault if you lose things? Try finding a place for everything and keeping it in that place.' She looked so stricken that he said immediately, 'I'm sorry, Laura, but you *are* untidy. I'll have to go. I'll be late tonight. Goodbye, love.' He gave her a quick kiss and left and Laura immediately found her keys in her handbag where she had already looked twice.

It was their first quarrel and she felt upset all day. She telephoned the bank but was told that he was unavailable and could only leave a message that she had phoned. She felt so miserable that she decided to call at her mother's house instead of going straight home. Anne was alone and had already had her meal but she fried egg and bacon for Laura and persuaded her to stay for a while.

She could see that Laura was upset and later as they sat drinking tea together Laura told her about the quarrel. 'It was all my fault,' she said.

'If that's your first quarrel you've done well,' Anne said. 'You've been married nearly two years.'

'No thanks to me,' Laura said. 'We'd have quarrelled often if Phil hadn't been so easygoing. I fly off the handle over nothing but Phil lets things pass.'

'Only trivial things though,' Anne said. 'You don't quarrel over anything fundamental, do you?'

'Oh no, nothing serious,' Laura said quickly. 'I'd never say anything to really hurt Phil.'

'Well, that's what marriage is all about,' Anne said cheerfully. 'Give and take. You cheer Phil up if he feels down and he makes allowances when you fly off the handle. You understand each other and do whatever's best for each other.'

'Is that how it is with you and Dad?' Laura asked, curiously. 'Give and take?'

'Yes, we understand each other, Dad and me. Dad's not perfect and neither am I but we suit each other.' She laughed. 'We must do. We've been married for thirty years in December if God spares us.'

Laura left in good time to be home when Phil arrived and as soon as she heard his key in the door she rushed into the hall. He dropped his briefcase as he saw her and flung his arms round her. 'I'm sorry, love. Sorry I was so snide this morning,' he said. 'I wanted to ring you but we've been up the wall all day.'

'It was all my fault,' Laura said. 'I found the damn keys in my bag as soon as you'd gone.'

Phil kissed her and they both said 'Forgive me?' at the same time. They went into the living room laughing, their arms about each other. Phil refused food and would have only a whisky and they went early to bed.

They made passionate love, both relieved to make up their quarrel, and whether it was due to that or to Rosa's theory, Laura soon found that she was pregnant.

Mary did not agree that Laura should hand in her notice when she was seven months pregnant. 'You're entitled to your maternity leave,' she said. 'At least have that and then decide. Girls often decide not to return when they've had maternity leave. They find that they don't want to leave the baby or can't make arrangements for it.'

'No, I know now I don't intend to go back so it wouldn't be honest,' she said stubbornly. 'I'll work until I'm seven months then leave. Rosa is making maternity frocks for me.'

The baby was born just before Christmas, a fair-haired, blue-eyed boy very like Phil in appearance. To Mrs Casey's delight they chose the name Michael Jonathan for him. He was a happy, healthy child and Laura and Phil felt that now their happiness was complete.

The baby did not disturb them at night until shortly before their third wedding anniversary when he began teething and then he often kept Laura awake. She tried to avoid waking Phil as he was still working very hard.

Rosa was making a dress for Laura and one Saturday morning she called with Fliss and asked Laura to try on the dress. They left the little girl collecting petals as they fell from the cherry tree. Then, while Rosa made alterations, Laura settled Michael in his pram and wheeled him up to the shade of the cherry tree. She had been awake several times during the night because he was feverish and fretful and she was thankful that he was asleep.

'Be careful you don't wake Michael,' she warned Fliss.

Phil came up the garden and Fliss ran to him squealing, 'Play with me.' Phil laughed and scooped her up in his arms then began to swing her round. One of her feet touched the pram and rocked it.

Laura started forward. 'Be careful, Phil. Have some sense,' she shouted.

There was no sound from the baby but Fliss flung her arms round Phil's leg. 'Don't you shout at my Uncle Phil,' she yelled, glaring at Laura.

Phil laughed but then he saw Laura's stricken face and swiftly plucked a wallflower and gave it to Fliss. 'Take this to your mother and stay with her,' he ordered and Fliss sped off, casting a frightened glance at Laura.

Phil put his arms round Laura. 'What is it love? What's wrong?' he asked gently.

Laura burst into tears. 'Oh Phil, I *am* like my dad,' she said. 'I would never believe it but I am.'

'But what if you are?' Phil said, puzzled. 'Your dad's a good man.' He drew her down on to a seat he had placed in the corner.

'It was like a flashback,' Laura wept. 'I saw the garden of our old house and the cherry tree and Gerry lying on the grass after he'd fallen from a tree. Dad shouted at Mum and I put my arms round her and yelled at him the way Fliss yelled at me. It all came back to me.'

'But that's nothing to worry about,' Phil said. 'I thought that was funny the way Fliss shouted. She was so small and so belligerent. Your dad probably felt the same way.'

Laura shook her head. 'No, I never forgot that. That's what made me want to take Mum away to live away from him.' Phil looked at her in amazement and she added, 'That's what I was saving for. You remember Mary talking about it.'

'But your mum and dad are very happily married,' Phil said. 'Your dad takes a lot on and it makes him a bit quick-tempered but your mum has the temperament to deal with that.'

Laura said nothing but she was thinking furiously. Gradually she had realised that her childish idea that her father was a bully and her mother a victim was totally wrong but now she felt that for the first time she really understood her parents. They suited each other perfectly just as she and Phil did. She remembered her mother's words about checks and balances and give and take and she stirred in Phil's arms.

He had been silent while she thought things out but now he said quietly, 'All right now?'

She nodded and they went to the pram to look down at their sleeping child.

'I wonder what sort of parents we'll be, Phil?' said Laura. 'I wonder what Michael will think about us?'

'Probably at times that we're great and at other times that we're a dead loss. Dinosaurs!' Phil said flippantly, then more seriously he added, 'We can only do our best and hope that he realises that we're not perfect but that neither is he. We'll do our best to be good parents and that's all anyone can do, Lol. Let's hope he recognises that.'

'I'll see that he does,' Laura said firmly.

Phil slipped his arm round her waist. 'I'm sure you will,' he teased her, and they went into the house laughing.

Acknowledgements

My sincere thanks to Clare Going and Sarah Thomson of Headline and Jennifer Kavanagh for their help and understanding, and to all my family my love and thanks for their support.